Judge

ALSO BY DWIGHT ALLEN

*The Green Suit*

# JUDGE

a novel

## DWIGHT ALLEN

A SHANNON RAVENEL BOOK

ALGONQUIN BOOKS OF CHAPEL HILL

2003

ʀ

A SHANNON RAVENEL BOOK

Published by
Algonquin Books of Chapel Hill
Post Office Box 2225
Chapel Hill, North Carolina 27515-2225

a division of
Workman Publishing
708 Broadway
New York, New York 10003

Chapter 5 first appeared in somewhat different form in the *Greensboro Review* and *New Stories from the South: The Year's Best, 2002* and chapter 6 in slightly different form in *Epoch*.

Grateful acknowledgment is made for permission to reprint from "What Do You Love More Than Love" by Dar Williams, copyright 2000 by Burning Field Music/ administered by Bug Music. All rights reserved. Used by permission.

Library of Congress Cataloging-in-Publication Data
Allen, Dwight, 1951–
    Judge : a novel / by Dwight Allen.
      p. cm.
    ISBN 1-56512-369-7
    1. Judges—Fiction.   2. Louisville (Ky.)—Fiction.   3. Judges' spouses—Fiction.
    4. Aged men—Fiction.   5. Death—Fiction.   6. Grief—Fiction.   I. Title.
PS3551.L39223J83 2003
813'.6—dc21                                                         2002038526

10   9   8   7   6   5   4   3   2   1
First Edition                                                             ·

The first thing a man remembers is longing and the last thing
he is conscious of before death is exactly the same longing.
I have never seen a man die who did not die in longing.

—Walker Percy, *Love in the Ruins*

Hey, what do you love more than love?

—Dar Williams

# Contents

Judge

# I

# The End

In Lucy Mulder's desk, in the drawer where she kept ibuprofen and scrunchies and a homemade turkey call that a United States marshal named Ray had given her, was a plastic canister of film—thirty-six 35-millimeter exposures. The film had been in her possession for a month or so. She'd found it, along with lens tissues and a 1981 Amtrak timetable, in the raincoat that Judge William Dupree, her late employer, kept in his chambers, the coat he sometimes wore on his lunchtime excursions, when he'd forgotten to bring his good one from home. It was this "tattered, dirty-at-the-cuffs" coat that got into his obituary, along with what the writer called a "golf cap." (The only warm-weather hat Lucy had ever seen the Judge wear, in her fifteen years as his clerk, was a floppy, broad-brimmed Australian bush thing, which his wife had demanded he put on whenever he ventured out into the daylight. He had tender skin, and he'd obeyed.) The coat and hat were details in an anecdote that a lawyer named Bemis (Sunbeam) Purdy passed along to the obituary writer. Purdy said that the Judge had been returning to the federal building from lunch one breezy, rain-spattered afternoon, walking his old man's thin-legged, tottery walk, when a wino who had just been picked up by the police for disorderly conduct shouted, "Look at him, look at that bum, he probably steals from old ladies, and here you are arresting me." Lucy suspected Purdy, a dapper Republican who had once been mentioned as a candidate for the district court bench, of a touch of malice in the airing of this story. Though she was also sure he'd claim—she'd heard him do so, at the gathering following the funeral—that the point of the story was that the Judge was a humble man, indistinguishable (at least from a distance) from the lowly and the bereft, the meek and the powerless. Anyway, she thought the Judge would probably have been amused by the story, had he seen it in print. Certainly he would have chuckled at the way Purdy or the reporter had rendered the wino's speech. As it happened, Lucy had been at her desk that afternoon, half-asleep from reading a motion to dismiss in a due process case, when the Judge returned to his chambers, his bush hat riding uneasily on his small head, the tie strings dangling loose. His face looked as if he'd fallen into a briar patch; he'd recently had a number of tiny skin cancers removed, and the surgery had left scars, red dots. He was frail, the collar of his shirt seemed a full size too big, and he listed to the left, which was the direction his decisions ran (or so some of his critics said). He was eighty-two. He stood before his clerk in his dingy coat and hat, the scent of rain and men's club food on him, and said, "A man on the street just called me— forgive me—a motherfucker." He said this word so softly, as if he had hardly enough breath to say it, that Lucy almost missed it. But there it was, like a fly stirring the drowsy air in which she labored on government business.

"He said I looked like the kind of you-know-what who steals from old ladies. But I don't think he could prove it in a court of law. Do you?" He peered at Lucy through his glasses—thick, fun-house lenses in unstylish black frames, the kind a mathematician might wear—the way he sometimes did with a lawyer who'd left the barn door open (in the legal sense). She looked at his face, creased and scarred and erratically shaven, and remembered for at least the thousandth time how he had kissed her one day two years ago and how she had kissed him back. His face had seemed to come momentarily open then, like a stuck door.

"Which charge?" Lucy asked now, teasing him. "Theft or the other?"

"Both, I suppose. Though the question was rhetorical." He smiled a partial smile.

"He'd need witnesses," she said, rhetorically. "Or evidence not of a hearsay nature." She took a sip from a can of Diet Coke. "And I assume neither could be found."

"There are some skeletons in my closet," the Judge said, removing his hat at last, almost hastily, as if to make up for his not having done so earlier. His white hair, once as pure as the proverbial snow, had yellowed a bit. It lay unneatly on his head, the part obliterated. "But none to suggest that I might have lain with my mother, like that Greek fellow, what's-his name."

"Oedipus," Lucy said. There had been times, early in her tenure, when she'd put a literary reference in a draft of an opinion. He'd let it stand, while noting, in his scribble, that the reference might be over the heads of some lawyers he knew, "including yours truly."

"Him. Yes. How did that old boy die? Do you recall?"

Maybe the Judge, on the way back from lunch at the Breckinridge Club, where he would have eaten a Hot Brown and played half-penny-a-point bridge with men who were known by their nicknames (Hateful, Stork, Prince Albert, Sunbeam), had fallen into thinking about his death, the great empty buzzing lot that lay before him, like the lot from which the old Chestnut Hotel had recently been razed and where perhaps he'd encountered the man who called him that obscenity. Who, at eighty-two, wouldn't have given thought, at least between meals, to extinction? Or, if you were a Christian believer, as the Judge was, to the sins the soul might drag with it into the next life?

"I'm not sure," Lucy said. She clearly remembered that Oedipus had blinded himself—with his mother's brooch?—after he'd figured out all the terrible things he'd done. But of what had finally become of him, she was less certain. It wasn't her favorite story. It was a bit on the sensational side. "I'm thinking that his daughter, Antigone, took care of him after he became blind and that he died of natural causes, whatever those might have been twenty-five hundred years ago." She would have gladly changed the subject.

"You might be right," the Judge said deferentially. Then he shuffled off, hat in hand, toward his desk, where he would take a nap, sitting upright in the enormous green leather chair that was purchased for him in 1972, the year of his appointment. Lucy watched him go, his legs barely moving beneath his raincoat. From behind, it appeared that he'd recently taken a seat in a mud puddle.

FOUR MONTHS LATER, in January of 2001, Lucy drove out to the Judge's home to see his widow. Lucy had the raincoat with her—uncleaned, in the state it had come back in the day the street person called him a thief and a motherfucker—and some other items from his office: photographs, desktop ornaments (the Everyjudge collection of ceramic and wood-carved owls; paperweights), two neckties, a tie clasp, old railroad timetables, plaques, one of his two robes (the traveling one, which came with a black leather case), a monogrammed satchel he'd never used, pens. All of this, aside from the robe case and coat, had fit into a couple of boxes, and was just about all that was left of his office possessions after the Judge's sons and his lawyer had gone through them. The lawyer, a square-shouldered, apple-cheeked man of fifty named Clifford Barnhill, who had clerked for the Judge several years before Lucy signed on, had been in search of stray insurance policies, stray stock certificates, any odd piece of intangible property that the estate could lay claim to. Judge Dupree, who had grown up in money and never lacked for it, had been notoriously casual about his finances; things weren't always where a more orderly person might have put them. In 1997, Lucy had found a dividend check dated 1981 in a volume of the *Federal Reporter*. His paychecks were known to have sometimes been deposited among the debris in the backseat of his car. Clifford found a check from the Commonwealth of Kentucky, a tax refund of $311, dated 1974, inside a ninety-five-cent paperback called *How to Play Slam Contracts*.

Crawford Dupree, the Judge's older son, had spent hours poring over his father's office possessions. He took boxes of stuff with him, whatever he could fit into his car. What he couldn't, he had Lucy mail to him in Wisconsin. He took desk diaries and personal correspondence (letters from senators and cranks and people his father had sent to the penitentiary; letters to his children and his siblings and a housepainter who hadn't finished a job) and superseded wills and photographs and official government memorandums and yellow legal pads with illegible notes about this or that case. Except for a few financial disclosure statements and an appraisal done on his mother's jewelry in 1990, there wasn't much that Crawford left behind. The owl knickknacks and paperweights and neckties and plaques didn't interest him much. Nor did the portrait of Justice John Marshall, peruked and prim. When Lucy asked him if he might like to have one of the robes, Crawford had hesitated. The robe not in the case, the so-called home-court robe, was in the closet, along with the raincoat and a pair of black rubber galoshes Judge Dupree had never worn. Crawford, gray haired, bags under his eyes, a crease between his pale eyebrows where dark thoughts were born, touched the sleeve of the robe tentatively, as if it were a relic with the scent of the deceased still on it. Lucy didn't say that Crawford's father had sometimes referred to the robe as his gallows costume. "With a hood and a sharp blade," he'd said, "I could go into business."

"I think I'll pass," Crawford said finally. "But maybe Morgan would want it." He didn't touch the raincoat, and mumbled unintelligibly when

Lucy mentioned that the coat was the one that had figured in the obit. It was said that Crawford had become erratic since he'd taken that whack on the head in New York not quite a year ago, in March of 2000. A bicyclist had hit him as he was crossing a street. He would check out all of a sudden, in broad daylight, disappear behind a scowl.

When Morgan came down from New York to go through his father's office things, he tried on both the robe and the raincoat. "I had a dream about this," he said to Lucy. "I put on my father's clothes, which were flapping in the wind on a clothesline, and everything fit perfectly. And then my ex-wife appeared and made a remark about what a fool I was." Morgan had once been a sportswriter, and now Lucy wasn't sure what he did. But you could see hope (or ambition or sexual energy) pulsing like a nerve afire in the middle of his brow; his long, thick, still-brown hair was swept back off his forehead so that the nerve or whatever it was would be clearly visible. In the robe, which was a bit short in the sleeves, he looked something like his father might have looked at forty-nine, had his father been more handsome and more vain. Morgan had been thinking of writing something about his dad, something along the lines of a memoir, which was one reason he'd come back home so soon after his father's funeral: he wanted to collect material. (He also seemed to hope to stake a claim to Lucy. He made her a little nervous, with his inquiries about her "situation," and she'd found an excuse for turning down his invitation to lunch.) It annoyed Morgan that his brother had made himself the repository for their father's papers. "Maybe I'll sue his acquisitive little ass," he'd said, though without vehemence. "Would you be willing to take the case on?" Lucy had said she wouldn't be a good choice. Morgan had packed up his selection of his father's possessions. It included a soapstone owl, a guide to New Orleans, a *Handbook for Judges,* a letter opener, the home-court robe, and an oil painting (a river scene) by his father's cousin Louis. The raincoat he'd left on its hanger. "Maybe Mom will know what to do with it," he said.

It was snowing the January morning Lucy drove out to Mrs. Dupree's house with the courthouse things. Snow wasn't exactly an oddity there at the extreme upper edge of the South, but many people drove as if each flake were a potential piece of an ice slick. Others, the owners of pickups and SUVs especially, drove as if the snow were a shower of dust motes, confetti, nothing. Lucy, whose car was a runty dinged-up Ford befitting a medium-grade government employee, drove in the slow lane, thinking about the Missouri River town in Nebraska where she'd grown up, where all the lanes were slow and some were dirt. The blacktopped one that went out of town, past the supper club and Cardew's apple farm and west toward Lincoln, was her favorite not only because it went somewhere but because it had a series of roller-coaster dips that her father, the proprietor of a motel and a movie theater until both failed, always drove with zeal, as if he were trying to separate Lucy and her mother from their stomachs. Lucy loved this, but her mother, who was prone to all sorts of maladies, did not.

Lucy got off the expressway and turned up River Road, a narrow, winding two-lane that followed the southern bank of the Ohio in a fairly rigorous way. It ran from downtown to near the county line. Judge Dupree, whose foot had contained no lead, had almost always taken it, rather than the expressway, to and from work. It was a road made for the Sunday driver, except where it shrank to one-and-a-half lanes in order to cross an ancient stone bridge that passed above Little Blue Creek, one of the river's tributaries, and then you couldn't dawdle. The Ohio was on Lucy's left as she drove east, behind a truck hauling pickles. There was nothing on the river this morning—no barges, no intrepid small craft. It was a blank slate, with snow swirling above it, the way one's mind swirls before it goes dropping off into sleep. In its winter state, the river reminded her of the Missouri as it slinked past her hometown, like some remote, unsociable, mumbling thing. In the spring, the Missouri, bloated with snowmelt, regularly climbed its banks and flooded milo and bean fields. Once or twice, she recalled, it got as high as the doorstep of her father's movie theater, which was down in a part of town that some people hoped the Missouri would take with it someday. The Ohio jumped its banks, too, some years. The Judge, who had grown up a half mile from the river, had told her stories about the Flood of '37, when for a month the only way off the Dupree property was by foot or rowboat. Of course, she, too, had seen the Ohio flood during her fifteen springs in Kentucky. She was thinking of the years gone by and tomorrow's appointment to get her hair cut, when the pickle truck turned off, into the Knights of Columbus club parking lot. She almost ran up its back, nearly skidded into the warty green monster dill painted on the rear. She liked pickles, they were a staple of her diet, though she preferred the sweet kind.

With both hands now on the wheel, Lucy drove down the whitening road, past the little club perched above the river where Protestant knights of business played paddle tennis and engorged their arteries with whiskey sours, past the bend in the road where there was a cross memorializing a car-wreck victim, past the road that led up to the Judge's boyhood home, where his sister still lived with her herd of Great Danes and free-roaming ducks and solitary ancient serving man, and to the now subdivided property where other Duprees and Mudges (the Judge's mother was a Mudge) had once lived. Between the road and the houses on the bluffs were meadows, fenced with the kind of dark creosoted horse-country fencing that horses could lean their heads over as they watched you shoot by in your tinny automobile, though Lucy had never seen a horse or any other animal along this stretch. What was a meadow in Kentucky without a horse? On a snowy day in January, it was an empty whitening space that made Lucy feel dull and sleepy.

She sipped coffee from a Kentucky Bar Convention travel mug and turned down the heat and switched radio stations from a classical one (soporific Telemann) to a rock outlet that would occasionally slip in an oldie between Limp Bizkit and Dave Matthews. Once on this station she'd heard an Elvis Costello song, which had transported her more swiftly than she might have predicted or wished to 1979, her last year in college, when she was reading lots of Henry James and was involved with her roommate and her roommate's boyfriend in a love triangle (it wasn't equilateral) in which she served mostly as confessor and go-between, and for her troubles was the recipient of four-hand massages. The boy, a physics major who had a cat named Schrödinger and a black birthmark under his eye that made him look like a pirate, had played Elvis Costello constantly. Now the station played something up-to-date, a male voice snarling behind snarling guitars, a terrible squall of sound. It led her to imagine for a moment being a boy listening to this music in his car, his thumpmobile, or in the privacy of his room, the room he'd had since he was six, the football pennants still up on the wall along with pictures of fighter jets and girls in spandex, saying, as the music punched him all over but especially in the holes in his ears that led through tunnels to his brain, "Yeah, yeah, oh yeah."

Lucy preferred the older guys. And also some of the dead guys, like Roy Orbison and Marvin Gaye. And all the jazz singers that her father had filled their little house in Nebraska with, who were also all now dead. (One of them, she remembered—was it Ella Fitzgerald, doing some wild upper-register scatting?—had always made Lucy's dog, Red, scratch at the door to be let out.) Sometimes, when she was out of range of the courthouse, Lucy would put Marvin Gaye or Sarah Vaughan in her tape player and, weather permitting, roll down the windows and sing along. She had an alto that wobbled among the notes enthusiastically. But the tape player in her eight-year-old Ford was broken now. She was at the mercy of the radio.

A few years back, she'd taken a car trip with Judge Dupree to Chicago. They were going to a conference on sentencing. This was two years before he'd kissed her and set in motion their peculiar, almost quaint affair. They'd taken the Judge's car, a Toyota sedan. He'd driven, a bit shakily, more than once inciting semi drivers to high dudgeon for not ceding a lane quickly enough. After lunch, Lucy had offered to drive. He'd have time to look at that bar journal article about forcible detainer she'd mentioned. It was boring as all getout, but germane to a case that was on his docket. Almost docilely, he'd dropped the clump of keys into her hand.

He nodded off no more than a page into the article. She drove up I-65 under a blue August sky in which not a cloud floated, past acres of corn and beans. She saw signs touting Jesus and herbicides and Dole/Kemp. The Judge twitched in his summer suit, like a sleeping dog dreaming of prey escaping, like a sleeping jurist dreaming of being reversed. Lucy turned on the radio and came upon a station that was playing Elvis Presley, nothing but Elvis Presley. Today, the deejay announced more than once, was the nineteenth anniversary of Presley's death. "Which if you go to Graceland, your tour guide will describe as the most gentle passing from earth to the next level you might wish for. He played a game of racquetball, you see, and then he sat down and quietly croaked. And if you believe that, I'll sell you some carrot juice that will increase your IQ by fifty points." Lucy thought the signal must be coming from a college campus—Purdue was in the neighborhood—unless the source was some airwave thief's trailer hidden in the cornfields. Anyway, the signal was strong enough that she heard a half dozen songs before the station began to fade. The Judge stirred during "Blue Moon of Kentucky." When he did, Lucy made a move to turn the radio off, but he said, "It's not bothering me. You can leave it."

So they drove past fields of tasseling corn and ditches full of chicory and fences dotted with red-winged blackbirds, who watched them go, and listened together to "Blue Moon of Kentucky" and "Suspicious Minds." Judge Dupree consulted a map, then cast his eyes forward again. He said, "Is this the man who said he was more popular than Jesus?"

"No," Lucy said. "That was the Beatles—John Lennon. This is Elvis Presley."

"That's right," the Judge said. He was still surfacing from his nap and his voice was husky. "The one who sang that 'Hound Dog' song. And was known as Pelvis, if memory serves."

"That's right," Lucy said, stifling a smile. She'd always assumed that his knowledge of popular music stopped at Gershwin or Hoagy Carmichael; he sometimes hummed snatches of one or the other at the office. But then again he had two children, from whom he hadn't insulated himself.

"I wonder if he took that as a compliment," Judge Dupree said. "Being identified as a body part."

"I imagine he got used to it." She steered around some carrion. This stretch of highway seemed to be full of it.

"In college," the Judge said, "I was known as Horse because my face had a certain equine quality." Lucy glanced at her employer. She'd not previously noted horsiness in his face, though it was true that it was narrow and unfleshy and his French nose was on the long side and his eyes, looming behind those lenses like objects underwater, sometimes seemed wary in a horsey way. "It wasn't a term of affection," he went on. "It got to me, I'm afraid, coming from well-bred East Coast boys with their fine manners and stickpins under their ties." Lucy thought the Judge's nap must have awakened something in him, some long-buried grievance. "I finally hauled off and slugged one boy. His name was Augie Weinglass. He was one of two dozen Jews in a class of five hundred. Augie acted like a character out of a John O'Hara novel, with everything he wore monogrammed. He was the only person I ever struck in my life. I did absolutely no damage to him; I hurt my hand more than I did him. I was a hundred-and-thirty-five-pound weakling." Lucy turned off the radio; static had overtaken the signal. "There were fifty other boys I could have punched, but I chose to hit Augie. He believed the reason I hit him instead of a Christian hockey player from

Andover was that I was an anti-Semite. He was right, though I like to think I've reformed."

Lucy wasn't quite sure how to take this story. In the twelve years of their association, he hadn't made her privy to much of his personal history, or, anyway, to that part of it that he couldn't relate as an anecdote of little consequence, though she'd heard stories (about his dipsomaniacal sister, for instance, and his bachelor artist cousin, Louis) from other sources. Did this confession mark a change in their relationship? As his days dwindled down, as he awakened from his naps, was he going to tell her about his missteps, his secrets, his laments, all that he hid (if indeed he did) beneath that gentle manner? The thought of having to revise her idea of him, of having to sift through all that he might be, scared her a little. She moved over into the passing lane to go around a truck carrying hot dogs and bologna and other meat products. She liked bologna. She'd been known to have bologna and pickle sandwiches for dinner.

The Judge shifted in his seat. He had more story to tell. "I saw Augie thirty years later at a bar convention in New Orleans. He was a civil rights lawyer in New York, but he was wearing one of those cream-colored planter's suits, almost like he'd been born to it. I said, 'Augie Weinglass? Is that you?' And he said, 'Horse? Well, I'll be damned.' He said he'd heard I'd been appointed to the district court and he wished me well. And then he slapped me on the back and said, 'Watch out for Jewish civil rights lawyers in planter's suits. They'll do everything they can to get an edge.' He turned up in my court some years later, not long before you arrived. He came down from New York with another lawyer to help represent a plaintiff who'd alleged discrimination, a woman who claimed she'd been denied a promotion by a chain of greasy spoons because of her color. Augie won. He would've won even if he'd worn his planter's suit. The facts were in his favor."

. . .

THE SNOW HAD PICKED UP. Lucy crept past a man and his dog walking by the side of the road. The man was in need of a hat. She turned off the radio. She went by Meehan's Bar-Be-Cue and Boat Dock and U R Hair and—she stepped on it here—over the narrow stone bridge that seemed to invite people to play chicken. She slowed down again and went past the Little Blue Creek fire station and the Little Blue Creek Baptist Church, a small white clapboard building with red double doors and a steeple that claimed a humble portion of the sky. It was almost like a child's drawing of a church, Lucy thought. A sign out front said, as it always did, Jesus Is Lord, in bigger letters than those used for the times of the services and the name of the preacher. Behind the sanctuary was a flat-roofed brick building where Sunday school classes met and the preacher had his office. On most Monday evenings for many years—right up until his death, in fact—Judge Dupree, a dyed-in-the-silk Episcopalian, had tutored children in reading and math in that brick building. It was for this sort of thing—as well as for the fact that a number of his major opinions had come down on the side of the weak and the afflicted—that Judge Dupree, a Republican whom Richard Nixon appointed to the bench, was known, in certain circles, as Judge Dugood or Judge Dugoody Two Shoes or Judge Duright If Your Idea of Right Is Left. To this, he'd said, "Well, it's better than being known as Dubad—or Dumal, if you want to get French about it." And then he had added, in an interview with the local newspaper of record, which appeared in the midnineties, around the time when he was thinking of retiring permanently (he'd long had senior status, a much reduced docket), "At the risk of offending some of my liberal friends, I admit to loving Jesus. Jesus is my Lord, and He influences my decisions inasmuch as He is the clearest example of love and mercy I've ever known." This remark—which had a rider that the newspaper didn't quote: "But I rule according to the law"—did get him in hot water, and he himself regretted his "too pious" tone. He also regretted speaking to the reporter, a young man who may have read the Constitution once, over lunch.

A mile beyond the church, Lucy turned right, up a road that, a sign said, was Private and had No Outlet. The road was narrow and had not been repaved, Lucy estimated, since before she became a federal employee. Perhaps the property owners were waiting for the day when the price of asphalt came down.

Lucy drove up a snaky incline, past a couple of driveways that were as long as landing strips, beneath old sycamores with their ghostly under-bark. The snow fell thickly now, lining potholes that Lucy bumped in and out of. At a blind bend in the road, there was a sign instructing her to sound her horn, but she didn't do it. She was thinking, not for the first time that day and probably not for the last, that she would soon be out on the street, without a job. She would receive her government paycheck until April, and then she would have to fend for herself. At forty-two and with her résumé, she was not the most marketable lawyer. Judge Dupree had long ago advised her—half-heartedly, to be sure—to pack up her briefcase and find more exciting work than tending to him in his dotage. Others, including Gene, her former boyfriend, had said she was com-mitting career suicide by spending her prime earning years with a judge who was semiretired and was handling fewer and fewer cases. It was time to put that expensive law degree to work. Lucy hadn't needed to be told that while it wasn't unheard of for lawyers to make a career out of clerk-ing, it also wasn't standard practice to clerk for a judge for more than a couple of years, much less fifteen. It had been whispered that she was hiding from the "real world" in her clerkish sinecure. But what was so wonderful about the real world? Most of the lawyers she knew who were in private practice complained endlessly about their jobs. Anyway, she would have clerked another dozen years for Judge Dupree, had he lived on. She'd loved the way he solicited her opinion. "Lucy," he would say, "I will be forever grateful for any light you can shed on this motion to dismiss." She'd loved the drugstore birthday cards he gave her. They all seemed to say, "You're the Greatest."

In 1998, for a period of about two months, he had come to see her at her apartment once or twice a week. The first time he came, he brought a jar of chicken soup that Ida, the Duprees' maid, had cooked. Lucy had been out of the office for several days; she'd caught a bug while visiting Gene in Washington. She'd not expected the Judge and when the door-bell rang, she was in her pajamas, the not-quite-sheer shorty pj's she'd bought on a lark, that for some reason she wore only when she was swollen-headed and feverish. She'd had the presence of mind to put a jacket on before answering the door, but the Judge, after telling her how much she was missed down at the courthouse, had left quickly, as if startled by the sight of her bare knees. A couple weeks later, after Lucy had returned to work, he turned up again at her apartment. It was a Saturday afternoon, Indian summer. He was wearing a short-sleeved pink shirt, and Lucy noticed how thin his arms were, how far up his forearm he wore his watch. He stood at Lucy's door and said, "My wife of forty-nine years has threatened to divorce me if I don't change my ways." He smiled only a little. She was properly dressed and she invited him in. She'd been repotting plants and watching football and waiting for her mother to call from her gated retirement village in Arizona and report on life with her second husband. (She was only one ahead of Lucy, though Lucy's first and only had been so brief that it almost didn't count, in the minds of either woman.) Lucy washed black soil from her hands.

"Who's winning?" he asked.

"Nebraska," she said. She'd grown up in a state where football was a religion. Even now, after twenty-five years of living away, she paid some attention.

"Go, Big Red," the Judge said, who, though unathletic, a hacker at the few sports he'd played (tennis, Ping-Pong), followed sports closely—too closely, in the opinion of his wife, who wished he would get out in the yard and water the trees. Didn't he know there was a drought going on?

Lucy said, "Mary Louise isn't really going to divorce you, is she?" She turned off the TV. The game was a slaughter.

"I think she might send me into exile for a while." He explained that his wife had been on him that morning for failing to organize the re-cyclables properly and also for neglecting to clean up a mess that the dog, an old West Highland white named Duff, had made in the breakfast room. The Judge had walked right through it and tracked up the kitchen. "I have bungled my sanitation duties, Lucy," he said, "and now I've come looking for sympathy."

Lucy brought him a Coca-Cola on the rocks and a plate of chocolate chip cookies, things he couldn't get at home. He came back a week later and again the week after that. He told her stories about his wife, his chil-dren, his long-ago youth. She fed him illicit foods. They didn't talk shop or discuss cases. Work was work, and this—whatever it was—was this. Lucy didn't tell anybody about the Judge's visits. She went to and from the courthouse and around town and, once again, to Washington to see Gene, with what felt like a state secret in her briefcase, though the secret was hardly earthshaking. They had conversations, the Judge spoiled his dinner by eating a Napoleon or a Krispy Kreme doughnut (with choco-late sprinkles), they watched football, the Judge gazed at Lucy with un-professional ardor and Lucy smiled or looked away or asked a question. The Judge's face was a flower blooming out of season, during some late, possibly fatal warm spell. At the courthouse, he kept this face mostly to himself, though it was clearly a struggle for him to do so. Once he threw caution to the winds and sent her a note through the interoffice mail. It said, "Would you be able to receive a caller on Sunday at four, by which time I hope to have obtained liberty from my keeper?" And once, in what was the climax to his visits, he leaned across the space between them on the cathouse-red sofa that Lucy had paid next to nothing for at a yard sale and kissed her squarely on the mouth. Lucy remembered his puckered, doughnut-sweetened lips traveling toward her slowly, as if the air were water and he were a fish, his eyes shut behind his glasses. She had seen this kiss coming for a long time, she had done nothing specific to discourage it, and she watched it land almost with relief, as if it were something to get beyond. What lay beyond, she hoped, would be a return to normal, in which she would be the trusty, diligent clerk, and he would be a senior judge, a little shabby and badly henpecked but a distinguished servant of the law nonetheless. So it surprised her when she kissed him back, though not hard and only, of course, with her lips. It must have surprised him, too, the way she leaned into him, for while a door to some neglected back room had suddenly opened, revealing light that was like the light at the top of the trees on a fall day, it shut almost as quickly. He stood up in a fluster laden with apology. Then somehow, while stepping away from the sofa, he fell and hit his forehead on the corner of her coffee table. Blood flowed as if from a faucet. Jumbo, Lucy's cat, came into the room and rubbed against him while he lay on the rug, and Lucy, kneeling, held a damp tea towel to the cut. He apologized for soiling her towel. He said his doctor had put him on a thinner a while ago for his heart, which maybe explained why he was bleeding like a stuck pig. He asked for her forgiveness, and Lucy, slightly irritated by his tone, said, "There's nothing to forgive, Judge." She cleaned the cut with Mercurochrome and put on a Band-Aid and walked with him outside to his car. He was quite pale; the bright October sunshine made him seem even paler. He said, "Do you have any advice about how to explain my mishap to Mary Louise? Or should I tell her the truth?" Lucy advised against telling the truth. He nodded in a sort of resigned way and said, "The truth would upset her, wouldn't it?"

The following Monday, he told whoever asked about the Band-Aid on his forehead that he'd run into the corner of a door in broad daylight. "Even on a weekend," he said to more than one inquisitor, "justice is blind." Lucy spent the day reading deeply in the United States tax code; a case in which the chief executive of a shadowy firm was hoping to recover certain sums from the IRS was soon to go to trial. When the case finally did come to trial, the Band-Aid was gone from the Judge's head. Lucy wrote a draft of an opinion that Judge Dupree praised for its clarity. A year or so later, he went into the hospital to have, as he put it, a piece of plumbing repaired. He came home from the hospital and peed streams of blood and went back into the hospital. A urologist from Bombay fixed him up, and after a period of enforced rest at home, he returned to the courthouse and solicited Lucy's views and remembered her birthday with a card from Walgreens. Some months later, Gene came down from Washington—he was a lawyer for the Nuclear Regulatory Agency—and told Lucy that he was seeing a man. Lucy went to Spain and slept with an Englishman, the owner of a chocolate factory. The Judge walked to lunch in his shabby raincoat and bush hat and heard a wino call him a motherfucker. In December of 2000, he fell while doing a sanitation job for his wife and landed in the hospital again. Lucy saw him there—a blood clot had been found in his leg and he had pneumonia —and in the course of their conversation about the Christmas party in Judge Norwell's chambers (Norwell, a fun-loving Democrat, had worn antlers), Judge Dupree brought up the subject of what he called their "extra-legal relationship." In a solemn voice, in the voice of someone making a deathbed speech, the Judge apologized to Lucy for what had happened between them and asked for her forgiveness and said that an old man's lust had corrupted him.

Lucy asked, "Was it really only lust?" She was afraid she sounded rude, but she hoped for a clarification.

He looked at her and then he looked past her, beyond her, as if the answer lay there. Or perhaps he hadn't heard her. There were times during the last few years when he'd missed testimony and such because he'd forgotten to wear his hearing aid or had left it in a coat that had gone to the cleaners. But he was wearing it today—it and his glasses and a hospital gown were all he was wearing. He weighed in the neighborhood of a hundred and twenty pounds now, fifteen less than Lucy, who was four inches shorter. He coughed while looking beyond her, and then Larry, a nurse whose strip of a beard was like a shadow on his long jaw, appeared and said that it was time for an oxygen treatment.

THE SNOW SPUN AROUND the Dupree house, whitening its red brick, filling the plant urns that stood on the porch. Lucy rang the bell, waited, caught a snowflake on her tongue, waited, fingered the holly in the wreath wired to the knocker, shifted the box of office doodads from one hip to the other, then put it down and went back to the car to get the second box. When she returned, Mrs. Dupree was at the door. She was wearing a long maroon sacklike robe—it put Lucy in mind of something a monarch might wander a drafty palace in—and fuzzy, pale blue booties. All that was visible of her were her hands and face. The lines in her face suggested that she'd reached some bitter conclusions about mankind long before this morning. Her nose was small and delicate, sensitive to anything the least malodorous, inclined to flare just before a rage came on. Her mouth was small, too; you had to look closely to see her smile. She was a tiny woman, no more than ninety pounds, counting her robe and slippers and the rings on her fingers, which often ached in cold weather.

"Oh, Lucy," she said. "It's you. I'd forgotten you were coming out. Excuse my appearance. I was up and down all last night, and now Ida has called, saying she doesn't want to get on the bus in this weather. There are a hundred things that need to get done around here. You'd think a big bus could make it through a little flurry, wouldn't you?"

Lucy did not attempt to correct Mrs. Dupree's impression that the snow now falling was only a flurry or note that it was a long way for Ida, who was pushing seventy and lived downtown, to come even in good weather. Anyway, the chances of getting a word in edgewise were not good. Talking to Mary Louise Dupree was like being caught in a downpour with no shelter in sight: you withstood it until it stopped.

"And I had an appointment to see Dr. Brinkman today." Dr. Brinkman was a chiropractor; Mrs. Dupree had sent her husband to him once, on the theory that an adjustment or two might improve his posture. "And I haven't had my hair done since I don't know when." With the tips of her fingers, she touched her hair, which was wispy but still dark. "Mr. Guilfoyle is on a cruise, of all things, and the last time somebody else did me, she nearly burned my roots, so I guess I'll have to wait until he gets back. Well, come in, dear, before we both catch our deaths."

Lucy brought in the boxes of the Judge's office things and set them down next to a chest on which a crèche sat. The baby Jesus, a thumbnail-size figure carved out of the palest wood, lay in a hank of blond hair. (Both Morgan and Crawford had once been fair-haired. Perhaps the manger hay was a remnant of their childhood.) One of the kings and his camel had tipped over. Lucy considered putting them upright, but decided against it. Better to let sleeping magi lie.

"I'm in a little boat on a big sea, Lucy," Mrs. Dupree said gloomily. Did she mean only that she was lost without a maid? Well, of course not. Her concerns were broader than that. She was grieving for her dead husband, wasn't she?

Lucy thought "I'm sorry" was not much solace, but it was all she could manage. The sounds of self-pity, at least as uttered by others, made her irritable.

A teakettle was whistling, high and insistent. Mrs. Dupree, who had a titanium ball and stem in her left hip, limped down the hall, leading Lucy past a portrait of a jowly, whiskery ancestor and past another chest on which the Judge's bush hat rested. She talked as she went. She said she needed to call the estate lawyer about something—she wished she could remember what it was. Clifford was such a slowpoke about doing things,

she said. "He's like hundred-year-old molasses, my dear. Sweet but slow."
In the kitchen, which smelled of burned toast, Mrs. Dupree remembered
what she needed to call Clifford about: a safety deposit key she'd found
in one of her husband's sport coats. "I never knew what I'd find in his
pockets," she said, turning off the kettle. "Peanut brittle. Vitamins he'd
forgotten to take. His hearing aid—I always told him he should have one
for the office and one for home, but he never got around to getting a du-
plicate." She poured boiling water into a bowl that contained a flaky,
grayish substance—oatmeal, perhaps. "Once I found something from
you, Lucy. If I hadn't known better, I'd've thought it was a love letter. It
was a card with a picture of a dog on it. I've got it somewhere, if you
want it back." She glanced up at Lucy, who had several inches on her.

Lucy was blushing, as much for her failure to remember what she'd
written on the card as for Mrs. Dupree's discovery of it. It must have
been a birthday card. "Your husband was a wonderful man, Mrs.
Dupree," Lucy said, her hands jabbing at the bottoms of her coat pockets. "He inspired me. He inspired everybody who knew him."

Mrs. Dupree stirred her oatmeal or porridge or whatever it was. The
loosening skin on her throat, above the ruffed collar of her robe, seemed
to vibrate, like a bird's. Lucy knew all about Mary Louise Dupree's temper, how she could fly off the handle in a moment.

"Some people think I didn't love him enough—my sons, to name
two. It was work sometimes, but I loved him more than they could know.
What could they know, living so far from home?" She said this in between spoonfuls of breakfast, her face turned away from Lucy, as if to
spare her husband's clerk some of the resentment she felt for her critics.

Lucy looked outside, at the snow whirling among the bare trees. A
crow came swooping toward the house, then angled off. Lucy told herself that she'd done her duty delivering the last of the Judge's things, and
now she was ready to leave. Then she realized that she'd left the raincoat
in the car, along with the traveling robe.

"They"—Mrs. Dupree meant her children—"just flew in and out and never saw what I saw. I had to train him to put his dirty clothes down the chute, for goodness sakes. He was off in his own world most of the time, thinking about cases or sports or Lord knows what else."

Lucy, who was becoming increasingly warm inside her coat, kept her tongue. She kept her coat on, too; she wasn't going to stay longer than was polite.

"Can I get you some tea, Lucy?"

Lucy declined. Mrs. Dupree opened a cabinet. There were a couple of boxes of tea among a sea of vitamin pill bottles. On the counter, in the dimness under the cabinets, were more vitamin bottles. Sometimes the Judge would come to the office with a bottle of vitamins—most of the alphabet, he said—his wife had packed for him to take at lunch. When Lucy had cleaned out his desk drawers, she'd found pills scattered about, a few in advanced states of decomposition.

"My sister said she slept with her husband's pajama top for months after he died," Mrs. Dupree said, taking up a new thread. "She wept into it every night. And then she remarried. Of course Vic was fairly young when he went. Sixty-one. And Betty is still young herself." She picked a tea bag out of the box—it was echinacea—and set it on the counter. Then she poured herself a glass of water from a ceramic pitcher gaily painted with jumping fish. "I have this fungus in me that I can't get rid of," she said. She drank only distilled water, Lucy knew; the Judge had been permitted to drink spring water, but of what came from the tap, the stuff doctored with who knew what, she had nothing good to say. "She came to the funeral. Flew in and flew out. Did you meet her?"

Lucy didn't think so. She had kept her distance from the family at the funeral.

The telephone rang. Mrs. Dupree answered on the fourth or fifth ring, after she'd finished her water. She told the caller how she was: "I feel like I'm in a little boat on a big sea, Dorothy." Lucy left the kitchen. She

passed the bedroom, noted the unmade bed with the comforter tossed
up like a crested wave, the drawn curtains, the tiny "lady's" desk in the
corner. Nothing of his was visible in the gloom. She gave the jowly ancestor a second look but resisted touching his descendant's bush hat,
which lay in its place like a stranded UFO. In the front hall, she stood before the mirror hung above the chest where the crèche was. She saw that
she was a clerkish color—pasty, wintry dull, the complexion, you might
say (she said to herself), of a single woman of forty-some years whose
footing in both the legal and extra-legal worlds was uncertain. She was
anxious and irritable and, though resigned to the fact that she was not by
any stretch beautiful or even particularly pretty, capable of making a face
at herself. She had a longish jaw and a hard little chin and a narrow nose
of the probing sort and she wore glasses that were more owlish than necessary. Her eyebrows were thin and gestural, more like concessions to the
idea of eyebrows than the real things. They gave her forehead more
prominence than she wanted, though she didn't attempt to hide her forehead with her hair. Her long hair, which until recently was a lovely chestnut color, she tied back with a scrunchy or occasionally put into a bun.
She had a good opinion of her hair, the creeping gray aside, and in a
weak moment she might have conceded that her mouth was wide and
full enough to qualify as "sensual." When she was a girl, her mouth—
and much of the rest of her, in fact—was an object of derision. A boy
once called her "Catfish," and she had made the mistake of saying back,
"A catfish has barbs, you know." She hadn't told the Judge much about
her past, nothing about her phantom ex-husband. He'd made polite inquiries, saying he hoped she wouldn't mind his asking, and she had offered up a few things and then changed the subject back to him. She
preferred his voice to her own, the elaborate courtesies, the kindly, me-
andering narratives (full of omissions, if you could put it that way) about
his family and his troubled relations, the occasional Southernisms (a
"bidnessman" was what his father had been, "supper" was what he called

dinner), the general absence of irony. If she tilted her head just so, she could hear him say, "Lucy, I would be forever grateful if you would cast your eyes on this brief."

Lucy turned away from herself and looked through a leaded-glass window that bordered the door. There, on the porch step, taking on snow the way a statue might, was Duff. Lucy let him in. He sniffed her with his ice-crusted muzzle and then trotted toward the kitchen. Lucy followed, hoping that Mrs. Dupree would be off the phone so she could say goodbye. In the kitchen, Duff shook himself vigorously, speckling things with melted snow. Mrs. Dupree, who had just hung up, instructed Lucy to go down into the basement and get a towel—"an old towel, in the laundry room, please." Lucy found the laundry room—it was next to the Judge's home office, a small bookish mess of a room—and a towel that looked older than new, and when she got back upstairs she began to wipe Duff off. Mrs. Dupree said, "Here, dear," and took the towel. She got down on her knees and wiped between the dog's toes. Duff submitted to this, while looking up at Lucy, as if in hope of an explanation. Mrs. Dupree scolded herself for leaving Duff outside in the snow, and then she began to talk about how her husband had walked the dog every day, up until the moment he fell down in the kitchen, right over there, by the refrigerator, when she asked him to wipe up some acidophilus he had spilled. She had made him drink acidophilus two times a day, in the belief it would be good for his GI tract. "I could have cleaned it up myself," she said. She started to cry and rose up from her knees in search of Lucy's arms. Duff ambled off.

Lucy held Mrs. Dupree for a moment, and then Mrs. Dupree let go and went to get a mug to put her tea bag in. Lucy went out to her car and brought the Judge's robe in. But she kept the raincoat and all the contents of its pockets.

# 2

# Hunting Pup

ON THE BENCH in his robe, Judge Dupree looked unimposing, not like a person vested with certain powers, able to say what the law was and wasn't. This was Crawford's opinion, anyway, when he saw his father in a courtroom in 1977. He looked less imposing than the prosecutor in his light summer suit making his pitch to the jury, less imposing than the U.S. marshal seated behind the defendant, an internist from Bowling Green accused of violating federal drug laws. Maybe it was the high ceiling and the great slab of burnished wood that Crawford's father sat behind that made him seem so wispy and unsubstantial. Or perhaps it was the fact that he didn't come close to filling up the high-backed leather chair. Maybe the proportions of the courtroom would have diminished any judge, even a bulky one who sat up straight. Crawford's father, who in his prime weighed a hundred and fifty pounds soaking wet, tended to sit at angles, tipped forward or sideways, leaning on an elbow. When his wife caught him in such a posture, she would reprimand him, as a mother would a child. He adjusted his posture for her, but out of her sight, even in grand settings like federal courthouses, he went back to being himself.

The courthouse where Crawford's father sat listening to the prosecutor sum up the sins of the Bowling Green internist was in Paducah, Kentucky. Judge Dupree tried cases there three or four times a year. He'd go down for a week, usually without his wife. He stayed in a motel called the Dogwood Inn. A couple of times, he had sent Crawford a postcard that showed the motel; no dogwoods were pictured, only a little square robin's-egg-blue swimming pool and cars from the fifties parked in front of an L-shaped building. In his arcane script—the letters tumbled into each other, like riders in a packed, jolting subway car—he would say that he'd slipped away from the lawyers one afternoon and done some railfanning (the Illinois Central yards were nearby) and that he missed Crawford's mother's home cooking (a fib—and, anyway, Ida did most of the cooking) and that he loved Crawford and looked forward to their next meeting.

In 1977, Crawford's father was fifty-nine, gray haired, six years from being eligible for senior judge status, ten years from being fitted for a hearing aid. (One of his clerks was Clifford Barnhill; Lucy had not yet graduated from college.) Crawford was twenty-seven, his long hair tied back in a ponytail. Crawford, who had taken six years to get his undergraduate degree, had quit law school in Oregon that winter, and was headed east with his girlfriend, Darla Frisch. Darla had a job lined up at a Washington, D.C., foundation. Her parents were Washingtonians, career government people. Crawford didn't know what he was going to do in Washington, aside from staying close to Darla.

Crawford had met Darla at a Mingus concert that spring. She was part black and part Jewish. He felt both intimidated and excited by her blackness and Jewishness. He had not believed his good fortune when, on their third date, she let him undress her in his moldy Eugene efficiency. Crawford thought he was just about over the hump then, safe in her affections. Later, when she called him "my little white hunting pup," he didn't feel uneasy, even if the implication was that he might be put outside for bad behavior. She'd laughed when she'd said it, and anyway he was happy to be hers.

When they'd checked into the Dogwood, Crawford tested the bed—Darla stayed on her feet—and then they drove downtown to the courthouse. They sat toward the back of the courtroom, next to a man and his straw hat. The hat, which had a soiled handkerchief in the crown, was upside down on the bench, airing out, and the man was dozing. It was midafternoon, a good time for a nap. Crawford saw his father shift in his chair as the prosecutor, in no great hurry, drawled out the evidence against the doctor. Words of a technical nature—"methylene dioxyamphetamine," "methaqualone," "phencyclidine"—hung in the air like vapors from a lab. Testimony had clearly shown, the prosecutor said, that the doctor had knowingly and intentionally imported and distributed Schedule III illegal substances. The doctor studied his hands. Judge Dupree removed his glasses and rubbed an eye.

Crawford had always found it unsettling to see his father without glasses. He looked naked and helpless, like a baby bunny that had wandered out of its nest. Crawford remembered one day in the early sixties, when he was twelve or so, watching his unspectacled father grope his way toward the swimming pool at the country club they belonged to, watching him step warily across the concrete apron, his eyes cast down, his mouth rather grimly set, the good humor with which he usually saw the world having vanished from his face because what lay before him was a blur of light and noise, a hundred voices, the acrid smell of chlorine, the faintly sexual smell of boxwood bushes whose tiny leaves littered the pool, the clotted summer air. His long swim trunks were cinched higher above his waist than was necessary or stylish, his body was as white as the moon except where black hair sprouted. Crawford had watched from the shallow end—Morgan was in the deep end, doing can openers off the high dive—and had wondered for a moment if he should go take his father's elbow and guide him down the steps into the water. And yet the sight of him looking so pitiful, like the kid who gets picked on in school, had annoyed Crawford. How could this man be the person who'd been elected in a landslide to a county judgeship, an office he would hold for another ten years, until Richard Nixon appointed him to a higher court? How could this pale person, this phantasm, be Crawford's father, the man who helped him with his algebra, who knew all the kings and queens of England and France from the Norman Conquest forward, who arbitrated disputes between Crawford and Morgan and between everybody and Mrs. Dupree (though, generally, it should be said, in Crawford's mother's favor)? How, Crawford had wondered, could his father be so different from him? When Judge Dupree finally entered the pool and began to do his version of the crawl, lifting his face most of the way out of the water when he took a breath, like a disoriented swimmer searching for shore, Crawford moved out of his path and watched him go by. Morgan, who had apparently spotted his father from the diving platform, swam over and greeted him. They horsed around. Crawford heard his father say, "Where's your brother?"

Now, in Paducah, Crawford's father put his glasses back on, as the prosecutor strolled before the jury box. Crawford leaned toward Darla and said, "You want to go back to the motel? Go for a swim?"

Darla frowned. "It would be rude to leave during this man's speech. And I haven't even met your dad yet."

When Judge Dupree announced a recess, they went back to his chambers. He had a view of the Ohio River and coal barges sliding south toward Cairo and the Mississippi.

Crawford hugged his father, felt his rough, whiskery cheek against his own. (This always surprised him; he expected his father's cheek to be soft, for some reason.) He noticed a hair growing near the tip of his father's nose like an alpine flower. Years of passing judgment and making rulings had worn parallel lines into his father's forehead; the lines were steady and resolute before fading out near his temples. The thick, complicated lenses of his glasses seemed to distort his eyes, cast unfavorable light on them, but this was an illusion: with his glasses he could see clearly, and without them he was legally blind.

Judge Dupree shook hands with Darla. He said that he was very pleased to meet her. His voice was warm and gentlemanly. What he actually thought upon seeing Darla—this cinnamon-skinned young woman with a bush of black, curly hair and round John Lennon spectacles—Crawford was not totally sure. He hadn't told his father or mother anything about Darla until shortly before he'd left Oregon, and then he told them only that he was bringing his girlfriend with him. To Darla, he'd said, "My dad is a moderate Republican. His great-grandfather fought with the Confederates at Murfreesboro. He grew up with servants and the usual prejudices, but he has tried to overcome them. Or most of them: his father told him when he was a boy that Democrats were scalawags, which most of them in Kentucky were, and I think he still believes that. I think he probably fears blacks who look like Angela Davis, and I've heard him use the word 'Jewess,' though he meant only to be descriptive. My mother is more of a wild card. She has a fair amount of Scottish cracker in her."

Judge Dupree said, "Are you all settled at the motel?"

Crawford said they had the room two doors down from his. "We might go back for a dip in a moment." Lodged in Crawford's head was a picture of Darla in a pool chair, sweat—lickable sweat—running down her chest and collecting at her navel.

"You're going to skip the defense's closing argument?" Crawford's father went behind his desk and picked up a folder. His face didn't suggest that the defense would be worth sticking around for, nor did it suggest the opposite.

Crawford noticed a photograph of his brother and himself on his father's desk. They were on a beach in Florida, in surfer's jams, circa 1964. Morgan, grinning, had his arm around his older brother, as if trying to console him for the defects in his personality. Crawford was squinting, looking as if he disapproved of the whole idea of a picture, and wanted only to go back to scouting the beach for girls. Anyway, he didn't want the particular girl he'd been gazing at to know that he had a family.

"I think we should stay," Darla said to Crawford. "How often do you get to see a courtroom as a spectator rather than as a defendant?"

Crawford grimaced. That winter, not long before he'd met Darla, not long before he'd dropped out of law school, he'd been arrested for urinating in a public place, a dank boulevard in Eugene. He'd been drunk enough to have upchucked on the policeman's shoes. He had apologized to the policeman for this last act, apologized profusely, but he'd spent the night in jail and had later appeared in court. The judge had stuck him with a fine and a hundred hours of community service, which, since Crawford had abandoned law school, he had plenty of time to complete that spring. He'd painted benches for the Parks Department.

"It wasn't anything much, Dad," Crawford said. "Just a misdemeanor. I didn't do any time."

Crawford knew enough about his father to know that his father wouldn't have wanted to know all the details. Anyway, the look of disappointment on his father's face told him that his father knew that the misdemeanor in question was likely to have been a consequence of drinking. At sixteen, after drinking nine Country Club malt liquor short boys, Crawford had crashed his father's Chevette into Mrs. Aurelia Crutcher's fifty-year-old magnolia—the Crutchers were distant cousins—and put a gash in his date's forehead. Drinking was what he'd studied hardest in high school. He continued to study it in college, along with dope smoking. Crawford's father hardly ever took a drink, not only, his son surmised, because he disliked the taste. There were people on his father's side of the family who were or had been in thrall to alcohol. There was, for instance, the rarely seen Uncle Ash, who had lived a virtual derelict's life in Mississippi, and Aunt Moira, who roamed her mansion by the river with a tumbler of bourbon in her grip. When Crawford was in town, she always invited him (but not her brother and sister-in-law) over for cocktails. And then there was Uncle Louis Mudge, his father's first cousin and best friend, who had spent a fair amount of time at drying-out places.

Crawford said, "Maybe we should stay and hear the defense. Maybe he'll be briefer than the prosecution."

LATER, WHILE DARLA took a shower, Crawford paged through the Gideon's. She had apologized for revealing his brush with the law to his father. It had just slipped out of her mouth, like so much nervous chatter. She hadn't meant to embarrass him, she said; she hadn't told his father any of the truly embarassing stuff.

Crawford didn't quite believe this explanation but neither did he question it. He was Darla's little white hunting pup: he would follow her anywhere, stand motionless in the woods until she said move.

He found the passage in the Bible he was looking for: Deuteronomy 1:16–17. When his father had been sworn in as a federal judge, he had placed his left hand on this page. Crawford's mother had held the Bible. The passage said, "Judge righteously between every man and his brother, and the stranger that is with him. Ye shall not respect persons in judgment; but ye shall hear the small as well as the great; ye shall not be afraid of the face of man."

Crawford had often heard it said that his father was above all else fair, that he did not respect the personage above the nonperson. There had been an editorial in the hometown paper not long ago to this effect— Crawford's mother had sent it to him—in which he had been praised for the way he conducted a civil rights trial. (His opinion, which the editorialist of this old-line Republican paper said was a stretch, went unpraised.) At home the rules of the courtroom didn't always apply, at least when his mother was a litigant. In arguments between Crawford and his brother, Judge Dupree appeared not to be swayed by Morgan's oral skills or by Crawford's lack of them, though Crawford felt that the record would show that his father had come down more often on Morgan's side. Crawford was older, his father had sometimes said, and should have exercised better judgment.

It was the conventional wisdom that Judge Dupree was a saint of sorts, but Crawford, a twenty-seven-year-old former law student with a better-than-average memory, could cite instances from outside the home when his father had seemed unfair to the less fortunate. Once, when Crawford and Morgan were of elementary school age and were walking to the car after a basketball game at the Armory downtown, their father said to a man who had asked for a dime for a cup of coffee, "It's not for coffee, it's for alcohol, and you know it." When the man said, almost plaintively, "I can't get a decent drink for a dime, sir," Crawford's father had shook his head in disgust. The panhandler was wrapped in a blanket, like one of the unhappy Indians Crawford had seen in TV westerns, and there was a black scab on his forehead. When they got farther down the block, Judge Dupree said, "Boys, let this be a lesson: don't ever try to have a conversation with a drunk." When Crawford said that the man didn't seem drunk to him—he'd seen Jackie Gleason and Red Skelton on TV, playing boozehounds—his father said, "His only purpose in life, Craw, is to collect enough dimes so that he can buy another bottle of liquor. He doesn't care about anything except his next drink." When Morgan began to lurch drunkenly down the sidewalk, Judge Dupree said, "It's not something to joke about." Not long after this, Crawford found out that his father had driven his cousin Louis to a drunk farm in Arkansas. In this case, Crawford judged, his father had apparently decided that it was OK to have a conversation with a drunk. Well, it was hard being consistent—and your children will always be there to catch you out.

Darla emerged from the bathroom, her hair wrapped in a towel and her torso in another. She was short, firmly made, with smooth little muscles she'd gotten from rowing on lightweight crews in prep school and college.

Unlike Crawford's father, Darla didn't look lost without her glasses. She crossed the room and pulled shut the curtains that had been open only enough to admit one crack of late-afternoon Kentucky sunshine. Then she sat down beside Crawford on the bed's nubbly, faded-white counterpane and took the Bible from him. "You shouldn't read in the dark," she said. "It'll make your eyes go bad."

Hairs, black and springy, poked out from under her turban. Crawford thought that if she undid her towels, he would be willing to expunge from his mind how she had embarrassed him in his father's chambers.

"Deuteronomy," Darla said, turning pages. "Moses cracks the whip."

"I was reading the part about God's instructions to judges." He kissed her on the neck.

"I'm looking for the part where God says 'Ye shall not lie down with those who eat crawdads and sheep intestines.'"

But she permitted Crawford, a lover of finless, bottom-feeding creatures if not of sheep intestines, to divest her of her towels.

Crawford sucked her nipples. They were hard little berries from some patch way back in the hills, blackberries swollen by the sun, nuzzled by bees; you had to go off the beaten path to find them.

"Ouch," she said.

He moved on top of her, his navel to hers, and then he quickly entered her, as if late for an appointment. He knew he ought to slow down, to breathe normally, to not go at it like a dog. The bed squeaked, which reinforced the idea that he was going at it like a dog. He tried to concentrate on the drone of the air conditioner, to fill his mind with the sound. Then he heard a rap on the door.

"Crawford? It's Dad."

Crawford stopped moving. He felt as if he were suspended above himself, above a buzzing body that might not actually be his. "Hi, Dad," he said.

"'Hi, Dad,'" Darla whispered into Crawford's ear, which always turned a hot pink during sex.

"I'm going to the pool," Judge Dupree said. "You can join me there, if you like."

"OK. We'll be there in a minute."

"Or two," Darla said. And then before Crawford quite knew it, she had put him on his back, under her. Darla was strong for her size. Oh, she was versatile. Even though she'd been a political science major, she could recite gobs of useless, beautiful literature, pieces from Byron's *Hebrew Melodies* or bits of Sappho or Whitman in a lather, all of which, Crawford supposed, would take her far. How would he, a spindly, ponytailed law-school dropout with no good idea of what to do next, keep up with her? She was bound to leave him by the side of the road.

THEY ATE DINNER at a Chinese restaurant, the only one in town. Judge Dupree was a regular there. When the owner shook Crawford's hand, he said, in an accent that had no southwestern Kentucky in it, "Your father is good man. Most good." Then he'd turned to Crawford's father and said, "You will be having Number eleven as always, Judge?"

"Number eleven, yes, thank you, Mr. Han." Judge Dupree was wearing a pink shirt and a madras tie with his pale blue poplin suit. His hair was combed and parted, and his cheeks glowed. He was a little overdressed for a Chinese restaurant on the banks of the Ohio, but it was his habit when going out in the company of women to put on his better things. Though the knot of his tie was, as always, not quite straight.

"And iced tea? Weak, so you sleep tonight, not like Chinese tea for dreams?" Mr. Han leaned toward Crawford's father, a grin lighting his moon face.

"Yes, weak, Mr. Han. Many thanks."

Darla and Crawford ordered beers.

When Judge Dupree's meal arrived—it was sweet-and-sour shrimp—Crawford watched him eat. Normally, he was a slow eater, capable of telling a story between bites, but he went at the shrimp with zeal. He used up all the sauce and asked Mr. Han for more.

"How does this stack up to Mom's home cooking?" Crawford asked.

"It's a change, Craw. But there's not much that can beat your mother's cooking."

Crawford had never heard his father be disloyal to his wife. What did his loyalty mean? How much love was in it?

Darla said she'd heard that Mrs. Dupree was into health food.

"She's a student of nutrition, Darla," Judge Dupree said.

Crawford said to his girlfriend, "My brother and I used to start our mornings with iodine in our milk and wheat germ in our cereal. We chased that with a saucer full of vitamins. Morgan and I flushed hundreds of dollars worth of vitamins down the john."

Crawford thought he saw his father lift an eyebrow as he transported a forkful of sticky rice toward his mouth. The shrimp were all gone. "How many vitamins does Mom give you every morning, Dad?"

"A goodly number," he said.

"It doesn't look like it's hurt you too much," Darla said to Judge Dupree.

"I'm doing all right for my age, Darla, thank you," he said. "Now tell me about your family."

Crawford sat silently while Darla talked about her parents, the Washington civil servants. For dessert, Darla and Judge Dupree shared a dish of peppermint ice cream, while Crawford chased his second beer with a cup of Chinese tea.

CRAWFORD AND HIS FATHER sat by the pool. The moon was out, looking somehow Chinese, beaming on two children splashing in the water. Under an umbrella, on the other side of the pool, were two men, neither of whom seemed to be related to the children. The men had out-of-state accents; the nasal tones hinted of the Midwest—Chicago, Flint, Wausau. They'd been fishing nearby—they'd caught mostly crappies, a word they pronounced with a flat, mocking *a*—and now they were drinking beer. Darla was back in the room, changing out of her dress.

"Well, Crawford," Judge Dupree said. "What do you think you'll do now that you've given up the law?" Crawford thought the disappointment he heard in his father's voice was due to the fact that they wouldn't be able to talk shop anymore. They struggled for ways to dispel the silences when they were with each other.

"I don't know," Crawford said.

"Do you have any job prospects in Washington?" Judge Dupree had taken off his coat and tie. It was a warm June night, one that a child in a motel pool might hope would last forever. Crickets chattered in the crabgrass.

"I'll find something," Crawford said. "I wasn't cut out to be a lawyer, Dad."

"Perhaps not. But sometimes it takes a while to grow into your work. My first few years as an attorney were dull as sin. I spent most of them in the library, napping. Now and then I would wake up and draft a will."

Crawford had heard this before. And then (the rest of the story went) the district attorney, a man Crawford's father had played squash with at the Y, had stirred him from his torpor and hired him as an assistant. And then somebody in the local Republican establishment, a man he served with on the vestry at St. John's-on-the-Hill, had suggested he run for judge of the circuit court, chancery division. Crawford remembered the "Dupree for Judge" flyers his father had handed out door to door, in neighborhoods where the doorbells played merry little tunes. Sometimes

Crawford and his brother went along. "Vote for my father," Morgan would shout as they hurried through a gap in a hedge toward the next house. Crawford's mother said that the picture of his father on the flyer looked like a mug shot; his cheeks seemed to be unshaven, his hair didn't sit down properly, and his solemn demeanor suggested he was guilty of something. "You won't get elected on this," Mrs. Dupree said.

Judge Dupree said to his son, "There's a man I know at the Washington *Star*. I went to college with him. Maybe he can help you out."

"Thanks, Dad. I'll be OK."

He watched the children in the pool. The older one, a boy, did play-by-play as he tossed himself a tennis ball. "And Bench hits a long one! He really tags it!" Crawford used to do this—be his own radio announcer as he shot baskets in his parents' driveway. He had liked the aloneness of it: rising off the asphalt however many centimeters, releasing the ball at the apex of his jump, seeing it swish in his own mind even before it actually passed through the hoop, hearing himself say "Dupree is hot tonight!" Sometimes he substituted names of the famous (Bob Cousy, Oscar Robertson, Cotton Nash) for his own. It annoyed him when Morgan would come out of the house and want to play. He felt as if his privacy was being violated.

One of the men sitting across the pool under the umbrella said, "I said to him, 'Charlie, how far you have to chase that jungle bunny to get that shirt?' It was the ugliest piece of crap I've seen in a long time—on a white man, anyway."

The other man snickered. "I think Charlie might be half-coon."

They went on like this for a while, squeezing their beer cans, making the metal pop, pitying Charlie, who, in addition to his poor taste in shirts, had a wife who was screwing half of whatever town they all lived in, it seemed.

Crawford wanted a cigarette, but even at the age of twenty-seven he didn't smoke in front of his father. He fidgeted in his pool chair, the bottom of which sagged. He was full of beer and Chinese tea and felt he might fall through.

Crawford's father got up from his chair and walked across the deck. His hands were in the pockets of his suit pants and his head was down. He walked slowly, stepping carefully around the towels and clothes the two swimmers had scattered on the pavement. His pink shirt caught the light that bounced off the pool. What was it about buttoned-down Southern men and pink dress shirts? Maybe there was something florid in their souls that needed an outlet, an ardor that was even greater than the desire to eat sweet-and-sour shrimp when away from their wives. Maybe it was just something they needed to run up the pole now and then, the flag of the island nation they inhabited.

Judge Dupree halted in front of the two men. One of them, the louder of the two, was tapping the butt of a fresh cigarette against the metal tabletop. Then he lit it with a lighter that gushed like a torch. His face was plump, his cheeks like bags in which nuts or seeds were stored. His sideburns flared a little. His friend was thinner and wore a cap, perhaps to protect his face from the moon.

Judge Dupree said, "I wonder if you gentlemen could have your conversation without using foul language." He waited for an answer with his hands at his sides. He was not quite six feet in his sturdy brown shoes.

"Who's wonderin'?" The speaker was the plump-faced man.

"We live in a free country," Crawford's father said, "and you may talk as you please. But common courtesy would hold that you watch what you say when you are in the presence of children or people who might find your language offensive."

"Oh, fuck you," the plump-faced man said almost wearily. "Fuck you twice. Why don't you go back to your rest home and take a nap."

Darla came through the gate in the fence enclosing the pool. "Come on, Dad," Crawford said, rising from his chair. "Let's go." Darla's rubber thongs flapped on the concrete.

"Yeah, scram, pops," the man with the cap said.

Judge Dupree, his head bent, turned and began to retrace his steps. The boy swimmer watched him. The girl swimmer was about to dive, her hands pressed together above her head prayerfully, as if she were trying to make an arrow out of herself. Crawford felt Darla alongside him, but he didn't look at her. He watched his father. His walk was slow and deliberate, his posture was some degrees shy of erect, a damp spot marred the front of his shirt. Was his father ashamed of him? Of course, even if he was, he wouldn't say so. He would never say so.

IT WAS TWENTY-THREE years later, January 2001, and it was snowing. Crawford had stopped somewhere in central Indiana, at a neon settlement surrounded by farmland. He could have gone on, driven around Indianapolis and then a hundred miles farther south to Kentucky, and if the snow didn't worsen, he might have been able to make it home by three or four in the morning. Maybe his father would have been still alive at that hour and able to recognize the elder of his two children through the fog that had collected where his mind had once been, obliterating a multitude of distinctions, a fog that Crawford's mother permitted the nurses to lighten with baby doses of Tylenol. Probably, Crawford thought later, he could have made it to his father's hospital room and sat with him for the last hour and even held his hand as he went wherever he was going with a tube in his nose and without his glasses.

But Crawford stopped. He went into a convenience store and picked out a six-pack of beer from the well-stocked cases. A million watts of electricity shined on the clerk's head, which had been shaved down to the scalp. Crawford asked him which of the local motels he should stay in; he had to choose from among four.

"They're all pretty much the same," the clerk said.

"Which one would you pick?"

The clerk looked up from counting out Crawford's change, as if he suspected that Crawford's questions might be preliminary to some drastic turn of events, as if he suspected Crawford—who was bleary-eyed, who had a pimple with a sesame-seed-like head on his chin—of carrying something in his overcoat. Crawford put the change in his pocket and took out a Kleenex and blew his nose. The clerk said, "If you want peace and quiet, I wouldn't go to the ones by the truck stop. The one over there"—he pointed in the direction of the Steak n Shake—"is OK."

"I'll say Rick sent me." The clerk's name was on his shirt.

"Kirk."

How had Crawford gotten "Rick" out of "Kirk?" Two out of four letters was not a high percentage for someone who wore corrective lenses that were only a few months old. Well, Crawford was tired. And then there was the matter of the blow to the head when the bicyclist hit him last year in New York. The accident had joggled him in ways that he couldn't quite get a handle on. He had headaches, he was slothful and passive, he had trouble remembering both remote and recent events, he would sometimes slur words.

"Kirk. Right," Crawford said. "She you later."

CRAWFORD CALLED HIS WIFE. It was eleven o'clock there, in the humpy moraine fields of southern Wisconsin. He had left home at four that afternoon, after his mother had phoned and said he'd better come before it was too late, after he'd decided not to fly because the weather was worse in the air than it was on the ground. Here, in the flatlands, beyond where the glaciers had advanced, where the wind was tossing the snow as if it lacked all substance, it was midnight, as it was in Kentucky.

Michelle said nobody had called since Crawford left, neither his mother nor his brother, who was back in New York. She said it was snowing hard now and that it was supposed to snow all night and that the schools would probably be closed tomorrow. Caroline, their daugh-

ter, was asleep. She and Philip, their twelve-year-old, were watching Jay
Leno. She was letting Philip stay up in anticipation of the snow holiday.
Crawford heard laughter, something that became a trickle of ha-has.
Michelle said Crawford shouldn't feel guilty for not driving on. Hadn't
he just spent two weeks in his father's hospital room?

"He knows you love him," she said.

Crawford twisted off the cap of his second bottle of beer. Michelle's
voice was soft and forgiving, a snowbank he could dump his head into.
When he'd married her, he'd known this much about her: that she
wouldn't ride him for his weaknesses if he permitted her hers, such as
they were. She ate junk food on the sly, she liked musicals, she believed
the most beautiful place in the world was a certain lake in the north
woods of Wisconsin, where she'd spent her childhood summers. She was
happy in a canoe, she was comfortable in a flannel shirt, she had sung
bedtime songs to her children in a tenderhearted voice. She was not impressed by smart people or wiseacres. But neither was she likely to hold
a grudge or work up a head of steam about some slight. She had imagi-
nation, but she didn't squander it. She saved it for her work, which was
teaching English to foreigners. Crawford sometimes thought he had
picked Michelle, following his unsuccessful first marriage, because she
would let him get away with being loving only when the mood was upon
him. And he had rewarded her, if that was the right term, with thirteen
years of almost complete loyalty. He had slipped only once, and even
then it was only a bobble. This was on the evening when the bicyclist—
a messenger, a Mercury—had struck him. Some of what had happened
immediately prior to the blow and the moment previous to that, when
a woman kissed him between the eyes, he had forgotten. But the kiss he
recalled without effort, as he did certain other facts and ambient sounds.
He remembered, for instance, sitting at a bar that also had a back-room
restaurant and a man in a jacket and tie playing piano. She was two
stools away, catercorner to Crawford. They looked at each other above

the rims of their wine glasses (red for her, white for him), during those moments when they rested their eyes from their reading material (the *Post* for her, the *Voice* for him), while cutlery clattered against plates and voices banged around in a New York way and the pianist, a light-skinned black man with a bushy mustache and steel-rimmed spectacles and a forehead that rippled when a particular sequence of notes tickled him, played tunes that Crawford thought he knew but could not name. Crawford was in town to visit his brother. Morgan was busy that evening, having drinks with somebody who might give him a job.

Crawford thought the woman drinking the red was a local. She was mid-winter pale. She looked as if she'd been knocked around by the day—blustery March winds, bruising cold, who knew what else—though not so thoroughly that she'd considered going back to her apartment, with its view of an air shaft, before having a drink or two. Her mouth sagged a little. Her throat was wrapped in a black turtleneck so that Crawford couldn't see the wine travel down it. He imagined it, however, soaking her tongue and sliding past her uvula and the spot where her tonsils had once been. He guessed that she was near his age, of the generation whose members had routinely undergone childhood tonsilectomies.

He was near the bottom of his second glass when the woman took a ringing cell phone out of her handbag and passed it across the bar to him. "It's for you," she said.

With this much wine in him, Crawford was usually capable of wit. But he said, "For me?"

"Yeah." It was as if a shade had just rolled up, and there she was, smiling above her black turtleneck. Pink and white her mouth was—a blossom that would keep if you kept it in wine, perhaps. "It's probably only a junk call."

The phone continued to produce its tittery jingle until Crawford found the right button to push. He traveled the streets of his midwestern city without a cell phone.

When he said hello, a voice said, "Evie? Evie? Who's this?" The pianist had just launched into a jaunty tune, something that Crawford recalled his father humming when everything must have been right with the world. Was it "I Got Rhythm"?

Crawford said, "It's Crawford."

"Crawford? Who the hell is Crawford?" The man pronounced Crawford's name as if it were a foreign substance he'd found in his soup. "Is this—?" He rattled off a number.

Evie took the phone back and squelched the connection. She'd moved around to the stool next to him. He noticed that she wore a gold wedding band and that her nails were chewed down.

"Thanks," she said. "It was an emergency."

They talked—about the bar (owned by gangsters, she said), about the bartender (a Russian named Timofey, who had worked on oceangoing freighters and eaten dog in Asia and monkey in Africa and been knifed by a man in Cádiz). Crawford looked at the bartender, his blond hair in a boyish sort of bowl cut, and did not see a man who had sailed the world and eaten monkey stew, but what did he know?

She said, "You remind me a little of Mr. Mears, my ninth-grade literature teacher. Maybe it's the eyes. Or the jacket."

The jacket was corduroy and soiled at the cuffs. Crawford admitted that he was a high school English teacher.

She saw that he was looking again in the direction of her wedding band. She held up her left hand and said, "It's supposed to keep certain kinds of men away. It's like an amulet."

"So you aren't married."

"Not right now," she said. She reached inside her turtleneck and pulled out a small black porcelain object that was hooked to a ribbon that went around her neck. It was a shoe, highbacked and clunky, like a workingman's boot, with little bull's-eyes painted on it. She said her *nonna*, who had come over from the south of Italy many years ago, had given it to her. Her grandmother had told her to rub garlic on the shoe to ward off evil, and she had, once or twice, when she was really afraid. "During a certain period in my life," she said, letting Crawford imagine brushes with mortality, a disease overcome perhaps. Then she explained that she'd once had a relationship with a guy in the recording business who turned out to be a stalker.

She asked Crawford if his wedding band was effective in warding off women.

Crawford said his wedding band was like a mosquito repellent that some mosquitoes had developed an immunity to. "It's not entirely effective." He meant to be humorous or charming or something, but the truth was that no woman had ever come on to him during his married life.

"I'm a bug?" she said.

"No," Crawford said hastily. "If you were a bug, you'd be like some beautiful species. I'd be Gregor Samsa. A cockroach. Do you know that story?"

She didn't. Despite whatever she'd felt for Mr. Mears, she apparently wasn't much of a literary person. She worked at a department store, though now, not quite a year later in Indiana, Crawford couldn't remember in which one or in which department. Possibly menswear or men's fragrances. But he did remember touching the shoe amulet that hung from the blue ribbon. And then he held it to his nose. Despite the material, it smelled flesh-warmed, slightly shoeish. And ungarlicky. Crawford took her response—a kiss on the forehead—to be forgiveness for the mosquito remark, or at least a desire to go forward in the curious way they were going. Though only a moment later she announced that she needed to leave. She said that maybe they could meet there at the bar the following night, at the same time. "That'll give you twenty-four hours to decide." She put her mouth next to Crawford's ear and said, "Buzz, buzz."

A few minutes later, he walked up the street toward Sixth Avenue. The day's winds had subsided. The air was almost placid, almost hospitable. Tomorrow was the vernal equinox, when it was possible, because of certain intersecting celestial forces, to balance an egg on its end. Or so he had read. He hummed a couple measures of "I Got Rhythm." When he crossed to the other side of the street, cutting between vehicles, a van and a compact, he was hit by the bicyclist, who would curse Crawford as he went down, calling him a dumb fuck.

MICHELLE SAID, "I DON'T see how you can still be awake. See if you can sleep some."

Crawford wandered around the motel room, touching the walls, the curtains, the television. He examined the print above the bed; it was an autumn scene, tawny colors, geese going south. He read the rate card on the back of the door, including chapter 145 of the laws of Indiana regarding the liability of hotels. He opened a drawer of the dresser and a fly flew out. He studied the pimple on his chin and decided not to pop it. He considered calling his brother, who had gone back to New York from Kentucky three days before Crawford had returned to Wisconsin. Morgan had said he couldn't take it anymore, the strain of watching their father die, and he had work to do—and work was respite from life. Crawford remembered his younger brother lecturing him, or seeming to, one day when they were coming home from seeing their father at the hospital. "Dad doesn't need me or you hanging around, muttering inanities like 'How's the custard, Dad?' and 'Those flowers the marshal's office sent sure are nice.' I can't help him cross the river, because I don't believe in the river or Jesus or an afterlife or any of that crap. I believe you do your best in life, and then it's lights out. He doesn't need me, Craw. Or you, either. We gave each other love in life, among other things, and now it's goodbye." Crawford was surprised at how angry Morgan was. His brother seemed to pride himself on staying cool; he'd perfected a sort of shrug, Crawford thought.

Crawford called Darla. He had all her numbers—office, cell, home, Maryland shore vacation cottage. They'd remained friendly after they'd split up, which happened not long after they arrived in Washington. Darla once said that Crawford would have been a good lover if there'd been no sex involved, if he hadn't been such an appalling mix of horniness and anxiety. She was only sort of joking. Three years into Crawford's first marriage, not long after his wife, Colleen, a veterinary school student who was beautiful with and without her glasses, had indicated a desire to leave Crawford for an industrial arts teacher, a man who was hoping to patent a coffeemaker that played "Hail to the Chief" when a certain button was pushed, Crawford had persuaded Darla to let him sleep over for a night. He was drunk and she made a bed for him on the couch. A few months later, after Colleen had concluded that her differences with Crawford were irreconcilable, Darla decided Crawford should meet Michelle. Darla and Michelle worked alongside each other at a liberal think tank. Michelle was a secretary and Darla was in PR. A plain white girl from the plains was how Darla described Michelle. Solid, modest, unneurotic. She played second base for the office softball team, distaff division. Darla played catcher. Darla liked being behind the dish. She liked to wear the gear and prop the mask on top of her head and survey the field like a generalissima, and she liked to chat up the batter. She would say to the batter, "Think about this, babe: I'm the first Afro-Jewish catcher in organized baseball, and I love the way those little green shorts fit you."

Darla's phone (home: an apartment not too far from DuPont Circle) rang and rang and then she picked up and said, "By the tenth ring, most people have given up." She didn't sound sleepy.

"It's Crawford. I'm in Indiana."

"There's a town in Indiana where some people go to bed at eleven, but across the street it's twelve," she said. "Or so I've heard. When the aliens land, they'll make Indiana the base of their operations, I hope you know." There was background noise, like a dishwasher shifting gears, hitting the scrub cycle. "What time is it in your part of Indiana, Crawford?"

He looked at the red digits on the clock radio. "12:39."

"Same as here," she said. "And you're in Indiana because?"

He explained. Then he said, "I need to be on the phone with somebody who isn't going to tell me that he's dead. I'm sorry to call you so late. Do you believe in the shoul?"

"The what?"

"Soul," he said, concentrating.

"I come from a short line of Afro-Jewish secularists," she said. "I'm really sorry about your dad. I liked him."

Crawford noticed that Darla had put his father in the past tense. Well, he was close to there—somewhere between here and there, if not in fact *there*. Crawford felt there should be a verb tense for his father's almost-there state—present imperfect, perhaps.

"He was brave," she said, "when he told those two guys to watch their mouths, wasn't he?"

Crawford said, "Yes, he was." When Darla had figured out what had happened at that motel pool—she'd had to wheedle the details out of her boyfriend—she had seemed to let it slide. She hadn't berated him for not coming to his father's aid, she hadn't put him outdoors. She continued to call him her little white hunting pup, as if in jest. Then one day when they were throwing the baseball around, which was not long before Darla started to see a political economist who worked at the think tank, she had said, "OK, bubba, OK, chickenheart, I hope you got your cup on because here comes the hard cheese." And then, a couple of throws later, while his eye was wandering in the direction of a woman walking by, she hit him on the thigh, though she claimed it was accidental.

Crawford knew that that throw—she had a good arm—was for all his bad traits. He knew Darla was going to dump him. But he was attached to her, as if by a leash. He wanted to be friends with her, and this was acceptable to her. She didn't dislike him, she just thought he fell short in some areas.

Crawford pulled open the night-table drawer. There was a black Gideon's and also a blue *Book of Mormon*. On the cover of the *Book of Mormon* was a water ring, where somebody had set a bottle or a glass— the sacred book as coaster.

"Jews don't believe in an afterlife, the soul going to some ultimate destination?" he asked.

"Some do. But you know how Jews like to argue and disagree."

Crawford was at the bottom of his beer. "I wish you were here, Darla."

"How's Michelle? Are you being good to her?"

"Yeah."

"You can cry, Crawford. It's OK."

"I don't want him to die," he said three times, in between sobs.


AT AROUND FOUR in the morning, after Michelle called to say that his father had died, Crawford put on his overcoat and went outdoors. The snow had stopped. Crawford listened to the sound of the traffic on the interstate. He tried to remember the name of the scientific principle for what happens to the pitch of sound when the sound-emitting thing approaches or moves away from the observer. Was a sound wave an actual thing, something you could see with a trained eye and the proper instruments, or was it a graphic representation of something theoretical? Crawford didn't know. He was a small body of ignorance standing in the parking lot of a motel in central Indiana on a winter night, shivering, unable to understand elementary things but capable of wondering if the strip club on the frontage road, next to the truck stop, was open, and if Kirk, the convenience store clerk, had gone home yet, to his girfriend or his mother or his dog.

Crawford stood in the motel parking lot waiting to hear a sound that wasn't a car or a truck or the wind or himself breathing.

# 3

# Apparition

FOR THE PAST FOUR SUNDAYS, Lucy had risen at 6:45, given the cat half a can of tuna-flavored food, showered and dressed, and then walked five short blocks to Grace Episcopal Church for the 7:30 service. She would sit in one of the rear pews, on the left side of the center aisle, usually, as it turned out, within a row or two of a black woman and her daughter or granddaughter, who was eight or nine and who always gave Lucy the once-over, as if she thought there might be a bird nesting in Lucy's long, not-always-tidy hair. Or as if—the girl wore black-rimmed glasses, the kind that signified studiousness or precocity—lack of faith were plain to see in Lucy's soaped-clean but still sleepy face. Lucy would smile an un-caffeinated early morning half smile, and later, during the exchange of the peace, offer the girl her hand. The girl shook it without enthusiasm, without responding to Lucy's "Peace," which Lucy once or twice almost made into a question ("Peace?"), and then passed the hand along to her guardian, a lady who wore on top of her marcelled blue-black hair hats bold with feathers and pins, hats that would have stood out even at

Easter or Derby Day, not to mention Lent, which was the season the church was presently toiling through. The lady, whom Lucy eventually learned was a young grandmother, gave Lucy's hand a polite shake and bestowed a polite "May the Lord be with you" on the rest of her before turning toward the preacher, who was advancing down the aisle in his purple and white vestments, hand extended, stomach swelling his surplice. The preacher always gave the girl a pat on her braided head and leaned close to the grandmother, one large, pale, unringed hand on her shoulder, as if he were exchanging with her something of even more importance than the peace. He nodded at Lucy as he passed her pew—Lucy always retreated to the other end of the pew after shaking hands with the black lady and her daughter, where she would sometimes encounter the soft, pious hand of an acolyte, an adult's; teenage acolytes were still in bed at this hour, it seemed—and Lucy nodded back. One Sunday, when the preacher nodded and she nodded back, she had the impression—it was stamped on her face, a glazed look—of having lived through this moment before. It was as if she were under a spell. She felt she would always be nodding at this man, the Reverend Alfred Lloyd (Sandy) Broyles Jr., like some davening Jew, and would never find the gumption to tell him that the reason she kept coming back and nodding at him was *him,* his pink handsome face in which she thought she saw doubt and faith contending. (She always left during Communion, without partaking, and thus never spoke to him when the service let out.) So, that Sunday, the second in Lent, she wrote her name and address—and a comment about the Reverend Broyles's previous week's homily—on a visitor's card, and dropped it in the offertory plate, along with a five. She regretted this immediately and considered chasing down the white-haired, blue-blazered plate passer and retrieving the card. But the deed was done. She was on record as having found the Reverend Broyles's homily on temptation to be "artful but not entirely persuasive."

On this Sunday, the third in Lent, she woke up at 6:45, with the cat hunkered on her chest, waiting to be served breakfast. Last night, she'd decided she wouldn't go to church, but now, in the light of day, looking at the remorseless black slits in Jumbo's green eyes, she decided she would. "Don't worry about making a fool of yourself once or twice a week," her father had said. "Most people do it eight times a week—twice on Sundays." Her father had been an avid nonbeliever. Her mother was a lukewarm Presbyterian.

So she met the cat's demands, showered, dressed in a fuddy-duddy plaid kilt and green sweater, tied a silk scarf around her neck, ate nothing even though she was starved, brought the paper in off the porch that she shared with her upstairs neighbor (a salesman of artificial knees and hips), put her index finger on the potting soil in which her temperamental begonia grew but did not blossom, watered it, and got her jacket out of the closet where Judge Dupree's raincoat hung, still dirty at the cuffs. She went out the door with the thought that if she'd been given a proper religious upbringing, something more rigorous than what she'd got from her mother's toe-in-the-water Presbyterianism, she would not be headed on this morning in March to any church. Had she had her fill of religion or at least enough to tide her over until her next crisis, she would have been headed toward Java Jimmy's for a cup of Sumatran and the *New York Times,* which she would read while hearing the ponytailed cabdriver, a Sunday morning regular, tell the tattooed coffee girl about his fares from the night before. Actually, Lucy was headed in the general direction of Java Jimmy's—at the corner of Mercer and Frankfort, you took a left to go to the coffee shop and a right for the church—and the thought that she could stop in for a quickie before proceeding to Grace occurred to her, as it had the previous four Sundays.

She walked down Mercer, her street, with its one- and two-family houses, squat brick ones and taller wood ones with screened-in porches half concealed by sharply slanting shed roofs. The morning was sunless and cool, the air prickled Lucy's shins, which she'd shaved last night during a marathon bath, but the daffodils that had sprung up during the last week, two weeks ahead of actual spring, stood straight, yellow and white throats open to whatever fell their way. Up ahead, at the corner of Mercer and Mason, in the yard where Buchanan for President signs bloomed every fourth fall, a Bradford pear blazed white, the kind of tree, with its upcurving branches, Lucy thought, that God might drape himself in, if He were inclined to make His presence known to some half-awake soul walking down the street in the Crescent Hill district of Louisville, Kentucky, in the second year of the new millenium, the first year of Little Bush. Though Lucy also thought that God, whose existence she was willing to posit for the sake of argument, was unlikely to disclose Himself to her, given His options and perhaps even His limitations: how many Bradford pears—and prickly pears and Seckel pears and Asian pears— could He be in at once? At the moment, the Bradford at Mercer and Mason was occupied by a stout-billed cardinal in high church plumage singing out something that Lucy first heard as "What cheer! What cheer!" and then as "Whatcha doin' here? Whatcha doin' here?"

Lucy hesitated at the corner of Mercer and Frankfort, and then turned left. She walked past the florist and the shoe repair shop and the store that seemed to serve as a graveyard for old computers and then entered Java Jimmy's. What she had in mind was a *café con leche*, something that might ease the thrumming near her left temple. A double would do it. Last spring, when she went to Spain, when she slept with the only man she'd slept with in ten years besides distant and wan Gene, she'd developed a taste for *café con leche*. She'd drink a couple cups in the morning and sail through churches and museums and Moorish gardens until lunch, when she'd have a little platter of Manchego and a glass of vino tinto and then go take a nap, except for the day she slept with the man whom she met under a royal palm in the gardens of the Alcazar in Seville. He was British, the owner of a candy factory, proud of his Spanish. As soon as he was finished with her, he left her room for the next town in Andalusia where he was peddling his chocolates. Lucy couldn't believe she'd fallen for him and had let him sleep with her. He wore tiger-striped bikini underwear, he smelled of a cologne or bath soap or shampoo that seemed to contain cocoa butter. He said he never took naps; he was too busy.

A bell tinkled as Lucy entered the shop. Heads turned to see what had come in off the street. One belonged to a woman in tight-fitting jogging clothes, whose mouth was at that moment full of scone or muffin, a Sunday morning indulgence perhaps: she had that pared-down, almost haggard look of the habitual runner. There was a guy sitting on the sofa over in the corner, mostly obscured by newspaper. And there, at the table closest to the cash register, was the cabdriver, untied hair running free down his back like that of a Plains Indian, silver stud in his ear, long whiskery face, a honker of a nose. There were two other early birds: Lucy had to stand in line to order her double *café con leche* to walk.

While she waited, Lucy listened to the cabdriver tell the young woman making the coffee (not the tattooed girl, this was a new one) and everybody else within earshot about a book he was reading, some sort of how-to book about communicating with the dead. "You're probably too young to even know any dead people," he said, hoisting his Java Jimmy's travel mug to his lips.

"My grandma died," the girl said, steaming a tin pitcher of milk. "When I was six. Does that count?"

"Sure, that's a start," he said, plunging ahead. "The point of this guy's book is that the dead are lonely, and they want to talk, they want to know what's going on, any little tidbit about life would, you know, make their day. So, what he's saying is that it's a two-way street. Like I want to say stuff to my dad that I didn't get to say before he passed and my dad wants to know about me: am I still driving a cab, how's the dog, did I see the Louisville-Memphis game the other night? My dad was a basketball junkie. He had a quadruple bypass the day the Cards were playing

Cincinnati, and the first thing he said when he woke up was, 'Did we win?'"

"What kind of dog do you have?" the girl asked, trying to keep up her end of the conversation while also trying to make foam for Lucy's drink.

Lucy said to herself, *Hound dog*. Didn't people own dogs that resembled themselves or some idealized notion they had of themselves? Lucy's little Nebraska dog, Red, which some hot-rodding boy ran over when she was ten, was pure mutt, frisky, itinerant, genial, much like Lucy's father, though Red didn't share his master's musical tastes.

"Part hound, part undetermined," the cabdriver said.

Lucy received her coffee from the girl and put thirty-one cents in the tips jar. She thought that if the girl received enough tips she might be able to afford a shirt that covered her lower abdomen. Not that she disapproved of bare midriffs—or navel rings, either: the girl had one—but she guessed that the sight of them made yakkers like the cabdriver even more talkative. Maybe the cabdriver regarded wherever he placed his hairy bottom—she supposed it was hairy—as the equivalent of the interior of his cab, a podium on wheels in which he freely spoke his mind to a captive audience.

Lucy was surprised at how crabby she felt this morning, and when she turned toward the door, she smiled at the cabdriver, as if in apology for her thoughts. The cabdriver said, "Hey! How's it going?"

Lucy stood on the sidewalk and sipped her double *café con leche*. She wiped milk foam from her lips, and waited for the thrumming at her temple to cease. On the railroad tracks on the other side of Frankfort Avenue, she saw a man walking, a suitcase of a bygone style and material in his hand, a hat the shape of a pith helmet on his head, and a raincoat, which was either tan or filthy, on his back. He was headed east, out of town, at a pace that wouldn't get him there until late next week at the earliest. He had this way of walking that was deliberate but tottery; he leaned a little to the left as if he were trying to hear a voice coming from that direction. She thought she knew him. She walked up the sidewalk, toward the church, keeping abreast of him, trying to rid herself of the thought, delusion, whatever it was, that the man was him or the ghost of him, her former employer, Judge William C. Dupree. She didn't believe in ghosts, the so-called spirit world, the souls of the dead strolling railroad tracks on a Sunday morning or any other morning—any more than she believed you could have an actual conversation with a dead person. (Or a dead animal: she'd tried to talk to Red, when Red was in his grave near the shed behind her house, and gotten nowhere.) She was a lawyer, if an all but unemployed one, trained to make distinctions, to analyze arguments for their omissions and missteps and half-truths and undocumented assertions.

Lucy stopped in front of the church. The person walking the tracks stopped, too. He set his suitcase down and turned toward Lucy, removed his hat (his hair was a wintry color: grayish-white), and raised his hand as if to wave. Or perhaps he was brushing a fly away from his face, though the morning was still too cool for flies to be at large. Unless one had been hiding under his hat, keeping him company as he walked out of town. After a moment of deliberation, Lucy decided he was indeed greeting her and she waved back. It was the friendly thing to do, even if the man was a spirit, a possibility she would now entertain for the sake of argument. Though the man's face was a bit of a blur from this distance —thirty paces, at least—she did see a resemblance in the shape of his head to that of her late employer. And he wore glasses, though the gold frames were not the kind the Judge had favored. But why would a spirit, if there were spirits, choose to reveal himself as the tattered person he was at the end of his life? Why shouldn't he appear as the boy he was, the college student he was, the middle-aged man he was?

She drank the dregs of the coffee, licked at the last bubble of milk foam, and then went up the brick path that led to the church's front door. Forsythia bloomed under the church's tall windows—a yellow so bright it made her blink. Some of the bricks in the path had heaved up, a fact she'd noted on previous Sundays but failed to account for on this gray morning. Anyway, she was turning around for a final look at the man or ghost on the railroad tracks while also stuffing the coffee cup into her jacket pocket when she stumbled and in the process of trying to right herself stumbled again and fell in the direction of a man— where did he come from?—whose shoes were so vividly polished she could almost see the look of alarm on her own face.

SHE SAT IN HER customary spot after being guided inside by the man whose shoes reflected aspects of the world—sky, church steeples, falling women possessed by demon caffeine. He told her that the brick walkway had come up for discussion at a recent meeting of the vestry. He said there was a faction that wanted to remove it and put down concrete, and another faction—"bricklovers," he called them—who wanted to pre-serve it. The church itself was brick. He was in favor of a concrete walk. They'd put in a concrete ramp for wheelchairs, so why not tear out the dadgummed bricks?

"I wasn't looking where I was going, I'm afraid," Lucy had said for the third or fourth time, wondering if the man was trying to elicit from her a declaration that she wouldn't sue. He had a rather firm grip on her arm as he led her into the nave.

She looked at the scrape on her hand, on the so-called mount of Venus. She felt old, though she was, with the exception of the spectacled girl, surely among the youngest of the congregants at this service. The heads in front of her were chiefly gray and white—those of widows and widowers, or married couples who'd survived a hundred illnesses and frights, men who'd fought in wars and women who knew what a rum-ble seat was, people whose children were close to retirement, people who had been up for hours before the preacher uttered his first "Blessed be God."

She was warm—coffee sometimes made her sweat—and she took off her jacket and scarf.

The hat the little girl's grandmother wore this Sunday was in the shape of a shallow cooking pot, like the caps that Muslim men in desert countries wear to keep their scalps from burning, except the material was black velvet and the velvet was sprinkled with colored beads and flashing oddments and a crescent of a silver moon. Space encircled her head. Lucy assumed the woman's hats were homemade. Maybe the woman spent Saturday nights preparing a covering for her head that God would smile upon in the morning. Or maybe she invented her hats willy-nilly, on whatever night inspiration struck. Maybe she had a husband, not a churchgoer, with whom she passed the night in front of the TV set, a husband who was unimpressed by her hats and held on to the remote like it was the one link to the future. Or maybe there was a boyfriend, somebody she let court her but not stay overnight. There was something staunch and formidable about her—it wasn't just her squarish figure or the hair that was so elaborately done up—and Lucy thought that whatever secret life she might have had was wrapped up in those hats. The hats were where she displayed what she withheld from the world in other ways. Lucy considered what someone might deduce about her own self from her uncovered head and the tumble of her hair. That, generally speaking, she preferred less hairy men to very hairy ones? (Gene had been unhairy, if little else.) That, like pregnant women, she liked to eat pickles from the jar, especially sweet bread pickles, and sometimes with bologna, while watching football or baseball on TV (she would die for Omar Vizquel, the Cleveland Indians shortstop, even though he appeared to be somewhat hairy)? That on the one occasion when she'd smoked pot, back in 1978, she'd also gone to see *Dumbo* and had fallen asleep?

Now, sitting up straight in the pew, her hands in her lap, she felt she was being watched, as if through a curtain that she'd failed to pull. It wasn't the little girl or her grandmother who was watching her. They looked steadily forward as the organist played a prelude, waiting for the preacher to emerge from the wings. Whoever was studying her was behind her. Lucy's face was flushed, and she pushed a strand of hair off her forehead. She wanted to turn around, but she resisted even when the Reverend Broyles and his two associates appeared and it came time for her to rise. When she did finally look back, following the collect, she saw the man who had picked her up off the sidewalk, winking at her, as if they were co-conspirators, members of the Anti-Brick League. And then she saw, several pews closer, a face she knew she knew but could not identify, a man who was grinning at her through a beard that was perhaps only a few days of not shaving. Was he a lawyer, somebody from the courthouse? Not many lawyers she knew, at least in the western district of Kentucky, wore beards that could have been mistaken for dereliction or let their hair dangle much beyond the tops of their ears or sported (in court or church, anyway) a milky pink pearl ear stud. Maybe it was some guy she'd seen at the gym she took her burgeoning thighs to every so often.

He gave her a waist-high wave and she nodded back as if in recognition. (Sunday was a day of resting *and* nodding, she'd concluded.) When she sat back down for the reading of the first lesson, it came to her that the man was Morgan Dupree, the Judge's younger son. When she'd last seen him, in January, in his father's chambers, he was smooth-faced and, as far as she'd been able to tell, unpierced. Probably he'd come down from New York to visit his mother. But what was he doing at this church, which, while of the denomination he'd been raised in, was not the family parish? That church, called St. John's-on-the-Hill, was out in the eastern part of the county, more or less in the direction the old man or ghost had been headed. William and Mary Louise Dupree had been married there, over fifty years ago, and Judge Dupree had been interred there not quite three months ago, in the garden, in a ceramic jar that had a pleasant yellow and blue design on it, something almost jazzy. She re-membered the neatly bladed hole into which the preacher placed the jar, the pile of coppery dirt beside the hole. The grass had been thick and dark green; it seemed to have been exempted from winter.

The grandmother with the hat that was a mirror held up to heaven read the first lesson (Jeremiah, in a take-no-prisoners mood) and led the as-sembled through the verses of the Psalm and then made her way, fearlessly and solemnly, through the passage in 1 Corinthians in which Paul preaches against unauthorized fornication. "What? Know ye not that your body is the temple of the Holy Ghost which is in you, which ye have of God, and ye are not your own?" Lucy wondered if the black woman's granddaugh-ter regarded her body, still somewhat short of budding past girlhood, as forever the home of the Holy Ghost. Was the Holy Ghost so omnivorous that it displaced all dreams and desires? The body was pretty demanding, after all, its wants not necessarily idle ones. You might say that it had a mind of its own. More than it wished for coffee or pickles or a hot biscuit, it sought another body to press against. Or so it seemed to Lucy.

Lucy thought unclean thoughts as the Reverend Sandy Broyles dis-cussed the passage from the gospel in which Jesus calls the unclean spir-its out from the Gadarenes in the mountain tombs and distributes them among a herd of swine. She thought of what it would feel like to lie alongside the Reverend Broyles, who was a divorced father of two and therefore available, or so she'd deduced from previous sermons. Because of the nature of the text, she thought more than once—it kept running through her head, like a tape—of a TV jingle about a local brand of ba-con: "Sam Macon's, we make bacon the Macon way." She thought of Morgan Dupree's ear ornament. Why a pearl—and a pink one at that? She didn't have a pearl to her name, not even a fake one. She didn't often buy jewelry on her soon-to-vanish government salary. She bought pick-les and low-risk mutual funds and exhaust systems for her car and dry cleaning for her collection of dark courthouse suits and health care for her cat and, in December, a fifth of Buffalo Trace bourbon, most of which she put into eggnog, which she served to the salesman of artificial knees and hips and to the fifteen or twenty other people who came to her annual New Year's Eve gathering. (The Judge and the Mrs. had come some years, but both had foregone the eggnog.) She wrote checks to a women's shelter downtown and a women's legal aid project and to the Humane Society and to the Cootie Williams Memorial Jazz Society (in memory of her father). In January, she'd written a large check to the railroad museum her late employer had founded. She lived modestly, at times thriftily, though she wasn't beyond imagining herself draped in a strand of cultured white pearls, which her one little black cocktail dress would go nicely with, if she could squeeze herself into it. She saw herself in the dress and pearls, hair in some sort of bun, the tender stalk of her neck exposed, legs poured into black stockings. She looked, in her opinon, not bad for a somewhat tall forty-two-year-old Nebraska girl too shy or too proud to wave a flag of distress here in this polite upper-South city. She saw herself standing in her apartment with the Reverend Broyles, who, a secular being by night, had exchanged his clerical collar for a turtleneck and a blazer; Cootie Williams played growl trumpet in front of the 1940 Ellington band, and the salesman of artificial knees and hips (who always drank too much and stayed late) danced, and Morgan Dupree, coarsely bearded and enigmatical, sat by himself. A moment later, she saw a multitude of swine, some in fine clothes, one in a black dress too small for it, plunging violently down a hillside toward the foamy sea. Should she tell Morgan Dupree that she'd seen a likeness of his father walking the railroad tracks this morning? Or should she leave now, before the exchange of the peace (or, as she sometimes thought of it, the shaking of the hands), even before the Reverend Broyles had wrapped up his sermon on the sinful and burdensome thoughts that nag at us, whose persistence requires regular purgings, healings of the most radical sort, such as Jesus performed on the tormented Gadarenes?

SHE CAME TO A STOP beyond the church door, her thoughts a little swarm circulating in the still sunless but promising air about her head. She was sweating under the arms and between her bosoms. She felt as if she'd left something behind. She checked the pocket of her jacket and found her keys and the squashed coffee cup and her snap-and-fold wallet. She wasn't big on purses. She had one for work and one for dress up, an antique black silk purse that she'd used maybe once in the last five years, at the Public Defender's Holiday Ball, to which she'd taken Gene, her gay boyfriend.

She took a breath. Why was she here, outside, on the uneven red brick sidewalk, instead of there, inside the church, reciting the prayers of the people? For one thing, she'd needed to flee the desire to look at the preacher in his vestments, to see his unpolished brown oxfords sticking out from under his robe, to hear the lulling music of the liturgy through his voice, a medium-slow upper-South drawl. She was grasping at straws—wasn't she?—thinking that church might do something for her. And then there was the presence of Morgan Dupree, with his pearl ear stud and raffish beard and tweed jacket that she recognized as having belonged to his father, whose invitation to lunch of two months ago she'd declined because, well, in part, there was something rather intense about the way he looked at her and also because she knew he wanted information from her about his father for his book or memoir or whatever it was—and what if, in a moment of weakness, she should reveal something about the period of unprofessional intimacy she shared with the Judge, chaste as it had been, which Morgan would surely distort for all the world to read and titter over? Was it an accident that Morgan had turned up at Grace? If not, how had he known to find her here? It was certainly jarring to see him. The whole morning had been rife with jarring sights, and she wondered if she should return to bed and start the day over.

She walked up Frankfort Avenue, hands in her jacket, past the bakery where she'd bought Napoleons (she'd fed one to the Judge), past the old movie theater (porn, wasn't it, at one time?), which had become an over-priced restaurant, thinking that what she heard in the not-so-distant distance was a train horn. The blasts of the horn, which were long and nearly continuous because this stretch of track was full of crossings, set loose in Lucy a feeling of dread. She saw the train approaching, felt the concrete on which she walked quiver, saw a boy nearly clip her as he went by on his bike with its banana seat and monkey bars and streamers flying from the handles. The thought occurred to her that the train, a freight pulled by four diesel engines, was gaining on the man or ghost who'd waved to her from the tracks not thirty minutes ago. She imagined him crushed, dismembered, his hat and flimsy suitcase all that survived him. But if he was a ghost—and she was now almost willing to accept that he was, because it was easier to imagine than the alternative—he wouldn't be harmed and she might even see him again. This eased her mind. She stopped and watched the train go by. She counted cars, as she'd done as a child and as she still sometimes did when caught at a crossing, because it was almost like a form of meditation. Or prayer— prayer that this, too, would pass. She was up to sixty-four when she saw Morgan Dupree. He had a way of walking that was a little like a cat walk-ing, if a cat could walk slew-footed, crossing the floor to the sunlit spot on the sofa where it took its late-afternoon naps.

He pulled her scarf out of his jacket and handed it to her.

"Oh gee, thanks," she said. "I thought I'd forgotten something."

During the course of their conversation, in which it was revealed that Morgan was an old friend of the Reverend Sandy Broyles—Sandy's fa-ther had been the rector of St. John's-on-the-Hill when Morgan was a boy—and that he, Morgan, was planning to move back to town, perhaps to this very neighborhood, at least for the time that it would take him to write his book, the clouds lifted and the sun came out. The March sun shined on Morgan's beard-in-progress and seemed to illuminate his

Hudson or along the Sound and into the dark countryside. Standing in clouds of steam, in the exhalations of a train just arrived from some far place, the name of the girl he'd been supposed to meet at the Biltmore was all but lost to him.

"This turkey is so salty," Mrs. Dupree said. "Don't you think so, Gina?"

"Maybe a little." Gina was Morgan's girlfriend. This was her first encounter with Morgan's family.

"Drink some water," said Crawford, who was on his third beer.

His wife, Colleen, whose cheeks and throat became rosy when she drank, which she did almost as enthusiastically as her husband, leaned across Morgan and said to Judge Dupree, "Crawford told me a story about how you all ended up at White Castle one Thanksgiving night and some guy held it up."

"It's an unlikely story," Morgan said. Colleen had her hand on Morgan's leg in what seemed to him to be an intentional way. Colleen was a person whose hands wandered, sometimes in explanation, sometimes in exploration. She and Crawford had met on the Washington Mall, shared a joint while watching some steel drummers from Trinidad. She was a waitress then and was hoping to go to veterinary school if she could ever finish her undergraduate degree. She was from a little town in southern Alabama. Her father was in the construction business, and they had a beach house on the Florida panhandle. She wore glasses and around her neck a gold locket that had a picture of a dog from her childhood. Dogs, though she presently owned none, were her passion. Morgan thought that his long-haired brother, who bore a resemblance to a sheepdog in search of sheep, might be a substitute. As far as Morgan could tell, sex was the grease that made their marriage go. Last night, Morgan and Gina had listened to Crawford and Colleen copulate on Morgan's living room floor. At one point, Colleen seemed to be speaking in tongues. In the morning, while Morgan stood in his tiny kitchen boiling water for coffee, Colleen had arisen from the floor like some groggy sailor girl and walked half-naked to the bathroom, her locket shining on her chest. She gave no sign that she noticed Morgan, though he was in plain sight. He thought that his brother was right about her: she was beautiful both with and without her glasses.

Judge Dupree cut into his turkey—white meat, no gravy—and said to Crawford's wife, "It's not a story I like to recall, if I can help it, Colleen." His voice was amiable and he even smiled a little, as if to suggest to Colleen that his reticence was perhaps simple modesty.

Morgan noticed gray whiskers under his father's chin, a patch his razor hadn't found. It gave him a bit of a billy goat look. Sometimes Morgan would look at his father and see someone who might, conceivably, somehow, because of a certain neglect of self, because of a tendency to wander off on his own, perhaps even because of some hidden desire to be somebody else, disappear, like that New York City judge (Crater, wasn't it?) who vanished during the Depression, and wind up among hoboes or with the homeless under Grand Central. Beneath the steward of the law and the gentleman and the loyal family man, Morgan imagined, was a wayward creature who could slip from all the tethers of bourgeois life. When Morgan had told his brother of his theory, Crawford had said. "There's no goat in Dad. There's sheep and there's this noble person. He's not like you or me."

Morgan said to Colleen, who had not let up on his thigh, "We try to keep that story in the closet." Though the truth was that he had told it, with variations and omissions, to friends, particularly to women (Gina among them) whom he had hoped to entertain or seduce or both. "Along with the other skeletons." Morgan glanced at his father, who was chewing his turkey, and then turned again to Colleen. Her face was so close that he could have licked the wine stain off the corner of her mouth almost without moving. The big square-framed glasses she wore seemed to magnify her green eyes, of which Crawford had once said to Morgan, "Imagine what it feels like to have them focused on you."

Colleen said, "I'd like to hear you tell the story, Morgan." He smelled beef on her breath as well as French red. She'd ordered prime rib instead of turkey. "You're the writer in the family."

"Would later be OK?" Gina was studying Morgan from across the table, while pretending to listen to Mrs. Dupree discuss the hazards of salt.

Colleen withdrew her hand. The subject of nuclear annihilation came up. Morgan's brother, who in those years was taking night-school courses toward a teaching degree, raised it. "I wonder where we'll all be when Reagan and the Russkies start dropping bombs. Will we be eating dinner in a hotel in New York? Will we be at the Modern, trying to make sense of Motherwell or Rauschenberg? Will we be back in Kentucky, chasing fireflies across the lawn with our jelly jars that have holes poked in the lids with an ice pick so the poor things can breathe while they expire?"

"Oh, Crawford," his mother said. "You're just talking through your hat."

"No, I'm not," Crawford said, resolutely.

Morgan had given up trying to understand why his brother almost always rose to the bait that his mother dangled before him. Arguing with her was a hopeless cause; she was invincible.

"And I'm not wearing a hat," Crawford continued. "Maybe you can reserve a space in Ron and Nancy's bunker in Virginia and watch old movies with them while the bombs fall. Maybe they'll show *Bedtime for Bonzo* or *Knute Rockne, All American.*"

"You seem so angry these days, Crawford," Mrs. Dupree said. "Maybe you should cut down on your drinking."

"Christ," Crawford said.

"Crawford is obsessed with Reagan," Colleen said to Mrs. Dupree. "He can't believe he won."

"Him and his harridan of a wife." Crawford got up from the table and walked off in the direction of the rest room. A moment later, his mother announced that she had a terrible headache, she'd had it all day, and was going to the powder room. When she stood, her husband rose from his seat, both in gentlemanly deference and to show sympathy for her plight, and said, "Maybe the mâitre d' would have an aspirin."

The mâitre d' was sitting at the bar, reading the *Post*. He had the demeanor of an undertaker who had stuffed his last body of the day and was ready to go home.

"I can't take aspirin, you know that," Mrs. Dupree said. "It upsets my stomach." She spun on her heels.

Colleen turned to Morgan and said, "Did Crawford just call me a harridan?"

Later, after they'd eaten dessert (Crawford had another beer instead, Mrs. Dupree had nothing), after the solitary diner wearing the ascot had dropped by the table to tell Crawford that he'd seen worse movies than *Bedtime for Bonzo,* after Gina and Mrs. Dupree and Crawford and Colleen had gone uptown in separate cabs, Morgan walked with his father to Grand Central. The station's proximity to the Biltmore was, after all, the reason they'd eaten at the hotel.

They walked under the immense ceiling speckled with stars and then through the gates to the tracks and out onto the platforms. Morgan's father surged ahead, as if in anticipation of seeing some railroading marvel preserved in the tunnels beneath Park Avenue, but there was little to see, aside from dingy, forlorn commuter coaches and the superannuated engines that pulled them.

Judge Dupree suggested they sit for a moment on a baggage cart at the head of a platform. A homeless man rolled his shopping cart by. It was heaped with debris—flattened cardboard boxes, black plastic bags containing who knew what, a TV with one rabbit ear. Farther away, a couple stood alongside a Hudson Line diesel and kissed. Morgan thought his father wanted to tell him something important—that his mother had come down with some dread disease, say, or that *he'd* been diagnosed with something terrible, or that something needed to be done about Crawford's drinking. But what Judge Dupree said was that he thought Gina was a fine girl and that he hoped Morgan would stick by her. Morgan had had inconclusive relations with a number of young women over the last few years. He'd started seeing Gina in the summer.

"It's probably not good to jump around a lot," Judge Dupree said, while looking toward the throbbing diesel and the couple alongside it. "From girl to girl, I mean. You only get so many chances."

"Sure, Dad," Morgan said, unable to disguise his annoyance. He would have liked to quote to his father what his father had quoted approvingly to him several times before: Justice Brandeis's defense of the right to privacy. Morgan knew it by heart: "the right to be let alone—the most comprehensive of rights and the right most valued by civilized men." It was a right that Morgan himself sometimes forgot to respect.

Judge Dupree gazed steadily out at the tracks. Morgan couldn't think of a precedent—not of a recent one, anyway—of his father sticking his nose into Morgan's business. On the rare occasions when his dad gave advice, it seemed he did so reluctantly, as if he had wrestled with the idea of saying nothing and lost. Some years later, it occurred to Morgan that his mother must have put his father up to this.

MORGAN WAS UNDER the blankets, reading, when Colleen came into the room. She shut the door behind her. "Crawford is snoring," she said.

Morgan put his book down. It was a collection of stories by an elderly Italian man who wrote for the *New Yorker,* where Gina worked. The book was inscribed to Gina, in Italian. Gina, who was Italian on her mother's side, was spending the night in her own little broom closet of an apartment. She was hoping to get some sleep before taking the train in the morning to Rhode Island to see her family.

Colleen was wearing a nightgown, if you could call it that, which came to about midthigh and was made of a shiny, synthetic material. It was the color of the moon, as colored by a child bearing down hard with a silver Crayola. She'd worn her glasses, but now she took them off and placed them on Morgan's desk, which was a piece of plywood that rested on two sawhorses. She stood next to the desk, not quite sure where or if to sit. The choices were the bed, which was a mattress on the floor, and the desk chair.

"Crawford snored when he was a kid," Morgan said. "I'd practically have to punch him to get him to stop. And he didn't always have a bunch of beer in him. But once when he did—he was about sixteen and starting to take up drinking in a serious way—I got a Magic Marker and gave him a new face. And in the morning he came down to breakfast without looking at himself first, and there he was, with a pointed beard and little red horns on his forehead—a hungover devil. My father and I were the only ones at breakfast at that moment. My mother tended to get up late. Dad kept glancing up at Crawford from behind the newspaper, and then he finally said, 'Crawford, I think you better go visit the washroom.' My brother just about killed me—it took him forever to clean it off."

"So your dad knew he'd been drinking?" The radiator, a quaint old thing, hissed like a teakettle. Even so, the apartment wasn't especially warm, and Morgan thought Colleen must be cool in her nightie. Her arms were folded across her breasts.

"I was never quite sure how much Dad knew about Crawford's drinking —or mine either, for that matter. But I imagine he was able to make some deductions from the time Crawford wrecked the car and also the time he came home and ralphed on the Oriental in the family room."

Colleen said, "He doesn't drink every night. Just sometimes he gets carried away." Morgan noted that she seemed to say this in sorrow, not in the hope that Crawford would become the person she'd thought she married.

Morgan had believed his brother's marriage was doomed from the beginning. Neither partner was a steadying influence on the other. He himself had no immediate plans for marriage. He was not yet thirty.

Colleen unfolded her arms and gripped the edge of the desk. "So, can you tell me the story now?"

Morgan was trying to concentrate on Colleen's face, but his position on the mattress made it difficult. He wondered if he should give her something of his to put on. His tweed jacket was right there, on the desk chair. "My brother won't tell you?"

"He did, sort of. But he said I should ask you about it. Since you're the writer." Morgan considered denying this, since what he wrote mostly—it was his job—were articles about the hotel industry. He worked for a trade magazine. On the side, he wrote about other things—sports, mainly. He was hoping to become a sportswriter someday, if, as he thought likely, he didn't make it as a fiction writer.

"Aren't you?" she said, tilting her head sideways. Morgan thought he saw her batting her big Alabama-girl eyelashes. Anyway, he couldn't deny that he had written a handful of stories, all unpublished, one of which was about the White Castle incident. That one was on his desk, under a coffee mug that held pens.

He got up from the bed—he was in his underwear—and took some pages of typing out from under the mug. Then he got his bathrobe out of the closet and gave it to Colleen before getting back into bed.

He said to Colleen, "It's kind of a long story. Don't you want to sit down?" He didn't pat the bed.

She sat in his desk chair, a ladderback made of bird's-eye maple, cane-bottomed, the one piece of furniture he'd brought with him from home. It was rickety from all the times he'd leaned back in it. Colleen tucked her feet under her, and then, perhaps because the position was uncomfortable, she untucked them.

"I didn't know you'd actually written a story about it," she said.

"Yeah." He'd written it long enough ago for it to have been rejected several times. So he'd lied when he'd said to her at dinner that it was a story that his family tried to keep in the closet, inasmuch as he was a member of the family. He hadn't even changed the names when he wrote the story. "Should I read it to you?"

"Sure." She abandoned the chair and moved to his mattress.

# 5

# "End of the Steam Age,"
# by Morgan Dupree

THANKSGIVING 1961. On the way home from the football game at the fairgrounds, my father suggested to his cousin Louis Mudge that we take a detour. Dad wanted to see a steam locomotive that was parked in the Louisville and Nashville yards, a 4-8-2 that the L&N, an all-diesel line by then, had borrowed from the Illinois Central for an anniversary excursion. He didn't seem to notice that most of the day's light had fled or that cold mist fuzzed the air. It didn't matter to him that he'd be riding the excursion train to Nashville a few days later; he wanted an early peek. I looked at the hair standing up on the back of his head, like a woodpecker's crest, and I thought that a person whose hair sat flat wouldn't have proposed a side trip like this.

Uncle Louis, whose brown felt hat was speckled with confetti, said that seeing the IC engine parked in the L&N yards would be like seeing a movie star in her house clothes.

My father said, "I'd pay full dollar to see Ingrid Bergman in dungarees."

Crawford, my older brother, who was almost twelve, spoke up from the farthest corner of Uncle Louis's Ford sedan, which smelled of to-bacco and dogs and old newspapers. "Who's Ingrid Bergman?"

My father didn't answer Crawford's question, perhaps because the prospect of seeing the IC engine had made him deaf to voices from the backseat.

I watched a raindrop slide down the window and thought about a halfback named Perryman jittering through a confusion of pads and helmets and then flying free across stadium dirt. Perryman played for Male High, a school my father and his cousin had attended twenty-five years before, when it was all boys and all white. Perryman's shoes had been wrapped with tape to make it look as if he were wearing spats, like a drum major. The Manual High defenders hadn't had a chance.

Uncle Louis chuckled, maybe at the idea of Ingrid Bergman in dun-garees, maybe at the earnestness with which my father expressed himself. Uncle Louis had been chuckling all afternoon, in between sips of coffee from a Thermos. Not too many months before, he'd been in Arkansas. I'd heard my mother say to somebody that he'd gone there to "dry out." I'd imagined him lying on a plank, baking in the sun. When I asked Crawford about this, about what it meant to "dry out," he said, with a certain authority, "It means he needs to get some air. His bones are damp and achy."

Our father had driven his cousin to Arkansas. On the way back, Dad had spent a couple hours in the rail yards in Memphis, taking pictures of rusting, coal-burning locomotives and their diesel replacements. That night, he'd written his cousin a letter on Peabody Hotel stationery. The letter, which mentioned a "beautiful" 4-8-4 Dixie Line locomotive he'd seen that early autumn afternoon, had ended up in the rear seat of Uncle Louis's sedan. My father had signed it, "Devotedly, Bill."

Uncle Louis turned off Second Street onto St. Catherine. The L&N yards were toward the west side of downtown, near cigarette factories and distilleries, not far from where Ida, our maid, lived. She'd spent the morning in our kitchen, helping my mother prepare dinner, and then we'd driven her home on the way to the game. When we drove through her neighborhood after the game, I didn't see anybody on the streets, except for a man who was looking under the hood of a car.

"They're rolling up the sidewalks, Billy," Uncle Louis said. "Hardly any place for us boulevardiers to go except the rail yards."

My father said, "We'll make it quick."

When we got out of the car, the mist had become drizzle. Uncle Louis pulled down the brim of his hat; it shielded his glasses but not the tip of his beak. He wore a long wool overcoat and baggy trousers held up by suspenders. Like my father's clothes, Uncle Louis's always looked as if they'd been tailored for his shadow, or for the person he might become if only he would eat three square meals a day.

My father didn't wear a hat or suspenders, but he bore enough of a resemblance to his cousin that they were sometimes mistaken for brothers. It wasn't just their noses or the glasses with the thick lenses or their slightly stooped, unathletic builds. They'd grown up next door to each other, on a bluff above the river, separated only by an acre of lawn. After they graduated from Male High, they temporarily parted ways: my father went to college out East and Uncle Louis attended an art school in Cincinnati. During the war, when my father was back home, studying law, and Uncle Louis was painting landscapes that looked as if they'd been done by someone with an astigmatism, they'd served together in the Kentucky militia. They'd trained on weekends. "We were going to mow down the Krauts as they boated across the Ohio River on a Sunday afternoon," Uncle Louis said. He also said that the brigade's commander had described my father as the worst soldier he'd ever seen and him as the second worst.

My father zipped up his plaid jacket and strapped his camera across his chest and led us toward the roundhouse, where he believed the IC engine was being kept. We passed between strings of freight cars that seemed to go on forever, into the gloom. Crawford said, "This is boring." He kicked at the gravel. He was wearing basketball sneakers he'd scissored the tops off of because he thought he'd look cooler that way. Our mother had yelled at him for ruining a good pair of shoes.

Our father, who moved at a meditative pace when not around trains, was traveling at a near trot now. Uncle Louis said, "Billy, if the Pinkertons come after us, I'm not going to be able to outrun them." Uncle Louis had always moved as if tomorrow was a fine time to get somewhere, and his stay in Arkansas hadn't made him any faster. He stopped to light a cigarette.

My father turned around and said, "The Pinkertons are having Thanksgiving dinner now."

Uncle Louis said to me, "Your father is a model citizen, except when it comes to trains."

The locomotive and its tender were, as my father had predicted, outside the roundhouse. An L&N diesel switcher sat some yards in front of the IC engine, almost protectively. I'd seen a number of steam engines in my short life, mostly by the light of day, and I didn't think this one was more impressive than the others. Or less so. It had eight driving wheels and they were all taller than me by a foot.

My father hopped back and forth across the tracks, shooting pictures from different angles, trying to stay ahead of the dark, which kept coming down, along with the rain. "I trust you opened your aperture wide," Uncle Louis said. He borrowed Dad's camera and had us stand in front of the engine, with its moon face and tarnished silver bell.

"*Père et fils sans chapeaux,*" Uncle Louis said, fiddling with the lens. "Soaking up the atmosphere in the L&N yards. 1961: near the end of the steam age."

"Say it ain't so," said my father, who smiled through the drizzle.

Crawford didn't smile. It was my older brother's policy to present a solemn face to the world, when he could manage it.

Uncle Louis put his hat on my head. For a second, I felt like I'd just walked into a warm, smoky room with big chairs to lounge in. My father asked Crawford if he wanted to pull up the hood of his coat, but my brother said he was fine.

We walked back to the car and got in. When Uncle Louis turned the key, the motor made no sound, not even a click. My father, who sometimes complained about the corrosive effects of the internal combustion engine on modern life but knew little about repairing one, said, "Must be a wiring problem."

Uncle Louis said, "Could be."

"Maybe it's the radiator," Crawford said. "Or the valves."

Uncle Louis said, "Could be."

We went to look for a pay phone. We didn't get far before Uncle Louis remembered that there was a pie in the trunk. Robert, the black man who kept house for Uncle Louis, had cooked it. Uncle Louis had intended to deliver it to a friend of his late mother on the way to the game.

Uncle Louis got the pie, and we walked out of the yards and along a dimly lighted street toward Broadway. My father led; he walked briskly, at close to his rail-yard pace. A skinny, sallowish dog waited for us at a corner, next to a bus bench. Uncle Louis said to me, "If it's mean, we'll give it a slice of pie." The pie was pecan.

When we passed, the dog lifted its nose slightly. Otherwise, it showed no interest in us.

"It was hoping for banana cream, I bet," Uncle Louis said.

We turned up Broadway, which was better lighted but not any less deserted. We passed a vacuum cleaner store, a loan company, a wig shop with silver and red hair hanging on eyeless plastic skulls. We found a phone in a White Castle, the kind of place my mother, who had never seen a french fry she approved of, might skin my father alive for taking her children into. There were two black men at the window counter, eating dinner.

I said we should call Ida. Maybe her son Alvin, who drove a garbage truck for the city, could come get us.

My father said Ida didn't have a phone.

"Duh," Crawford said.

Uncle Louis ordered Cokes for me and my brother and a coffee for himself while my father called my mother. Dad said "Honey?" and then explained where we were. Eventually he said, "We'll just hail a cab."

"Sounds like you're in the doghouse, Billy," Uncle Louis said.

Dad called a Yellow Cab and then bought a nickel carton of milk and sat down on a window counter stool between me and Crawford. He wiped his glasses with a napkin. Without his glasses he looked grim, as if he were waiting for the next blow to fall.

The two black men finished their meals and lit cigarettes. One saw the purple Male High booster button on Uncle Louis's coat and asked if Male had won.

"Thirty-four to thirteen," Uncle Louis said.

"Perryman ran wild," my father added.

"That Manual coach don't have the brains of a housefly," one of the men said. They got up and went out the door.

A radio was playing in the back of the restaurant. It was tuned to a station that Ida sometimes listened to when she was ironing in our basement. I watched out the window for the cab. Crawford sucked at the last drops of his Coke through a straw, as intent as a scientist working on an experiment. Uncle Louis sipped coffee and picked confetti off his hat. Then he asked me if I'd ever heard the story about the goat my father's family had kept when he was a boy.

I didn't recall any stories about goats. I was trying to listen to the song on the radio—some man trying to say how much he loved a girl. My brother sucked on his straw until Dad said, "Crawford, that's enough now."

Uncle Louis said, "Well, your grandparents had a goat named Cyril.

He was named after a fellow your granddad and my father played bridge with."

My father said, "That goat was the sorriest creature." The recollection seemed to have cheered him up.

"In the summer," Uncle Louis said, "Cyril liked to sleep under a car, where it was cool. Oil would drip all over him and he'd get filthier than he already was. So then he'd decide he needed a bath and he'd amble over to our house and take a dip in the pool."

I didn't understand how a goat could decide it needed a bath, but I didn't say anything. I watched a man wearing a hooded blue windbreaker come through the door. The drawstring in the hood was pulled so tight you could see only a portion of his face. He went to the order window and asked for a hamburger.

"Just one?" the lady asked. Most people ordered six or seven at a time; one was about one bite's worth.

"Yes, ma'am," the man said.

"Anything to drink?"

"No, ma'am."

When she brought him the hamburger in a little white box, he asked her to put the box in a bag. She did, and just when she was about to hand it to him, he said, "Give me everything you've got in the register, except for the pennies and nickels and that kind of shit. Just put it in the bag, please." He was pointing something at her; it was hidden under the windbreaker.

My father and his cousin were laughing. Now they were talking about a dog Uncle Louis had owned a long time ago, a terrier, that somehow got trapped in a utility pipe and had to be extracted by a plumber.

"Don't give me those fuckin' quarters," the man in the windbreaker said. "They'll break the bag. Just the bills."

"Yessir," the woman said.

I tapped my father on the arm and said, "Dad?" I noticed that he had nicked himself shaving, just above his Adam's apple. I glanced back at the man in the windbreaker. He was looking at me, at all of us. Only the center of his cold-reddened white face was visible.

My father and Uncle Louis didn't stop talking about the terrier until the man in the windbreaker said, "Don't do anything dumb, mister." He sounded like somebody trying to sound older than he was, like my brother did, when he tried to explain to me a scientific principle like gravity, for instance. The man in the windbreaker was addressing a large man in an apron and a white paper hat. The robber was backing up toward the door, the hamburger bag with the money in one hand and a silver-barreled gun held high in the other. The gun looked like one I no longer played with, a cowboy six-shooter that came with a tooled leather holster that had a thigh string. When the man was abreast of us, Uncle Louis, who was closest to the door, swiveled on his stool and said, "You don't need to hurt anybody. Just take your money and go." Uncle Louis was between me and the robber. My nose was close enough to Uncle Louis's overcoat that I could smell the whole day in it—that and my own fearful breath coming back at me. On the robber's nose, I saw a red dot, like a pimple or a boil.

Uncle Louis later said that his first mistake had been to open his mouth. His second was to open it again. He said to the robber, "Why don't you take this pie along, too? It's pecan." Then he reached behind him for the plate.

AT THANKSGIVING DINNER six years later, my second cousin Gee asked Uncle Louis to tell the story that my mother sometimes referred to as "A Series of Bad Decisions on Your Father's Part." My father took a drink of milk from a green goblet. Gee's mother, whose husband had died the year before, said, "Maybe we should save that for after dinner, Gee." Everybody in the family, even the second cousins' second cousins, knew the story—or parts of it.

Gee said that Martin might like to hear it. Martin was a high school student from England who was spending the fall semester with us. He was handsome and self-confident, with smooth cheeks and a wide mouth that a steady flow of mockery had seemed to warp slightly. (To annoy me, Martin would refer to Ida as "your Negro slave.") It had taken Gee, who was two years younger than Martin and me, about five minutes to fall in love with our guest from overseas. Before dinner, she'd gone into the bathroom to make herself look more stunning than she was in her miniskirt and boots. Martin had said to me, "The lipstick is a bit whorish, but she's not bad for fourteen."

My father hadn't yet said the blessing. We were waiting for my mother to emerge from the kitchen with the turkey, which she was carving with a new electric knife. She wouldn't permit my father to carve the turkey, because she believed he would make a mess of it. She thought I had a future as a carver of meat but that my day had not yet come. I was sixteen and lacked finesse. Crawford, who was at college out West, as far away as he could get, was not a candidate for other reasons.

My grandfather, my father's eighty-two-year-old father, jiggled the ice in his glass, in the hope that more Scotch might somehow materialize. He'd had his limit, and unhappiness was growing in the fold between his white eyebrows.

Martin said, "I'd love to hear the story, especially if it's sordid and violent."

Uncle Louis lowered his chin to the napkin tucked into his collar and chuckled. Martin amused him, it seemed—a guy who didn't know jack about anything, except what he'd read in books or seen on the movie screen.

Granddaddy said, "Is this the story about Louis falling asleep at the Toddle House? In that plate of eggs and hash browns?"

"No, Dad," my father said, sitting a little taller in his chair at the head of the table, as if by doing so he might somehow absorb Granddaddy's question and cause it to disappear. "Why don't you tell Martin about Cyril the goat? He might enjoy that."

"God save us from goats," Granddaddy grumbled. The crease between his eyebrows deepened and he sank into silence.

Gee said to Uncle Louis, "I'll show you my etchings if you tell the story." She fluttered her eyelashes. They were long and swooping, worked on.

"Oh, Virginia," her mother said, using her daughter's given name. "Don't be so silly."

Uncle Louis laughed more than was called for. His shoulders shook under his cardigan; the soft flesh under his chin vibrated. Perhaps, I thought, believing I was wise, he laughed to hide his disappointments. I'd learned a few things while leaning in doorways, skulking around the house. I knew, for instance, that Uncle Louis had forgotten to pay his taxes the last few years. I knew that he'd lost all but a couple of his private art students and that an artist whom he'd rented space to in his house had made off with a box of heirloom silver when she moved out. I knew that my father had driven Uncle Louis back to Arkansas again, two years before. I knew that to help his cousin my father had commissioned a painting of a steam engine. (The result hung in my father's basement office, not being suitable, in my mother's view, for a more prominent wall.) And now I knew, as did everybody else at the table, that Uncle Louis had passed out drunk at the Toddle House, though whether this incident was post- or pre-Arkansas I couldn't have said. Tonight, anyway, Uncle Louis was drinking water.

My mother said from the kitchen, "Go ahead and say the blessing. I'll be there in a minute."

Dad said, "We'll wait, honey."

My grandfather came swimming up out of his silence and, snorting derisively, said, "They caught him with his pants down."

It was unclear whom Granddaddy was referring to. It might have been a politician—sixty years before, he'd been beaten up by thugs when he was working as a poll watcher; he hated politicians, particularly Democrats —or he may have been thinking about somebody at the nursing home. Anyway, nobody asked. My father told Granddaddy about the football game he and Uncle Louis had attended that afternoon. I'd begged off and gone with Martin to see *Bonnie and Clyde* at the Rialto.

"Male is in decline," my father said. "Manual seems to have all the horses nowadays."

My grandfather considered this, lifting his chin high, and said, "You still have that dog, Louis?" I wondered if he meant the dog that had got stuck in the pipe.

My father said Louis had two boxers now.

"They're supposed to be guard dogs," Uncle Louis said. "But they act like pussycats."

"I wish that place would let me keep a dog," Granddaddy said. He meant the nursing home.

My mother came in with the platter of turkey, saying, "I don't see what's so great about an electric knife." My father said grace, his holiday version, which went on for a bit. Then Gee announced with her red lips that Uncle Louis would tell the story of the time he offered a pie to the White Castle thief and nearly lost an eye.

"That again?" my mother said.

"I'll tell the expurgated version," Uncle Louis said, putting a scoop of stuffing on his plate.

LATER THAT EVENING, after I'd taken Granddaddy back to the nursing home, Martin asked me to tell him the unexpurgated version.

We were in the den, watching a TV variety special that featured Dusty Springfield and Burl Ives. My father and Uncle Louis were downstairs in the rec room, looking at slides of trains my father had photographed in Europe that summer. The women, except for Gee, were in the kitchen.

"The robber called Uncle Louis a 'fucking four-eyed faggot,'" Gee said. She giggled. Her bare thigh was within an inch of Martin's leg.

"'Fuck-faced,'" I said. "Not 'fucking.'" When the robber swore at Uncle Louis, I'd lifted my nose from the damp wool of his overcoat and turned to look at my father. Light bounced off the lenses of his glasses, the hair in his nostrils seemed to quiver, his Adam's apple rose and fell, but his mouth was shut tight.

"And then the bloke hit your uncle in the eye with the cap pistol?" Martin said.

"He's my father's cousin, actually," I said. "We just call him 'Uncle.'"

"So the bloke hit your dad's cousin, right?" Martin said impatiently.

"Yeah." The robber had swung the gun, knocking Uncle Louis's glasses to the floor and opening a cut under his eye. The gun was a toy—or so we found out later—but its parts were metal. Cheap, tinny metal, but metal nonetheless.

"And then," Martin said, "the Negro bloke, the cook, descended from the flies like a deus ex machina and saved the day, right?"

In Uncle Louis's description, the cook, who was built like an icebox, wrestled the robber to the floor and sat on him until the police came. Under his paper hat, which fell off when he jumped on the robber, the cook was bald. His skin was a purply black shade, the color of some vein of ore deep within the earth, a rich and fearsome color. When he had pinned the robber and the robber had stopped flailing, the cook said, "If you say one word, pus-head, I'll put my fist through your motherfuckin' face."

The cook's comment hadn't been included in the Thanksgiving table version of the story. Nor was Uncle Louis's confession, made to my father while holding a handkerchief to his swollen eye in the back of the police cruiser that took us home. He said he'd been so frightened he'd thought he was going to soil his trousers. My father, who had his arm around me and held the pie in his lap, said, "You deserve the *Croix de Guerre*, Lou."

My father was shivering. Crawford sat up front with the policeman, asking him questions, whether he'd ever been in any high-speed chases, for instance.

Now Martin said, "I love America. So violent and yet so sentimental." And then he flopped around on the sofa like a rag doll, eyes popping and warped mouth agog, the way Bonnie and Clyde had done, in slow motion, at the end of the movie, when the Texas Rangers pumped them full of bullets. When Martin was finished, he laughed in self-appreciation. Gee laughed, too, of course.

I went outside to smoke and discovered that the crumpled pack in my pants was empty. I wondered if there might be a cigarette in Uncle Louis's car. He still smoked, as my mother would sometimes note when my father came home from a night of cribbage with him. I explored the front and back of Uncle Louis's Ford wagon, the car he'd bought to replace his old sedan. I looked on the dash and in the glove compartment and under the seats. I found an ice scraper from Mr. Wendell's Sinclair and a tin of peanut brittle and a Thermos and some *National Geographics* and an empty box of Parliaments. In the luggage space, there was a fifty-pound bag of dog food and overalls dappled with paint. In a pocket of the overalls, I found a pistol.

I sat in the backseat and looked at the pistol under the car's dome light. There were no firearms in our house, aside from the BB gun my father had bought at the urging of my mother for the purpose of shooting at a Great Dane that ran loose in the neighborhood and sometimes attacked Felix, our dachshund. (The gun was in my father's basement office, still in a shopping bag.) The pistol had a pebbly grip and a short barrel that I couldn't quite fit my pinkie into. Had Uncle Louis bought it for protection? Perhaps the White Castle thief turned up in his dreams. When he'd told the story at the dinner table, he'd made a comedy out of it, cleaned it up the way he'd cleaned up stories about my father and himself in the Kentucky militia. He'd claimed he hardly ever thought about the incident, except when he drove past a White Castle. I didn't believe him. What else would have led him to buy a gun?

I pointed the pistol out the door at the dark. Then I put it back in the overalls.

I took a longish butt from the ashtray and smoked it down to the recessed filter. I went back into the house, through the rec room door. The slide projector was on, beaming a picture of a SNCF electric locomotive onto the stand-up screen. My father and Uncle Louis had gone down the hall, into Dad's office. I could hear them talking.

"Here it is, Lou," my father said. "I sometimes read this for consolation." I tried to think what my father read for consolation, aside from histories of railroads and the meditations of certain jurists. He attended church, of course, but mostly, I'd always assumed, out of duty.

Uncle Louis was silent. Then he said, "Some earnest fool tried to convert me at that drunk farm. I said, 'It's hard enough giving up bourbon. Don't make me give up my disbelief, too.'"

"Jesus was a wise man," my father said, though not with any fervor. He didn't have a future as an evangelist.

"But does Jesus know anything about sinking funds and outstanding debts?" Uncle Louis made an odd, gassy noise, like a chuckle spoiled by indigestion. Then he said he was thinking of selling his house and moving away, possibly to New Mexico.

"I hope you won't do that, old bean," my father said.

"I might, Billy. I might move out there and paint steer skulls, like Georgia O'Keeffe."

"I hope you'll paint more train pictures," my father said.

UNCLE LOUIS DIDN'T SELL his house or come within five hundred miles of Georgia O'Keeffe. He did try to go out West for a month's vacation in the summer of 1968, but his dogs were stolen from his car at a diner in Missouri and then the car died in Kansas, so he gave up and came home, only to discover that Robert, his housekeeper, had had a stroke.

Not long after, Uncle Louis was hired to teach art at a girls school. With my father's help, he was able to pay off taxes in arrears. He bought a new car and got a dog from the Humane Society.

By 1969, the year I left for college, he had acquired a new housemate, a young woman who did the cooking in exchange for room and board. Cora was from Floyds Knobs, Indiana, across the river. She was a teacher's aide and did volunteer work for a downtown jobs program. She was also a potter. Uncle Louis said to my father, "I don't think she's going to run off with what's left of the silver."

When I came home from college that November, my mother was laid up with a bug and Granddaddy was feeling too low to venture out of the nursing home, so it was decided that we'd have Thanksgiving dinner at Uncle Louis's. We'd take some dishes Ida had made in advance. Cora, whose virtues didn't seem to include good relations with her family across the river, had agreed to cook the turkey. Not that I'd be able to eat it. A month before, in a conversion inspired by some late-night reading, I'd decided to become a vegetarian. Crawford would eat my portion— eat it and say something smart.

Even though I was an intellectual now and had lost interest in football, I went with my father and Uncle Louis to the Male-Manual game. (Crawford skipped it; he didn't get up until noon, anyway.) My father drove his gray three-on-the-tree Chevrolet sedan, a car so drab he hadn't bothered to have a rear-end dent repaired. The radio had only a tuning knob, no buttons. When Uncle Louis got in the car, he said to me, "It's good for the souls of our elected officials that they not ride around in style." Uncle Louis's own soul appeared to have departed him during the night; under his brown hat he was pale and drawn.

It was a bright fall day, a day that felt like the last warm breath of the year. Uncle Louis said Cora had kept him in the kitchen all morning, shelling chestnuts and crumbling stale bread for stuffing, when all he wanted to do was sit outside in the sunshine with a cup of coffee and watch for the pileated woodpecker that lived in the woods below his house. "You know all the trouble you have to go to just to shell one damn chestnut?" Uncle Louis said.

My father let the clutch out too quickly as he turned onto River Road, and the car bucked a little. We drove in silence past the Pine Room and the KingFish and Mr. Wendell's Sinclair, the bountiful sunshine lapping at the car. Then Uncle Louis said, "I tied one on last night, Billy. Cora gave me a taste of her Mateus and one taste led to another, as they say. I fell off the wagon onto my pitiful face." He turned around to look at me. "Did your dad ever tell you I'm a grisly old boozer?"

I saw that a stem of Uncle Louis's eyeglasses had been secured to the frame with a gob of black electrical tape. Perhaps he had actually fallen on his face. I said, "No."

"Your dad is the epitome of discretion," Uncle Louis said.

Dad said, "You've gone a long time without taking a drink, haven't you, Lou?"

"A long time would be accurate if you don't count a number of episodes you don't know about."

My father told his cousin not to give up the ship.

"This old ironclad?"

ON THE WAY BACK from the game, my father took a route that led us past the railway museum he'd helped found a few years before. The museum, which was on a patch of once-industrial riverside, had just acquired an L&N steam engine, a 4-8-2 Baldwin that had carried passengers around the Southeast between the world wars, and my father wanted to show it to his cousin.

"It's on the homely side," Dad said, pulling into the dirt parking lot and stopping next to the chain-link fence that enclosed the museum.

"We need to give it a coat of paint and spruce up the cab." He asked Uncle Louis if he wanted to take a closer look at the engine. He had a key to open the gates.

Uncle Louis said, "I think we better get home and check on the turkey." There was confetti on his hat and raincoat. He'd sat stiffly in his seat for most of the game, sipping coffee. Late in the second half, he turned to me and said, "The problem with football is that there are too many discussions and too many people falling down too often."

As my dad attempted to put the Chevrolet in reverse, he ground the gear and then stalled the car. "Doggone it," he said.

"Give me an automatic any day," Uncle Louis said.

When we got to Uncle Louis's, my father remembered he needed to pick up the dishes Ida had prepared. He dropped us off and drove away, stirring up leaves, narrowly missing a boxy old Rambler parked beneath a sycamore. Uncle Louis didn't know whose car the Rambler was. It didn't belong to Cora, who drove a VW.

As we went up the cracking, moss-laden brick steps to the front door, we heard music, and then Uncle Louis remembered that Cora had invited a boy to dinner.

When we went inside, he said, "It's her only serious flaw." I thought he was referring to Cora's choice in boyfriends, but he meant the music. "I think she might have a tin ear." The music was *In a Silent Way*, by Miles Davis. I owned the record myself; I'd found the melancholy trumpet consoling.

Uncle Louis laid his hat on a low, wood chest that was long and deep enough to store a knight's armor, or so I'd imagined as a child. But when I'd lifted the heavy lid, it had contained only yellowing newspapers and an umbrella. Probably it still did.

We walked through the sitting room, where the hi-fi was, and into the kitchen. Cora sat at the table, peeling the skins from cooked yams. Steam rose from the yams, whose flesh was a dark, lush, underworld orange.

"So, who won the game?" Cora asked, after Uncle Louis had introduced me. Cora had long, straight, dark hair parted in the absolute middle of her head and sharp cheekbones that made her seem older than she probably was. She was pretty, in a country kind of way.

"Manual won," Uncle Louis said. "We were about the only white people there."

"Hmm," she said, pulling a strip of yam skin free. She had long fingers. I imagined her throwing pots, the wet clay rising, dilating, fluting.

Uncle Louis asked where Jacques, the dog, was. Cora said Jay had taken him for a walk.

"Jay? Did I hire a dog trainer named Jay?" Hatless, his gray hair matted, his stomach sticking out beyond the panels of his raincoat, Uncle Louis looked as if he'd spent the afternoon asleep in a movie theater. He went into the pantry.

"Jay's my friend," Cora said, glancing at me. "He's having dinner with us. Remember?"

"Yes, your friend. You told me about him. Though I could use a dog trainer, if he's available." A cupboard door, its wood swollen, scraped open. Glass clanked against glass.

"He's studying welding at JCC," Cora said. JCC was a community college. "But he likes dogs."

"A dog is man's best friend," Uncle Louis said. I heard the glug-glug of liquid flowing into a receptacle.

"I'm going to excuse myself and go take a bath," Uncle Louis announced. I watched his raincoated figure slip out of the pantry, tumbler in hand.

Cora said, "I think we may be all out of cooking sherry now, but I have some beer Louis doesn't know about, if you'd like one. Jay brought it." She was slicing the skinless yams, making wheels of them.

"I could go for a beer," I said. I would have to drink it before my father arrived, however. I wasn't legal—you could be drafted in Kentucky at eighteen, but you couldn't drink—and my father minded about such things. Even Crawford, who was a year and a half closer to being legal, didn't drink in Dad's presence.

Cora spooned a sauce over the yams. It smelled lemony. Then she put the sauce pan down and went into the back hall. When she returned, she said, "Louis went down to the Pine Room last night after I made the mistake of giving him a hit of wine." She saw me looking at the embroidery bordering the neckline of her thin white peasant's blouse. I adjusted my gaze upward. "I didn't know he had a problem." She handed me a can of Sterling.

"It's not your fault," I said, pulling the pop-top.

The back door opened and Jacques entered, followed by Jay. Jacques was some sort of terrier mix. His ashy-gray coat was stiff and harsh, and he had goatish chin hairs. Jay undid the leash, and Jacques shot out of the kitchen, as if he'd just seen a cat stealing through the sitting room.

Jay had long hair and a patchy beard that didn't conceal a skin condition, and his eyes would have been visible through fog. I thought he might be stoned. I thought there was an unpleasantness in the fixity of his mouth. I also thought I'd seen him before, a long time ago. I was sure of it.

CORA ASKED ME TO CARVE the turkey. I said that I didn't think I should, since I was a vegetarian. Crawford said, "But he wishes he wasn't." Then she asked my father if he would do the honors and he said, "I'll give it a try." While at home, fetching Ida's dishes, he'd put on a necktie, a blue one decorated with the C&O cat nestled in a quarter moon. It flopped against the turkey's browned skin as he hacked meat from the breast. Cora lifted the tie from the turkey, brushed it off, and tucked it inside Dad's shirt.

Crawford stood over by the stove. He'd come with a girl he'd known in high school named Libeth. He was stoned. He was sucking a Life Saver, and kept touching his earlobe, as if its existence baffled him.

Jay stood by the refrigerator, drinking a beer, looking steadily at Crawford's date. Libeth went to college in Boston. She was a serious girl, who was known to laugh in your face if you said something ignorant. When he wasn't drunk or stoned, Crawford was a serious person, too, and he must have enjoyed the idea of having someone to laugh at the ignorance of humanity with. Three years on the East Coast seemed to have sharpened certain parts of Libeth's face. She stared back at Jay.

Jay pulled at the collar of his flannel shirt and scratched his beard. He'd hardly said a word since entering the house. Then he said to me, "The last turkey I had was at Eddyville. It tasted like crap."

My father looked up from his carving. Eddyville was a state prison.

Jay opened the refrigerator and leaned in, as if he wished to escape from his confession, which was loose in the room like a bat.

Libeth said, "What'd you do? Knock over a store?" She was wearing a Peace Now button on one lapel of her blue-jean jacket and an Eldridge Cleaver button on the other.

Crawford giggled. Too much pot made him giggle.

"Something like that," Jay said, refrigerator light washing over him.

Cora said, "Jay made a mistake and he paid for it and now he's doing fine."

When Jay shut the refrigerator and I saw his eyes again, the dark gleam of them, I understood why I thought I'd recognized him earlier. I believed he was the guy who had come through the door at the White Castle, eight years before, his face all but hidden under his windbreaker hood. I wondered if my father recognized him, or if the beard threw him off. Neither my father nor Uncle Louis had testified at the trial; Uncle Louis had even asked that the assault charge be withdrawn. I remembered my father saying after the White Castle thief had been convicted and sent away that the boy who had done it was barely eighteen. But he'd had a juvenile record, and he'd been given a stiff sentence. The judge hadn't been moved by the fact that the weapon was a toy.

Had Jay recognized my father? When Cora introduced them, had the name Judge Dupree given Jay a jolt? Whatever the case, my father, a proponent of keeping the conversation flowing away from danger, started telling the story about Cyril.

Cora stirred gravy. She had a busy, mistress-of-the-kitchen look on her face. The kitchen was very warm and I could see sweat building up under her blouse. "Goats are the most useless animals," she said, as if she'd had a lot of experience with them. "I don't know why anybody would want to keep one."

She asked Jay to get a basket for the rolls out of the pantry. He seemed happy to have something to do. I was relieved when she sent me upstairs to fetch Uncle Louis.

CRAWFORD CAME WITH me as far as the staircase. I said, "It's him, that guy, the one who stuck up the White Castle. I swear. Don't you recognize him?"

"No." Crawford's pupils had taken over most of his eye sockets.

"You're so messed up, you wouldn't recognize yourself if you bumped into you."

"It's how I get through these family dinners." He grinned. If there was a positive side to his increasing use of drugs and inebriants, it was that it had made him more amiable for certain stretches of time. (Two summers later, when he became a Buddhist and a vegetarian in a bit of an about-face, he became grouchy again.) He said, "Last night, Libeth and I made it. Even though she has a boyfriend in Boston. Even though I could hardly get near her in high school. It was so great. I couldn't believe it was happening. What'd you do last night, Morg?"

• • •

JACQUES LAY ON Uncle Louis's unmade bed, his tail whisking the headboard. Uncle Louis was in the bathroom. The door was open a crack. Water dripped into the tub—*buh-lip, buh-lip.*

I said dinner was ready.

"The turkey has been burned to a proper crisp?" I heard him rearrange himself in the tub.

"Dad's carving it," I said, studying a framed black-and-white photograph on the dresser. It was of my father and his sons—*père et fils sans chapeaux,* soaking up the atmosphere in the L&N yards, November 1961. The picture was grainy, a bit underexposed, but my father's happiness was evident.

"Tell him to save a drumstick for me," Uncle Louis said.

I said, "I met Cora's boyfriend." Jacques regarded me with terrier ears upraised.

"Is he a vegetarian like you or a dirty old meat eater like me and your old man?" He farted, rippling the water like an outboard starting up. *"Excusez-moi."*

"Meat eater. And an ex-felon. He told us the last turkey he had was at Eddyville."

"Cora has an ex-felon for a boyfriend?" Uncle Louis seemed less shocked by this revelation than by her taste in music—or perhaps it only confirmed something about her taste in music. "What'd he do?"

I saw him again, the cold-reddened center of his face. "He looks like the guy who popped you at the White Castle."

"Is that right?" He sounded almost amused. Then he said, "Are you sure? I thought that boy's name was James. James Becker. Or Beckett. Something like that."

"Maybe I'm wrong." I didn't recall Cora having mentioned Jay's last name.

"It would spoil dinner if you're right," Uncle Louis said.

Water sloshed as he moved in the tub. "I hope you won't ever find yourself in a situation where you have nothing to drink but cooking sherry. It's god-awful. And you have to drink a gallon of it to feel the least bit giddy." He chuckled. "However, it's probably better for you than aftershave or Sterno juice."

Though I'd never tried aftershave or Sterno juice, it seemed probable to me that I would turn out more like Uncle Louis than my father, who never drank anything stronger than a Coke, who didn't take the Lord's name in vain, who lost his head only in the presence of trains, who would drive his cousin down to an Arkansas drunk farm at the drop of a hat and write him letters of encouragement on hotel stationery. I might turn out to be an improvement on Crawford, but I still didn't feel it was within me to aspire to what my father seemed to represent: sobriety, honor, loving-kindness. I didn't think I stood a chance of becoming like him.

I said, "Maybe we should pretend we don't know who he is—the robber. If it's him, I mean."

"We could do that," Uncle Louis said. "It might make dinner go more smoothly."

I'd opened the top drawer of the dresser, not quite absentmindedly. It was a weakness of mine to want to open other people's drawers. In Uncle Louis's, I found a heap of thin silklike socks. This style of sock, which my father wore, too, which had to be held up by a garter, seemed dandyish for a man who was so careless of his appearance. Perhaps it was all that was available at the downtown men's store where he and my father shopped. Or perhaps Uncle Louis felt tenderly about his feet and ankles. I'd heard it said that he was a homosexual. (Martin, the foreign exchange student, had said, "Your dad's cousin seems like a poufter. Is he?") I wasn't uninterested in this aspect of Uncle Louis's life, and yet it seemed less interesting than some of the other things I knew about him.

Near the bottom of the drawer, I found a handful of bullets. I held them in my palm and felt their weight and purpose.

Uncle Louis lifted himself out of the tub, dripping, groaning. "I guess I should come meet the company."

I put one of the bullets to my nose. It had a cool pleasant smell.

"Goddamnit," Uncle Louis said. He'd hit his foot or leg against something.

"You all right?" I put the bullets back.

"I'll be fine as soon as I can get some real alcohol in me," he said.

WHILE WE WAITED for Uncle Louis to come to the table, my father told the story of how a horse Uncle Louis's parents had owned had wandered next door onto my grandparents' property and dropped dead. The horse, Isabelle, had remained in my grandparents' yard for several days, rotting in the summer heat, until somebody could be found to haul her off.

"Isabelle had two gaits," Uncle Louis said, entering the dining room. "One was standing still and the other was walking in the direction of food. I think she was hoping to eat some of your mother's flowers before she passed on."

My father laughed and said, "I think she was revenge for Cyril."

Uncle Louis was wearing a clean white shirt and khakis held up by suspenders. He'd shaved. His shaggy gray eyebrows flickered above the rims of his eyeglasses. He greeted Crawford and Libeth. He asked after Libeth's mother, whom he used to see at the opera in the days when he went. We lived in a big upper-South city that was actually a small town, I realized.

Cora introduced Jay to Uncle Louis. She said, "This is my friend Jay Beckman."

Uncle Louis shook Jay's hand and said it was nice to meet him. Neither gave any sign of recognizing the other. But Uncle Louis excused himself and went into the kitchen and then out of the house. Maybe he was going to get a bottle he'd remembered he'd hidden in the garage some years ago. Or maybe he was going to drive down to the Pine Room and spend the evening there, without his relatives and without Cora and her ex-felon of a boyfriend. It would be simpler to sit on a bar stool, having removed oneself from the complications of life, its idiotic coincidences and mean symmetries, having cast aside all ambition except that of drinking oneself senseless.

After a while, my father said, "Maybe I should go find Lou." He got up from his chair. His tie was still tucked inside his shirt. The white napkin he clutched in his hand suggested a small nightgowned figure, a puppet ghost.

"I'll get him," I said, looking at Crawford, who had found something in the middle distance to gaze at. My father sat back down.

I met Uncle Louis coming back inside through the kitchen door. He had one of Jay's Sterlings in his hand. He looked confused. He said, "I can't remember where I hid my gun."

"You have a gun?"

"I bought it at a truck stop near Covington. Don't tell your dad. He wouldn't approve."

"Maybe we should eat now. We can find the gun and shoot Jay later, if necessary."

"I suppose that would be more polite." He took his glasses off and inspected the crudely taped stem. "I used to have an extra pair, but I couldn't find them this morning."

When we returned to the table, Uncle Louis with his beer in a glass, my father said grace, the holiday version. When he was done, Crawford, suddenly roused, said, "And while you're at it, God, how about stopping the war in Vietnam. *Merci beaucoup.*"

"Amen," Cora said. The *a* in "amen" was soft as a pillow, as sweetly formed as the breasts beneath her peasant's blouse.

"Right on," Jay said, not loudly, almost as if he were muttering to himself.

My father and his cousin were silent for a moment. I spooned yams onto my plate. I didn't want to discuss the war. My father always routed me when we argued. (He routed Crawford, too, but my brother didn't recognize it.) I wanted to put Cora's yams into my mouth. I wanted Jay to disappear.

"As soon as we pull out," my father said somberly, "the Communists will gobble up the country like seven-year locusts."

"We're killing peasants in rice paddies while propping up a corrupt government," Libeth said. "It's shameful."

"It gives me a headache just to think about it," Uncle Louis said, rising from his seat. He'd polished off the beer and was heading to the kitchen for another. My father watched him go. Perhaps he'd decided that he couldn't keep his cousin from blinding himself and walking off the edge of a cliff. Perhaps he'd decided that all he could do was wait at the bottom for when Uncle Louis stopped falling. And then maybe he could get him to go back to Arkansas.

Crawford, who was warming to the subject, said, "Who cares if the Communists take over, Dad? It's their country."

"They're just a bunch of slopes," Jay said. "Fuck the war and fuck them."

My father stiffened. He had a long face, which became longer when vulgarities disturbed the air around him. I heard a hiss: Uncle Louis opening a can of beer.

"Jay!" Cora said. "God!" Her cheeks and throat had turned a becoming pink.

Jay stared at the chunks of turkey on his plate. The middle of his face was knotted with anger, as if he knew Cora wasn't going to be able to save him from whoever he was. She'd dump him sooner or later, and then he'd just be an ex-felon trying to get a job as a welder if he could first pass the course at JCC. He wasn't the kind of clay you could really work with.

Jay got up from his place and went toward the kitchen, his boots digging into the thin Oriental. Cora followed.

A draft from somewhere made the candle flames shiver. Uncle Louis's house wasn't exactly airtight.

Libeth said, "He's kind of scary. I wonder why she hangs out with him."

"Maybe she likes a challenge," I said.

Crawford said, "Are you sure it's him, Morgan, and not just another homicidal maniac we get to spend Thanksgiving with? Or maybe it's his twin."

"What?" my dad said, breaking his silence. "Whose twin?"

In the kitchen, Cora said, "Where do you think you're going, Jay?" She sounded like my mother when furious.

"Do you like being around these rich people and listening to their dumbshit stories about goats and horses? This is too grand for me, Cora." He took a breath. "Maybe if you bang him, they'll let you be a member of the family."

Crawford giggled.

My father got up from his seat, shooting a look at me. Had he assumed, as I had, that it was me Jay was talking about Cora banging? Did he even know the term "banging"?

Uncle Louis said, "You can't talk like that here. Please leave my house."

"Is that my beer? You can't drink my beer, you fuckin' alky faggot."

"Stop it, Jay," Cora shouted. "Don't do that."

My father went toward the kitchen with his napkin in hand. Crawford and I got up from our seats and stood around like rubberneckers. By the time our father reached the kitchen, Jay had gone out the door, with

Cora right behind him. They yelled at each other in the dark. Then they drove off in their cars.

Uncle Louis came back into the dining room. His shirt was splattered with beer, and there were spots on his trousers. "Excuse me while I go change," he said. But he didn't come downstairs again.

# 6

# Woman with Manikin

ON THE WAY to Rosa's place, Crawford saw a woman carrying what from a distance looked like a manikin. It was life-size, approximately, and unclothed. Crawford was on his bicycle, headed east, on the rutted dirt path that ran alongside Feather Lake. It was 6:30 on a Sunday morning, the first Sunday after Easter—Low Sunday, as it is sometimes called. The Resurrection had come off without a hitch and now spring was beginning to stir here in the upper Midwest. The wind was blowing in such a way that Crawford could smell cow pastures thawing. Soon May apples and weedy nightshade would rise from beneath mats of leaves. By June the lake that the wind now so gently ruffled would become a pot of algae and duck crap and farm runoff. Crawford used to swim in the lake, once or twice a summer, until the day he came eye-to-eye with a three-foot-long dead carp.

From the rear, Crawford judged the manikin to be male. Its torso didn't narrow much at the waist, and its buttocks were flatter than a female manikin's were likely to be. It looked to be made of the sort of lightweight plastic that pool toys are made of. It was a pinkish-brown color, like a Band-Aid. The woman, who wore a long, formal, lavender gown, held the thing upright, around its waist; its feet were several inches off the ground and its bald head floated just above her own. Her hair, which was cut short, was blacker than a crow's feathers. She walked in the clunky brogans that young people of both sexes seemed to favor nowadays, though hers were at least a size too large. Crawford thought it was odd that the woman had no wrap, no sweater or jacket to keep her from shivering in the morning air, but then again a person who would be out walking at dawn with a manikin could be expected to overlook some details of dress.

Crawford was dressed as if for church—clean chinos, blue button-down shirt, and a blazer that his late father had worn. Crawford had left a note on the kitchen counter saying that he was going to church, but where he was actually headed was Rosa Murrado's house. Rosa was principally a hair stylist. She cut Crawford's hair every two months or so. When he arrived for his appointment, at the salon in the strip mall, she always said, "Won't you come to my station, Señor Dupree?" And then she would cover his front with a black sheet that fastened at the nape and lay her hands on his gray head, like a priest bestowing a blessing or a fortune teller consulting a crystal ball, and say, "Is it time again to make you beautiful?"

On the side, to supplement her income as a hair stylist, Rosa did massage therapy in her home. It was uncertified, off-the-books massage therapy. She said, "You need to go to school to know how to rub someone? Hehehe." Her laugh was high and piercing. There was a jungle bird in the hair salon that imitated it, and it was sometimes unclear to Crawford who was laughing. Rosa described her service as "healing massage, no funny business, no Swedish lady in hot pants." An hour cost thirty dollars, well below the going rate, and it also included what Crawford regarded as a form of talk therapy, though it wasn't the sort of talk therapy that Michelle, his wife, had proposed he seek. Crawford had gone to Rosa once before, on the third Sunday in Lent, and on that occasion he had come close to crying while telling her stories about his dead father.

The woman with the manikin walked with her head lowered, as if absorbed by the nuggety gravel and tree trash embedded in the path. She walked in the middle of the path, unmindful of the space she was taking up. Of course, this early on a Sunday morning, there was no traffic, except for Crawford on his almost-new Giant Yukon, a fifty-first birthday gift from his wife and children, which replaced the bike he had backed the car over last fall when he was in a hurry to make a doctor's appointment. Crawford usually wore a helmet, mostly to mollify his wife and children, who would say things like "What if you fall on your head again, Dad?" but he was without it this morning. Not wearing it was something between an oversight and heedlessness. First, he'd put on a helmet that turned out to be too small—it was Philip's, his son's—and then he couldn't find his own among all the junk in the garage. So he rode off, with the cuffs of his chinos flapping close to sprocket and chain, his gray hair blowing in the cow shit–scented breeze, humming a song that had been in his head for days.

Crawford tacked toward the lakeside side of the woman and her companion. When he came within a few yards of them, he observed bicycle protocol and sounded a warning. "On your left!" he said. He said it firmly, surprising himself a little, for his voice was soft and low, of a timbre that often left his wife and children asking him to repeat what he'd just said. The moment he announced his intentions, he noticed that the space between the woman and the edge of the path had narrowed. He thought of veering back to the right, but he was practically on top of the woman, close enough, anyway, that he could see what he supposed was a tattoo on her shoulder. (Was it a butterfly? It had wings.) So he kept pedaling leftward, the sound of his voice preceding him, and, as he went, the woman spun, counterclockwise, bringing herself and her partner into Crawford's path. He hit the brakes as he came face-to-face with the manikin—it had a slash of a mustache and a putto's round cheeks—but he was a moment late. He glanced off the manikin and skidded off the path into a thicket of leafless honeysuckle bushes. As he fell, he heard a seagull complain. *Keraw, keraw!* Then he saw the woman standing above him, still gripping the manikin at the waist. He thought he recognized her, but he could not find a matching photo in his cluttered, jumbled files. He knew she was in the Acquaintances of the Last Several Years section. Was she a former student? No, his former students, both those who had thought *The Sound and the Fury* had sucked and those who had thought otherwise, he tended to remember. He had some inkling that he'd encountered the woman in a retail situation. Her expression was one of annoyance.

Crawford had some rough edges, but he was always polite to the young and the elderly (his mother being a possible exception), especially to young women and more especially to young pretty women. He was a bit of a snob in that regard, though he was never deliberately unkind to young unpretty women. The young woman in the lavender ball gown was somewhere between pretty and less than pretty. He guessed that she might be hungover. He heard himself say, "Do you know the song 'I Can't Get Shtarted'?" He was embarrassed when he slurred a word, but rather than apologize for it—or correct it—he kept going forward. "By Ira Gershwin and Vernon Duke? It was one of my dad's favorites." Crawford remembered his father singing bits of this tune while they were in a boat on Kentucky Lake, singing it to the blasé bass and crappie.

WHEN PHILIP WAS SIX, seven, eight, nine, and he got up in the morning before his parents did, he would sometimes stand beside their bed and watch them sleep. He tried to resist waking them with his voice or by touching his mother, who slept nearest to the door and therefore to him and his sister. He believed that his presence alone would rouse them, that his mother, the lighter of the two sleepers, would somehow detect his scent through the veils of sleep and dreams that lay on her face. Sometimes Philip thought he could see movement behind her eyelids, like something flickering in the predawn dark. Or her mouth would twitch, like a fish's seen through glass. He would be unbudging, motionless, a little soldier in pajamas, intent on not signaling his presence except by force of his stillness. He had some idea—from his father?—that stillness was a state both desirable and powerful. At any rate, he tried to practice it. He saw that it won him points from some adults, when, for instance, they compared him to his younger, extroverted sister, Caroline. Of course, it was also true that Caroline won points for the way, when she wasn't venting steam or being ornery, she bounded around like a kangaroo with horseradish in its nose. (That phrase was the invention of his Uncle Morgan, who lived a thousand miles away, in New York.) It wasn't Philip's style to bound much. Even on the tennis courts, where he was becoming something of a terror, he tried to move silently, as if he had fins.

Philip felt a sense of accomplishment when he was able to wake his mother without so much as touching her or breathing a word. He liked to hear her say, slowly, as if she were only then learning to make sentences, "Oh, Philip—what—isn't—can't you—for Pete's sakes—it's hardly morning." Sometimes his father woke up, too, looking as if he'd spent the night in a wrestling match. Naturally, it pleased Philip when both parents wakened, but one was enough to start the day with.

One morning, when the sky was just beginning to lighten, Philip had gone into his parents' room and found his mother lying naked on her side, her back to him. His father was under the sheet. Perhaps he had spirited the sheet away from her. Or perhaps she had thrown it off. It was summer. The ceiling fan was spinning slowly, its motor ticking like a bug. Philip stood an arm's length from his mother, studying the notches on her spine, the jut of her shoulder blade, her hip rising like a wave, her booty like a big, round loaf of bread sliced down the middle. Philip turned his head sideways to observe more closely her crack, dark and mysterious. He'd seen his mother naked before, accidentally, fleetingly, but there'd been no opportunities to inspect her at such close range. (He was nine that summer, a string bean lengthening, growing untender as the Midwestern sun beat down.) His mother often saw him naked—in the tub, usually, where he sometimes told her about dreams he'd had or schoolmates who had made him angry—but she hadn't until now returned the favor. Not that it was his goal in life to see her spread out before him, like a fold-out picture. Anyway, she wasn't really spread out now. Her legs were drawn up toward her chest and her hands were tucked between her thighs. She'd made herself compact, perhaps in order to slip through a hole in her dream. Turning his head more sideways, like a person looking under a bed for a shoe, Philip saw the dark fluff at the base of her crack, right where he supposed his bloody head had poked through all those years before. (At his request, she had described some aspects of his birth, how slow he'd been in emerging but how determined she was to have him the natural way instead of via a slit in her abdomen, which is how Caroline would come, popping right out like she couldn't wait to go swimming in the fluorescent lights of the delivery room, how good Philip had looked in his red, white, and blue skullcap, which he'd received as the first baby to be born on the Fourth of July in this particular south-central Wisconsin hospital.) Philip was pondering the mystery of his mother's sex, his heart beating fast, like that of a scientist on the verge of a discovery, when he heard a voice that seemed both distant and quite near. He realized it was his mother's, all husky with sleep and yet not unfirm. She'd said, without twisting around to look at him, without attempting to cover herself, "Philip Dupree, will you please take your bloomin' face out of my crotch." It was not a question. He'd fled. The word "bloomin'," one of her peculiar expressions, stayed in his head all day, a buzzing in his ears.

Soon after this, Philip decided that while stillness might be worth as-
piring to, invisibility, as hard as it no doubt was to achieve, was more
worthy of pursuing. At any rate, he stopped coming into his parents'
bedroom in the mornings. Sometimes he'd go downstairs and pour himself a bowl of cereal and eat it with his fingers in front of the TV. Sometimes he'd go into his mother's office, a cove off the dining room, and
play a computer game or look at her e-mail (boring) or visit the Web site
called Totallyjengreen. (Jen Green was an actress and swimsuit model.)
Sometimes he'd go up to the attic, where his father had an office and
where Button the cat sometimes slept. He'd pet Button, if Button was
there, while looking at one of his father's picture books. Crawford had
one that was a bunch of old yellowish photographs of men hanging by
the neck from trees and bridges and lampposts, mostly black men, their
ratty trousers sliding down their hips, their heads lolling, their mouths
ajar. Some of the pictures showed white people in coats and ties and hats
staring at the hanged man, like he was something that had fallen out of
the sky and caught himself on a tree.

Early one morning last summer, the summer he turned twelve, he'd
taken a couple dollars out of his combination-lock safe and walked down
the street and across the railroad tracks to the strip mall that had a copy
shop and an acupuncture clinic and a hair salon and a coffee shop called
Ariosto's. His father bought his bags of beans here. Philip was interested
in the blueberry muffins, which, if he came early enough, would be
warm. For a while, he came every morning at 6:35, unless he somehow
overslept. On the fourth or fifth morning, the woman who usually
served him said, "Let me guess. A double espresso and a lemon scone?
No?" She had a stud in her nose and hair that was blacker than a Halloween cat's. On his seventh or eighth visit, she handed him a sack with
a muffin in it before he could place his order, even before he could say
"Hello." She said, "Here you are, *mon petit*," and he paid her and thanked
her and sat on the curb outside the shop, as he always did, and ate the

muffin bit by bit, beginning at the smooth, flat bottom, then chipping away at the fluted sides and the interior that was both fluffy and inky-dark with mooshed berries, saving for last the heavy, crusty, sugary top that was the shape of a toadstool cap, wondering all the while what "*mon petit*" meant. "Kid"? "Junior"? "Sonny boy"? The next morning he over-slept and the morning after that he and his father got up early so they could drive across the state to a tennis tournament and not long after that school started. He visited Ariosto's several times during the school year, usually with his dad and not early in the morning, but the girl with the stud in her nose was never there and the one time he had a blueberry muffin it didn't resemble those muffins he remembered eating on the curb when hardly anybody was awake, except for him and the guy at the gas station across the street who was setting up his display of tires.

Now, on this Sunday in April when the light came slicing through his blinds and crows had gathered in the maple outside his window to argue about what tree they would sit in next, Philip went downstairs without any good idea of what he was going to do, except probably eat some-thing. He took a roundabout route to the kitchen, however, when he saw his ten-year-old sister, ordinarily a late riser, sitting in front of the TV with Button in her lap. He petted Button, who was thirteen and enjoyed the attention, while also accidentally on purpose blocking Caroline's view of the TV.

"Move!" she said.

Caroline had a voice like a pip-squeak dog, Philip thought—like the Effs' papillon with its goony ears. Sometimes Philip couldn't believe Car-oline was related to him, but there was no getting around it. All you had to see were their narrow frames on which dark heads sat.

Philip continued on toward the kitchen, passing through the dining room, where, last night at dinner, his father had asked him if he knew what the square root of 169 was. Philip had said, "Huh?" His father had said, "Well, I'll give you a hint: soon you'll be the square root of 169."

Philip knew the answer then, but he let his sister, her mouth full of barbecued turkey dog smeared with ketchup and relish, say it. Philip didn't know why his father had brought up his birthday, which was two and a half months off, close to an eternity. Perhaps Crawford had been thinking about when he was thirteen. (Philip had seen pictures of his father at thirteen, but they had not quite persuaded him that his father had actually ever been that age. They looked doctored somehow.) Or perhaps his father had been trying to connect with him, on a mathematical level. They'd not been connecting lately. Philip, hoping to engage his father in conversation, would say, "Dad, have you seen my Cardinals cap?" and his father would answer with one word ("No") or two ("No, sorry"). Philip could pose the same question to his mother and have a colloquy concerning the misplacement of articles of clothing and the state of his locker at school and the science project that was due next week and the candy wrappers on the floor of his bedroom. Not that he enjoyed these exchanges, but he preferred them to his father's silences or occasional queries out of left field.

Philip opened the refrigerator door and saw juice and milk and pickles and a bottle of pink medicine for an eye infection that Button had. (Button had at first been called Dick Button, because when Button chased his tail he had somehow reminded Crawford of the ice skater, but over time the cat had lost its first name as well as its desire to chase its tail.) Philip took a container of strawberries off the shelf and sat down at the counter and ate the strawberries slowly, putting back those that were damaged or not as firm as he liked, while watching his tetra swim through the murk of its fishbowl. It was his job to clean the bowl. Maybe he'd do it later. Then, as he was swiveling off the stool, on his way to check the bread box for whatever might be in it, he noticed a yellow Post-it on the counter. It was in his father's handwriting, a curious slanting print in which backward *c*s masqueraded as *s*es and *r*s looked like *v*s and *w*s like *u*s or *w*s that failed to live up to their potential. The note said,

"Gone to early service at St. Jimmy's. Back around 10. Love, Craw/Dad (almost as tasty as a lobster)." It took a moment for Philip to understand that his father was being whimsical, joking around, being the Good Old Dad that he'd so rarely been of late. Though it was true that he occasionally, mostly for the benefit of Caroline, did his mating-call-of-the-bandersnatch imitation, which was actually just a four-note whistle that Philip could do himself, if he felt like it.

Philip found the pad of Post-its, and in print that was erect and un-slanting, the letters cleanly if not elegantly articulated, wrote, "Gone biking. Back sometime. P. W. Dupree." He stuck his message next to his father's. He stared at what he'd written and saw that something was wrong, but he let it go, whatever it was. He went into the back hall and found his tennis shoes and put on his mother's hooded gray sweatshirt when he couldn't find his own hooded black one. He went out the side door into the garage. He surprised a squirrel that was eating birdseed spilling from the bag. The squirrel looked at Philip, then ran away, jerkily, seeming to freeze every few feet, as if it were playing a game of Statue. Philip found everybody else's helmet before he came upon his own, on a shelf given over to insecticides and plant food. He strapped the helmet on and rode off toward Feather Lake, thinking that he might go all the way downtown, maybe have a hot breakfast at McDonald's.

MICHELLE HEARD THE CROWS—so loud and so rancorous so early in the day. They ruled the neighborhood from the crowns of maples and oaks and pines; they heckled squirrels and cats and humans as they went about their business. Once Michelle had seen a gang of them, twenty or thirty at least, set upon a horned owl that had had the temerity to set up shop in the Effs' backyard; the owl hadn't returned.

Michelle heard the crows, moaned, registered the light that seeped through the blinds, noted the absence of a bedmate (up early, wasn't he?), and rolled from her side to her back, a maneuver complicated by the cast on her leg. The cast was made of fiberglass but at certain moments it felt as heavy as old-fashioned plaster. (She'd had one of those as a girl, when she'd broken her leg, the other one, skiing in the U.P.) She'd hoped that the orthopedist, a smug ectomorph who wore a tie decorated with crested Road Runners, would put a lightweight cast on her leg, one of those contraptions with Velcro straps, which she could remove at night. But the break, in the tibia, was apparently severe enough that he thought the bone should be immobilized round-the-clock. "We'll have you up and dancing in no time, Michelle," he'd said. It had bothered her somewhat that he addressed her by her first name. It had bothered her even more that he seemed to be amused by the fact that she'd broken the bone while dancing.

She'd done it at Parents Talent Night at Caroline's school—or, rather, at the dress rehearsal for Parents Talent Night. Dancing wasn't a particular talent of Michelle's, but Eva Bigelow had talked her into it. Eva's daughter, Sonya, was Caroline's best friend. There had been a number of alternatives to dancing, or so her family had informed her. For instance, she could recite a poem in German. (She knew German.) She could do the Hula-Hoop and simultaneously recite a poem in German. She could explain the Infield Fly rule. (Crawford had proposed this, and that she wear her old Washington, D.C., softball uniform, with the shorty shorts, while doing it.) She could explain the No Elbows on the Dinner Table rule. (Philip proposed this.)

Ho, ho, ho, she had said. But she had given in to Eva, a lawyer, who was imposing both in her dark courtroom suits and out of them. She agreed not only to dance in a chorus line with a half dozen other middle-aged women but also to wear a costume that consisted of fishnet stockings and spandex leotard and spiked heels and a bowler. The number was the title song from *Cabaret,* and the hoofing it demanded wasn't too strenuous—just a bunch of leg kicks. But Michelle had practiced the steps at home, in the basement late at night, when everybody was in bed.

Then, on the second go-through the night before the show, her heel caught in a divot in the stage floor and her ankle turned over. She heard a bone snap, as clear as a drummer's rim shot, and went down. Two men, one a tubaist with the local symphony, the other sporting a fake Abraham Lincoln beard, carried her to a car and drove her to an urgent care outlet. Crawford had been at home, grading papers while watching basketball on TV, a talent that, along with his others, he wasn't going to share with Caroline's school community.

That was three weeks ago. Michelle had another five or six weeks of taking showers with the cast wrapped in a plastic garbage bag, negotiating the world on crutches, finding a not uncomfortable position to sleep in. On her back, which was the least uncomfortable, she snored, according to Crawford, a snorer himself, who would squeeze her thigh (or shoulder or hip) when he caught her at it. She noted again the unoccupied space beside her. She could smell his absence in his wadded-up pillow. Perhaps he'd gone to church. It was Sunday, wasn't it? Yes, she could tell by the way the light slipped through the gap in the curtains that it was. On weekdays, when there was sunlight, it shot through the gap. On Saturdays, it came somewhat more slowly, but on Sundays it seemed full of idlement, a puddle to loll in. Sundays had not always been so. When she was a girl and her mother had marched her and her two brothers to the nine o'clock service at St. Paul's Lutheran, the light, even when the sun was shining brightly, had seemed thin and dull, like a lesson to be learned, like a wafer to be eaten. When she was released from Sunday school—every June, she received a pin for perfect attendance—she could not help noticing that the light, even when the sun wasn't shining on her section of Wisconsin, was of another consistency, something that made you want to say "Hooray!" Once after church, when they were getting into their Valiant, the car that her father drove all over the state selling milking equipment to dairy farmers, her mother had said, under her breath, "I need to get out of this girdle." Michelle had hoped that this declaration prefigured some change in routine, that her mother had seen the wisdom of taking a Sunday off now and again, but this had not come about.

At college in Minnesota, one founded by Lutherans, Michelle had never attended church, though she had taken a couple of religion courses —one called Modern Spirituality and the other called Elements of Buddhism (better known as Om One-oh-One). Over the next decade, she had firmed up her disbelief to the point that she had insisted that her marriage ceremony be a civil one, only later to cave in to her mother and the Duprees and even Crawford, who revealed a streak of Dutiful Boy that she hadn't previously known about. When Crawford had suggested that Philip be christened, she'd said "Fine, OK." Just as she'd said "Fine, OK" when Crawford had argued for circumcision and against a boy's most precious thing looking like it belonged in a freak show, at least as seen from the point of view of the circumcised masses; Crawford didn't want his son being laughed at in the locker room. But why Crawford periodically stumbled off in the dimness to church, she wasn't sure. It was some sort of secret with him, something that she was reluctant to pry into. Lately, she suspected that his going had to do with his father's passing, as well as with the blow he'd taken to the head, which had jiggled his memory and speech and made him even less accessible than he already was. He had always been not quite within her reach—even on those increasingly rare occasions when he had been inside her, she could see him walking down some lonesome road, kicking at stones—but she had decided early on to accept this about him, the secretiveness, the brooding silences, like whole nighttimes, which were not worth knocking her own head against. He had his virtues, which included loyalty, though into this, too, she did not care to peer deeply, for wasn't her loyalty to him hanging by a thread? Wasn't it true that she was a little attracted to Rolf Unger, the symphony tubaist who had carried her to his car when she had broken her leg, who was built, as seemed to be required of tuba play-

ers, like a Greco-Roman wrestler, whose height and bulk were as pleas-
ing to behold as a shade tree, whose head was large and fuzzy on the top,
and whose mouth looked to be an organ of some complexity? It had
been disappointing to see that his car, a Sonata (alas), had a bumper
sticker that said Tuba Players Have Big Lungs, but more troubling was
the fact that he appeared to be in love with his wife, a reedy Taiwanese
who worked in a genetics lab. At any rate, Michelle had often seen them
holding hands, this odd pair whose offspring, a pint-sized boy, suggested
that her genes were the dominant ones. Though it was also true that
Rolf, when he had seen Michelle at school not long ago, just before
Easter break, had, while pretending to inspect her cast, touched her bare
pale forty-seven-year-old kneecap, and then had promised, when she for
some reason began to inquire about the classical tuba repertoire, to bring
her some recordings. There was a lovely tuba concerto by a British composer, he'd said, and also some chamber pieces she might like. He'd yet
to bring them to her, however. Maybe he would turn up this morning—
right now, say—and she would banish the children with the magic wand
that she kept in her bureau under her underthings, and she and Rolf
would listen to some of the tuba music and then he would carry her upstairs, cast and all, to where she now lay, on her back, hearing the crows,
not missing her husband or the pinches he gave her when she snored or
the grunts he made in response to her inquiries, her eyes open to the
light that so gently licked the five unclean toes that poked out of her cast.

"I HAD A LITTLE ACCIDENT," Crawford said to Rosa, as he stood
inside her door, breathing air scented with coffee and cigarettes. And
then he remembered—Rosa brewed strong coffee—where he had previously run into the young woman with the manikin. He'd bought bags of
French roast from her at Ariosto's. He remembered that once, when he
went in for a pick-me-up, after he'd put some change in the tips jar, she'd
told him that his shirt was on inside out and on another occasion that

she'd been reading *The American Way of Death,* by Jessica Mitford. But none of this went very far toward explaining why she'd be walking with a manikin early on a Sunday morning or on any morning for that matter. Crawford hadn't asked her about the manikin, and to his question about the Duke Gershwin song his father had often hummed, she'd said, "Huh?" And then he'd walked his bike up the honeysuckled slope and climbed back on and pedaled the rest of the way to Rosa's place, the less than mild air nipping at the scratches on his face and at the kneecap exposed by the tear in his chinos.

Rosa lived two blocks in from Feather Lake, above a Laundromat, next door to an electronics shop. From the bathroom, where Crawford went to clean his face and undress, you could see a portion of the lake and on the far side of it the state hospital for the criminally insane, an early-twentieth-century pile made of yellow limestone. He imagined an inmate at his cell window, looking wistfully in his direction.

Crawford came out of the bathroom wrapped in a sheet. He went down a hallway, past Rosa's bedroom, holding the sheet off the floor. In the living room, he saw Sombra on the sofa. Curled up, Sombra was about the size of a throw pillow. Rosa had found him in a parking garage, in a box with a note that said, "This is Little Dude. He needs his shots. He likes ramen noodles." Rosa had changed his name right away—he was a smooth-haired, mostly black feist, with pointy Boston terrier ears and the stubby body of a beagle—and taken him to be vaccinated and fed him heartier things than ramen noodles. For Valentine's Day, Crawford happened to know, Sombra had received a six-ounce steak, cooked medium rare. He was four years old now, in the prime of life, but whenever Crawford saw him, he seemed to be napping. Sombra looked at Crawford long enough to determine that Crawford didn't want to share the sofa with him and then he tucked his moist black nose back into his belly.

Crawford lay down on a mattress that was on the floor, between the

TV and the coffee table. The mattress was lumpy, full of little fists. He swam around on it for a moment, searching for smooth places. He pulled the sheet up to his shoulders and settled his head. Looking down on him, from a perch on top of the TV, was a photograph of President Bush. It was autographed: "To Rosa Murrado, With Best Wishes." Rosa had a cousin in Austin who ran a lawn care service, who had obtained the picture for her. The last vote Crawford's father had cast had been for Little Bush, or so Crawford had surmised from conversations that Thanksgiving, which was the last time Crawford saw his father upright, not on his back in a hospital bed. His father, that putative liberal, had voted all his life for the party that had put him on the bench in the first place. And why shouldn't he have? Judge Dupree's view of Democrats had been shaped by his father and that story of how he'd been beaten by a Democratic mayor's thugs, back before the First World War, when he was serving as a poll watcher in Louisville for the other party. Crawford had a photograph of his grandfather with his head wrapped in a bandage, one eye swollen shut, the other also swollen but held open by anger and suspicion. Crawford had found the picture in his father's courthouse files, in a folder labeled "Dad." He had also found files labeled "Crawford" and "Morgan" and "Louis" and "Lucy Mulder" (there was a postcard from Spain and an uncashed 1987 check for $38.19) and "Ida" and "Bridge." Most of the files Crawford had sent on to his brother, who was writing something about their father, but others he'd kept: his own thin dossier, for one, and the photograph of Granddaddy Dupree, which Crawford tacked to the wall of his home office to remind him that head injuries ran in the family.

From the kitchen, Rosa said, "Are you ready for me, Señor Dupree?"

Crawford said he was, and Rosa came into the living room preceded by a cloud of smoke. In Mr. Stanley's Hair Studio, she refrained from smoking and chewed Juicy Fruit. He wondered how many massage clients Rosa had. All her business was, as she had put it, "by mouth to ear only." Was Crawford's ear the only one to find its way to Rosa's mattress?

Rosa extinguished her cigarette, and then asked, as she had before, if Crawford would care to hear some "*música*" while she worked on him. Before Crawford could say, "Sure, why not?" she had put on, as she had the other Sunday, a Guatemalan crooner known as El Jaguar.

Rosa wore a thin, blue, sleeveless frock that buttoned down the front; it looked institutional, like what a cleaning lady might wear to work. In Houston, where Rosa had been briefly married to a man named Fernando, she had worked as a maid while attending a college of cosmetology. Rosa kneeled down beside her client, sighing a little as she did. Crawford didn't know how old Rosa was, but he guessed she was closing in on fifty, a virtual contemporary, someone whose knees probably creaked, as his had started to. She was a plumpish woman, bosomy, with cocoa-colored skin, small, undelicate hands, a face that in the cheeks and around the eyes suggested frogginess, hair that had been dyed strawberry. Her eyes were brown and deep and mournful, the kind of eyes that one could imagine El Jaguar singing to.

Rosa pulled the sheet down to the top of Crawford's buttocks. In her palms, she put oil that smelled of a tropical something and rubbed them together. Listening to this, Crawford thought of the word "lubricious." He shut his eyes. Rosa asked him how his headaches were—he got them all the time, especially on school days—and he said he didn't have one right now.

"How are your children?" Rosa was kneading his upper back, where Crawford stored disappointments and grudges, where his headaches ended up, after they'd finished with his head.

Crawford said they were fine.

"And your wife?"

Crawford said she was fine, except she was tired of going around with her leg in a cast.

"And your mother? She OK?" Rosa was working her way down Crawford's back, pushing her thumbs in deep. He was bare clumpy ground, and she was loosening it up. He'd be siftable dirt when she was done.

"My brother moved back home, so my mother will have someone to look after her, in addition to Ida, the lady who cleans and cooks for her. My mother likes to be tended to." Crawford groaned as Rosa pressed the base of his spine. "She told me she quit her hairdresser the other day. She said he'd been mean to her because she was late for an appointment, and she didn't like the chemicals he put in her hair, even though she'd been letting him do it for years, and when she finally asked him to stop, he said, 'I am a professional, Mrs. Dupree, I will not be dictated to.' And she said, 'Well, I am not a lawn to be treated with your sprays, Ted.' So now she goes to this woman who uses vitamin E spray and is nice to her even if she shows up twenty minutes late for her appointment."

Rosa said, "Mr. Stanley says the customer is always king or queen, depending on whether it's boy or girl." Rosa laughed her strange, high, birdy laugh.

Had she made a joke? Crawford wasn't sure. He laughed just in case.

Rosa went at Crawford's upper back again. She breathed her tobaccoey breath on his neck. He listened to El Jaguar, who was light voiced, like a bossa nova singer, though every now and then he made a throaty growl, like a cat asserting its true nature. Hence, Crawford supposed, the name. Sometimes Rosa hummed along with El Jaguar. Once, when she made a sound that was like a growl, Crawford felt as if he were part of a religious rite, and that when Rosa had finished with him, turned him to pulp, Sombra would jump off the couch and eat what was left.

Crawford's heart beat faster when Rosa removed the sheet and began to work on his bottom and legs. In certified massage therapy, he knew, the therapist uncovered only a portion of the client's body at a time. But Rosa was a gypsy therapist, a freelancer. And he was just a slab of gringo flesh. Anyway, he took this moment as a signal to start talking.

"Did you go to church as a girl, Rosa?"

"*Sí.*" She filled her palms with more of the aromatic oil. "Every day in Guatemala City I wash my face and go to church with my mother. When I am done with this, I will wash myself and then go to the *iglesia* by the football stadium. You know it? It's for Spanish people. I always pray for you, Señor Dupree."

"You do?"

"*Sí.*"

Crawford waited for her to elaborate, but she didn't. She was kneading a hamstring.

He said, "When I was fifteen, my mother arranged for me to play tennis with this man who belonged to some evangelical Christian athlete organization. I was a troubled teenager in my mother's opinion, and she thought this guy, whom she'd found through her network of Christian friends, could set me straight. My mother was Episcopalian, but she had fundamentalist tendencies."

"What is Episcopalian?" Rosa asked.

"It's like Catholic," Crawford said, "except there's no Pope and the Virgin Mary is a minor figure and there are no confession boxes. Episcopalians make a general confession of sins in the service itself. We say things like, 'We have followed too much the devices and desires of our own hearts,' and 'We acknowledge and bewail our manifold shins.'" At one point, twenty years ago, while his marriage to Colleen was collapsing, Crawford had briefly considered going to divinity school. When he'd told Darla of this notion, she'd said, "You? Divinity school? How will you save souls with a hangover?" And Crawford had said it was his impression that drinking and preaching went hand in hand in the "Piscopal Shurch." That was the night Darla had let him sleep on her sofa and advised him to think about getting on the wagon.

"I will always go to the *iglesia,*" Rosa said firmly. "It makes me feel better to say prayers and light candles."

Crawford wondered if he ought to continue his story about the tennis-playing evangelist in view of Rosa's confession of piety. But she had her hands squarely on his bottom now, still a tender spot despite the depredations of time, and there was a junky, B-fantasy side to Crawford before which he sometimes felt quite helpless. He was getting a boner. He started talking again.

"So I hit some balls with this guy, who said he'd played for a Big Ten team. I guess Jesus had helped him with his forehand—and his hop serve that hopped like a damn Super Ball. When we were done, he drove me home, except first he needed to stop at the house where he was staying. He was like an itinerant evangelist, you see, except all I knew when my mother set me up with him was that he played tennis. He invited me in for lemonade, and then he asked me if I wanted to get down on my knees and pray with him. Even though I was a rebellious teenager, I was still kind of polite, so I got down on my knees on this nice pale blue carpet." Crawford didn't know how much of this Rosa was taking in, or if he was offending her religious sensibilities in any way, but he kept going. "He wanted me to say a prayer, something from the heart, to ask Jesus for forgiveness for all my bad behavior and for help in my tennis game if I wanted to add that, but I said I didn't feel like it. Then he said, 'Why don't we say the Lord's Prayer together?' I said I really didn't feel like it."

"The Lord's Prayer—El Padre Nuestro—is my favorite," Rosa said. She said something in Spanish that got lost in the croonings of El Jaguar. And then she translated. "In English you say, 'Señor, take us away from the devil, keep us away from evil.'"

Crawford said, "Right." He could feel the sunlight on his cheek from thirty-five years ago. When he and the evangelist had kneeled on that immaculate blue carpet, they had kneeled in wholesome spring sunlight that poured through spotless windows.

"You want to turn over?" Rosa said. "I do your front."

PHILIP ORDERED A McFlurry and a piece of apple pie. He'd never had a McFlurry or apple pie this early in the day. Bicycling in the cool morning air had sharpened his appetite.

He sat down at a table with his breakfast, and then he got up to fetch a fork. On the way back to his table, he saw a black-haired woman eating next to a thin, bald man, who was slumped against her. Then, when he looked again, he saw that the man was a dummy. The black-haired woman, who was dressed as if for a dance or a wedding, Philip had recognized immediately. She had presented him with the warm blueberry muffins at Ariosto's. She looked about the same, except she didn't seem to occupy her face; it was blank, like she'd moved out and taken up residence elsewhere. In the meantime, she was eating a McMuffin. And sharing a table with a dummy.

Philip watched her as he ate. He had two theories about the dummy. One was that it was a door prize she'd won at a party. The other was that the dummy was a dummy only by daylight, that the man inside the dummy slept until darkness fell. Usually the woman didn't make the mistake of staying out too late with him, but last night she had. Philip figured the couple never talked about what the man inside the dummy became during the day. Anyway, he was dead to the world when the sun was out, incapable of all discussion. At night he was good company, his bald head shining like her own private moon. She loved him for all that he was at night but was not embarrassed to be out in public with him when he was a dummy, even though she generally avoided it, because some people stared and some people, such as the old ponytailed guy sitting two tables from her, said things. What he was saying now was, "Well, at least you don't got to worry about him talking too much, complaining because you didn't ball up his socks nice like he likes them. The first thing you got to worry about with me is I talk. I talk a stream. I talk from the get-go. I talk to dogs and strangers and judges who want to put me in jail for talking. I talk when I sleep, I hear, whole long sentences finer than anything any three-piece lawyer can produce while awake and standing on his hind legs before His Honor. Everybody wishes I was like your friend there, Miss—quiet, reserved, boring." The ponytailed man, whose skin was the color of a brown paper bag, who wore a bandanna around his neck, paused to take a sip of his coffee. "Except the ladies. The ladies like it that I'm more frisky than your friend, that I can keep up my end of things, so to say." He leaned his head suddenly to the side, like a dummy that had nodded off. "And I like to keep the conversation flowing even at those most intimate times—there is always something that ain't been delved into enough, always something worth exploring."

The black-haired woman slid out from her seat. She had come back into the fine little house that was her face, and it was as if she'd found it turned upside down. She was pissed, Philip could see. But she didn't say anything or even look at the ponytailed guy. She gathered up the dummy and went out the door in her long dress and thick-soled shoes that seemed too big for her.

The ponytailed guy said, "Some women look a gift horse in the mouth and be afraid."

Philip waited until the woman was out of sight, and then he went outside with his half-finished McFlurry and unlocked his bike. He intended to trail her.

THE CROWS HAD DRIVEN Michelle into the shower. She stood under the water, with her left leg wrapped up to her knee in a black thirty-three-gallon Hefty Cinch Sak, and attempted to compose a list of matters to be addressed today or sometime soon. But water is a slippery medium, and her mind soon wandered from the phone calls she needed to make (to her mother, to her mother-in-law, to Philip's math teacher, a Vietnamese man whose English was like trying to follow a small animal through dense woods) to what Rolf would make of her breasts. Not that they were peculiar in any way. They were of a nice, manageable size and had a nice, classical shape and X rays had shown them to be free of disease. She rather liked them, even if, being a modest and practical midwestern woman, she didn't like them excessively. They had briefly fed two children and they had pleased the handful of adolescent and postadolescent males and one female with whom she had lain during the past thirty years. They were somewhat veiny now, and the nipples had a kind of chewed-upon look, though nobody had even mouthed them in months. Crawford had been a less than avid partner since the accident in New York a year ago, and had had no interest in sex since his father died.

She listened to the sound of water pattering on the Hefty bag. She washed her neck and behind her ears and in her armpits, where tufts of black hair had thrived for years. Originally, she'd cultivated the armpit hair for vaguely political reasons (and because it was an easy way to annoy her mother), which was also why she'd also gone around with hairy legs for a while, at least until she'd gotten that clerical job at the Washington think tank, a hotbed of liberalism except when it came to unshaven legs on female staffers. It was Darla, Crawford's old girlfriend, who had advised her to shave them. She said one of the think tank's benefactors had complained. "Millions of dollars ride on those hairs, girl. Better take them off." This wasn't quite true, but it did seem to matter to the benefactor, who also owned the O Street townhouse where the think tank was installed, that women's leg hairs not be visible to him. A few weeks later, her legs shaved like a Republican girl's, Michelle was at Darla's apartment. It was late and they were drinking Black Russians and listening to Stevie Wonder. The shaggy-haired boy-man who had come for dinner, who had been Darla's boyfriend before he married someone unsuitable, had gone home. And then Darla had put her hand on Michelle's knee and said, "I don't have any etchings, but I could show you my old Washington Senator baseball cards." And Michelle, who was both curious and docile, had let Darla take her by the hand into the bedroom, where they had lain under a poster of President Reagan saluting a monkey. When they were done, Darla had brought out her Senator cards and they had exclaimed over the chaws in the mouths of Harmon Killebrew and Ken Aspromonte and Roy Sievers.

It was a holiday weekend, and when they returned to work it was as if nothing had happened between them. Michelle didn't know if she was relieved or disappointed that Darla all but ignored her. But Darla called the shots and Michelle, despite her hairy armpits, had a mousy side. At some point, they resumed the pretension that they were buddies, though what this actually meant was that Michelle was Darla's pale-girl sidekick from the Midwest, a companion but not an equal. Michelle came for dinner again and there was the shaggy-haired boy-man as well as a nicely groomed East Coast think tank male for Darla. Darla seemed to be offering Crawford as a gift to Michelle. Or was he a booby prize? Or was Michelle the gift or booby prize who was being offered to Crawford? Michelle's instincts told her not to acquiesce in this transaction, and she didn't initially. She took Crawford to be the sort of person who would fade away after a couple of rebuffs. But along with the somewhat forlorn demeanor, there was a streak of stubbornness in him, more than a touch of pride. He fell short of the charmingly flawed but persistent romantic hero who gets the reluctant girl in the end, but then where did you find such men anyway, except in movies or fiction? And he was not unkind, if a little (she discovered later) temperamental. And when they made love for the first time, she didn't feel the presence of his former girlfriend and her onetime bedmate. Or, mostly she didn't. Eventually she asked Crawford about Darla, but he said little. (About his ex-wife, Colleen, who had left him for a shop teacher, he was more expansive; he told her how once, when Colleen was angry with him, she put a bunch of ice cubes in a tea towel and lay down with the ice on the bridge of her nose, where her headache was centered, and said, "I wish I had a dog instead of you.") When Crawford asked Michelle about her old lovers, she told him about them all, except for Darla.

Darla was the only one of her former bedmates Michelle ever missed. (Two of the other four, both of whom she'd screwed in cars, were right here in Wisconsin. One was now the owner of a sports bar who, on the side, did voice-overs on local TV commercials. Every time she heard him do some rapid patter for a snowmobile dealership or his own establishment, she would also hear a seventeen-year-old boy going "Unh, unh, unh" in the backseat of his father's Delta 88.) Michelle tried not to miss Darla and generally succeeded in spite of Crawford's continuing relationship with her, most of which was conducted by e-mail. Michelle supposed Crawford confided in Darla and that Darla, for her part, humored him. Michelle pretended not to be very interested. Darla was just an odd hunger that came over her at odd times, such as on a Sunday morning when the world yawned and stretched, such as when she was standing in the shower with her leg in a garbage bag. Rolf was an odd hunger, too.

"Mom?"

Michelle started. Through the shower door she recognized her daughter. She was a long, thin shape, stretchy like taffy. Caroline's mood was always right there to behold in her face, but now her face was a smear in the steam.

"Yes?"

"You've been in there for an hour."

"Not quite that long." But Michelle turned off the water and pushed open the door.

"Everybody's gone. Dad went to church and Phil went biking. He spelled 'biking' with an *e*. That's wrong, isn't it?" Caroline was a star in school, unlike her brother. She'd almost caught up with him in math. She wasn't any good at hiding her competitive streak, which contributed to the high color in her cheeks.

Michelle ignored the spelling comment. She said, "Well, we'll have to rely on our imaginations and figure out something to do."

"What's that?" Caroline pointed to her mother's chest, to her heart-side boob.

Michelle lowered her chin and looked. "What?"

"That spot." Caroline delicately placed a finger on the outside of her mother's breast. "Like a burn."

Michelle saw a penny-size spot that was the color of a fairly recent hickey. It was a little puffy. How had she missed it earlier? She wasn't sure how to account for it. She failed to imagine Crawford sucking on it during the night without her knowledge. It had been a long time since he'd done that—half-asleep midnight plunder. It was true that she had been massaging herself in the shower, but only gently. An incubus would be a possibility, if she believed in such things. Maybe a spider had gotten her while she was asleep. She believed in spiders.

"It's probably a bug bite," she said. It was a superficial thing, she thought; it didn't portend anything dire. Woman with broken leg bitten by bug—that was all.

PHILIP FOLLOWED ABOUT a block behind the black-haired woman and her companion. They went along deserted shop-lined streets and across the six-lane avenue that split the city up the middle, and into a district that he didn't recall ever being in, at least not on a bike. He went past an electric substation where, within the chain-link fence, he saw a cat wandering. He worried about the cat, but kept going, past a hospital. He didn't see anybody entering or leaving the hospital. It was an immense, silent, many-winged thing. He remembered going to see his grandfather in the hospital in Kentucky. He remembered how one day he'd had to put on a paper mask and gown and rubber gloves before he went into his grandfather's room and how his father, also gowned and masked and gloved, had read to his father from the Bible and had kept on reading even though Grandpop fell asleep almost right away.

When he looked away from the hospital, Philip didn't see the black-haired woman. He assumed she had turned off. He pedaled to the next corner and stopped and straddled his bike and peered down a street full of parked cars and leafless trees and old wood houses with muddy yards. He still didn't see her, and he suddenly felt guilty of something—conspicuousness, perhaps. He pulled the hood of his mother's sweatshirt over his helmet, and steered his bike slowly along the sidewalk. He hunched over the handlebars to make himself even more discreet. In the middle of the block, a voice said, "Hey!"

She was sitting on porch steps, in the shadow of a trash-festooned evergreen bush. Supine on the steps was the dummy. "Didn't I just see you at Mickey D's?"

He didn't deny it. She didn't seem to be accusing him of following her.

"You used to come in to Ariosto's to buy lemon scones, right?"

"Blueberry muffins," he said.

"I stand corrected." But she didn't rise. She was taking off her shoes.

Philip wondered if it was safe to ask a question. He had several in mind. He kept looking at her in her lavender dress and thought, That dummy is so lucky.

Finally, she said, "I'd invite you in, except I'm tired." She grabbed the dummy by the wrist and rose from the steps. The sun had climbed in its steady fashion and it now illuminated the upper story of where she lived.

Philip could already feel her absence. He squeezed the hand brakes on his bike and said, "How come you're going around with him?" His voice sounded high and fluttery.

She said, "I'm glad you asked. This is Sir Lancelot of the Lake. Though some people confuse him with Wayne Newton. You know who Wayne Newton is?"

Philip shook his head.

"He's a no-talent singer, a Vegas cheeseball. Lance is a person of substance." She settled Sir Lancelot of the Lake against her lavender hip and said, "Say hello to the boy, Lance."

Philip was somewhat offended by the reference to his youth, but he didn't let her see that.

In a voice that was somewhere between a tenor and an alto, Lance said, "Hey, dude, how's it going? Cool bike!"

Even from ten feet away, Philip could see the woman's lips move. He said, "You're like a ventriloquist." It was almost a question.

Lance said, "She's working on it. I keep wishing she'd get me a suit so I don't have to perform naked."

"Oh, get a life," the woman said to Lance. She picked up her shoes. There were a half-dozen things that Philip was uncertain about, but he couldn't think of what to ask next.

"Come back sometime and I'll show you my other dummies," she said. "And I'll teach you the basics, if you want."

"Are you like a professional?"

"Semi," she said. "I'm hoping to be in the Yellow Pages someday. Well, see you, *mon petit.*" She climbed the porch stairs and disappeared into the house.

WHEN HE TURNED onto his back, Crawford shut his eyes. This way he could avoid observing the boner that troubled the sheet—this hadn't happened on the previous occasion, that Sunday in Lent, when he'd been so gloomy and Rosa had rubbed him in a manner that was so workmanlike it almost seemed penitential—and also avoid looking into Rosa's eyes.

So now, with Rosa bearing down on his thighs, he talked with his eyes closed, somewhat like a child saying his prayers. El Jaguar had fallen silent.

"The guy, the evangelist tennis player, finally gave up on me and drove me home. But before he let me out of the car, he said, 'Don't be afraid to call on God, wherever you are in your personal journey. The world is His house and He's always home.' And then he patted me on the shoulder and gave me his card and said, 'And remember when you're serving, keep your ball-toss hand up in the air for a second. That prevents you from dropping your head and dumping the serve into the net.'"

Rosa clucked, possibly at Sombra. Crawford guessed Rosa had not been paying close attention to his story. He wished she would work on another part of him—his feet, say.

"When I went inside my house, I found my father listening to one of his railroad sounds records. Whistles, brakes squealing, steam hissing, crossing gates dinging—that kind of thing. He loved trains and he had a collection of these records, but he played them only when he was alone. It was Saturday afternoon and everybody had scattered, though Ida was there somewhere, cleaning or ironing and listening to the sound of a double-header coal train climbing a mountain. My dad had turned the volume up so loud the house seemed to shake. He was sitting in the living room, where all the antiques were, where nobody sat except to listen to music, because the hi-fi speaker was there. His back was to me. His hair stood up all funny in the back. He had a cowlick."

"He come to me, I fix it for him."

"He's dead," Crawford said, perhaps too sharply. He knew she knew his father was dead; she just didn't move easily among English verb tenses.

"*Lo siento.* I am sorry. I am sad for you, Señor Dupree."

"It's OK, Rosa," Crawford said. He opened his eyes. He saw Sombra curled up in his spot on the sofa, his black triangular ears flopped over. Then he saw Rosa. She was bent over his thigh, diligently kneading it, squeezing and prodding its hairy sponginess. She was sweating. There were sweat trails on the back of her smock. The sheet was bunched up at his crotch, like a diaper.

He placed his hands on his chest, as if to hide at least that part of him-self, and closed his eyes again. "My dad would have been in his late for-ties then. We didn't talk much. He talked more with my brother, who was less of a social misfit than I was—easier to talk to, anyway. I'd al-ready determined that I wasn't going to grow up to be like my dad, who was eccentric but also a straight arrow. And virtuous—good-hearted, not a mean bone in his body, though he disapproved of drunks, which was one thing I was planning to be when I grew up. In fact, I was well on my way at age fifteen.

"He didn't hear me when I came in. He was lost in the sound of those locomotives blasting the hell out of his ears. He must have been happy sitting there, no thoughts about his work and the divorce and custody cases he presided over, no thoughts for the moment about the list of tasks my mother had no doubt recommended he do that weekend, no thoughts about his teenage boys.

"I went upstairs to my room and closed the door and put a record on my record player and turned it up loud. Then I burned the card the evangelist had given me. It was satisfying, Rosa."

"Thank you," Rosa said, baffling Crawford for a moment.

She had left off his thighs and was now rearranging the sheet, cover-ing his legs. By accident, presumably, in passing, she touched his boner. She made no comment. Crawford's heart leapt into his mouth. He felt he might go off at any moment. I will always be fifteen, he thought.

"Now I do your head and then we finish," Rosa said. She moved around behind him and propped his head up on her knees.

"Eventually, I heard a knock on my door. My dad was the only person in the house to knock first and actually wait until you invited him in. He asked me how the tennis game had been. I was not responsive, as lawyers say of certain kinds of witnesses. But he sat down on my bed, the way dads do when they want to have a little talk."

Rosa's meaty fingers massaged Crawford's ears and scalp and temples and the place between his eyebrows where bad thoughts were hatched. "My dad wasn't particularly good at tête-à-têtes. At least not with me and my tête. With lawyers and the rest of humanity, he was wonderful. Not that he was unreasonable with me. He was just sort of hesitant. What's the Spanish word for 'head,' Rosa?"

"*Cabeza*," Rosa said. The word sounded almost tropical. He imagined a coconut in a tree. A droplet of sweat fell from Rosa's face onto Crawford's eyelid, popping it open. Crawford saw another drop pending at Rosa's fleshy chin. He shut his eyes again.

"I don't remember what we talked about exactly. I know I didn't tell him about how the tennis evangelist got me down on my knees or about how angry I was at Mom. I was pretty sure he'd been out of the loop as far as arranging the thing. I sort of preferred to nurse my wound in private rather than expose it, you know? Anyway, my dad would have defended my mother, partly out of husbandly duty, partly as a survival tactic. Her temper was famous and we all mostly quaked in front of it, though I less than my brother or father. Anyway, at the end of whatever we talked about, my dad asked if I wanted to play Ping-Pong. I said I didn't feel like it. I could see he was disappointed. So then he got up from the bed and said, 'We love you, Crawford.' He said this from time to time. It was kind of the parental 'we.' Not that he was necessarily speaking for my mother. He just found it hard to use the first person singular in certain circumstances. At least that's what I thought for a while."

Rosa began to worry the skin along Crawford's jaw and around his mouth, which inhibited his talking. She ran fingers gently over the scratches on his cheeks. Then she leaned forward and slid her hands down to his chest. Her matronly bosoms hovered above his mouth. She did some sort of uncertifed massage therapy thing with his pectorals, which made his nipples tighten and tingle. He'd thought his head was to be her last stop. He was right there at the edge again.

He shut his eyes more tightly. "But later I decided the 'we' referred both to the person who for practical purposes was my father, who would be loyal to me and my brother and my mother no matter what, who was sort of a sheep and yet a very good one, and also to this man who lived apart from all of us, who had his own concerns and peculiar desires, a judge who was a railroad hobbyist. Even this person, who wasn't obliged to love me, did. 'I' would have covered both components, but he was shy, so he said 'we.'"

It was the way Rosa did his nipples that tipped him over. He watched her face, as best he could, as it was happening, as his gush was dampening her sheet. He thought he saw Rosa smiling a little, though his perspective was of course upside down. Crawford pulled his knees up a bit, hoping this would obscure his embarrassment, even while being sure it wouldn't. There was really nothing to be done about his wretchedness, except apologize for it.

"*Lo siento,*" he said. He wished he'd accepted his father's long-ago invitation to play Ping-Pong. Had he done so, he might have turned out differently. That was his hunch, anyway.

# 7

# Digging

LAVELL LEFT THE DOG on the patio in its shroud when he went down to the woods to dig the grave. He carried the shovel against his shoulder and walked in a way that reminded Mrs. Dupree of a baseball player strolling to the plate—no swagger though, just a man on his way to his job. He wore dungarees and a green collared shirt that was snipped off at the shoulders. It was left over from his stint at Walt's Tree Service; his name was stitched on it.

She didn't mind the shirt or the tattoo of the playing card joker on his upper arm because he was steady and he looked after her flowers and trees and lawn as if they were his own. She'd gotten his name off the bulletin board at church. He went to AA meetings there. He'd been with her for about two years now, since the spring of 1999, which was longer than the tenures of the three previous yardmen put together, one of whom had also come from the church bulletin board, and she'd never smelled anything on him except peat moss and male perspiration. Sometimes he would be hard to get on the phone—he worked for another woman at church, a real estate agent—and Mrs. Dupree might catch herself wondering if he'd gone off on a bender. Once an alcoholic, always an alcoholic: she knew that much. But she would let the thought go, before it corrupted her belief in him, usually before he called back. Down deep, she felt, he was a good Christian man. She'd concluded that he'd tried to be attentive to his mother, who had died of lung cancer, even though he'd been, by his own admission, drinking most of the time that she was ill. Now, he looked after his father, who was all but crippled from thirty years of bending over at the Ford plant. And he supported his daughter, Kendra, who was a special-needs child, whose mother, his ex-wife, was, he once put it, a special-needs kind of woman. (He'd taken that comment back almost as quickly as he'd let it out. "I ain't so perfect myself," he said.) He'd told her these things as he watered or weeded or mulched. Sometimes, she'd kept him on way past his quitting time, talking to him about her own bout with cancer and how she'd overcome it or about the deficiencies in the diets of American children or about the problems she had faced in trying to keep her husband healthy. Lavell was a good listener. He would listen to her even as dusk was falling, even as his truck sat in her driveway growing rust in the damp river valley air. And he could be counted on to come over if she had an emergency, as she had had yesterday evening, when she'd found Duff convulsing on the patio.

This happened after she'd returned from taking Ida to the bus. She remembered coming into the kitchen and pouring a glass of distilled water and then mixing a teaspoon of powdered vitamin C into it. She had a frog in her throat. When she'd spoken to Ida that day, she'd talked in a raspy whisper. The sounds she produced had made her anxious, as if she'd been trapped inside an imposter.

When she'd finished the glass of water, she'd gone into the library to put on a CD. She often listened to music around dinnertime. Sometimes she listened to the local classical station, though the host at that hour was a bit of a modernist and there was only so much of that she would willingly give her ears to. She was set in her ways, she supposed. She liked the old repertory. Beethoven thrilled and shook her, Puccini could make her cry, Mozart cheered her up. During her husband's last week on earth, she had listened to music all the time. (She herself had been ill during that period, and had hardly been able to drag her body out the door to his hospital room.) Her elder son had complained about the volume at which she'd played the music—Beethoven, Christmas carols, *The Messiah*. "How about we listen to nothing for a moment," Crawford had said. It wasn't a question. When Crawford and Morgan were children, she'd sometimes played music at dinner and asked the boys to identify the composer. Crawford would always guess wrong.

Yesterday, before she found Duff convulsing, she'd put on a Beethoven piano sonata, the D minor, with its dark chords and moments of near silence and sudden plunges at the heart. Morgan had given it to her for her birthday last month, her eightieth. He'd taken her out to dinner, a bistro over on Bardstown Road owned by a woman he'd grown up with. For her husband's eightieth, she'd rented the ballroom at the country club and invited three hundred people. It had been a surprise—he was easy to fool—and praise and love had warmed his face as he made his way around the ballroom with a glass of Coca-Cola in his hand. A couple days later, she'd had to tell him that it was time for him to come down from his cloud, from his Coca-Cola high; it was time for him to get Duff to the vet for a bath and a nail trim, it was time for him to take her car over to the vehicle emissions inspection station, it was time for him to call the Better Business Bureau about that carpet cleaning service that had gypped her. After her birthday dinner with Morgan—no dessert, she couldn't eat sugar—she'd come home and watched *Larry King Live*.

She'd gone into the kitchen during the adagio movement. It was then that she'd seen Duff. He was lying on the patio, next to the wrought iron bench she'd bought in New Orleans some years ago, which nobody ever sat on because it was too uncomfortable. Six o'clock sun fell on Duff's small white body and on the hibiscus that had bloomed feverishly ever since Lavell had repotted it.

Duff was nearly fifteen, one hundred and five in dog years, as she explained to friends and children and deliverymen alike. He had become incontinent during the last year or so, and she'd kept him outdoors during the day when the weather was good. Recently, there'd been a stretch of weather so beautiful—it was May now, the week after Derby—that she had actually lifted her arms in praise one morning. The skies had been as blue as those at the beginning of the world must have been, and the air was full of sweet smells. Two nights ago, after a meal of scrod and spelt bread and then a walk around the yard, she had lain on her bed, which her husband had fallen off of three times during his last months, the smell of pittosporum on her clothes from when she'd brushed against it, and slept for two solid hours, until she heard a weak, croaky bark. She'd left Duff outside. He'd not even been able to keep up with her as she'd hobbled around the yard, cane in hand. When she'd let him in, she'd apologized and given him some leftover scrod, which he didn't touch. Later, she'd put him in the cage she'd had to buy because of his incontinence.

When she saw him convulsing on the patio, she felt as if she'd taken an arrow in her hip, right where the orthopedist had inserted the titanium ball and stem. When she finally got to him, he was stretched out to almost beyond his full length, as if he were trying to escape from his old, ruined body. Jolts of electricity seemed to pass through him. The jolts lifted his head off the flagstones and curled his lip and she saw his gums and yellow teeth. When the convulsion stopped, she lowered herself to her knees, a procedure that she rarely attempted these days (at church she prayed seated and took Communion standing), and put her hand on his taut belly. "Oh, Duffy," she said. Duff had been mostly her husband's dog, and she'd sometimes been brusque with him, as she had with Bill.

She had a short fuse. She was prickly and thin-skinned and grudge bearing and mad about a thousand and one things. For some of these sins, she asked for God's forgiveness almost every day.

She'd called Morgan first. He'd moved back to town several weeks ago. She'd been excited when she'd heard he planned to do so, for neither of her children had lived anywhere near her for the past thirty years. Then Morgan had informed her that the move was likely to be temporary. He hadn't come home to take care of her in her dotage. He was doing research for a book—a memoir about his father. The idea of this had left her feeling flushed in the face. She guessed she'd come off badly in the book, though probably not as badly as she would if Crawford were the author. Morgan was more like his father, she believed. Crawford bore her imprint. Perhaps she would be dead before the book came out, if it did. How many more years did she have?

Morgan hadn't answered the phone. She talked to his machine. She didn't like talking to those things. They made her feel ghostly, like she wasn't all there. She said, "Morgan, Duff is dying." She tried clearing her throat. "He's convulsing. Outdoors. I can't lift him. This is Mom. Please call me."

She might have tried the vet next, though it was after office hours, or phoned a neighbor—Gerald Boardman, for instance, one of her husband's bridge cronies, who had professed his desire to serve her in whatever way he could. Pitt Miller, the assistant minister over at St. John's-on-the-Hill, would have come. It was him she'd called the night her husband had fallen in the kitchen and could not get up. But she phoned Lavell instead. Lavell lived two miles away, in one of Adele Barr's shabby creek-side rentals, property that Adele planned to convert to condominiums. Adele was a wheeler-dealer, in Mary Louise Dupree's opinion. She didn't approve of Adele's huge car, which you practically had to be airlifted into, or of Adele using her cell phone in the church parking lot on Sunday morning. Or of how hard Adele seemed to work Lavell.

Which was why Mrs. Dupree could get him for only one afternoon a week, sometimes two, if it was a week when his boss was letting him breathe a little. Lavell would say to her, "I sure would like to come see you on Thursday, Mrs. Dupree, but Mrs. Barr's got me booked solid. I'm going to promise you Friday afternoon." And he would come as he'd promised, in his blue truck that looked as if it had been in a hundred hail storms. She liked the sound it made as it came rattling down her driveway.

Lavell wasn't home, so she was forced to talk to another machine. It was somehow easier talking to Lavell's than to Morgan's, though she went on for too long and was cut off. Probably he'd gone out to dinner, to eat the fast food that she'd told him was just like putting poison directly into his system. Or maybe he'd gone to an AA meeting. There was one at seven o'clock most weekday nights.

She'd stood at the patio door and watched Duff quiver and then she'd gone to get his towel. She'd wrapped it around him so that only his head was showing. It was the old beach towel that he slept on in his cage. She sat on the wrought-iron bench and talked to him as he continued to convulse. She said, "It's all right, Duff. You'll be with God and Bill soon." She told him about a dream she'd had about her husband, how she'd seen him walking along railroad tracks in an old raincoat. She believed Bill knew where he was going; he wasn't lost or at loose ends. He wasn't wearing his sun hat, either. "His beautiful white hair was combed," she said to Duff.

It became dark and the convulsions seemed to intensify. Twice she leaned forward and touched Duff and then she sat back and talked to him through her tears. She could feel the night through her thin shirt. She was a wisp of a woman, ninety pounds in her walking shoes. The phone rang and she nearly tripped going in the door to get it.

When Lavell arrived at her house, Duff had stopped moving. Lavell carried Duff into the garage and laid him under the shelves she kept her gardening things on. They decided he would come back tomorrow, during his lunch break, to bury Duff.

"That won't be too late, Lavell?" She imagined animals gathering outside the garage door during the long night, trying to figure out how to get in. The next-door neighbor had looked out her kitchen window one day this past winter and seen a coyote at the head of her driveway.

"No, ma'am, he'll be all right in here for a few hours." The reason Lavell hadn't come over until now was that he'd gone to a conference at his daughter's school. And then he'd taken her to play mini-golf and eat a cheeseburger. He was wearing a nice plaid cotton shirt with sleeves and clean dungarees. She couldn't have guessed from what he said about the conference that Kendra had recently bitten the special-needs teacher on the ankle or that his ex-wife, Claudette, had said to him afterwards, in the parking lot, while lighting a cigarette, "I tried one of those patches, but it didn't work." But Mrs. Dupree could see in his posture that he was worrying about something. He hadn't told her much about Claudette, but she did know that Claudette was about to marry a mechanic at the Toyota dealership where she was a secretary.

They stood in the doorway of the garage. Her husband's car was gone—she'd given it to Morgan—but she still parked hers over to the right. She still slept entirely on her side of the bed, too. The extra space filled her with dread. It was like space that would swallow her if she tried to occupy it.

She said to Lavell, "My husband used to get up at six-thirty in the morning to take Duff out. Right up to the end."

"Yes, ma'am," Lavell said. He was edging the tiniest bit toward his truck. It was thoroughly dark now, except for where she stood, in the light from the garage. "I sure am sorry."

She felt dizzy for a second, and she almost reached for Lavell's arm to steady herself. It was hunger that made her this way, she thought. She hadn't eaten in hours.

THE BEACH TOWEL Duff was shrouded in dated from when she and Bill had taken the boys to Delray Beach, in Florida. This was in 1964. They rented a house two blocks from the Atlantic. It was a shack, essentially, with a little screen porch and a sand yard in which a couple of shaggy palms grew. It disappointed her; she thought they could've done better. The roof over the porch was tin and when it rained—there was a doozy of a storm during their stay—it clattered wildly on the roof, as if they (and she in particular) were under siege, as if the sky were releasing pent-up devils that broke to pieces as they fell. She was like that back then, nervous with ideas, prone to frightful dreams that she kept to herself. Late at night, during calmer weather, it was possible to hear the ocean—if Bill wasn't snoring, that is. She was always the last to bed. One night she put down her book—was it one by that bishop in California, Pike, the man who later disappeared in the Judaean wilderness?—and put on a sweater and walked toward the beach. She was still in her dinner clothes, though she'd exchanged her heels for sandals. She'd had scallops for dinner—she shouldn't have, because they always gave her bad dreams. (Both the boys had eaten lobster tails and for dessert banana cream pie. Crawford had tried ordering a Coke with grenadine, but she'd made him have milk.) When she left the house, she didn't have a plan, except to walk on the beach and feel the ocean air on her sunburned body. She hoped to tire herself out. But the way the waves curled and foamed made her feel eager and untired, and when she came abreast of the Del-Mar Hotel, with its lengthy veranda, she had an idea that there was someone waiting for her to walk onto it in her dress, which was printed with magnolia blossoms. On the sidewalk she brushed the sand off her feet and slipped her sandals back on. She crossed the street— jaywalked right in front of a police cruiser—and mounted the steps to the hotel porch. Older voices, men's, were discussing Castro and the Communists in bitter tones. One man said mysteriously, "Think what they could do if they got hold of the goddamn orange juice industry."

Mary Louise Dupree herself was a staunch anti-Communist, as was her husband, though unlike Bill she'd first flirted with the other side; at college, she'd drunk strong coffee at the house of an economics professor, who had a circle of friends ("townies," mainly) who were said to be party members. She wondered if the men on the veranda could possibly detect that about her, how easily she'd been sucked in. She saw one of them studying her, and she went on into the lobby, where the man she had imagined on the beach, the one who would take her away and listen to her describe the kinds of dreams she had when she ate scallops, was sitting on a sofa, reading a magazine and smoking. (He'd have to give up smoking; she couldn't permit it.) He was wearing a sports jacket over a polo shirt and his hair was dark and wavy in a European kind of way. He looked up when she came through the door, and in his nod to her, which was a nod she felt all the way to her toes, she saw his gentleness and intelligence. It was clearer than day that he'd been expecting her. She may have actually smiled at him, she wasn't quite sure now, but she kept going, into the powder room, its walls pink as the inside of a conch. She splashed handfuls of water on her face and then sat in a stall for several minutes. She left the hotel by another exit, and the next day, when she went to the drugstore to buy lipstick and sunburn lotion, she also bought a straw hat for Bill (she was tired of seeing him in the soiled porkpie tennis hat that didn't even protect his nose from the sun) and the beach towel that Duff was now wrapped in. The towel was an idle purchase, not a necessity—they had four—but an extra one might come in handy. It was blue, with a border of cockleshells.

SHE GOT UP from the table where she'd been eating her oat-flake-and-lecithin porridge and yeastless toast. It was past noon. She hadn't got out of bed until eleven—Ida didn't come on Saturday—and she was still in her bathrobe. She stood at the patio door and looked across the green yard toward the green woods. Lavell, having apparently finished digging, stood with his shovel next to a young holly, where the grass gave out and turned into creeping charlie and pokeweed and brambles. She used to go walking in the woods in early spring, before the snakes came out and the undergrowth rose up, and after Thanksgiving, when the snakes slept and the undergrowth had subsided. There was a fallen tree, down by the trickle of a creek, where she sometimes sat, trying not to think of her cares or the life that was slipping away from her, where, while birds discussed the weather, she sometimes said St. Francis of Assisi's prayer, "Lord, make me an instrument of thy peace." But she'd not gone down there for years, and she was not likely to ever go again, with her hip the way it was, unless she was to be carried on a litter. The thought of herself on a litter, two strong men hauling her through the woods, made her feel almost light-headed.

She walked with her cane when they went down to the grave site. It was an extra something to hold on to as she negotiated the slope. Lavell had his arms full of Duff. He carried Duff on his forearms, palms up, as if Duff were something being borne along a church aisle. A corner of the beach towel hung down, revealing her dog's forelegs, and she felt an urge to tuck it in. But she was distracted by a molehill. She slowed to squash the upheaved earth beneath her black shoe. She'd had a couple of her former yardmen set traps for the moles, but she'd just about given up on trying to get rid of them. They dug relentlessly—Lavell had said one six-ounce mole could undo sixty feet of earth in a day—and she had to admit that she admired their industry. And whenever she thought about moles for too long, a picture from *The Wind in the Willows* came into her head: she would see Mole picnicking on a riverbank with Ratty, spectacles on his sensitive snout, curlicuing slippers on his feet. And then she would think of the moment in the book when poor Mole, on some ill-fated adventure with Ratty, tripped and cut his shin. Sometimes when she stomped on a molehill—when she was alone, that is—she would say it wasn't personal.

"I meant to try Morgan again this morning," she said. "I wonder where he is."

"Yes, ma'am," Lavell said.

"Beau ran away one time," she said, not thinking to identify Beau for Lavell, thinking only of the wandering collie that had so complicated her existence forty years ago. "That was before the time he ran away for good. Crawford was so upset. He yelled at me, telling me I shouldn't let Beau out or else I should put him on a leash in the yard. And Morgan, who was about ten then, said, 'He'll come home, Craw, don't worry.' Morgan was always trying to calm his brother. A lot of people thought he was the older one. He wanted things to go smoothly, you see."

"That's how I like them to go, too," Lavell said. "But not much does most of the time."

She glanced at him. It always caught her by surprise when Lavell said something a little on the bitter side. Sometimes he'd take it back, like when he made that comment about his ex-wife being a special-needs kind of person. Usually he was so quiet. When he was down on his knees in her garden, with his hands in the dirt, head bowed to his work, she imagined a man who had found his way out of trouble—all those days and nights of drunkenness, blackouts, pain—to peace. She imagined he had cast bitterness aside to get there.

Even so, she didn't think Lavell was wrong about the way things generally went. She believed in God, she felt His presence in the very air she breathed, she felt Him lead her to the right words when she prayed, but nothing on earth hardly ever did go smoothly, did it?

"We have to have faith," she said.

"That helps," Lavell said, a stick cracking under his boot.

They were at the bottom of the slope. To the right was a sinkhole, which over the forty-odd years she'd lived here had widened to the point that she now thought of it as a maw. Some years ago, on the advice of a landscaper with whom she no longer did business, she had planted flowering trees around the perimeter, but only one, a redbud on the lower side, had not been lost to it. She had filled the hole with yard debris for a while. Then Lavell had cleared it out and seeded it with wild grasses. The hollow wasn't really visible from the ground floor of her house. Only when she walked past did she let herself contemplate the dank underground spaces—there were caves beneath her property, experts had told her—to which the sinkhole led. These were places where even a mole, even a slippered and spectacled one, would not be tempted to go, even on a frolic.

They traversed twenty yards of solid green earth—the grass was abundant here, comforting—before reaching the grave site. She said, "Of course, Morgan wasn't attached to dogs the way Crawford was. Crawford loved dogs more than people. 'They don't criticize you,' he said." She lifted her cane tip off a clump of old leaves and set it down among stalky, downy-headed dandelions. "Now he's got a cat. 'Dogs are too much trouble,' he says."

"They are some work," Lavell said. He stood beside the hole he'd dug, Duff still in his arms. It was warmer today, a little humid, the sky puffy with the possibility of rain. The hole was twice the size of the one into which her husband's jar of ashes had been placed. She was going to go into a jar, too, and then into a little square hole that Frank, the sexton at St. John's, would dig next to her husband's. She wondered what sort of jar—urn—her sons would choose for her. Crawford had picked a ceramic one for his father. When he had come home from the funeral home, he'd said to Morgan, "The guy was hoping I'd pick the six hundred dollar walnut urn with the brass handles, suitable for the cremains of a federal judge, but I picked the three hundred dollar crockery jar, the second-cheapest one in the display case. 'That's a very nice choice, sir,' the guy said. I also made 'a very nice choice' when I picked out the second-cheapest casket to burn him in."

"You want me to set him down now, Mrs. Dupree?"

"I guess it's time." The frog had gone from her throat, hopped out overnight. But she still didn't feel in the clear. She had to be so careful about what she put into herself—a drop of vinegar, not to mention a pinch of sugar, could send her up the wall—and there were so many viruses and bugs waiting to catch her out, if she should let down and not keep up with her regimen of vitamins and herbal potions. Sometimes— today, for instance—she believed she could see in the sky, in the shapes of the clouds, that something was about to befall her. The clouds seemed glutinous, even phlegmy.

Lavell knelt with Duff, then looked up at her and said, "You want me to leave the towel?"

"I think he should take it with him. He slept on it."

"Yes, ma'am." Duff fit easily lengthwise, but the hole was snug width- wise. It seemed to her that Duff didn't lie quite flat.

Lavell, who had a certain gift for anticipating her requests, said, "You think I should make it a little bigger maybe?" He rested his hands on his dungarees. There was a smear of dirt high on his forehead. He was fast losing his hair, she was sorry to note. One thing about the Dupree men was that they were blessed with more than enough hair to hide their skulls. Lavell was going to be down to skin and bone in a couple years. It was a prejudice, but a bald man always made her feel a little skittish. There was a man down the road, a retired actuary, whose head was as bare as a bird's egg, who could not help telling off-color jokes in mixed company.

"Maybe we should," she said. "If you don't mind."

"No, ma'am. I misestimated there." He lifted Duff out of the hole and laid him next to the pile of dirt.

They were silent as Lavell made the hole more commodious. A single

bird, a cardinal, called from the woods in front of her. She couldn't lo-
cate it. Then a mockingbird took over, flooding the air with everything
it knew.

Lavell returned Duff to the hole. "That seems better."

"Thank you, Lavell."

"No problem."

The mocker went on and on, sweetly retailing gossip. The other day,
one had flown smack into her dining room window, while she was sitting at the table, answering sympathy notes about Bill. She'd received
hundreds and had fifty more to acknowledge. Mockers were fiercely ter-
ritorial; they would attack their own reflections. They wanted to be all
birds at once, the only bird on the block.

Lavell picked up his shovel again and said, "Are you ready for me to
cover him?"

She gazed at the lump wrapped in the faded blue towel. She saw the
ocean, heard it soughing in her ears. She saw her husband stumbling
out of the water, pushed forward by waves that had started over by
Africa (according to her younger son's theory), a slender, unmuscled
man, white or pink where he wasn't hairy (but mostly white, because
she'd made him cover up on the beach), no threat to fish or children,
a man who as a boy had spent a week in a hospital bed with his head
immobilized between sandbags after an eye operation and who could
later, without his glasses, see only a hallucinogenic version of the
world, who had been blindly in love with her from the very beginning,
who called her "Gorgeous" or "Sweetheart" even on days when those
terms were far from accurate. She watched him pick his way among
beach umbrellas and sunburned flesh, his swim trunks clinging to his
narrow body, and then he was there, all of him that she could see or
hear—his dripping paleness, the wen on his shoulder, the news that
the water was "invigorating."

"I thought we might say a prayer first," she said.

"Yes, ma'am," Lavell said. "That would be good."

"Dear Lord," she said, shutting her eyes, waiting for God to sit down next to her in the dark that filled her head. "Thank you for giving our little dog fifteen years on your beautiful earth, and for letting him keep Bill and me company as we have moved closer to you. Thank you for keeping him out of harm's way all those years, except for a few scrapes that couldn't be helped. Thank you for letting him spend time with Morgan and Crawford and my three dear grandchildren, especially little Caroline, who loved him so, who loved to come down here and sit with him under the dawn tree. Thank you for letting him know Lavell, too, and his quiet, steady ways. And Ida, whom he followed around the house and gazed up at when she was at the stove, in hopes of a treat. Please take unto yourself, dear Lord, our little dog's soul, and let him walk again beside you and the man he loved."

Lavell had kept his eyes shut and his head lowered until she'd mentioned his name. And then he'd looked up, also because he'd heard a door slam. When he heard a door slam nowadays, he almost always thought of his ex-wife slamming the bathroom door in his face when he told her he couldn't live with her anymore because she'd been unfaithful to him and his child. He'd quit drinking by then. She'd slammed the door in his face twice, the second time after calling him a goddamn loser. Now the world was silent, even the birds had hushed, and Mrs. Dupree's face was wet with tears. He was hungry. He'd not eaten lunch before coming over.

Mrs. Dupree reached into the pocket of her slacks and pulled out a little square of paper. She hung her cane on her forearm and unfolded the square. "I copied this down from the prayer book last night." But she couldn't read it—she didn't have her glasses with her—and she thought she would foul it up if she tried to say it from memory.

"Would you mind?" she said, giving him the prayer.

Lavell had some trouble with her handwriting—particularly with the word "fellowship," which she'd abbreviated "f'ship"—but he made it through.

"Amen," she said, firm in her belief that God would grant Duff, as the prayer so beautifully put it, "an entrance into the land of light and joy."

But she turned away when Lavell began to scoop dirt onto Duff. "I'm going up," she said.

"Yes, ma'am, I'll be done here in a moment."

She turned back and said, "Maybe we can plant something there one of these days. Witch hazel might be nice if the darned deer would leave it alone."

She went past the sinkhole that like a pitcher plant sucked in everything that came near its lip and she continued on up the hill. Above her, on her patio, she saw a man in a pink shirt and glasses. She knew it was Morgan, but for a moment she saw her late husband inhabiting her son's slouchy thinness. He, her husband, was awaiting her as she trudged up the slope with her metal cane and her day's worth of complaints—her back hurt, her hip hurt, a spring cold was stirring in her chest even though the frog had gone out of her throat. But as she came closer the resemblance between her son and husband faded. It was only Morgan on the patio, her diffident, divorced, elusive but not unreliable son, who would return to his New York "bachelor's pad," as she thought of it, when he was done with his book project. She often wanted to tell him things, tell him all her heart's troubles, but there was something in his face that usually kept her from it. She wanted to tell him, for instance, how she had seen his father in a dream walking along railroad tracks with a little suitcase in his hand, and how he was smiling even though he was alone and in his shabby raincoat. God had granted him an entrance into the land of light and joy. That was how she read it, anyway. The tracks disappeared into light as rosy and tender as baby's skin. The suitcase was an odd detail, though—it was round, a blue bag sprinkled with paste-on stars, like what a little girl of fifty years ago would take on an overnight.

"I'm sorry about Duff, Mom," he said. "I didn't check my messages until too late. I was out to dinner with Lucy last night."

For his book? She didn't want to probe into his private life too much, so she didn't ask.

"Lavell helped me out," she said. "He came over last night and took off from his lunch today." She heard a harsh note in her voice. She was a little winded from the hike up. She gazed at the espaliered magnolia that grew against the sitting room wall. It always made her think of herself in a girdle and shoes that pinched. But it blossomed without fail.

"Maybe you should get another dog," Morgan said.

"No, I'm too old for that. I wouldn't have the time or strength to house-train a dog." She turned and saw Lavell coming up the hill with the shovel on his shoulder. She had faith in Lavell. He'd show up and dig holes for her when she needed him to. Maybe she'd write it in her funeral instructions that he was to dig the hole that she would go into.

# 8

# On Vacation

UNCLE LOUIS STOOD before *Starry Night* for a long time, longer than he'd stood before Monet's *Water Lilies* or Matisse's nude dancers or any of the other paintings he'd come to New York to see. Morgan wandered off, and when he returned, Uncle Louis was sitting on a bench, cleaning his glasses with his necktie. Morgan thought he saw the trail of a tear on Uncle Louis's dark cheek, but perhaps it was a gleam of light. Among the gallerygoers, Morgan had noticed, were a number of women who wore silver or gold things in their hair or around their throats or wrists. It was as if these women, both the tall, languid ones and the short, bustling ones, had all awakened on that spring day in 1984, when the air trembled with promising ideas, and decided that the light should reflect off themselves, wherever they went.

Uncle Louis settled his glasses on his nose and said, "I hear a rumbling in my stomach, Morgan. What do you hear in yours?"

Morgan, who was thirty-three and a day, who had celebrated his birthday with his girlfriend at a French restaurant in the West Forties the night before, said, "I could go for a cup of coffee." When he'd wandered off, he'd stood in front of a Rothko painting for a moment or two. The dark bands of color had seemed to throb. It wasn't a painting to look at when you'd had a lot of wine the night before. Neither was *Starry Night*, with its pulsating moon and stars and its cypresses that were like blackened tongues of flame. Nor, for that matter, were the stripes of Uncle Louis's seersucker suit a sight that Morgan found easy to behold.

Uncle Louis rose from the bench. He was sixty-six then, two months older than Morgan's father. He had a paunch upon which the end of his tie (striped, also, alas) lay. At one time he'd fed his stomach mostly alcohol, but he'd been completely sober for the past half dozen years, since the late seventies, and his stomach had almost seemed to swell in response, in joy or relief. When Morgan had seen Uncle Louis a couple Christmases ago, he had looked, next to Morgan's slender father, the more robust of the two. And then last spring, when Louis began to have night sweats and to experience pain near his left eye, it was discovered that he had lymphoma. He lost weight and had to tighten the red Christmas suspenders that he wore almost year-round. During the summer, he was given radiation treatments, and by the fall his doctor had declared him to be mostly clean of the disease, except for a few minor pockets. The lymphoma was said to be "indolent."

Uncle Louis had subsequently decided to light out for distant places. That winter, he had seen the sun rise in Cádiz and Tangier and Dubrovnik and Istanbul. In the summer, he was planning to take a train the length of Sweden to Lapland and paint the Lapps and their reindeer and the white nights. Now he was on his roundabout way to a Mexican beach. He'd said he was going to point his belly at the sun and paint the sky and the palm trees from that perspective. He said he was going to call it the Fat Vacationer series.

Uncle Louis patted his stomach. "Coffee it is. With a bagel and cream cheese on the side."

As they descended the stairs to the museum lobby, Morgan imagined his father's cousin trying to paint while lying on his back. It would be awkward, though Michelangelo and Tiepolo and all those guys had done it, hadn't they? A man who had given up drinking ought to be able to paint on his back, surely.

They retrieved Uncle Louis's hat from the cloak room and passed through the revolving doors onto Fifty-third Street. Uncle Louis somehow got caught in a busload of Japanese tourists. When at last he wriggled free, he said, "The one place I won't ever travel to is Japan. I haven't forgiven them for attacking us. And I don't care for raw fish."

They walked toward Fifth Avenue. A garbage truck swallowed black bags of garbage, car horns sounded, a jackhammer undid a piece of concrete, but there was something unmistakably sweet in the air, something that even Morgan, with his postbirthday hangover, could detect. Some hint of lilac or cherry had wafted down from Central Park, perhaps. Or maybe all the women in the city, when they left their apartments that morning, had released into the air some secret perfume. When Morgan had seen Gina go off to work at quarter past nine—he was still in bed— he'd noticed that she'd pinned her hair up off her neck and was wearing under her unbuttoned baby-blue cardigan a low-cut shirt. All that sleep-softened flesh was awake! He imagined that as she'd walked out of the building into the April sunlight some sort of chemical event had occurred, something even a doorman, had there been a doorman, wouldn't have failed to observe. She was a beaker of compounds exposed to radiant energy.

By the walls of St. Thomas, a man was selling wind-up puppies that turned in frenzied circles and spun their tails. Uncle Louis bought two. One was for Jacques, his very old dog, and the other he presented to Morgan.

"Happy birthday a day late," he said.

They walked down Fifth Avenue, Morgan with his wind-up dog and

Uncle Louis with his, in the direction of a coffee shop where Morgan had lunched before. Morgan worked near Grand Central, for the magazine that covered the hotel industry, but he sometimes wandered uptown in search of a grilled cheese sandwich to write home about. He'd taken off work today.

People sat on the steps of St. Patrick's, enjoying the sun, listening or not listening to a man in a houndstooth hat and too-short checked trousers preach against wickedness. Morgan had seen the man before and heard his sermon about how God had rained fire and brimstone on Sodom and Gomorrah and the other cities of the Plain. "Lo," he said, in a high, sharp voice that strived against the noise of the street, "the smoke of the country went up like the smoke of a furnace."

Uncle Louis said, "I trust that I won't run into these religious fanatics in the afterlife."

"Maybe there'll be a special room for them," Morgan said, though his actual view of the afterlife, as best as he could imagine it, was that it was pure nullity, a zero without even the line that circumscribes it. Normally, he tried to avoid the thought of this—everything (love, blue skies, the squeeze bunt) erased—for it struck terror in his heart.

"It's fun to imagine, isn't it—the Ayatollah Khomeini and this peckerwood exhorting each other in languages unintelligible to each? Ho! It cheers me up, Morgan."

Uncle Louis looked upward at the spires of the cathedral, needles in the haystack of tall things. Morgan wondered if Uncle Louis actually entertained the possibility of an afterlife. If so, did he imagine a room—or something grander, perhaps—where bachelor uncles such as himself, closeted gay men, would spend eternity? An image of laughing, naked men sprawled beside a pool from which steam picturesquely ascended filled Morgan's head. The preacher in the houndstooth hat had left the cities of the Plain to smolder and was now foretelling the end of the world in general.

Morgan asked about his father. A few weeks ago, he'd had a cataract operation.

"He's still drinking milk and following your mother's orders. I beat him in cribbage the other night."

Small puffy clouds, like those in a children's pop-up book, were moving eastward, but the sun ruled the sky. It gave a glow to Uncle Louis's shaved but shadowy cheeks and made the lines in his forehead seem distinct as a philosopher's furrows.

"And of course he is meting out justice again, with two mostly clear eyes." Uncle Louis had flipped the clip-on sun lenses down over his glasses.

"Not respecting persons in judgment? Hearing the small as well as the great?" Morgan had several times heard his father recite this bit of scripture, his head held level, his French nose tipped neither up nor down.

"Naturally," Uncle Louis said, as they proceeded up the street, away from the end-of-the-world man. "When we played cribbage, he told me about a Vietnamese fellow he tutors. Your parents' church adopted the family. Your dad said he took Mr. Vu to the Rexall store, so Mr. Vu might become familiar with American toiletries." Uncle Louis chuckled. "I think your dad has a shot at sainthood if he keeps it up."

Morgan smiled at the thought of his father leading his Vietnamese pupil along aisles full of analgesics and salves and ear-wax remover and Ace bandages. He imagined his father and Mr. Vu standing before the array of hair products, chanting "Shampoo! Shampoo!"

Uncle Louis put a quarter in the cigar box of a blind man who was standing outside Saks, in front of a window containing a jumble of bare manikins.

Uncle Louis thumped his forehead. "I just remembered I need a bathing suit for my Mexican adventure." He flipped up his sun lenses.

They wandered around Saks with their wind-up puppies, slowing down at the perfume counter so that Uncle Louis could sniff ("Oleander?

Bougainvillea? Dubrovnik at dusk?"), fingering raincoats and neckties and dress shirts. Uncle Louis did the fingering. Morgan hoped only for a cup of coffee and a couple of Tylenols. They rode the escalators and at last found a table devoted to men's swimwear. The style in men's swimwear that year seemed to be no style: no plaids, no paisleys, no gaudy stripes. A few of the suits made nods in the direction of the tropics. Uncle Louis picked a modestly cut, pale blue one.

"Excellent choice, sir," the hovering salesman said. "Anything for your companion?"

"My nephew is all set, thank you," Uncle Louis snapped. Morgan had never heard this tone of voice from his father's cousin. It made him wince in sympathy for the salesman.

As they descended to the ground floor, Uncle Louis said, "I know you aren't, technically, my nephew, but I think of you as such." He put his hand on Morgan's shoulder.

Morgan again thought he saw a spot like a tear on Uncle Louis's cheek, unchecked sentiment glistening, though the store was so full of light bouncing off shiny surfaces he couldn't be sure. He said, "So, what did you think of *Starry Night*? I've always thought it looked like the work of a deranged child."

"Well, yes," Uncle Louis said, chuckling in his peculiar, almost private way that was like something bubbling underground. "I believe he painted it not long after he presented his ear to a prostitute. It is a little childlike and perhaps a little mad—or visionary might be kinder—but I would trade all my worldly goods, except for Jacques, to be able to paint one brush stroke like van Gogh. Then I could die."

On their way out, they stopped for a second time at a table of men's dress shirts. The shirts were yellow and blue and lavender and pink and the green of a Granny Smith apple. Uncle Louis selected four. They were for a friend of his in Mexico, he said. "I hope I have his right neck size." He offered to buy Morgan a shirt for his birthday. "Do you like this blue one? It's almost a van Gogh blue. Or this pink one? If men wore pink more often, there would be fewer wars."

Morgan didn't own a pink shirt then and he was against all wars except for the just ones, so he accepted Uncle Louis's gift on the condition that Uncle Louis let Morgan pay for the coffee.

"And a bagel with cream cheese. I'm starved," Uncle Louis said.

THREE MONTHS LATER, Morgan and Gina flew down to Louisville for a long weekend. It was ninety-eight degrees the day they arrived. In the evening, Mrs. Dupree enlisted Morgan and his father to help her water the yard. Everything was parched, she said. Gerald Boardman's retriever had come over that morning and dumped his head in the birdbath and then slept in the English ivy below the dining room window until she sent him packing.

On their second night, Morgan and Gina went to see Uncle Louis and his new friend Lazaro. They shook hands with Lazaro, and then Lazaro retreated to the kitchen. Uncle Louis sent Morgan and Gina upstairs to his bedroom to change into their swimsuits. "Jacques will be there to attend to your every need," he said. Uncle Louis wore a striped beachcomber shirt and he had scattered cologne (possibly a bit too much of it) among the creases on his neck. The lenses of his glasses were smudged, but the blue of his eyes was clear. It seemed to Morgan, as he and Gina climbed the stairs, that Uncle Louis was as happy as Morgan had ever seen him. Perhaps Uncle Louis had had a moment at the easel when something mysterious flowed down his arm into the hand that held the brush, when the resulting square of yellow on the canvas could pass for a box of God's finest light. Perhaps he was still reveling in this. Or perhaps Uncle Louis's state of mind was due to the presence of, as Morgan's mother called him, "the Mexican houseboy." Morgan's father had said, "Lazaro has brought some spice into Louis's life." There was a hint of regret in Judge Dupree's voice; it seemed that he and his cousin played cribbage less often.

Jacques was asleep on Uncle Louis's bed, his grizzled part-terrier's head on a throw pillow of lively south-of-the-border colors. When Gina sat down to pet him, Jacques didn't lift his head or open his eyes more than a slit.

Morgan said, "He's fifteen at least. Uncle Louis got him at the animal shelter."

Gina put her nose close to Jacques's moist black sniffer and said, "I forgive you for ignoring me."

Uncle Louis's room was neater than Morgan remembered it being when he was last in it, on that Thanksgiving in 1969. Perhaps Lazaro had taken a hand to it. The bed was made, anyway, and the tops of the dresser and night tables had been straightened. There was a stack of clean laundry on a chaise longue. The closet doors were shut tight. A panama hat had come to rest on a bedpost. Had Jacques been a decade or so younger, he would have jumped up, snatched the hat in his jaws, and eaten it in three or four bites.

Morgan picked up a guidebook to Sweden that was on a night table, then put it back, on top of a guidebook to Brazil. He was sweating through his shirt. Uncle Louis didn't have air-conditioning, though there was a fan in the window. Morgan turned it on. Jacques raised his head an inch, as if in gratitude.

Gina said, "Hey, I think I recognize this kid." She was looking at a photograph on the dresser, the one that showed Morgan and his brother and their father standing beside a steam engine in the Louisville and Nashville yards on Thanksgiving Day 1961. Though the picture was a touch fuzzy—dark had been falling when Uncle Louis snapped it, and rain, too—Morgan could discern his father's smile, as well as the cowlick that the drizzle didn't flatten. Crawford slouched and frowned, having for his own reasons renounced cheerfulness. Morgan saw in the tilt of his own ten-year-old head—buzz cut, with jug-handle ears and eyes a little raccoonish—a desire to please while not giving away too much.

"How did that little bald monkey turn into you?" Gina said, finding an ear beneath his long hair to tweak.

"Wheat germ for breakfast, organic peanut butter for lunch."

Gina went into the bathroom to put on her suit.

Morgan, who still sometimes found it hard to resist violating other people's privacy, opened the top drawer of Uncle Louis's dresser where, all those years before, he'd found bullets for a pistol. What had happened to that pistol? Maybe Uncle Louis had hidden it where he couldn't find it. Or maybe he'd discarded it when he gave up drinking.

Trying not to look at what his hand was doing, as if it were picking a name out of a hat, Morgan fished among balled pairs of silky hose.

"Lazaro is certainly a beauty," Gina said. She'd left the door open.

Morgan said he guessed he was. He'd seen Lazaro only for that moment downstairs, a slight, dark young man with sharp cheekbones like an Indian's.

Morgan found a pair of sock garters and one cuff link and a small round latticework box made of pale, delicate wood. When he opened the box, a piece of the latticework broke off. There was nothing inside.

"Do you think everybody in Louisville supposes they are lovers?" Gina pronounced the city's name the local way—*Lou-uh-vull*—while making it plain that she found the pronunciation amusing.

"'Sinners' is the word some Louisvillians would use," Morgan said, though it wasn't obvious to him that his father's cousin and Lazaro were lovers. The story Morgan had heard was that Lazaro had arrived in Kentucky a couple weeks after Uncle Louis had returned from his trip to the Yucatan. Lazaro had been waiting tables at a hotel on Isla Mujeres. He was hoping to study business at an American university, and Uncle Louis had promised to pull strings. In the meantime, Lazaro was minding

Uncle Louis's house and working on his English. "Though maybe their relationship is completely chaste."

"If I were Uncle Louis," Gina said, "I'd want Lazaro to lie down next to me at least twice a day."

Morgan wondered if the box might be a cricket box. He'd had one as a child. It had sat on the red rolltop desk in his bedroom for many years, gathering dust, never a way station for a cricket. He hadn't been the type to collect insects.

Gina came out of the bathroom. Her black two-piece suit—it was too modest to qualify as a bikini—was polka-dotted. Morgan had been in love with Gina for four years now. He always fell more in love when he saw her navel. Her navel was an inny, as sweet as a morning glory's funnel, and he'd been known to linger there, like a bee with all the time in the world.

He said, "I'm thinking of getting down on my knees and kissing you. Would that be OK?"

"It would be OK if you closed the door all the way." Sometimes he couldn't believe his luck that out of all the men in New York, dashing men with impressive résumés, literary men and artistic men and men with trained voices and guys who juggled on crowded sidewalks, she'd picked him, who had taken trumpet lessons barely long enough to learn the scales, whose drawings of people made them look like bugs, who wrote articles for a magazine dedicated to the hotel industry.

He closed the door and they made love on a wool throw rug of many colors, another souvenir from Mexico, it seemed. He didn't linger at her belly button. It went quickly; the colors of the rug bled into each other for a moment and then separated again. Their kisses and sighs didn't rouse Jacques from his nap.

Gina said, "When do you think you'll be ready to be the father of my child?"

"We should probably get married first, don't you think?"

"We could do that," she said.

He could get his mind around the idea of marriage, even if it did seem an awkward thing, like trying to get a bulky piece of furniture through a narrow door and then up a couple of flights of stairs. (Unmarried love was easy; you hardly needed furniture.) The idea of being a father, however, caused him consternation. Wouldn't a child reject him on the grounds that Morgan had no experience being a father?

"Uncle Louis is going to wonder where we are," he said, getting up to search for his swimsuit.

"I doubt he'll wonder too much," Gina said, wriggling into her suit bottom.

"Is a cricket in the house good or bad luck?"

"Good, I think. Do you hear one?"

"No. What if it's dead?"

"Then it's a cricket whose luck has run out."

"When do you want to get married?" Morgan, still naked, was on his knees, looking under the chaise's skirt for his suit.

"Are you proposing, Morgan?"

The wind-up puppy from New York was under the chaise. Morgan turned the key and the puppy jittered about on the floor, its stiff little tail rotating. Jacques raised his head two inches for this.

"Morgan? Is that a proposal?"

"When would you like to get married?"

"Would before I fall in love with Lazaro or somebody else be a good time?"

LAZARO CAME ACROSS the lawn carrying a trayful of drinks. He was wearing a long-sleeved white dress shirt and blue jeans that looked new. Morgan watched him from the diving board, trying to decide if Lazaro lay down beside Uncle Louis twice a day or once every other day or not at all. Lazaro walked slowly, with his head tipped to the side, as if he were trying to remember a verb conjugation. His face was coppery.

The lawn was a midsummer brown—the color of toast—where the sun struck it all day. The sun was low now, and it hit Morgan between the eyes. He bounced on the old, springless board covered with a disintegrating mat made of jute and dove into the pool, hearing in the moment he was airborne Uncle Louis's voice and a bird he couldn't identify. Morgan's father had swum in this pool fifty years ago, when it was built, and so had Cyril, the goat that had belonged to Morgan's grandfather. Five feet under, there was nothing to be seen but murk; neither the bottom nor the sides had ever been painted. The pool was a little concrete hole into which Uncle Louis put some chlorine that kept unwanted organisms at bay.

Boxwood grew unpruned at the corners of the pool, and when Morgan surfaced, he found himself among a constellation of leaves. Lazaro was setting the tray on a table between Gina and Uncle Louis, and Gina was gazing at Lazaro, as if she were trying to see herself in the lustrous black hair of his bent head. The bird that Morgan had heard when he dove was in the honey locust over near where Uncle Louis kept his rabbit hutches. Its voice was rapid and agitated.

"You want to go for a swim, Laz?" Uncle Louis asked.

"I prepare the dinner," Lazaro said, edging away from the table.

"Is it something good? Hamburgers with your wicked guacamole sauce, I hope?"

Lazaro smiled a little, vaguely, and then turned back toward the house. He had left behind beers for Morgan and Gina and a glass of Coke for Uncle Louis and a bowl of cashews for all.

Morgan climbed out of the pool. The water had not soothed the postcoital ache in his groin. If he married Gina, would they still have quickies on other people's rugs? What if she had twins or triplets or quintuplets? The bird continued to complain.

Morgan took a swig of beer and asked Uncle Louis if he'd painted any paintings while lying on his back on the beach in Mexico.

"You mean for my Fat Vacationer series?" He chuckled and his body shook gently. "I did a few sketches, but I was mostly just lazy. I've hardly picked up a pencil since I've been home, except to draw Laz. He indulges me." He scooped cashews from the bowl and filled his mouth with them. Then he got up, stripped off his beachcomber's shirt, placed his eye-glasses on the table, and announced that he was going to do a cannon-ball before dinner.

Morgan watched him pad through the grass in his blue Saks trunks, disappear behind a boxwood, and then, hairy belly foremost, reappear on the diving board.

"He told me that he's afraid the lymphoma might be coming back," Gina said to Morgan. "His eye hurts."

"Really?" Morgan saw Uncle Louis rise on his toes, do a dainty test bounce. The Mexican cricket he'd brought into his house had not brought him luck. But the cricket had at least—or so it seemed—brought him happiness. "Maybe he's mistaken. Maybe the problem is unrelated to the cancer."

"Bombs away," Uncle Louis said, grabbing at his knees as he jumped from the diving board. The water received him, rose in droplets that sparkled in the sunlight and rushed in waves toward the sides of the pool.

LAZARO WANTED TO see New York from the Empire State Build-ing, so there they were—Lazaro, Uncle Louis, and Morgan—eighty-six floors above the street. It was breezy, and Morgan, who was afraid of heights, felt certain that the building was swaying. He looked down at his white Adidas with their stylish black racing stripes, the shoes that he'd circled the Central Park reservoir in, in an effort to lose his love handles, the shoes that had carried him around puddles and people living in boxes on the street and turds dropped by horses ridden by policemen in jodhpurs and helmets. Why was he up here, messing with gravity? He didn't look down. He looked straight out at the sky, a piercing October blue.

Uncle Louis handed Morgan his point-and-shoot camera and stood beside Lazaro at the edge of the observation deck. Uncle Louis was wan and thin; he'd undergone another series of radiation treatments during the summer, not long after Morgan and Gina's visit. The doctor had strongly recommended that Uncle Louis also take chemotherapy, but he'd declined. Instead, tomorrow, he was going to fly down to Belize to meet with a doctor who treated cancer patients with hormone shots and herbal remedies. "He promises I won't lose my hair and won't be upchucking all the time," he'd said last night, at dinner at an Indian restaurant, where he'd contented himself with tea and nan bread. In the meantime, Lazaro, who was having visa problems, would stay in New York with Morgan. Morgan had bought an English-Spanish dictionary for the moments when English failed them.

"Say *queso*," Morgan said.

Uncle Louis, who had worn his panama out into the morning sunshine, said, "*Queso* it is."

Lazaro, whose eyes were hidden behind sunglasses, whose thick black hair the wind stirred only a little, whose cheekbones the sun glanced off of, was busy smoking a cigarette and didn't say anything. Uncle Louis laid a hand on his shoulder and said, "Smile for posterity, Laz."

Morgan pushed the button just as Lazaro opened his mouth. "I say New York, New York," he said.

"One more," Uncle Louis said to Morgan, putting his arm around Lazaro's waist. Lazaro took off his sunglasses and Morgan saw again why Laz liked to hide his eyes: he didn't want his hopes to be mistaken for foolishness.

Morgan saw Uncle Louis's old, stained teeth and Lazaro's young ones, white against his dark skin. He pushed the shutter release button. At that moment a wind came up, shifting (Morgan felt sure) the concrete under his feet and also picking the panama off Uncle Louis's head and flinging it out into the blue void. The hat traveled westward, toward Macy's, toward Penn Station. It caught an updraft and it mounted the air in a rush, as if it were looking for a cloud to alight on. It was a hat without a home before it became a speck, then something the day had absorbed.

# 9

# Guess Who

IN APRIL OF 2001, a little over three months after his father died, Morgan rented an apartment on Cumberland Court, in the Crescent Hill section of Louisville. It was the second floor of a frame house, and at the back, off the kitchen, was a miniporch, where he often sat, reading, tending his hibachi, gazing in the direction of Lucy's house, on the next street over. Pieces of Lucy's house—three lots to the left—were visible through a tall sycamore that a man named Jerry sometimes sat under in the evening. Jerry had a straw-colored flattop and he would sometimes scratch it when he wasn't tipping beer into his mouth; then he would look at his fingers to see what, if anything, he'd raised. He smoked 100-mm cigarettes and often coughed between puffs. Morgan knew the man's name was Jerry because a woman would sometimes call to him, telling him to come to dinner or get the phone or go buy her a fly strip because she'd never seen so many flies in her life, they were all over her kitchen, damn it, Jerry. She had a voice that was like something that had gotten loose from a coop, a voice that would have scared children and solicitors from the yard, but it hardly budged her husband. Jerry sat in his green metal chair under the sycamore, and contemplated the fading daylight, the dusk, the darkness gathering in the grass that his big white feet grazed in.

Sometimes Morgan stayed on his porch past dark, by which time Jerry would have shambled off to his supper or his TV or perhaps the Last Stop, a tavern on Frankfort Avenue where Morgan had recently had a beer with the Reverend Sandy Broyles. When dark fell, when lightning bugs began to speckle the air and bats flew out from hiding places to swallow whatever was so foolish as to be still airborne, certain pieces of the house where Lucy lived became more visible. It was as if the house, a slumberous, wasp's-nest gray, had awakened from a long afternoon's nap. The windows, depthless black holes by day, lighted up. With his naked eyes, which were hazel and hyperopic, Morgan could see five windows, four in the lower rear half of the house, which Lucy occupied, and one above, winking through the branches of the sycamore. One of Lucy's windows was the frosted, bathroom kind, and blinds or shades were often pulled over the others, so what he could actually see of the interior of Lucy's house was nothing more than the odd shadow. Most nights Morgan had to content himself with studying simple squares of light, which left him to consider the alternative of going inside his own apartment to read or wash dishes or dance with himself as he listened to Al Green or clean Mr. Jet's kitty litter or call his son in New York or write the first chapter of his memoir about his father. Once, on a beautiful, warm early June evening when Morgan had been drinking bourbon and was in love with the entire Commonwealth of Kentucky and all the clovery breezes that blew through it, he thought he saw a man at one of the windows on the first floor (the blind was up). Morgan had then gone inside to get his binoculars. Even though he'd never set foot in Lucy's apartment, even though he'd practically had to beg her to go to dinner with him, he had come to regard her as someone to watch over. He felt he owed it to his father to look after her, this tallish lawyer-bachelorette. It was wrong, he knew, to spy on her, but he couldn't help it. His hands trembled a tiny bit as he focused the binoculars, which he'd bought in New York to take to sporting events but had also used for illicit purposes, especially after he and his wife had broken up. When he got a bead on the window, he saw Lucy, a mug of something in her hand. She stood stock-still, as if fixed in the frame of the window. He could swear that she was looking straight at him and could see clear through the lens of the binoculars into his head, which was empty except for a man treading in the black pool of his desire.

BACK IN MARCH, before Morgan had left New York, his mother had called and said, "We'll fix up Dad's basement room and you can write your book down there."

"I don't think that would work, Mom," Morgan had said. He was watching a miniskirted woman and her skin-and-bones greyhound turn the corner. With his binoculars, he'd once found this woman on her apartment sofa, eating a bowl of globby pink stuff. It was amazing what people ate when they were alone.

"Or you could put your computer and whatnot in Crawford's room and sleep in your own. You'd have the run of the upstairs. I have a lot of my old summer dresses in your closet, but Ida can move them. We'll find a place somewhere. Which reminds me. Do you think you'll want any of Dad's suits? Some of them are quite handsome, you know. I can get Mr. Witkin over here to alter them if you think you'll want any of them. You can try them on when you come down."

Morgan said, "I don't have many opportunities to wear a suit, Mom." He owned a single dark one, his wedding suit, and he hadn't worn it to his father's funeral. He remembered that Mr. Witkin, who was short and gruff and had eyebrows that looked like slashed-on chalk marks, had come to the visitation and had said, as if his mouth were even then full of needles, "Fine, fine man your dad was. My sympathy."

"He has some nice seersucker ones," she said.

"We'll see," Morgan said. When he attempted to express his true thoughts to his mother, they came out fluttery and thin, like moths doomed to expire in lamplight.

"When do you think you might move in?" his mother had asked.

MORGAN SPENT ABOUT ten days at his mother's place before he found the apartment on Cumberland Court. Morgan had brought little with him from New York—clothes, hibachi, laptop, Mr. Jet, binoculars, boom box, a waffle iron given to him by Uncle Louis and Lazaro—and so he had to furnish his apartment with things from his mother's house. She gave him some retired sunroom furniture—two wicker chairs and a love seat. In the basement, they'd uncovered his boyhood desk, the red rolltop, into which he'd rashly carved the initials of a girl who dropped him a few weeks later, and into which Crawford had carved "Morgan bites." From his father's basement office, he took the daybed, which had served as a catchall for railroad books and timetables and mail and photographic equipment and Christmas candy from courthouse cronies and tennis balls and years-old dividend checks. Once, while idly pawing through the stuff on the bed, Morgan had come across a black-and-white glossy of his father shaking hands with President Nixon. It was taken at the White House, in 1973. Morgan's father was wearing a mussed raincoat and a camera was slung over his shoulder and his graying hair stood up on the back of his head like a clump of wild grass. He was smiling broadly at Nixon, whom he had voted for three times, whose sagging, glum face seemed to be asking, "How'd this yokel get in the door?"

From his mother's kitchen and pantry cabinets, where several sets of flawless bone china were stored, no plate of which had had anything edible on it for decades, if ever, Morgan had taken some dining car dishes issued by the Baltimore and Ohio Railroad company back in the days when trains were the way to travel. He also took some coffee mugs (one had scripture on it, another he had drunk iodine-flavored milk out of when he was a child) and a set of four tall, ribbed inky-blue glasses, which used to appear on the dinner table in the summers, filled with mint tea.

"I always loved these," Mrs. Dupree said.

"You don't want me to take them?" She had glasses by the dozens, all now for one mouth.

She wrapped them in bubble plastic for him.

She gave him her coffee percolator and a gateleg table to eat off of and some bathroom supplies, including monogrammed towels and a toilet plunger. You never knew when you'd need a plunger. She had an extra, from the time when her husband had a bleeding spell following a bladder operation and he'd tried to flush his safety diapers down the toilet. Actually, the plunger belonged to her neighbor Gerald Boardman. Gerald had come running with it when she'd called, when she couldn't find her own. Bloody toilet water had swamped her bathroom. Crawford had been there that weekend. He'd reported to Morgan that their mother had been hysterical. Crawford's wife and Gerald had handled the sanitation problem. Crawford had driven his father downtown to an emergency room and stayed with him until five in the morning, when he was admitted to the hospital proper.

"I don't think Gerald would mind if you borrowed his plunger," she said. "He came over in his pajamas that night, you know. Did I tell you that he offered to take me to the orchestra next week? We both have season tickets. But I said no, I didn't think I could make it. Dad's been gone for barely three months. It seems too soon. What do you think?"

"I don't think Dad would mind if you went to the orchestra with Gerald Boardman."

"They *are* playing Beethoven. I don't know." She was looking into her husband's medicine cabinet. "Is there anything from here you want? His brush? Epsom salts you probably don't need. Baby powder? Look at all this baby powder. Styptic sticks? Probably not since you don't shave anymore."

Morgan took the brush. It still had some of his father's hair in it.

HE PUT THE BINOCULARS back in the case, on the gateleg table, where Mr. Jet lay, with his black nose next to the blue picnic-size Morton's salt dispenser. Morgan had given up trying to keep Mr. Jet off surfaces where humans ate and prepared human food. Mr. Jet was a pasha who lay where he pleased. When Morgan and Gina had divided up things, about two years ago, she had claimed Mr. Jet for William, their son, who had named Mr. Jet (shortened from Mr. Super Amazing Black Blazing Jet, which he once was, before he became middle-aged and sedentary) and had slept with him many of the nights of his childhood. It had been decided that William would spend the bulk of his time with his mother, but William said he didn't want Mr. Jet at his mother's house. When Morgan had asked his son why, William had shrugged and gone into his room and put his ears under headphones. Later, his mother bought him a dog.

The phone rang. Morgan went into the bedroom to get it. He thought it might be his mother and then he thought it might be Lucy calling to tell him she was going to report him to the police for peeping. Didn't she wear those serious black-rimmed glasses through which she couldn't miss seeing other people's flaws? At dinner with him the other night, their first and only date, which was over at ten sharp, she had removed her glasses while eating her appetizer and he saw under her eyes places darkened by doubt and worry. She saw him peering at her, and before the main course arrived, she put her glasses back on.

The phone, a pale blue Princess model, rotary style, from the downstairs guest room in his mother's house, rang seven times before he picked it up.

"You motherfucker," a woman's voice said. "I should've killed you when I had a chance and put you out on the lawn for the vultures to sup on. Except they would have died from food poisoning in about ten seconds, you miserable chickenshit shithead. And I have economic concerns."

Didn't she mean "ecological concerns," Morgan wondered, while searching his memory for a match to the voice. It was not his ex-wife's. It was a slightly twangy voice, a Kentucky voice, though the diction ("sup," for instance, and "lawn" instead of "yard") was a little on the urbane side. He didn't recall any girls from his youth here, on the banks of the Ohio River, who talked quite like this, none whom he might have so offended that she'd call him thirty years later to fill his ear with obscenities. And then he remembered that at Kroger's the other day, near the dairy case, he had bumped into a woman who had told him that she was Sarah Gilbert, who had been his girlfriend for a few months in tenth grade. She didn't look much like the girl he had talked to about *Siddhartha*. She looked as if she'd slipped through the cracks; her face was puffy. She'd told him she was divorced and unemployed. Sarah clearly had "economic concerns," but her voice, though twangy, was unlike the caller's. Sarah's voice was soft, like sawdust, like defeat.

"Unlike you, you rich prick, you son of a fucking judge, with all your lying bullshit about how you're going to take care of me and my baby—or should I say your baby who's going to have about zero chance if you don't live up to your promises, you lying shithead."

"Who is this?" Morgan finally said.

In the past, Morgan or his brother had occasionally been confused with the son of a judge named Sackrider. Morgan and Crawford and Peter Sackrider had, to make things even more confusing, all gone to the same school for boys, a place of much hilarity and little learning. Morgan, whom an older boy had dubbed Morgan Le Fay when Morgan was in the sixth grade, became known in the upper grades as Your Honor, mostly because he was a good student. Crawford was sometimes referred to as Judge D's Lesser and Messier Spawn. Sackrider was sometimes addressed as the Dishonorable Pete.

But it wasn't really plausible, was it, that the caller was confusing Morgan with some other son of a judge? Maybe she had said "you son of a fucking noodge," though it seemed unlikely that Yiddish would be among her languages. Or maybe she'd said "son of a fucking drudge." Which, granted, would have been an odd choice of epithet.

"Who is this?" the woman's voice mocked. "It's the angel of death, brainless."

She clicked off. Morgan backed away from the phone. He was standing in darkness, except for the light that came from the kitchen. He'd been living alone for some time now, and he had almost become accustomed to finding himself in unlighted rooms, wondering what next to do with himself. On occasion, in his New York apartment, he'd gone into the bathroom and undressed and masturbated in front of the full-length mirror. "I'm being kind to myself," he said once, to Mr. Jet, when the cat had walked in and given him an inquisitive look. This was not so long ago, about a month after his father had died. William had just returned to Gina's house, after spending the weekend with Morgan. It was the bottom of winter. New York was frozen and mean, steel and concrete and hard piles of dog turds and people who would snap at you if you brushed against them. Morgan's apartment smelled like burned waffles (dinner), the wind rattled the early-twentieth-century windows. He had put aside his book—the *Handbook for Judges: An Anthology of Inspirational and Other Helpful Writings for Members of the Judiciary*—that he'd found among his father's office possessions, and gone into William's room to look at his things. For some reason, he didn't turn on the light. William's things emerged as the darkness peeled back. Morgan saw the behemoth Macintosh that was William's "away" computer. He saw the unmade bed, a turmoil of sheets and comforter and pillow and stuffed animals that had accompanied William out of childhood into the swamp of adolescence. He saw the bookshelves, which were half empty, because his son had taken his favorites with him to his mother's house. He touched the basketball jersey hanging on the back of the desk chair—it was a Ray Allen, number 34, shiny white with purple trim, almost as elegant as an ecclesiastical garment; Crawford had sent it to him—which he wore as a night shirt. Then Morgan left William's room and sat down and resumed reading an article by Judge Learned Hand. Then he got up and went and stood naked before the bathroom mirror.

Now, here in the Crescent Hill district of his hometown, he got down on the floor and did twenty-seven sit-ups and twelve push-ups, the modified kind, where you lift yourself from your knees instead of your toes. Then he went into the kitchen to make coffee. Mr. Jet still had his nose flush against the Morton's salt dispenser. Morgan said to Mr. Jet, "What is the equivalent in the cat world to somebody you don't know calling you up to say that she's the angel of death and you're a motherfucker? Can you tell me that?"

He rinsed out the percolator. When he'd told the young woman at Java Jimmy's that he needed his French Sumatran ground for a percolator, she said, "Wow, that's way retro." The percolator wasn't calculated old-fashionedness. It was just what his mother had pressed on him, along with his father's seersucker suit, which now hung, in need of some tailoring, in his closet, next to his father's home-court robe. (Once or twice, he had considered wearing the robe around the house like loungewear, but then he'd thought, No, that would be too weird.) On the other hand, he was, despite the long hair and the beard and the pink pearl in his ear, somewhat conservative in his tastes, maybe even a little stuffy. He didn't like the music his son filled his ears with— hard, banging, tuneless, hip-hop jibberish. There was no joy in it, you couldn't dance by yourself to it, it wasn't about love or heartbreak, you couldn't hum it while brushing your hair with your father's brush that your mother had bought from the Fuller Brush man thirty years ago.

His son would be here in a couple weeks, at the end of June. He'd stay until mid-July. Morgan hadn't figured out what they were going to do. William was almost a teenager. His voice had recently fallen from above his soft brown eyes to a dark, echoing passageway in his chest.

Morgan leaned against the refrigerator and listened to the percolator perk. It was like the sound of rain being sucked upward out of the earth —time in reverse. He remembered that his mother—or Ida, if she was there, which she usually was—had always perked coffee for the bridge and dinner parties she gave when Morgan was a boy. The percolator would sit on a silver trivet on a lowboy in the dining room. Bone china cups and saucers would be arranged alongside, like a fleet of sailing ships, with a silver pitcher of cream and a fluted silver bowl of white sugar cubes, which were otherwise hidden under lock and key. (The sugar that Morgan and Crawford were allowed to put on their morning wheat germ and shredded wheat were brownish crystals, which Morgan imagined to have been mined from rocks rather than extracted from cane.) At these parties, Morgan and Crawford were required to shake hands with all the guests, and, after they did, after they'd waded through the clouds of cigarette and pipe smoke and the queries and the comparisons ("Your brother's just *shot up*, hasn't he?") and jokes ("You all look so much alike you could pass for brothers!"), they would go upstairs to their separate rooms or go into the kitchen to see Ida and try to talk her into giving them an extra dessert, which, for occasions such as these, were made with regular white sugar. Sometimes, later in the evening, Morgan would pinch a sugar cube or two and sit on the stairs and listen to the conversations in the so-called living room, which, when the party was over, would revert to being a museum for antique furniture. He would hear bids of three clubs and four hearts and cries of dismay or glee and men talking about Eisenhower or Kennedy or the damn Democrats or the damn Russians and he would hear his mother and her friends talking about an art exhibit in Chicago or a dress bought at Byck's or the

Reverend Alfred Lloyd Broyles Sr. over at St. John's having to bail his sexton out of the drunk tank. Sometimes Morgan sat there for a long time, waiting for the moment when his mother would begin to discuss him and his brother. But it would be worth the wait, because he, Morgan, the younger child, who did so well in school and was so well behaved, always came out on top. Morgan would hear a woman named Hildegarde Gray say in her voice that had originated somewhere south of Louisville, that was composed of equal parts of cotton and sugar, "You have the most darling children, Mary Louise." To which Mrs. Dupree would reply, "If you only knew about Crawford's temper." Or, "They're darling, but my older one can be so difficult sometimes." And then she would tell some long story, which, if you were a listener, was like traveling a back road that kept looping off somewhere, veering away from a destination that was possibly not even on the map, until a voice, always a male one but not Morgan's father's, would say, "It's your lead, Mary Louise." The Duprees weren't often paired together at the bridge table, at least not when Morgan was eavesdropping. It was rare that Morgan heard his father's voice at all. He had the impression his father was concentrating on his cards or thinking about a legal problem or an upcoming railroad trip in which he would ride for hours in the vestibule with the window open.

Morgan sat down at his childhood desk with the scripture-emblazoned mug (Matthew 10:42) of black, sugarless coffee (half decaf, half not). Above the desk was Uncle Louis's painting of a steam engine pushing through smoke and hazy impressionist light, the one that had hung for years in Morgan's father's basement office. The picture made Morgan think about time and extinction, though the light was a solace.

He turned on his computer. In his files was a document called "Dad: Chapter One." He clicked on it. Those three words were the sum total of the so-called document, which, until Morgan had given in to computers (he was a latecomer), he'd thought of as a tactile thing, like an old letter, say, that smelled of love or sweat and could inflict a cut if the paper hadn't gone too soft around the edges. He'd found such things in the drawers of his little childhood desk. One was a Putt-Putt scorecard (he'd beaten Crawford); another was a scrap of paper with Don Ameche's autograph (his mother had gotten this, on a train, in 1959); another, on fake parchment, was a dollar-fifty reproduction of the Declaration of Independence, which he'd bought at Monticello when he was a boy; and another was a Valentine from his father.

Morgan stared at the blank document on his screen and then he took his father's Valentine out of the drawer. It showed a sheepish man in rags setting his immense thumping heart at the feet of his lady love, who peers at it through a lorgnette. The caption inside read, "Please accept this token of my affection." Below, in his peculiar script that always seemed in danger of going horizontal, that looked like a big wind had swept through it, his father had written, "To Morgan. With love, Guess Who." Morgan had received the card in 1964, when he was almost thirteen. His father had mailed it, from downtown Louisville, the postmark on the envelope showed. He would also have mailed a card to Crawford. Morgan smiled at the idea of his fourteen-year-old brother, the sullen boy who had carved "Morgan bites" into the top of this desk, finding in the mail a Valentine from their father, who would be home that night to ask Crawford how he'd done on his Latin test and to tell his wife that he'd reserved two sleeping car compartments for their Easter vacation trip to Florida.

Morgan stared at the blank document on his screen and then he went outside to the porch with his coffee. He wished that he could see his father's former law clerk climbing over backyard fences and crossing property lines to reach him, to inform him that she would stay with him all night and tell him everything he wanted to know about his father.

# 10

# "Chapter One: Dad"

IN 1983, MY FATHER, the chief judge of the United States District Court in the Western District of Kentucky, issued an opinion in the case of *Hummer v. Brown,* Hummer being an obstetrician/gynecologist and Brown being the governor of the state as well as the former chief executive officer of Kentucky Fried Chicken. Dr. Hummer and several of his colleagues in the medical profession had petitioned the court to declare Kentucky's antiabortion statute unconstitutional. My father did not assign himself this case; he drew it by lot. My mother, a fervent antiabortionist, suggested he recuse himself, because of what she imagined his beliefs to be, but he said it was his duty to hear it. This rebuff, polite though it no doubt was, did not keep my mother from lobbying my father during the time that the case was before him. One of his law clerks has said, "She dogged him. But he ruled according to the law of the land, to what the Supreme Court had ruled about a woman's right to privacy. When it was over and the hate mail started pouring in, I expected to come across a letter from your mother."

In 1983, I was living on the Upper West Side of New York with my girl-friend of three years, Gina Lang. Gina was from Providence, Rhode Island. I once spent a number of hours writing a limerick about her provenance, as a kind of birthday present to go along with the actual present, which was a tiger's-eye-maple jewelry box handcrafted in Appalachia, and when she took it out of the box and read it, she said, "I once knew a boy from Kentucky, who was the result of a little fucky, between a judge and his pet monkey." She was quicker than me at just about everything. She killed me in Scrabble and chess and in debates about whatever. She saw the squeeze bunt coming before I, the apprentice sportswriter, did. Sometimes I would say to Gina, "I know you're going to leave me for a smarter man someday." And she would give me one of her Mona Gina smiles, no teeth peeking out, and say, "First, I think I'll have your baby. When do you think you might be ready for fatherhood?"

I liked to imagine that Gina's superior mind was purely the result of the union between her father the German professor of anthropology, whose specialty was assassin cults within Amazon Indian tribes, and her mother the Connecticut novelist descended from Italian nobility. At any rate, it seemed fair to assume that this collaboration of genetic material gave Gina a leg up on the competition. She attended fine East Coast schools, had far-flung adventures in the summers with her father's anthro cronies, and after arriving in New York, brown and sinewy from six months of digging for Neanderthal tools in France, quickly landed a job as an assistant to a fiction editor at the *New Yorker*. Her mother happened to be a friend of this editor, though I'm sure that Gina would have gotten the position on the basis of her charm and brains alone.

The first time I saw Gina was outside the Thalia, where I'd gone to see a Jean Vigo double bill. When I came out, it was raining hard. I stood under the marquee and watched the rain come down. The air was sweet and cool. Trash rushed along the edges of the street as if on the back of a mountain stream. A few feet from me was a young woman who observed the storm with the detachment that only New Yorkers can muster for natural marvels. That is, she would periodically look up from her magazine to see what the lightning might have struck or if the wind that accompanied the rain had blown anybody significant off his feet. She was pretty, with a small, wry mouth, a firm chin, a clear, confident brow, auburn hair. Hadn't I come to New York in the hope that I would find myself under a marquee during a rainstorm with such a person? And also in the hope that I and this woman of my cinematic dreams would leave together and run through the rain toward some dry place where, an hour or two later, we would lick beer foam off each other's lips? This didn't happen—she made a sudden sprint for Broadway and I didn't follow—but I ran into her again, on a Sunday morning, at a Greek coffee shop on Columbus Avenue. I sat down on the stool next to her, and I said, even before ordering eggs or glancing at Red Smith, "I saw you at the Thalia the other night and I wanted to ask you what you thought of *Zero for Conduct*?"

"I saw you, too," she said, as if she'd been waiting for this conversation to happen. "I liked it. What did you think?"

"I liked it a lot," I said. "I liked that scene where the boys stand the dorm master's bed on end. I like movies about kids rebelling in school because I never did and I wish I had."

"You could always take an adult education course and act up," she said. She shook salt on her scrambled eggs. "Did you like the moment after the pillow fight when all the feathers were floating down like snow?"

"Yes, I did," I said. "I thought it was great."

And then, after another bite of her breakfast, she departed in a rush, as if struck by inspiration.

But when I saw her one more time, on the same stool, on another Sunday, she didn't flee. My head was full with what I'd collected and saved up to tell her. I think that when she went back to her apartment, she wrote down everything I'd said. It all came out in a book some years later. But all I cared about was that she gave me her telephone number. I wrote it on the palm of my hand.

By that fall we had become lovers. I couldn't think of a time when I'd been happier, even though my day job, writing piffle about the hotel industry for a trade magazine, did not thrill me. Gina didn't seem to mind that I had a dinky job or that my ambitions ran to writing about sports. Once, when she caught me moping, she said, "I fell for you because I liked your pretty face and all your hair and the spot in the middle of your forehead that throbs when you're anxious. And you tip excessively, which is a nice trait." She took me to parties given by her *New Yorker* friends, and I felt envious and drank more than was decorous, and then we came home and put music on the stereo and lay down in a heap together. Once, about a year after we met, as I was kissing her belly, she said, "If we were, say, characters in a novel, and you were the author of it, what verb would you use to describe what we are doing now, here, on this scratchy carpet scrap on the living room floor with the anticrime streetlights seeping through the slats of the blinds? 'And then they came home and' what?"

I lifted my head from her belly, which was rumbling, sorting itself out; within was Thai stir-fry and tamarind sauce with coconut milk and several bottles worth of beer. She enjoyed eating and drinking.

She said, "Made love? Noodled each other? Poured their souls into each other? Went at it like dogs?"

I had put Al Green on the stereo and he was singing in his near-falsetto range, where you couldn't distinguish agony from love.

"If the characters were us," I said, "if I were writing autobiographically and was also trying to be sort of honest, I might say, 'And then they came home and he kissed the place directly below her belly button from which threads of dark hair flowed like something faintly Japanese, a delicate trickle of hirsuteness, which he had come to worship, as he did all other parts of her.'"

"Golly," she said.

I had found my way inside her. I was dizzy from our night on the town, but there I was. Gina was only the third woman I'd ever been inside. I was about to turn thirty. I'd almost slept with—if that is the right phrase—my brother's first wife, Colleen, on that Thanksgiving night when I read her my story on my bed, when Gina was sleeping in her own apartment. Colleen had offered herself, but I didn't want to be inside anybody except Gina, not even Crawford's amazing goose of a wife.

"How would you put it," I said, "if we were, say, characters in your autobiographical novel and I was inside you?" Inside Gina had no correspondence to the outer world that I could think of.

"Oh," she said, "I might say, 'And then we came home and he came before I came, but I was happy anyway. I chewed on his silken earlobes.'"

IT WAS IN THIS CONTEXT—we used birth control, my sperm went to its death almost daily—that I learned about my father's abortion ruling. My mother sent me the newspaper clippings, along with a note on her "From the Desk of Mary Louise Dupree" stationery. The note said, "He says he ruled according to the law of the land, but what about the unborn children, God's children, who are being killed because of the 'law of the land'? I don't think people should be given a license to murder just because they don't want a baby, do you? What if I'd decided to do that when you or Crawford were inside me? When it comes time for you and Gina to have a child, whenever that should be, you'll understand how precious your baby's life is from the instant of conception. On the bench, Dad can only concern himself with abstractions, I'm sorry to say."

When I talked to my father on the phone about his decision, he said, "Well, it wasn't an easy case, Morgan, but the Kentucky statute was plainly unconstitutional. Justice Powell said in *City of Akron* that the right to privacy guaranteed in the Constitution gives a woman the right to decide whether to terminate her pregnancy."

In the background, I heard a clanking—my mother at the stove, I supposed, knocking a spoon against a pot. Like a judge with a gavel. She said, "Tell him about those calls you've been getting."

"What calls are those, Dad?"

"Just some people unhappy with my decision. Let me give you our new number."

"It's such a doggone nuisance having to change our number because of that decision," my mother said. She seemed to have moved close enough to the phone that there was a threat of her commandeering it.

"It is a nuisance," my father concurred. After he gave me the number, he asked if I thought the White Sox would win it all that year and whether there was any chance of Gina and me coming down for Thanksgiving. He said that Crawford, who had remarried that summer, was planning to go to Wisconsin to be with Michelle's family.

"We hardly ever see your brother," my mother, within inches of the phone, said. "Except when he gets married."

"Well," Dad said. "I'll turn you over to Mom. My love to you."

GINA AND I WERE married in the spring of 1985. The Reverend Sandy Broyles flew up from Kentucky to do the ceremony. We did it in a Unitarian church in whose soup kitchen Gina sometimes worked. Then we all traveled to a loft on Houston Street for the reception. My parents rode with Gina and me in a cab driven by a Sikh. My father sat up front and attempted to draw the driver into a conversation about trains in India but failed. The Sikh was too busy weaving through the late Saturday afternoon traffic.

My mother wore a hat that took up much of the airspace in the backseat of the cab. Silk flowers bloomed at the base of the hat's crown and somewhere among them was a silk hummingbird, sucking nectar through its filament of a beak. At the reception, Dieter Lang, who had flown out of the Guyanan jungle and arrived in New York only a few

hours before, said to my mother, *"Quel chapeau!"* My mother related to
Dieter the history of her hat, how my dad had sat on it, how she had it
reblocked, how it had traveled to New York in its own special box, and
then she said, "I had my doubts they'd ever do it."

Dieter asked, "Who'd ever do what?"

"Our children," my mother said. "Marry. I had my doubts."

Gina's father was wiry, almost bony, un-German in build. Jungle life
had whittled him down even further, it seemed. He was dressed in a pale
lightweight suit, no tie. Around his neck was a string of colorful beads.
His beard and hair were lavishly unkempt, copses in which wild things
possibly hid. He told my mother about the use of flutes in Indian
courtship rituals, how a man in pursuit of a woman sought to dazzle her
with music like birdsong, how the woman would lie down with the man
posthaste if the music was beautiful enough. *"Eine kleine Liebmusik,"* he
said. "In hyperrationalist white European societies, the woman is sometimes slow to lie down with the man—in the sanctioned, institutional
way, that is. Since, of course, marriage signifies the end of love. And what
hyperrationalist wants to acknowledge that love is over and that all that's
left is the simple desire to produce the next generation?"

I thought my mother was going to argue with him, tell him that love
persists, even if my father did sit on her hat, even if she did carp at him
almost daily. I also thought she might at least invoke Jesus and sacrificial
love, but she withdrew to the shade beneath her hat.

Later, while my father danced with Gina's mother, while Crawford
(full of wine but in an accommodating mood) danced with my mother,
his face shining moonlike above the bower of her hat, while Gina danced
with her boss, the *New Yorker* fiction editor, while my cousin Gee
laughed at some man's comment, I sat on the fire escape with Dieter
Lang and drank a beer. He said, "This is the moment when I tell you a
story or a joke that will contain wisdom about marriage. Or I could tell
you a story about Gina as a child." He drew on his cigarette, a European

brand. Two flights below us, on Houston Street, cars moved through the dusk, honking, jockeying from lane to lane, their drivers hoping to speed up their journeys to wherever by a half-second or so.

"A story about Gina would be nice," I said. I saw the fiction editor, a Mr. Wineapple, a man of sixty, put his lips next to Gina's ear. He was short and gray and impeccable, the wrinkles under his eyes the merest tracery.

"You must know the philosopher Schopenhauer," he said. "He was a bachelor all his life. He wrote, played the flute an hour each day, traveled little, probably masturbated a lot, and doted on his dogs. He loved dogs more than humans. He addressed each one as *'Mein Herr'*—'Sir.' He believed, as you probably know from your studies—tell me again where you went to college?"

"A small school in Ohio called Draper. It's known for its music conservatory and the hard sciences." I had told him this before, in exactly those words. This was only the third or fourth time I'd seen him in the five years I'd known his daughter. It did not appear as if he was going to tell me a story about Gina's childhood.

"Out there. *Ja.* Where the Miami and the Shawnee and the Iroquois used to roam." I saw a flickery light in his blue eyes, a little campfire burning in the distance. What was it about Middle Europeans that stoked their interest in savage tribes? I wanted to ask him, but he had the lectern. He tapped ash from his cigarette and said, "Schopenhauer, my gloomy countryman, believed that romance is merely two people sizing each other up for procreative purposes. He said that the function of so-called love is to produce the next generation—a healthy, handsome one, if possible. He himself reviled marriage, believing that while it might result in excellent little Hanses and Hannahs, it would otherwise make us quite unhappy. Surely you, Morgan, have noticed how quickly *tristesse* follows upon the heels of fucking, if you will pardon both my French and my English. That's the devil's laughter you hear in the background, while your face is buried in the neck of your partner. 'That marriage and passionate love should go hand in hand is the rarest stroke of good fortune,' Herr Schopenhauer said. Which is a rather gentle way to put it, don't you think?"

"I haven't had a lot of experience at marriage," I said.

"I'm sure you will produce beautiful children, all your pleasant Anglo-French genes mixing with Gina's German and Italian ones. Maybe you will produce a handsome little sportswriter." He clapped me on the back.

"Maybe," I said. I still worked for the hotel industry rag, but I had recently published my first sports article, about a New York softball league made up entirely of academics. It was meant to be humorous.

"Or perhaps the German gene will prove to be dominant—you know us Germans, always wishing to be on top—and a lovely little anthropologist will emerge. She or he could work in the field with me, if you get started now."

"I don't know how soon we'll have children." Gina's boss, who was married to a woman in her early thirties, his third wife, a proofreader who was a poet by night, kissed Gina on the forehead before releasing her to another well-wisher.

"Have them now," he said, "while you are still in love."

"I will always love Gina," I said.

"You are a gallant boy, Morgan. I wish for happiness for you and Gina. I hope you will prove Herr Doktor Schopenhauer wrong."

I looked down and saw a young black man riding a bicycle along Houston Street, no hands, crazily placid in the whizzing traffic.

DURING THE SEVENTH month of Gina's first pregnancy, when, as she put it, she felt like "La Vache Qui wants to eat the whole pasture," I went down to Florida to do a story about a new professional baseball association made up of recently retired big leaguers. This was in 1988. I had an assignment from a jazzy new New York monthly that did not confine itself to New York stories. I got the job because Gina knew the editor from her college days; in fact, they had known each other intimately, if college students who sleep together a couple of times can be said to know each other intimately. The editor, Eric Hitchcock, a thin, red-haired man, who was attired in high-top black Converses and a white button-down shirt on the day I met him in his SoHo office that smelled of fresh paint and Chinese takeout, told me that his mother had not, due to some oversight or quirk, given away his baseball card collection, that he had a cat named Brooks Robinson (he'd grown up in Baltimore), and that the best approach to writing about these ex–big leaguers getting together to play pitch-and-catch would be, well, not entirely straightforward but not entirely ironic, either, if I knew what he meant. When I went home and laid my cheek against Gina's amazing belly and asked her what Eric had meant, she said, "He means you can write about 'tweeners and ribbies, but the whole thing is a bit of a joke after all—old men in caps and spikes who might as well be across the street selling Dodges."

"Did you really sleep with him?"

"He left his girlfriend for me. And then he left me for someone else. Go figure."

"Is it time for a 'tweener?" I was kissing her belly and our baby through the knit of her pregnant woman's dress. I said, as if to a press-box mike, "And Dupree hits one up the gap. Nobody's going to get that one, ladies and gents."

"But no, hold on, fans," she said in her pleasant play-by-play voice that had a hint of crisp New England in it. "Dupree is going to be thrown out at second. Lang played the bounce off the wall perfectly." She tapped her belly. "We're tired."

I spent a week in central Florida, moving from Winter Haven to Kissimmee to Clearwater to Bradenton. The Golden League teams played in the ballparks used by the Pirates and Phillies and Red Sox during the spring. Ten days before Christmas, on Moss Sweeney Seat Cushion Night, there were 321 paying customers at McKechnie Field, for a game between the Bradenton Sea Dogs and the Miami Conquistadores (better known as the Conks). The corrugated-tin press box above home plate contained five reporters, one from a local paper and the other four from up north. Two had book contracts, and they sat at opposite ends of the press box. One, a Boston writer, was reading a primer on Zen that a Sea Dogs pitcher, a lefty who had thrown a one-hitter for the Red Sox in 1979 while high on an assortment of illegal and prescription substances, had recommended. The other, a young woman named Melanie Grossman, the daughter of a New York journalist who was known to have made big city pols wince and stutter, studied stat sheets and sipped coffee. Melanie was twenty-seven, ten years younger than I. When she was a child, her head had been patted by John Lindsay and Willie Mays and Frank Sinatra and Everett Dirksen and a high-ranking member of a mob family, who also gave her a pack of candy cigarettes. She had gone to Wellesley and become a Marxist for a couple of semesters and then she got a job in the sports department of her dad's newspaper. She was on leave now. I'd met her in Winter Haven, at the beginning of my trip.

After the game, I'd gone to talk with the manager of the visiting Conks, a veteran of minor league parks who was still hoping that one of his pals in Los Angeles or Chicago or Atlanta might hire him as a coach. His name was Norton Hands. Among the players he was known as Hands On for his aggressive managerial style. The reporter from Boston had told me that Norton Hands was a waste of my time, but I was interested in baseball lifers who would likely never make it out of Double A. Hands was from my hometown, and I figured we could talk about that fact before going on to weightier matters.

"I haven't thought about that place in years," he said. Louisville was a Triple A town. "What's the name of the magazine you say you write for?"

"*Skylark.*"

"What is it—a bird magazine? A car magazine?" Hands was sitting behind a metal desk in his underwear, his feet up. He hadn't removed his aqua-and-peach Conks cap, which he wore uptilted, revealing all of his tanned, rutted brow. "What the fuck are you doing here if you're a bird writer?"

"It's a magazine for the literate masses," I said. "The name is from the song by Hoagy Carmichael." Eric had told me this. "It's supposed to suggest something whimsical, I guess, and not too serious. Kind of like Golden League baseball."

"You don't think this is serious?" he asked. He took his feet off the desk and slid his chair forward. On his forearms were moles that looked as if they might be cancerous. He lit a Merit. "You think this isn't serious because those guys"—he pointed to the clubhouse behind me, where naked men were laughing and swearing and listening to music—"aren't playing in the fucking show anymore, because they're making a few hundred bucks instead of hundreds of thousands?"

"That was kind of my next question," I said. "How seriously do you take the losses?" The Conks were the worst team in the league.

Hands straightened up. "I hate losing. I hate it worse than death."

I wrote that down.

Melanie came into the room. "Hey, Norton, is it true you beat your wife after every loss? That's the scuttlebutt out there." She cocked her head. Her face was sheltered by a cloud of black hair, a mass of ringlets. She peered out through round-rimmed, scholarly spectacles. She had an angular newshoundish nose, tender at the tip, and a mouth that sometimes pursed when she wrote in her notebook. She was small. She made me think of the rabbit that gave Mr. McGregor so much trouble, sneaking through his fence, eating his lettuce.

"Your book is going to be full of falsies, Mel," Hands said, "if you rely on my players for information." The sight of her had made him somewhat more cheerful. He leaned back in his chair and put his sockless feet on the desk. I guessed he didn't get to entertain a lot of female reporters from New York during the regular season, when he was minding twenty-year-olds in Shreveport and Winston-Salem.

"'Falsities' is the word you're looking for, Norton," Melanie said. "'Falsehoods' also works."

Hands said, "You're the writer, Mel." He took his cap off and scratched his graying buzz cut. Then he put it back on.

They bantered like this for a while and seemed to establish that after losses Hands did not beat his wife or even his dog—he only kicked lockers (with his spikes on, however) and upset tables of food. Then the questioning turned to important baseball matters—why had Hands bunted with his number-three hitter in the seventh?—and when we were done, the manager reached across the desk and shook my hand and told me good luck with my article for *Skybird*.

"It's *Skylark*," Melanie said. "It's a nice magazine, but it would be way over your head, Norton."

Some nights later, as we sat in the Bradenton press box watching Hands stroll to the mound to consult with his forty-five-year-old pitcher, Melanie said, "He really did beat his wife, you know. It went to court and he got a slap on the wrist and she came back to him after less than a year."

"Did he know you knew that when you asked him about it the other night?"

"I think he hoped I was joking."

"Are you going to use it in your book?"

"I haven't decided."

We had dinner the next night, at a restaurant that was on a pier on Longboat Key. We ate fried shrimp out of plastic baskets and drank beer and watched a pelican ponder the dark from a piling.

"What will you name it if it's a boy?" Melanie asked. She wasn't married. She had a part-time boyfriend ("an oxymoron," she said, "but one I can live with") back in New York. He was with a network news department.

"It's under discussion," I said, "but I'm for William, after my father."

"You could call him Willie Dupree and make up rhyming songs about him. 'Little Willie Dupree, he sat in a tree, eating red spaghetti.'"

One of the things I found attractive about Melanie, both in the candle-light of a shrimp place on the Gulf and in the bug-flecked fluorescent light of the press box, was how the delicacy of her skin contrasted with the wild thickety growth of her hair. And her eyebrows were dense and comical. And, like my wife, she had a flair for doggerel.

I had had just enough beer to be able to say, "I could lean across the table and kiss you except I would probably singe myself on the candle and possibly also bring my marriage crashing down."

"That seems dramatic," she said. "Anyway, how would your wife know?"

The waitress arrived with my dessert—banana cream pie, my favorite. I had first eaten it at the Blue Boar Cafeteria in Louisville as a boy—my father had taken Crawford and me to dinner there one night when my mother was sick—and I had often tried to replicate the experience.

"She could see it on my face."

Melanie leaned across the table and with her coffee spoon helped her-self to the pie. "She could see one kiss on your face?"

"Maybe not only one."

"Ah," she said, sticking her spoon back in.


WHEN MELANIE'S BOOK came out, she invited me and my fam-ily to a party. It was in a bar on the Upper East Side, where the occasional Yankee or Met, smelling of pine tar and dirt, was said to stop in for a glass of milk. On the walls were pictures of Yankees and Mets and mem-bers of the New York press (including Melanie, above whose head Davey Johnson made rabbit ears) who covered baseball. William, who was one and a half, wore a red-billed, white-crowned Cincinnati Reds cap that I or Crawford had worn back when baseball players wore flannel. William wore the cap until we got to the door of the bar, that is, and then, like Billy Martin (or Norton Hands) protesting an umpire's decision, he flung it on the ground. It was a hot summer night. The bar was as cool as a cave, despite the crush of people.

Melanie's book was called *The Old Boys' Game.* It was a straight-forward piece of reporting. She didn't mention the charge of spousal abuse against Norton Hands, but she didn't do much to make him look like a warm human being, either. There wasn't much that could be done, it seemed. The hero of the book was a pitcher from Cuba named Garcia, who, she discovered, was actually nine years older than the *Baseball Encyclopedia* and every other authority said he was. There were a few references to other reporters, though not to the one from Boston who was her chief competitor. Near the middle of the book, she described entering Norton Hands's "cubby-office" and hearing him "browbeat a fledgling writer from a fledgling New York magazine." She did not mention the kiss that she and the writer shared on the Longboat Key pier. She kept her eye on the ball, like a reporter from the prememoir age.

Melanie was wearing a long, low-waisted summer frock, scoop collar, a sort of Englishwoman-in-the-garden thing, and a Conquistadores' cap, which looked like flotsam that had temporarily come to rest on her beautiful bush of hair. When I introduced William to her, she said, "It's Willie? Wee Willie Dupree? Hit 'Em Where They Ain't Willie? Shortstop for the Sheboygan Chairmakers?" She attempted to shake hands with him, but he kept his face buried in his mother's neck, his hands to himself.

Gina said, "Morgan says your book is very good. Congratulations!"

"It's OK for a book about bats and balls. It's not literature by any stretch. It won't make Roger Angell nervous." Gina was getting stories published here and there, including in the magazine for which she and Roger Angell worked. Melanie turned to me and said, "Did I tell you that I'm moving to Los Angeles this fall? My boyfriend got a job out there and I'm going to tag along. Maybe I'll take up Rollerblading. Or Buddhism."

I pulled at the skin under my jaw. Even though I hardly knew her, even though we'd rarely seen each other in New York, the idea of Melanie living at the other end of the continent, where the earth shook and moutains sheared off on sunny afternoons, made me feel melancholy. I said, "Why would you want to Rollerblade when you can watch Mookie Wilson and Lenny Dykstra hit triples and dribble tobacco juice all over themselves?" Gina looked at me.

"I also have to go into locker rooms full of naked assholes." She put a hand over William's ear. "I'm tired of pro sports and all the bores who write about them. I bore myself."

Had my *Skylark* sports articles bored her? I'd sent her a couple.

"I keep telling him he's underachieving," Gina said.

"Yours are nice, though," Melanie said to me. "I liked the one about the world championships of Ping-Pong."

"Somebody had to write about it," I said.

Gina handed me William and went to get a drink. Later, while riding in a cab across the park, she said, "You want to tell me something?"

"What?" I flinched. The driver, another Sikh, tore through the dark. He had the radio tuned to a station that was playing Peggy Lee.

"I knew when you came back from Florida that time that you'd fucked somebody. You were so shy with me all of a sudden. And it was her, wasn't it?"

"That's not accurate." I didn't know whether to admit to having kissed Melanie. It was a long kiss. A man was fishing off the pier about ten feet from where we stood. The Gulf bumped against the pilings. During the time we kissed, the man caught a fish, a sheepshead. We watched him land it.

"Which part isn't accurate?" William sat in his mother's lap, murmuring, as the Sikh, steering the cab through the park's curves, sang along with Peggy Lee. I saw his mouth moving under the tumble of his beard. "Fever," he and Peggy Lee sang. "You give me fever."

"You're the only woman I love, Gina." We came out of the park onto Central Park West. Twenty-three blocks north and we'd be home. If the driver hit twenty-three greens in a row, I'd be tempted to give him a really good tip.

"But you fucked her anyway?"

"No." Here came the kiss. It was a Peggy Lee, is-that-all-there-is? fast-ball. "We had dinner and kissed goodnight. That was it. I sent her a birth announcement. She sent me an invitation to her party. We're in the same trade."

"Was the kiss on the lips or on the cheek?"

"Cheek," I said. The tail end of it was in fact on the cheek, at the moment when the man started to reel in his sheepshead, his line whining as he tugged against it, right after Melanie had said, "Who taught you how to kiss? Not that I mind your tongue searching out all my cavities." She was shaking a little and so was I. But she could talk while shaking.

THE BEACH HOUSE my parents rented on the Florida Panhandle in 1995 was a couple hundred yards from the Gulf and maybe a hundred yards from a crafts shop whose owner kept peacocks. There were certain hours of the day and night when the peacocks seemed to cry out, like muezzins calling the faithful to prayer. My mother, who watched TV with the volume turned way up, said the peacocks disturbed her sleep. "You would think there'd be some sort of ordinance against them in a little resort town like this." She looked reprovingly at my father, as if my father's jurisdiction extended this far south.

"An antipeacock ordinance?" Crawford said. His face was sunburned. He held his glass of iced tea against his cheek. "Are you serious?"

"I don't see why not." We were out on the deck, having a three o'clock lunch. (My mother had had breakfast at eleven.) Philip and William were chasing lizards in the sandy scrub below. Caroline was on Michelle's lap, sampling the crayfish salad that Crawford had prepared and that my mother wouldn't eat because she said she was allergic to it; when she'd last eaten crayfish, on a trip to Biloxi in 1959, she'd broken out in hives. The sky was blue and the Gulf was blue and calm. Earlier, I had allowed Philip and William to bury me up to my neck in the white sand. The night before, while the peacocks called to the lovelorn and the lost, Gina had put a hand on my belly and said, "Are we going to have another baby or not?" She moved her hand down. My pecker rose politely—a woman had come into the room. "Have you made your mind up?"

"How've you been sleeping, Dad?" Crawford asked.

"Not too bad, Craw." The table umbrella protected him from the sun, but he wore a hat anyway, a Foreign Legion desert job that my mother had picked out. He'd worn it that morning, when he and I and Crawford and Michelle had played tennis. He'd been happy shuffling around in the gray clay in his whites, his socks clinging to his hairless shins. Once when he didn't stretch enough for a volley, he'd said to Crawford, his partner, "That was a Browning shot, I'm afraid. My reach exceeded my grasp."

Now, out on the deck, under the shelter of the umbrella, he touched his ear. "One of the blessings of hearing aids is that you can take them out before you go to bed."

"I think you could be deaf as a post and hear those silly creatures," my mother said. "Did you know that man keeps a monkey, too? The poor thing's in a cage hardly big enough for a parakeet." She took a bite of cracker, on which she'd spread a very thin layer of organic peanut butter, then said to my forty-five-year old brother, "You should cover up if you go to the beach this afternoon."

Crawford and I cleared the table and washed the dishes. Then we walked down the road toward the beach, past houses whose first floors were ten feet off the ground, safe from the Gulf when hurricanes stirred it up and pushed it landward.

"I don't know how Dad takes it," Crawford said. He wore a shirt but no hat. No dark glasses, either. He was making an offering of his eyeballs to the sun.

"Maybe he prefers to overlook her flaws. It makes life go more smoothly."

"But what does he see when he overlooks her flaws?"

We were walking west, toward Destin. Apartment towers rose out of the sand like cemetery monuments.

"I think she loved him," I said, "and then he became an illustrious man who was also regarded as a kind of saint, and that complicated her feelings for him. His fame left her in the background."

"She ain't going to play second fiddle to a man who can hardly see to shave himself in the morning, you mean?"

"Something like that."

"Do you resent Gina for her fame?" Gina had published a book of stories the previous fall. The stories were about her husband and family, with the exception of one, which was about a man who leaves his wife and kids for a dentist who is a closet transvestite. The book had gotten good reviews and she'd traveled around promoting it. Once, when she returned from a trip to New England, I felt sure she was having an affair. It was something about the way she would pull her lip or scratch her throat or otherwise touch herself, as if to confirm that her lover had indeed kissed her there—and there, at the temple, beneath her still mostly auburn hair. But I didn't ask. And by Christmas she had calmed her hands.

"I'm jealous, but I don't resent her."

"How did you get to be so goddamn easygoing?" A prop plane flew low over the Gulf, pulling an advertisement for Sid's Fish House. "As the older child, I'm supposed to be the calm and controlled one."

"But I'm churning inside, Craw," I said, hoping to cheer him up. "I prefer to hide my messes. You leave your crap all over the room, I push mine under the bed."

He paid scant attention to this, which was, after all, a rhetorical answer to his rhetorical question. He was looking at the flesh cooking in the sand. It was pink, glorious, flabby, firm, tender, the color of a suspect mole, the color of a Brazil nut, glistening, wrinkled. Someday it would all be ash and bone, but not now. I saw a pregnant woman, maybe six months gone. She stood with her hands on her hips, her belly a child's toy globe pushing against the shiny blue fabric of her swimsuit. Gina had been lovely with William swimming around inside her, fresh light dawning in her face. But William was enough children, in my view. Not that that conviction had kept me, the night before, from dumping myself into my wife's unprotected, forty-two-year-old womb.

"Have you ever cheated on Gina?" Crawford asked, while studying two naiads around whose knees the Gulf foamed. "And if not, have you ever been tempted to?"

"You're full of questions," I said. The naiads were a milky color, like something that had been shot out of the pale northern sky. They were holding on to each other excitedly, happy to have landed so far from home. "You should have gone into journalism."

"I leave that to you, Red." It amused my brother to address letters to me "Morgan (Red) Dupree, Dean of Sportswriting, *Skylark* Magazine." Crawford was a prolific letter writer. I didn't write him back as often as I should have. "Don't worry. I'll hold your answers in confidence."

"Age before beauty," I said.

"The answers are no and I gave up temptation for Lent." He turned toward me. He didn't look much like the sort of pappy who was content simply to have his spot on the sofa, the evening paper in his hands, the kids making a ruckus, the wife with her needle and thread upstairs. He looked like someone who wanted to escape out the door, go stand in a field under a black sky and mutter. Or walk on a beach until the sun scorched his eyeballs. But he probably wasn't lying, at least as far as the first question went. He wasn't much good at lying.

"Your first wife tried to seduce me, but I turned her down," I said. "It was hard."

"I'll bet it was. And I'm grateful for your loyalty. It sets you apart from most of the other men she was attracted to. But that preceded your marriage. Have you kissed only Gina since then?"

I didn't often tell my brother my secrets. I didn't trust him. So, it surprised me when I heard myself say, while watching a sandpiper hurry along the wet hard-packed sand on legs that were like pencil strokes, "I kissed a woman named Melanie a few years ago. I'm probably still in love with her. Though I guess I won't know until I see her again. If I ever do." She was still in California. She and her husband—a lawyer of Chinese descent who had left his wife for her—had produced twins. "It was a long time ago."

"Just kissed her? That's pretty old-fashioned, if it's true."

"It is." I looked straight into the four o'clock sun, though unlike my brother, I wore sunglasses. "We're probably going to have another child, Gina and me—I, whatever the pronoun is."

"I thought your reproductive years were over, son." He bumped me with his shoulder.

"We'll find out."

Three pelicans passed over the beach and headed out to sea. They seemed half invention, half prehistoric creature. When they were beyond the breakers, they banked right, westward. They sailed into what little breeze there was, and then one plunged straight down, making a splash that seemed immodest even in the vastness of the sea. When it surfaced, it bobbed in the waves, everything that it wanted swimming in the pouch that hung from its enormous bill. Or so I assumed.

. . .

GINA HAD A MISCARRIAGE toward the end of July, during a week of sweltering weather. She didn't cry, at least not that I saw. She and William went up to Providence to see her mother and sit on the beach. When she came back, I said, "We'll try again." But I wasn't sure I wanted to try again.

My dad declared unconstitutional a Kentucky law that prohibited the use of Medicaid funds for all abortions, a law that criminalized all publicly funded abortions, except those performed to save the life of the mother. He said that according to a federal directive, an indigent woman who had been raped had a right to a publicly funded abortion. My mother sent me the newspaper clippings, along with a note in which she complained about the holes in my father's memory. She said that when she sent him on errands she wrote everything down for him, spelled it all out in boldface, and still he bought the wrong kind of dishwashing soap when she had specified *lemon- scented.* She wanted to send him to a neurologist. "I think he may have had a little stroke, unbeknownst to him," she wrote.

Two weeks later, *Skylark* went down the tubes—or, as they put it in the media column of I forget which paper, "The sweet little literary birdie has expired from lack of nutrition (money) and attention (readership). Maybe there were one too many articles about Ping-Pong and singing waiters."

Some weeks after that, around Labor Day, when Gina and I came home from a dinner party given by one of her mother's friends, a party at which I had used the word "frankly" often and for reasons I couldn't fathom, almost as if it were a kind of verbal tic, my wife said, "Would now be a good time to attempt procreation? I'm in the mood. Frankly." I was on the bed, reading a memoir by a woman whose father, a preacher of some fringe Protestant faith, had raped her repeatedly, in adolescence and on into adulthood. I read this with my mouth half-open, like an idiot. I looked up at Gina, my wife of ten years, the mother of our six-year-old

boy, who was across the hall, sleeping with Mr. Jet and twenty stuffed animals and a bowling pin. Gina was standing perhaps five feet from the
bed, wearing nothing except a wristwatch. She had put away several
glasses of wine at her mother's friend's Upper Fifth Avenue apartment
but she wasn't wobbling. She stood between me and a floor fan, stealing
my breeze. I envied the breeze. I loved my wife. She was smart and kind
and funny and successful, with no terrible habits and only a few annoying ones, such as stepping out of her shoes in the middle of the kitchen
and leaving them there until somebody tripped over them and then saying, when sombody complained, "Well, move them if they're in your
way." She had size 8C feet. She favored sturdy shoes, because she liked to
walk to her office, forty-some blocks to the south, which kept her in
shape. Her feet weren't pretty, but her legs were. Probably her belly and
breasts would give in to time and gravity, but she'd walk off the earth on
firm legs. Did I want her to walk off the earth now and leave me to my
devices? If I loved her, why did I want her to disappear, if I did? And if I
wanted her to disappear, why did I want to kiss that faint trickle of hair
that descended from her navel? What was wrong with me that I didn't
want to have another child with such a person as Gina?

We had unprotected sex. Gina kept her wristwatch on. I heard it ticking near my ear when we were finished. It was a drugstore watch. The
watch I'd given her the previous Christmas she'd lost on the beach in
Rhode Island.

Several weeks later, in late November, I saw Melanie. She'd come to
town to visit her parents. She'd left the twins in Los Angeles with her
husband. I'd been writing her. I'd told her about the demise of *Skylark*,
I'd told her about my morning naps, about what I did after waking from
my naps (weather permitting, I went to a bench in Central Park and read
a detective novel), about my weekly visit to the bearded Upper West Side
psychologist whose basement office was so drably lit and furnished I
wondered if I should add a tip to his hourly fee so he could buy another

lamp or a sunnier abstract painting. I'd arranged with Melanie to meet in front of the Metropolitan. It was cold but I didn't want to go in and look at paintings or amphorae. We walked south. The sky was a snowy gray and my head was bursting with things I wanted to say to her. I felt like I was fourteen. I wanted to hold her hand. But she kept her hands in her jacket as we walked and she told me the details of her life in southern California. She had a grapefruit tree in her backyard. She had an African gray parrot that could say "Go, Dodgers." Joe and Jamie, her twins, her jaybirds, were taking violin, she was learning Chinese, and her husband, David, an entertainment lawyer, grew daikon and bok choy and bird chilis in his garden. He was a good cook. She was still in the sports journalism game—she was writing a book about a retired NBA player, now a drug addict living in a trailer park—but she did it mostly out of habit. She said, "I can't complain. I'm healthy, life is sweet. I even have a tattoo on my ankle that says 'Love & Happiness.' I got it when I was falling in love with David. I'd show it to you if it didn't involve taking off my boot and sock."

We were in the lower seventies, near the Frick and the co-op building that had turned down Richard Nixon when he applied to be a resident. Nixon was in the ground now, in Yorba Linda.

I told Melanie about a boy from my elementary school days, a squirmy burr head named Roy, who while riding the school bus licked the soles of his fellow passengers' shoes at the rate of five cents per sole. He did a lot of business. Roy had cheerfully put his tongue on the bottoms of my sneakers, but I hadn't paid him.

Melanie said, "That's interesting. Why'd you tell me this?"

"I was thinking about shoes. And guilt. I go to a shrink. He talks into his beard. He has forty-watt bulbs in his lamps. When I'm there, I feel like I'm in a cave and that I should go out and shoot a wolf for dinner."

"Ah," she said. Or maybe it was "Pshah." Traffic was pouring down Fifth, taxis bleating.

We walked. There were sights to be seen. A man in a mint-green body suit and ballet slippers balanced on the park wall and ate fire. Below, a woman in a buckskin jacket held his cape and the box in which he kept his fire sticks. When flame gushed from his mouth, like a cartoon caption, the woman made a gesture with her hand, as if to say, "You see what you can do if you put your mind to it." Her mouth was stretched to what might have been a smile.

A guy in the audience said to a companion, "He uses Coleman lantern fuel. It don't hurt. It's cooler than the regular shit."

We walked until we were across from the Pierre. I said, "You want to go in? There's a tea room, I hear. Is it tea time?"

We sat down at a table and then I went to the bathroom. When I came back, she showed me her tattoo. It was a challenge reading it in the poor light beneath the table, but I could see that words encircled her ankle and that the ampersand between them had a Cupid's arrow through it. When I sat up, the couple at the next table, clearly tourists, were staring at me.

"Love and happiness is what I wish for you, Morgan. And a writing assignment, a book contract, something to keep you off the streets."

We kissed outside the Pierre. She went down to FAO Schwarz to shop for her twins, and I walked across the park toward my psychologist's office.

"HAVE YOU TOLD your wife that you don't want to have another child?"

"Sort of. I mean, I said I didn't think I could handle it."

"And how many months pregnant is she now?"

"Three. She throws up in the morning."

"Did you tell her that you didn't want to have another baby before you got her pregnant?"

"No."

"And what was her reaction when you told her that you weren't prepared to take on another child?"

"She wanted to know why I hadn't said anything during the past nine months, when she was trying to get pregnant and I was, you know, assisting her."

"Do you know why you didn't?" A bulb in the lamp on his desk seemed to flicker.

"Because I'm a coward?"

"Do you believe you're a coward?"

"More than likely. It gets dark so early now. I mean, it's hardly four o'clock and it feels like the bottom of night."

"It's December. It's almost the shortest day of the year. Do you think your relationship with this other woman, your friend who writes about sports, has anything to do with your feelings about becoming a father again?"

"She's married. She loves her husband. She has twins. She lives in Los Angeles. Grapefruits fall off her trees. Her married name is Ng"—it sounded like I was swallowing when I tried to pronounce it—"two consonants plucked from the middle of the alphabet."

"You've said before that you felt you were in love with her."

"Yeah. But it's love in a vacuum. She doesn't love me. She's happy with her life. Anyway, I love my wife, too. I'm just having some stupid midlife crisis that involves not having any more babies, if I can help it."

"Maybe categorizing it as a 'midlife crisis' won't help us to get at the possible sources of your depression?"

"I'm depressed?"

"What are you and your wife going to do about her pregnancy?" When the light on his desk flickered again, he took his pen from his shirt pocket and made a note on the pad in his lap. New 40-watt bulb?

"It's her decision."

"And you'll support her if she chooses to have the baby, despite how you feel about it?"

"I don't know."

WE HAD AN ARGUMENT. Gina threw a shoe at me and hit a painting on the living room wall, breaking the glass. It was one of Uncle Louis's pictures, a riverscape, summer haze on the broad and mighty Ohio.

I said, "Well, let's have the fucking baby, if you want."

William had come down the hall in his Mets nightshirt. I said, "William, you should be asleep."

"Don't yell," he said. "You shouldn't yell. Or say 'fucking.'"

Gina took William back to bed. They read one of the Moominland books. After William fell asleep, Gina left the apartment. She did this the next several nights, too, after William had gone to bed. She slept at the apartment of Eric Hitchcock, the editor of the recently expired *Skylark*. She said she slept on his sofa bed. She came home early in the morning, before William awakened.

Early in January, she went to a women's clinic in the Village and got an abortion. Eric went with her.

# I I

# Saturday Night, June 2001

LUCY WAS IN BED, reading *The Portrait of a Lady,* when the phone rang. She was at the point where Madame Merle explains to Isabel Archer what it feels like to be over forty, how emotion "had become with her rather historic," but how her age had earned her the right to "judge." Lucy wondered if it was true that one's capacity to feel deeply faded after forty, or was Madame Merle just blowing smoke? The other day, she had seen Judge Dupree's widow at a Swifty gas station out on U.S. 42. This was only the second time she'd encountered Mrs. Dupree since the day in January when she'd delivered the Judge's courthouse things. (The first was at a baby shower for the clerk of court.) On this afternoon, Mrs. Dupree was dressed like a doll on her way to a tea party—polka-dotted dress, white stockings, straw hat with a ribbon that tied under the chin. It was much too hot for the stockings, too hot for small talk at a filling station. Lucy watched Mrs. Dupree's face tighten as she inserted her credit card again and again into the slot on the pump. She withdrew the card quickly, snatching at it, as if the slot might contain teeth, but to no avail. Eventually, Mrs. Dupree looked in the direction of the attendant's booth, threw up her hands in a way that seemed not entirely an appeal for help, and got back in her car and drove off, with her gas tank flap open. Lucy, who would turn forty-three later that month, had for an instant considered following Mrs. Dupree home, to make sure she got there, but then had thought better of it. She had not lost the capacity to feel unkindly toward her former employer's widow.

On the fifth ring, Lucy picked up the phone.

"Lucy?" It was a man's voice but she didn't recognize it. She didn't get a lot of calls from men.

"This is Morgan—Morgan Dupree. Sorry to be calling slate." He might have meant "so late." He might have had one too many.

"That's all right," she said, though it wasn't, really. She'd been content in her bed, with the window air conditioner humming and gurgling. It was Saturday night. She'd had a late dinner—two pickle-and-bologna sandwiches. Now, along with her James, she was having some chardonnay in a pharmacy glass.

"I'm having kind of an emergency." He got his mouth nicely around that last article and noun. "A bat bit my mother."

"Are you at your mother's now?" Her eye wandered the olive walls of her bedroom and landed on the picture of her father outside his movie theater on the banks of the Missouri. The Rivoli it was called. (Some of her schoolmates called it the Ravioli.) He was a thin, wavy-haired man with glasses. He stood with his arms at his sides beyond the shadow of the little wedge that was the marquee. "MAN WOMAN," the marquee said. He hadn't had enough *as* to display the whole title, *A Man and a Woman*, on both sides of the marquee. His was the only theater within a five-hundred-mile radius that was showing this romantic French film, and nobody came. Which was perhaps why he looked so lonely in the mid-day sunshine.

"I'm at home, in my apartment. I can see your window." Her blinds were pulled, but she crossed her ankles anyway. A couple of times, she'd raised the frosted bathroom window—the view was best from there—and looked in the direction of his house. Once she'd seen him on his little porch, poking at his grill.

"Listen," he said. "I'm wondering if I could persuade you to go with me to my mother's. I kind of went over the limit tonight, you know, so, well. Plus I thought I might need a hand capturing the bat, if you were in the mood for a late night adventure. I apologize for getting you into bed."

"You mean out of bed, I think."

"Yes, I do," he said. "If you're willing."


She didn't think he looked very far gone when he got into her Escort. Maybe he'd recovered in the fifteen minutes between when he called her and now. His hair was wet and combed and his beard was groomed. He smelled of soap. The pink pearl in his ear looked as if it had just then come out of the sea. His polo shirt was tucked into his shorts. He had brought along two bottles of honeydew-flavored fizzy water. It felt to Lucy like they were going out on a date, except she was driving and they were going to capture a bat. Presumably they'd have to kill the bat, too, so that a lab could examine its brain for the virus.

"I really appreciate this," he said. "My mother was exhibiting some of the symptoms of a rabid person over the phone."

Why did all the men in this family seem so helpless around this woman? Well, maybe Crawford wasn't afraid of her. Lucy couldn't say. She didn't know Crawford very well.

She drove along Frankfort Avenue and then into St. Matthews, past the White Castle and past a bar where she once spent two hours with a divorced attorney, who told her about all the pranks he'd pulled as a juvenile, perhaps in order to persuade her that he was fun-loving, that he was ready to pull one with her. Like driving onto someone's lawn and peeling out?

She turned left and then right along the railroad tracks. Before she turned again to cross the tracks, the gate came down.

"Damn," Morgan said.

Ahead of them was an old-model Firebird with black privacy glass and a sticker on the bumper that said It Don't Matter How Deep You Fish, It's How You Wiggle Your Worm. The driver's arm hung out the window, a cigarette at the end of it. Lucy almost said something about stupid bumper stickers, but decided against it.

The freight, hauled by three engines, inched along, but since Lucy had company she didn't count the cars. Morgan took a swallow of water. She hadn't touched her bottle. Flavored fizzy water was always a disappointment.

Morgan said, for the second or third time, "I apologize for taking you away from your evening." He drummed his fingers on the hairy skin above his knee.

"Fortunately I wasn't doing anything except reading."

They discussed Henry James. Morgan claimed that reading him was like taking a long walk with a vase or something balanced on your head.

"I don't understand," she said. "Why would you take a long walk with a vase on your head?"

"To improve your posture?" he said. "To see if you could do it?"

"I like him," she said. "He understands women. And men."

"There are no dirty breakfast plates in his books. Or annoying insects —chiggers, say. Or bats. Or scenes at railroad crossings."

The arm and cigarette hanging out the Firebird retreated inside. It was a humid night. The damp air got under the neck of Lucy's T-shirt and made her scratch herself. Boxcars and tank cars and flatbed cars rolled by. Some were graffitied in the style that made puffy, bloated things out of letters of the alphabet; the letters tumbled sideways into each other. She couldn't decipher the names, if that's what the letters amounted to.

Morgan said, "I used to be prograffiti. Now I'm antigraffiti. I like a clean boxcar, a clean overpass, a clean subway car. I must be getting old." The pearl in his ear seemed to suggest that he wished this wasn't true.

A clean boxcar, one with the Southern Pacific seal on it, clanked by, and in it, a step or two back from the open door, stood a man wearing what looked like a convict's striped pajamas—a convict from another era, that is, since contemporary ones wore orange jumpsuits. Or perhaps what he had on was a seersucker suit. On his head was a broad-brimmed hat. Her first thought was that the man was Morgan's father disguised as either a Southern dandy or a convict from another era. He was distinct, like a figure in a dream, and yet he had all the substance of a phantasm.

She looked at Morgan after the SP car had faded away. He gazed straight ahead, giving no sign that he'd seen anything but a long, slow-moving train, an almost quaint obstruction that lay between him and the chore of tending to his mother.

She opened her bottle of fizzy water and thought, I need to exercise more.

THE HOUSE WAS ABLAZE with lights. Lucy thought of a cruise ship out on the dark sea, with Mrs. Dupree, its only passenger, pacing the decks with her cane, barely hearing the dance band that played in the empty ballroom.

Morgan said, "Aliens will have no trouble finding her house, should they decide she's one of them."

Lucy parked in front of the garage. Moths swirled around a spotlight. Did moths hang out near lights because the dark was such a horrible alternative? Were they safe from predators there? But many of them burned up in the bulb's heat, didn't they? She remembered as a child finding their papery corpses beneath the porch light of her Nebraska house. She had kept a collection of dead insects for a while. She put them in an old fishing tackle box, each in its own compartment. The collection was mostly cabbage moths and tiger moths and monarch butterflies and cicadas and a couple of beetles with green tints in their shells. Once she left the tackle box open out on the front walk and a wind came up and blew the contents away, like dust. She didn't start over.

Insects buzzed and whirred and crackled, like they owned the night, like they were rallying to take over the world. She followed Morgan into the house. Music was playing, something classical. Beethoven, wasn't it? The Ninth?

They went down the hall, past the portrait of the jowly ancestor, past the chest where, five months ago, she'd seen the Judge's bush hat resting. Morgan said, "Mom? Mom?" Lucy studied his back. He was narrow in the shoulders, narrow in the hips, a bit slouchy. What could you tell about anybody from behind? She supposed she could see that Morgan wished he wasn't walking where he was walking, that he wished his shapely legs were somewhere else.

Mrs. Dupree was sitting on the couch in the library. Her chin was on her chest, her small veiny hands had let go of the book in her lap, which was about to slip between her legs. The music, which was at a volume that was a factor in Lucy's halting in the doorway, came from the TV. There was a mighty roll of kettledrums, then the orchestra leaped forth. Morgan stood in front of his mother, seemingly uncertain of his next move. At last, after saving the book from the floor, he tapped her knee.

Mrs. Dupree's head rose slowly, reluctantly. Her face was veiled as if with a pleasant morning haze, but a complaint was taking shape in the vicinity of her mouth.

"I'd just about given you up for dead," she said to her son. Her eyes found her late husband's law clerk in the doorway, though she was still sleepy enough to doubt her senses. "Lucy? Is that you? What are you do-ing here?" She looked back at Morgan.

"I brought a lawyer, in case we decide to sue the bat." Morgan took the remote from beside her leg and lowered the volume on the TV.

"It's no laughing matter," Mrs. Dupree said. The haze had lifted. "If the bat's rabid, I'll have to have all those shots. I'm old, Morgan—my body can't tolerate that kind of thing."

"Don't worry. Everything'll be OK." Morgan said. He was bent down, studying his mother's hand, like someone poring over an ancient text. "Where is it?"

"It's right here," Mrs. Dupree said, wiggling her left index finger. Lucy came over and, removing her glasses, saw two minuscule tooth marks on the tip.

"How did it happen?" Lucy asked.

"I was lying down in there"—she indicated her bedroom, next door—"with the lights off. I'd been in the basement, riding the bicycle. I was tired. I've been tired all week, all this heat and pollution. I should wear one of those surgical masks when I go outdoors. I don't how I made it to Frankie Bagshaw's birthday luncheon. It was her eightieth, you know. Her daughter came up from Atlanta to arrange it. It was over near where the Bard Theater used to be, at whatchamcdougal's, that little place with the French name. Tom Thumb would have gone away un-happy, the portions were so small. Not that it mattered to me. I wasn't very hungry and I probably shouldn't have gone in the first place. I didn't sleep at all last night. But I'm very fond of Frankie. You remember when she held you on her lap because somebody left you out of a game and you were crying?"

"Not really," Morgan said. Lucy wondered if she would ever hold a hot, tearful child in her lap. It was getting late, and it didn't help to wonder.

"Well, you do," Mrs. Dupree said, refusing to grant him a lapse in memory, if that's what it was. She was sitting up straight now. A little gold cross lay flat against her chest. The skin on her arms was falling away from her bones.

"How did the bat get into your bedroom?" Morgan asked. There was agitation in his face, between his eyebrows. Perhaps the memory of himself crying in Frankie Bagshaw's arms had been jarred loose.

"It must have come in through the bathroom window. The screen was torn, and Lavell took it to get it fixed. He's on vacation this week. He and his daughter went down to Kentucky Lake to go fishing. I would have called him tonight if he'd been around, instead of dragging you all the way over here, Morgan. And poor Lucy! I hope he didn't get you out of bed. What time is it, for goodness sakes?"

LUCY PUT ON A plaid windbreaker Morgan found in the front hall closet and a pair of wool gloves. Both had belonged to the Judge. Morgan wore his father's raincoat—the good one, a Burberry with epaulets—and a pair of his leather gloves.

He took his father's bush hat from the closet shelf, examined it, and then offered it to her. "You need a hat? You know how bats are attracted to women's hair." He grinned. "Dad wouldn't mind."

"No, thanks."

"Heigh-de-ho then," he said, leading the way toward his mother's bedroom, his bare calves flashing below the hem of the raincoat.

He carried a bucket and a dustpan and a besom. Lucy had a broom and a grocery bag. She was a hatless Halloween witch in drag, shopping for a bat to put in her black pot.

Morgan closed the door behind them. Lights were burning everywhere. Lucy felt as if she had walked into some sort of shrine. There were so many photographs—on the dresser, on the walls, on the desk that you had to be a tiny lady to sit at. Several generations of Duprees and Grissoms—Mrs. Dupree was a Grissom—were here, gazing out from expensive frames. Morgan said, "Should we spread out or work in tandem?"

"Maybe we should spread out," Lucy said, "and if I find it, I'll let you know by shrieking." She heard a chorus singing the "Ode to Joy." Mrs. Dupree had turned up the TV again.

"Why don't you go thataway"—he pointed toward the bathroom— "and I'll search the boudoir." She zipped up the jacket.

Between the bedroom and bath was a dressing alcove, with closets and a bureau. Lucy surmised that this bureau, which was crowded with pictures of Duprees and Mudges, had been the Judge's. She saw a tie clip that he often wore, one with the Louisville and Nashville logo on it. The L&N was gone now, having been absorbed by another railroad, one whose initials Lucy couldn't recall. She remembered the Judge lamenting the decline of the American rail system, telling her about riding trains called the Flamingo and the Phoebe Snow and the South Wind. And then she remembered him telling her, during the period when he was stopping by her apartment, of an excursion to the L&N yards on a Thanksgiving in the early sixties. "What a calamity," he'd said. He and his sons and his cousin the painter had somehow, after their car broke down, ended up at a White Castle and witnessed a stickup. He'd gotten in dutch with his wife for that one.

She searched behind the curtains and peered into a closet full of dresses shrouded in plastic. Would she in fact shriek if she came eye to eye with the bat? She remembered reading that bats clean their teeth with a hind foot. Well, at least they cleaned their teeth.

She went into the bathroom and sat down on a little wicker bench and massaged her eye with her thumb. Her head ached. She wondered what the Reverend Sandy Broyles was up to on this Saturday night. Was he writing tomorrow's sermon? Was he watching TV? Was he out on a date? Morgan had told her, when they were on *their* only previous date, that Sandy was seeing a woman he'd grown up with. Morgan had said,

"A hot little Presbyterian divorcée, if you can imagine that." She imagined it, but it didn't deter her from continuing to attend church. It had almost become a habit with her to go, and now she could also inspect the preacher for marks the divorcée might have left on him. Would there be a Sunday when she would see, peeking out from above his clerical collar, like a sun rising, a love burn?

The door of one of the medicine cabinets on the wall was ajar and she opened it further in the thought that the bat might have secreted itself inside. She saw a razor and a jar of petroleum jelly and a styptic pencil and baby powder and several bottles of pills prescribed for William C. Dupree. She didn't see the bat or any headache medicine.

When she found the bat, clinging to a man's blue cotton robe hanging on a door hook inside the part of the bathroom where the toilet and the tub were, she didn't shriek, but she did say, "Oh, gosh!" It was a soft brown color, about the size of her palm; it hung upside down, with both its forelimbs and hindlimbs drawn in. It had sweet, perky ears. Lucy pushed the door shut with the broom. Then, gingerly, she extended the bristle end of the broom toward the bat. The bat took to the air. There was hardly space for it to work up any momentum, and it flew gracelessly, like some blundering thing drunk with fear. Several times, it came close to Lucy, who sat on the edge of the tub holding her gloved hands on her head, but it didn't touch her or any other solid thing. It had a gift for avoidance. At last, it landed on the window curtain. The curtain, made of a gauzy material, was a translucent white; the bat looked like a splotch on a hospital monitor, a blight, something that would have to be cut out.

The thought that she could open the window and free the bat to eat moths and mosquitoes again had passed through her throbbing head. But that would mean Mrs. Dupree would have to get all those shots— were they still given in the stomach?—and Lucy didn't dislike her so much that she would wish that on her. Mrs. Dupree was a strangely bitter person, full of resentments that Lucy didn't quite fathom the sources of. Why had Mrs. Dupree bullied her husband, a man Lucy had loved as much as any she'd known, except perhaps for her charming failure of a father, now dead for twelve years? They'd never met, her father and Judge Dupree. Her father had spent his final years driving around the country in an old laundry truck whose interior he'd outfitted with a bed and an armchair and a Coleman stove. He'd visited her in Louisville only once, a year or so after she became Judge Dupree's clerk. She made dinner for him and put Duke Ellington on the record player, and in the morning, after he took a shower, which he'd badly needed, he'd left. Two years later, he was found dead at a rest stop at the Arizona-Nevada border. He'd had a heart attack. Recently Lucy had imagined him driving down the highway in his laundry truck refurbished for the afterlife, listening to "Concerto for Cootie" or "Jack the Bear" on his special audio system. She hoped that if he should ever see a fellow spirit walking the railroad tracks in a raincoat or (who knew?) a seersucker suit, he'd pull over. They could go have a picnic somewhere.

"Lucy? You doing all right?"

"I'm in here with the bat." She had the sense that she sounded disconsolate. She needed to find a job, rediscover the pleasures of the legal profession. She'd been adrift for several months now, officially unemployed since April. On Monday, she had an interview at the public defender's office.

Morgan opened the door partway and peered in. On his upper cheek, just beyond the fringes of his beard, was a pimple or boil, some eruption. He was self-conscious about it; he'd touched it often in the car, as if touching it might make it go away. His mouth was small, like his mother's, though not prim; it would stretch, she thought, to accommodate happiness or astonishment.

"It's over there," she said, pointing at the window. She was hot inside the Judge's jacket and she unzipped it a little.

"You want me to kill it?" he asked. He didn't sound eager.

"I guess you have to."

He sat down on the edge of the tub and took off his gloves. Then he reached into the pocket of the raincoat and said, "Look what I found." He pulled out a timetable (Chesapeake and Ohio, 1947, the mascot kitty snoozing on the cover) and a roll of film and a balled-up handkerchief.

"I have some film of your dad's that I've been meaning to give you." Actually, she hadn't thought about it in a long time. At one point, when she'd cleaned out her desk at the federal building, she'd thought she'd get the film developed. Now it was in her closet, where Judge Dupree's old raincoat hung.

Morgan smoothed out his father's handkerchief, then folded it. "My dad used to sneeze really loud sometimes, like he was expelling a month's worth of bad thoughts. It was the biggest noise I ever heard him make."

"I doubt he had a month's worth of bad thoughts his whole life."

Morgan unfolded the handkerchief and then refolded it, making the edges flush. "You and Dad were quite close, weren't you?" He kept his head lowered.

"I worked for him for fifteen years," she said in a firm voice, wondering if anybody at the courthouse had told Morgan anything. Not that there was much to tell.

"Yeah," Morgan said. "Well, I guess it's time to do the deed. I hope it's not a baby."

"YOU WANT TO GO somewhere for a drink?"

She didn't, really. It was close to midnight and her head hurt.

"There's that barbecue place down on River Road. Or the Pine Room, where my Uncle Louis used to go."

The Escort's high beams pushed the dark aside. Bugs danced in the stream of light. "Shouldn't we get the bat into your refrigerator as soon as possible?" Lucy asked.

It was in a Ziploc bag at Morgan's feet. The way he had killed it was that he had got it into the grocery sack and then, after the broom proved to be an ineffective weapon, smashed it with a shoe from his father's closet, a black dress-up shoe. The bat had made peeping sounds as it died. Morgan was going to deliver it to the department of health lab— tomorrow, if the lab was open. Also tomorrow he was going to take his mother to an immediate care clinic, after she went to church. She hadn't wanted to go to an emergency room tonight. "I won't go to those places. They just fill you up with drugs and things. Look what happened to Dad when he went to the hospital. He caught that staph infection. No, thanks." They'd left her in the library, drinking water with powdered vitamin C in it, watching a movie that starred Don Ameche and Mary Martin.

"We'll have them put it on ice for us," Morgan said.

THE FIRST GIN and tonic eased her headache and the second washed it away. Amazing were the medicinal properties of alcohol! Morgan, who limited himself to a single beer, drove her home from the Pine Room. When they arrived, her upstairs neighbor, the salesman of artificial knees and hips, was sitting on the front porch. He was eating something crunchy out of a bag, his feet on the railing. Bugs milled about the solitary porch light. As they mounted the stairs, Lucy took Morgan's hand, the one not holding the bag with the bat, not because she felt unsteady, but because she wanted to take possession of him outdoors. Indoors would be different, she thought; she was a little scared.

"Hey, Lucy," the salesman said. "What's happenin'?"

"Not much, Brent," she said. "You?"

"I lost a hundred and eighteen bucks at the track today. I put one of those exacta wheels on a dog in the Stephen Foster and got burned."

"Sorry to hear that," Lucy said. She let go of Morgan's hand and unlocked her door and went inside without introducing her companion.

"Night," Brent said.

She led Morgan into the kitchen. She took the bat from him and put it in the freezer, next to the package of crappie that one of the marshals at the courthouse had brought her last summer from Reelfoot Lake. The marshal, Ray, had filleted them, too.

She took a shower. It was, she realized, her third of the day. She heard again the peeps the bat made when Morgan smashed it. She considered whether to insert her diaphragm now or to wait. She waited. She put on her bathrobe and exhaled deeply, as if she were about to present her case to a jury.

Morgan sat on the edge of her bed, dressed, reading *The Portrait of a Lady.* Jumbo, her cat, was perched on her bureau like an owl, contemplating Morgan's back.

Morgan read, " 'Goodwood meant to go away early, but the evening elapsed without his having a chance to speak to Isabel otherwise than as one of several associated interlocutors.' He kind of writes like a lawyer, don't you think? Not that I have anything against lawyers. 'There was something perverse in the inveteracy with which she avoided him; his unquenchable rancour discovered an intention where there was certainly no appearance of one.' I mean, I wouldn't mind having Henry James as my lawyer. Except he's dead. My first choice among the living would be you."

He stood up and walked toward her. He was trying to pretend that he was walking without any particular destination or intention.

She wondered if he would ask her again about her relationship with his father. He hadn't asked at the Pine Room. They'd discussed, among other things, the crank calls he'd received of late. She'd said she'd almost not picked up her phone tonight.

She touched his earring and said, "You look good in pearls." She wondered if she sounded foolish, but then she'd already said to him, in effect, You can have me. Under her bathrobe was nothing.

"I bought it after I got my divorce. It was an impulse purchase." The boil, cyst, whatever it was on his upper cheek was quite inflamed, but it was possible to not notice it if she kept her eyes on his. Though his, hazel and mild, kept sliding away, like a skittish deer's.

"What did your father think of it?"

"I think the only time he might have seen it he was in the hospital. He didn't say anything."

Morgan reached for her hand and then he kissed her quickly, as if he couldn't get his head through the space between them fast enough. When he let her go, he said, "I don't mind that you were my father's lover."

What hearsay, if any, had led him to conclude this? "I loved your dad, Morgan, but I wasn't his lover. Don't forget to check your facts with me before you write your book." She meant to sound helpful.

"I don't think I'm ever going to write that book. Anyway. Well. We'll see. Thank you for coming with me tonight."

She thought he might actually turn and go. But he leaned forward again and put his mouth on her neck.

# 12

# States That Begin with *I*

SIDNEY, WHICH WAS her actual as well as her stage name, was telling Crawford about her mother's first husband, not Sidney's father. This man, a Greek named Takis, had been an amateur ventriloquist. By day, he was a baker in Boston. When he died—he was stabbed seventeen times by the husband of a woman he was seeing on the side—Sidney's mother had put his dummy in the trash. Some years later, Sidney, whose full name was Sidney Greenblatt (she and one of her dummies, an anti-Semite called Jayne, had a routine involving her name), found a box of photographs among which were several of Takis in a garish tux, his wide-mouthed wooden companion on his knee. Sidney prevailed upon her parents to buy her a dummy, though her mother resisted. "Mom said, 'What's wrong with ballet? You like to dance.' But I thought it would be cool to make my voice come out of this inanimate thing. I also wanted to learn to eat fire. I think my mom might have been happier if I'd done that, particularly after she saw me do a routine with a dummy I called the Jolly Greek Baker. He wore a toque, which kept falling off. I

When Crawford took Philip to his first lesson—he wanted to meet the teacher—Philip told him that Sidney had formerly worked in Ariosto's, where Crawford bought his coffee. Crawford said, "Is that right?" The young woman at Ariosto's, black-haired, mouth of a critical shape, the one who had told him that his polo shirt was on inside out, had also been the woman he'd nearly run into on the bicycle path that Sunday morning back in April, and he supposed that the chances were good that she would turn out to be Philip's ventriloquism teacher as well. The Wisconsin city he lived in was smaller than he sometimes wished it might be.

When he'd introduced himself—it was her, sure as shooting—she said, "I remember you, yeah, you were a latte guy." Actually, he drank more Americanos than lattes, but he didn't quibble. She didn't bring up their encounter on the bicycle path—did she even remember it? had it been more than a blip in her day?—and neither did he. Nor did he ask her what the tattoo on her shoulder was supposed to be. Butterfly? Bat? He handed her a twenty-dollar bill, the cost of Philip's lesson, and sat in the car. He had recently started taking an antidepressant, but it had not kicked in. When he got up in the mornings, he wanted to go back to sleep, though usually, with enough coffee, he would make it until early afternoon before succumbing. It was three, past his nap time. He reclined the driver's seat and shut his eyes and watched himself slip down a rabbit hole that led to a soft, pillowy underworld. Somewhere on the way to sleep he heard his father singing "I Can't Get Started" on a boat in Kentucky Lake. This was when he and his brother were young boys and it seemed that a stringer without fish on it, a stringer still in the tackle box after four hours of fishing, was an impossibility. There had to be one dumb crappie in this huge lake, didn't there? And Crawford had begun to blame his father and wished he wouldn't sing that song or any of the other songs he knew because it sure wasn't helping. And they had all gotten sunburned and gone back to the motel fishless and forty years later Crawford had nearly struck a woman walking with a manikin on a lakeside bike path in Wisconsin and, as he untangled himself and his bike from honeysuckle, had told her that "I Can't Get Started" was among his father's favorite songs. He had actually said "I Can't Get Shtarted," one of those slips of the tongue that had rarely occurred before the bicycle messenger hit him in New York. He didn't recall what she'd said in return, though his memory had preserved the look of bewilderment on her face.

Now, three months later, he was driving her to a convention of ventriloquists in Fort Mitchell, Kentucky, across the river from Cincinnati. Her car was in the shop and the only way she would get on a plane, she'd said, was if she'd had enough tranquilizers to knock out an elephant. Crawford had said he would be glad to take her as far as Louisville, where he and Philip were going to visit family. Then he had said, What the heck, he'd take her all the way. The antidepressant had started working by then, or, at any rate, his desire to sleep during the daytime had slackened. He sometimes even felt eager and curious when he got up in the mornings. He could certainly manage a couple extra hours in the car with Sidney and her dummies. (She had not brought Lancelot of the Lake, but she had packed Jayne the Anti-Semite and Mrs. Chedwick, the mother of thirteen children.) He and Philip could stay overnight in Fort Mitchell, and Philip would be able to watch some vents perform and also check out the world-class collection of dummies that a man in Fort Mitchell had amassed. When Crawford had told his wife of his plans, of this detour to a part of Kentucky where the good Germans of Cincinnati used to go to have a sinful time, Michelle had said, "I trust Ms. Greenblatt will have her own room." Crawford said that he assumed she would. Three people and a bunch of dummies in the room he'd booked for himself and Philip would be a crowd.

THEY HAD A PICNIC at a rest stop in central Illinois, between Le Roy and Farmer City. Crawford had prepared it: bagels with cream cheese and red onions, rabbit food for dipping into homemade baba ghanouj, fruit. They sat at a table under a hickory and held on to their paper plates and napkins as a wind from the southwest blew. All around them, to the horizons, were cornfields, green and shimmering. Crawford felt as if he might have been at sea, with no land in sight.

Sidney said, "The thing about the Midwest is that the open spaces will either make you kind of philosophical or kind of crazy. Like the highest thing around here is a silo or an overpass or a tree, which is also known as a lightning target." She glanced up at the hickory, a pignut, whose narrow leaves danced in the wind. "At least in Wisconsin we have a few hills. They calm the eye, you know."

Crawford said, "The glaciers left little bumps of debris behind in Wisconsin. Illinois is like the floor of some ancient sea. I think that's right." He scooped baba ghanouj with carrot.

"I don't even like corn," Sidney said. "It gets stuck in your teeth."

A leaf fell onto Crawford's bagel. He plucked it off. The flagpole rigging banged against the flagpole, and a straw hat was blown from the head of a lady walking her corgis near the rest area property line. It was gone, that hat, over the fence and into the green fields.

Philip, who had two baby hairs sprouting from the mole on his chin, who had draped the headphones to his Discman around his neck, said, "You can't be philosophical if nothing makes sense. Like I had to write this poem for Language Arts in school." He was talking to Sidney, or to the tattoo on her shoulder, which Crawford had concluded was a bat. It had red jewellike eyes. It was partially hidden by the strap of Sidney's lime-green tank top. "The poem was supposed to be about life. You were supposed to use similes and imagery and stuff. Such as: 'Life is like a highway.' I wrote, 'Life isn't like anything. Except sometimes it's like a hair ball the cat spits up. It's a mess nobody wants to clean up. It just sits there.'"

"Life doesn't always feel like that, does it?" Crawford asked, in a tone

that was somewhere between plaintive and philosophical. He didn't recall Philip having shown him the poem during the school year—not
that Philip was inclined to show him much of his work. He also didn't
remember Philip having talked so much in his presence in a while.

Philip didn't answer his father. Sidney said, "I hope you got an A for
that."

"C," Philip said. "I was supposed to write eight lines or more."

"Typical," Sidney said. She took a swig from her bottled water—she'd
brought her own supply of it—and Crawford watched her pharynx and
esophageal sphincter do their work. He remembered that his father had
been given a swallow test during his last days, though he couldn't remember what this test was supposed to prove or disprove. Anyhow, the
test had not revealed any irregularities—and then two days later his father caught a staph infection.

Crawford, wishing to be supportive of his son, said, "Brevity is the
soul of wit." This chestnut had sometimes come back at him from those
of his students who felt that five hundred words were several hundred
too many to sufficiently analyze, say, the theme of alienation in "The
Love Song of J. Alfred Prufrock."

Sidney said, "I agree with you, Pip. Life isn't like anything. It's just, you
know, there or here—this carrot I'm eating and this picnic table that
some probably mass murderer ate a candy bar at in 1989 and that guy
over there in the XXL basketball shorts with that little feather duster of a
pooch. Except sometimes life is like a big fat guy in basketball shorts sitting on top of a little dog, and you're the dog."

Philip laughed. Crawford wished that Sidney would cut back on the
references to murder; they seemed to be a staple with her.

Sidney excused herself from the table and walked toward the building
that housed the restrooms, her green tank top outshining everything in
sight, her hair black as a musical notation. She took her bottle of water
with her. People going around with bottled water, Crawford thought,

were like toddlers with pacifiers, or like how people used to be with their cigarettes, when America was a nation of smokers. Philip extracted a dollar in change from his father and ran after Sidney. When he caught up, she turned and placed her free hand on the middle of his back. In the instant of this gesture, Crawford saw his son as Sidney's dummy, in thrall to her, as if there were a cord in the middle of his back that she could pull to make him open and shut his mouth. But Crawford quickly banished this notion from his head: Sidney was odd but not sinister. The wind blew their laughter back to him, two distinct laughs. Sidney and Philip were just a couple of ventriloquists, teacher and apprentice, yukking it up off I-74 in central Illinois.

THEY DROVE PAST the motel in western Indiana where Crawford had stopped the night in January his father had died. It was next to a body shop called Stan's Collision, across the state highway from a truck plaza and other motels and a long shedlike building that offered "Live Female Dancing." (What would "Dead Female Dancing" look like? Crawford wondered.) He had stopped at that motel even though, as it turned out, he could have made it to his father's hospital bed before he died—something his mother had pointed out when he arrived in Louisville the following morning. He remembered the motel clerk, a dark-skinned man who was from India probably, behind the Plexiglas partition that separated the office from the lobby; the man had been watching the *Andy Griffith Show* on a small TV.

Sidney, opening a new bottle of water, the bottle hissing as she twisted the cap off, said, "I know this woman who does lap dancing in Boston. It's to support herself while she gets her Ph.D."

"What's she getting her Ph.D. in?" Up ahead, to the east, the sky was gray and muzzy. Wind swayed the blurs of roadside flora, patches of Queen Anne's lace.

"Public administration or something."

Crawford remembered that when he reached his parents' home, six hours after his father died, his mother had given him a little hug and then pulled back and said, "All he needed was one baby Tylenol. He didn't have much pain. He was peaceful. I wish you could have been there with me. You were only three hours away, weren't you?" And then she'd turned her head aside. Crawford had said nothing, not even asked how it was that she knew that a "baby Tylenol" was enough to ease his father's pain. Anyway, she was right: he could have made it. But he'd been afraid.

They drove toward Indianapolis. The skies to the rear looked bleak, the color of a fresh bruise. Crawford thought rain would catch up with them by the time they reached the outskirts of the city. He saw a goat standing next to a mailbox, as if waiting for the postman to bring him news, something to chew on.

Soon, farmland gave way to suburban developments, a golf course, an industrial park. He said, "Ten points if you can name a famous Indianapolis native."

"I give up," Sidney said.

Philip, his head temporarily free of earphones, said, "Larry Bird."

"He's from French Lick. South of here." Rain was spattering the windshield.

"I'll give you a hint. His name starts with V. He's a writer."

Sidney said, "I remember from college, from my Twentieth-Century American History course, that Indianapolis was, like, a big place for the KKK. Like one of the capitals of racism and anti-Semitism."

Crawford recalled reading that, too. Philip wanted to know about the KKK, and as the rain began to beat against the car, Sidney told Philip about the men in their white robes and hoods with the eye slits, how they would lynch innocent people, mostly black, but some whites, too, Jews especially.

"Like in that book you have," Philip said to his father.

Crawford was unsure of what Philip was referring to. He searched through his memory for a book devoted to the KKK or lynchings or Jews. He surveyed the spines of books on the shelves in his attic office, and then he spotted it, under a pile of stuff on the top of a file cabinet, a volume of photographs of mostly black men and women hanged by laughing mobs of white men and women and children. There were pictures of lynchings in Kentucky and Georgia and Indiana and Nebraska and Ohio and Illinois and Florida and North Carolina. Some of the photographers had used the pictures for postcards: on the back of a silver gelatin print of a man hanging from an oak, you could write a message to your cousin in the next state. Crawford had kept the book in his attic office because the photographs were so horrible. It wasn't something you put on the coffee table for your children to flip through. But Philip had discovered it, apparently.

"Right," Crawford said, giving Philip a quick look in the rearview, wondering if his son had also found the copy of *Tropic of Capricorn* (well thumbed, but not read in its entirety) and the anthology of literary erotica. It was OK if he had, Crawford supposed. He remembered finding *Lady Chatterley's Lover* in his father's basement office, among railroad magazines and law journals, and reading it in his bed early in the morning, before anybody else in the house was awake. He had looked in his father's library for other books of an erotic slant but had found none. His father had apparently limited himself to this one classic and had perhaps not even read it. The book, a fifty-cent paperback, had been in pristine condition when Crawford got hold of it.

"Christ! Look out!" Sidney said.

Crawford saw what Sidney saw through the rain that was coming down hard now, a greenish blur of a car off his front right bumper, one of those tippy, high-riding Jeeplike SUVs the color of a fruit Popsicle, which had emerged from the access ramp as if shot from a cannon. Crawford hit the brakes and simultaneously, instinctively, flung out his right arm as if to keep his son from flying forward. He caught Sidney, who had put a hand on the dash to brace herself, in the chest. The Subaru began to slide as it skidded, turned maybe thirty degrees, but he righted it somehow—just luck, because he'd always been uncertain about which way to turn the wheels when the car skidded in snow— and then he saw that the offending sultry-green vehicle was no longer within inches of his bumper. It was racing ahead, through the downpour, switching to the outer lane to pass a truck full of market-ready hogs.

"Jesus, Dad," Philip said. Crawford didn't know whether this was an expression of relief or criticism of his driving. Or perhaps it was both. He was trembling a little and didn't say anything to his son. Sidney was silent.

He eased by the truckload of hogs, smelling them even though the windows of the Subaru were shut tight. Were there slaughterhouses in Indianapolis?

He said, "The famous Indianapolitan, if that's a word"—and it had come stumbling out of his mouth as if it wasn't—"I was thinking of is Kurt Vonnegut."

"I've heard of him," Sidney said. Crawford was glad to hear her voice again.

"He lives in New York now. He moved on."

"I'm not surprised," she said.

THEY HAD A FLAT on the east side of Indianapolis. Crawford was going to wait until the rain relented to put the spare on, but the rain didn't relent. Lightning flashed, fissuring the late-afternoon dark. The rush-hour traffic went by at a creep. Philip put his earphones back on and listened to a PJ Harvey CD Sidney had brought. Sidney took her cell phone from her handbag and punched in two numbers but reached only her mother's answering machine. She offered the phone to Crawford. "You want to call your wife? Before we have to start paddling?"

"I'll call tonight maybe." Michelle and Caroline were flying down to Louisville later on. Caroline was at a sleep-away camp until Sunday.

Crawford, to pass the time, as if talking might slow the rain, told Sidney about how his mother had been bitten by a bat the other week. It had come in through the bathroom window, where a screen was out, and she had got her hand too near while trying to shoo it. It nipped her on the finger.

"Did she have to get shots?"

"The bat wasn't rabid. Lucky for her." He rubbed a porthole in the condensation that had built up on the windows. "It doesn't look like it's going to let up anytime soon. Maybe we should just get it over with now. You game?"

After they moved the stuff in the cargo area, Crawford got the spare and the jack out of the well and squatted down before the deflated tire. Sidney hovered above him, holding a beach towel as a shield against the rain. It took only a moment before they were soaked. Crawford handed Sidney his glasses; he couldn't see through them.

"Where's a NASCAR pit crew when you need one?" he said, turning the jack handle the wrong way, then the right way. At least he'd found the point where the jackscrew was supposed to fit. At least the flat wasn't on the highway side of the car.

Sidney said, "What?" The wind was blowing the rain sideways. The traffic sizzled in the deluge.

The Subaru rose with Philip (still headphoned) in it—a danger Crawford was willing to risk. If the car slipped off the jack, it would likely be he, not his son, who would be maimed. He undid the wheel nuts and handed them to Sidney. She had let go of the sopping towel. His glasses she'd hooked onto her tank top. She stood there glumly but stolidly.

Trying for levity, he said, "You look like someone who won't come in out of the rain."

"Thank you," she said.

Crawford lifted the spare onto the wheel rim. It was one of those light-weight temporary tires, which you weren't supposed to drive on for more than a few miles.

"May I have a nut, please?" he said.

She placed a wheel nut in his palm and said, "I just had a brainstorm. I've been looking at you and looking at you for weeks and thinking, you know, like, where else besides Ariosto's had I seen you. Before I met you formally, I mean."

He put the nut on the bolt and held out his palm for another. "Where?"

"At the movies. I went to the Egyptian to see this movie that a friend had told me about because there was supposed to be a ventriloquist in it, a Japanese guy. It was the five o'clock show, hardly anybody there, except for the ticket kid and this guy sitting in the lobby with his bicycle helmet in his lap, reading a book. I wouldn't have noticed you, except some guy on a bike had nearly hit me two weeks before, when I was walking on the path over by the lake, and even though I was kind of hungover when that happened, I had a memory of your face. So I bought a box of Junior Mints and watched the movie, which was twenty percent talking and eighty percent sex, which you know because you saw it, too, and it pissed me off that the ventriloquist was this fringe character who performed for audiences of two and three and told only fuck jokes, which is how we're always depicted in movies—as psychos, basically." She swiped at her face, which shone despite or perhaps because of the battering from the rain. "When I came out, I saw you—I mean, I saw this guy who I now think was you—fiddling with your bike lock and stuff. But I wasn't go-ing to say anything to you. I don't go talking to men I don't know, even if I've run into them before." She dropped another wheel nut into his hand.

"You saw that movie?" Crawford said, trying to remember what he might have been reading in the lobby of the Egyptian and failing, remembering that he sat in the very last row of the theater and counted seven heads below him, seven dark spheres on seven necks, each with a row of its own, each watching the bruising entanglements of flesh on the screen and subtitles now and then flickering over the bodies. This was in May, two months ago. He remembered that he'd had his backpack with him, full of papers to be graded. He'd bicycled downtown after school to pick up a new pair of glasses, and then on a lark, life sometimes being a lark and sometimes a crow cawing at you and sometimes a turkey vulture circling above, he'd decided to see a movie that the poster said was "searingly erotic." He didn't have a clear recollection of the ventriloquist who told the dirty jokes—it must have been a very bit part. He had no recollection of any of his fellow moviegoers' faces. Out of the dark of the theater, he'd kept his eyes averted.

"I don't usually go to the movies on a weekday afternoon," he said.

"It seems like we were kind of fated to be here, you know, changing a flat in a monsoon in Indiana." She squatted down beside him. She was close enough that even in the poor light he could see a hole in the alar groove of her nose.

"You believe in fate?" she asked. She put on the last wheel nut herself.

"Character is fate, somebody said. Some Greek guy, I think."

"So I have a bunch of encounters with a person I don't know because of my character?"

"Or mine." Crawford turned the jack handle to the left—the right way—and the spare settled on the concrete. "It's not the moon, anyway."

"Maybe it is," she said, pushing herself up, using his knee as a lever, leaving him to tighten the wheel nuts. Lightning flashed, about a quarter mile away judging by the thunder that made him start a second later. Sidney was grinning, as if she and the heavens were in league. Crawford thought of the Count on *Sesame Street*, the numbers-mad Transylvanian with his black cape and Peter Lorre haircut and batty teeth. Crawford had watched *Sesame Street* with Philip and Caroline long ago, way before the bicycle messenger in New York ran him down and jiggled his brain, afflicting him with headaches and spotty recall and slurry speech. He wondered if Sidney could do a Transylvanian accent.

THEY MADE IT TO the Indiana-Ohio border by 8:30. Darkness was everywhere, but the rain had stopped. Sidney, whom Crawford had let drive, said, "Farewell, states that begin with *I*—farewell and so long like a hot dog and good riddance."

Crawford, studying a map under the handy overhead map-reading light, said, "Actually, if we take the bypass around Cincinnati, we spend a few more minutes back in Indiana. But we get to Kentucky faster."

Crawford looked down at Sidney's legs—at the gas station where they'd had the tire repaired, she changed into a blue-jean skirt and a T-shirt that said "Have you hugged your dummy today?"—and saw that she was driving without her shoes. But she managed to steer the car across the Ohio River and into Kentucky and then, after a couple of wrong turns that were the navigator's fault, to the Huddle Inn in Fort Mitchell. A sign out front said, "Welcome Vents!"

It turned out that the Huddle Inn Crawford had made a reservation at was in Fort Thomas, over in the next county. The one in Fort Mitchell had no vacancies. The desk clerk, who, with his black string tie and salt-and-pepper goatee, bore a resemblance to Colonel Sanders, said, "Actually, with all the dummies present, we may be overbooked." He smiled at his joke and then licked his forefinger before using it to tap in a telephone number.

It also turned out that Sidney hadn't made a reservation at the Huddle Inn or anywhere else. She was planning to stay with another ventriloquist, a friend from Cleveland, when he arrived sometime the next day. Tonight she was hoping to shack up with Crawford and Philip. She'd pay the roll-away charge. She said she'd even do a little bedtime show for them. "It'll be a warm-up for Saturday night." She was scheduled to perform at the convention, with a group of young ventriloquists, in a program called New Voices. "I have this routine I'm going to try out with Jayne. It seems that she is part thampire."

"Thampire?" Crawford asked.

"Vampire. Dummies have trouble with their *vs*."

Philip said, "Like, 'The thestal thirgins are thery thicious when prothoked.'"

"Right," Sidney said. "Except you want to choke off that *p*, squish it into a *t*. So 'provoked' is like *trothoked*. Did you see my lips move?"

Philip shook his head. They were standing in the parking lot of the Huddle Inn in Fort Mitchell—Crawford, his thirteen-year-old son, and his son's ventriloquism teacher. Crawford was hungry. His lips said, "I'm starthed."

AFTER THEY HAD finished the pepperoni pizza—or *tetteroni tizza*, as a dummy might render it—Sidney went into the bathroom to change. Crawford had gotten a room with two double beds, no roll away. The motel was in Covington. (It was closer to Fort Mitchell than the place in Fort Thomas was.) It was a motel that had possibly seen better days—back, say, in the fifties, which appeared to be the vintage of some of the furniture. It was called the Wishing Well; there was a small, round, roofed-over structure in the grassy oval out front, which was perhaps what the name referred to. Philip had said, "I don't know, Dad—it looks kind of crummy." But Crawford, who had a soft spot in his heart for old motels, for the kind that have those springy metal chairs to take the air in outside your door, said, "It's probably OK."

"You want to warm the audience up for me, Pip?" Sidney said. Crawford glanced up from his reading, a Chamber of Commerce guide to Covington, and saw a sliver of Sidney through the open bathroom door. She was in her underwear. He looked back down at the picture of the

Goose Girl Fountain, which was in the MainStrasse part of Covington.
"You brought your dummy, didn't you?"

"Yeah," Philip said. "But I think I'll pass."

"You sure? You ever show your dad what you can do?"

Crawford turned to look at Philip, who was on his back, contemplating the ceiling. On occasion at home, he had heard Philip talking in his bedroom with his dummy. Once, he had gone into his son's bedroom and taken the dummy out of the box and held it, this thing with which Philip had intimate conversations. It was plastic, with a very wide, sausage-lipped mouth and cheeks like a baby's fists and eyes like saucers. It was some sort of knockoff of Mortimer Snerd. Philip, apparently with some assistance from Sidney, had named his dummy St. Philbert the Abbot of Nuts. On the untonsured skull he'd put a helicopter beanie. But he had yet to do a performance with St. Philbert, not even a private one for his family. He'd said he wasn't ready.

"Maybe some other time," he said to the ceiling.

"It would be fun to hear you," Crawford said to his son, wishing that Sidney would hurry up and do her show so he could brush his teeth and lay his head down.

"No, thanks, Dad," Philip said.

Crawford got up to adjust the air conditioner. It was an old window unit, and the cool air it produced was like the air found in a damp corner of a basement, in the vicinity of a cat box. Or so Crawford imagined. Ever since the bike accident in New York, he'd been prone to picking up smells that others did not detect.

When at last Sidney came out of the bathroom, she was in a short, baby-blue, sacklike dress that looked like something Twiggy might have worn. On her head was a plaid tam-o'-shanter. She'd put the stud in her nose and had colored her lips a not very attractive purple shade. Her toenails were green. There were so many styles in this getup—ghoul, schoolgirl, swinging sixties London lassie—that Crawford couldn't decide what Sidney was trying for. Whatever it was, it also seemed to be what she was aiming for with Jayne, the dummy, whose costume differed from Sidney's only in the color of her dress, which was pink and had a bow under the bust.

Sidney sat down on the desk chair and settled Jayne on her knee. Jayne was about three feet tall.

"That's a mighty skimpy frock you have on, Jayne," Sidney said. "Was it discounted?"

"I got it at Marshall Field's," Jayne said, with a sniff. Her voice was lower than Sidney's, a little rough, suggesting a history of smoking and drinking. "And how far did you have to chase the little girl to get yours, my dear?"

"I got it off the rack at Kohl's," Sidney said brightly. "Do you like it?"

"I won't shop there," Jayne said. "It's a Jewish enterprise."

Sidney turned her head sideways, as if this might enable her to see into Jayne's brain. "Is that so? I'm a Jew, you know."

"That's your trodlem, dear," Jayne said, sitting up stiffly. Jayne had chubby legs, those of a person who didn't get enough exercise.

"My what?"

"Trodlem, I said. Trodlem. With a name such as Sidney Greendlatt, you have a dig trodlem."

"Green*blatt,*" Sidney said. "Have you been drinking, Jayne?"

"I had my usual," Jayne said. "And a cut o' dlood on the side."

"And where did you get the *cup o' blood,* if you don't mind my asking?" Sidney gave Crawford and Philip an appalled look. Then she turned back to the dummy. "I hope not at Marshall Field's. I have friends who work there."

Jayne, collecting her thoughts, stared at Crawford and Philip. Then she said, "I sucked it from a dummy I know. He thanted to make loth to me, and I said, 'Dring it on, dig doy.'"

"How would you describe the dummy, Jayne?"

"Gentile," Jayne said. "Handsome, uncircumcised."

Crawford flinched, Philip chuckled.

Jayne said to Sidney, "Let me ask you a question. You're always testering me, so now it's my turn. Do you wear your dresses so short so doys may see your tanties?"

Sidney tugged at the hem of her dress. Then she pulled up Jayne's and said, "At least I wear panties."

Crawford worried about the direction Sidney's performance seemed to be heading in. He wished she would pull Jayne's dress back down.

"Would it be fair to say, Jayne, that you are a blood-sucking, anti-Semitic whore?"

"And you have nether slept with a dummy?"

Sidney lifted her chin, made herself taller. "One or two, maybe."

"You should not cast stones, if you live in a glass house and are wearing a little dress."

"I'll remember that," Sidney said, huffily. Then she said to Crawford and Philip, "That's the short PG-13 version. I figured I shouldn't do the raunchy routine."

"Thanks," Crawford said. "I mean, thanks for the show."

"Yeah, cool," Philip said.

"Do you make your own costumes and stuff?" Crawford asked.

"I do, yes. I'm a ventriloquist who sews. So, if I fail to make a living at this, I can always get a sweatshop job." She grinned, her purple mouth glistening like a bitten-into plum.

CRAWFORD AWAKENED FROM a dream and stumbled off toward the bathroom. His wife had been in the dream, singing "I'm an Old Cowhand" while eating crackers. The occasion seemed to be a talent show. Crawford peed, examined the bottle of throat gargle Sidney had left by the wash basin, and returned to the bedroom. He sat on the edge of the bed he shared with Philip and watched Sidney sleep. She slept on her stomach, her mouth mushed into the pillow. The lurid red digits on the night-table clock glared at him with the news that it was 2:22. How could it be so many hours from dawn and his wake-up pill? He again noticed the scent of cat urine from the air-conditioning. He put on his bermudas and loafers. Philip was sprawled out in the center of their bed, his growing body having already discovered the space his father had abandoned.

It was an August night in the Ohio Valley and the air was thick and still warm. Crawford walked out of the motel parking lot and up the street, past a milk plant, which was quiet, though a plastic cow, spotlighted, turned slowly on a rooftop pedestal. Crawford was hungry; the pizza had not filled him up. He had his heart set on a plate of hash browns, crisp and salty, like he'd eaten at the Toddle House long ago, when he was a teenager. He'd gone there late at night with Sandy Broyles, after they'd dropped off their dates and after they'd run out of beer. The Toddle House had had about ten stools, no tables, and the stools at one in the morning would be filled with drunks, most of whom were, unlike Sandy and Crawford, of legal drinking age, some of whom were loud, some of whom were quiet, some of whom stubbed their cigarettes out in ashtrays, some of whom stubbed their cigarettes out in their ketchup-and-eggs. It was a story not often told that Crawford's Uncle Louis had fallen asleep in a plate of Toddle House scrambled eggs. Crawford had sometimes ordered scrambled eggs at the Toddle House, along with a cup of coffee, but it was for the hash browns that he came and sometimes stood and waited until some old drunken fart finally vacated a stool.

Crawford stood in the parking lot of the strip mall where they'd bought the pizza and, like a dog that had wandered out of its neighborhood, held his nose high, trying to pick up a scent. A sign in the window of Mr. Duane's Hair Studio and Day Spa, one that spelled out in blue neon the name of a beauty product, flickered. Instead of fried food, Crawford would have settled for hair to bury his nose in. The soft hair of his wife might have calmed him. Or even—the thought was there, nagging at him like a tiresome toddler—the black hair of his son's ventriloquism teacher would have done, just for a moment, just long enough to relieve him of the anxiety of standing in a parking lot in Covington, Kentucky, at 2:30 in the morning.

He ventured onward, toward the bright lights of a twenty-four-hour gas station. As he walked, hands in the pockets of his shorts, he saw on the other side of the street a man keeping pace with him. The man wore a light-colored coat that came to around his knees and a light-colored broad-brimmed hat around which insects circled as if it were illuminated from within. He was carrying a little suitcase that was the shape of a lady's hatbox. Had it been daytime, had it been 1935, he might have passed for an itinerant salesman, his bag full of notions and nostrums. But it was the dead of night, it was 2001, and the man resembled his late father too closely for Crawford to ignore the possibility that he was an apparition. Though not a believer in the spirit world, Crawford understood the tremor in his jaw and the way his heart leaped into his throat to be belief, at least of a temporary sort. He walked faster and he noticed that the man, the spirit with the hatbox-shaped valise, struggled to stay abreast. His gait was ragged and unsteady, an old man's, though there was valor in it, too—clearly it took some effort for him to keep going.

Crawford went into the gas station store and a bought a six-pack of beer and two Hershey's chocolate bars and yesterday's edition of the *Cincinnati Post*. When he returned to the street, he saw his father—well, the ghost of his father—on the other side, sitting on a bus-stop bench. The ghost greeted Crawford with a salute, like the salute Indians on old TV westerns used when meeting a white man. Crawford had a hand free, but he didn't wave back. He nodded, as one might nod to a stranger; it was the best he could manage under the circumstances. He felt that if he waved, he would cross some line, he would lose himself in vaporous nonbeing; it would be like accepting Jesus into your life maybe, something he'd never been inclined to do, though he did sometimes go to church and wrestle with the mystery of Him. If he waved, the person he was wouldn't make it back to the motel; he would be transformed beyond recognition, and Philip and Sidney would be forced to call the police. And the police would divest him of his beer and candy bars and belt.

When Crawford got back to the motel—the ghost, possibly too tired to go any farther, hadn't left the bus-stop bench—Sidney was sitting outside their room. She was wearing her Twiggy dress, no shoes. The remnants of a dream were scattered about her face, in her matted eyelashes and right in the middles of her cheeks. A bottle of water was set between her legs.

"Couldn't sleep?" Crawford asked—a surefire late-night conversation starter.

"I kept smelling cat pee in there," she said.

"And I thought I was crazy." He took a beer out of the bag, a local brand called Hudepohl. "Long, long ago, in the early sixties, my dad took my brother and me to see the Reds play baseball at Crosley Field, which was razed before you were born probably. How old are you, anyway?"

"Twenty-six."

"Before you were born, yeah. And there was this beer vendor, a black guy, who would cry out, 'Get moody with a Hoody, get moody with a Hoody.' You care for one?"

Sidney held up her bottle of water.

They talked—about baseball, about Philip, about Sidney's mother, about the murdered Greek baker-ventriloquist, but not about the specter Crawford had just seen—until somebody drove up in a new-model pickup and got out and knocked on the door two rooms down and said,

"Hey, baby, open up." Crawford and Sidney walked to the grassy oval where the wishing well was. The opening was boarded over.

"Not accepting wishes at this time, it seems," Sidney said. She handed Crawford her water and boosted herself up on the rim, which was concrete with pebbles stuck in it. Her legs were much more beautiful than Jayne's.

Crawford handed Sidney her water and his beer and boosted himself up. She took a sip of his beer and returned it to him. He said, "Your routine with Jayne reminded me of something."

"Yeah?" She borrowed the beer back.

"My first real girlfriend, the first one I made out with, in sixth grade, was Shewish. Jewish." He shouldn't have been telling her this. It would have been safer to tell her about his father's ghost.

"There are Jews in Kentucky?"

"A few, yeah." He watched a city bus go by. There was nobody on it, not a soul.

"Tell me about her," Sidney said, touching him on his back, near where he supposed the cord would be if he were a ventriloquist's dummy.

# 13

# Smudge

LAZARO CARRIED THE URN out onto the bridge. He walked slowly, carefully, not only because he was leading a funeral procession (if four people can be called a procession) but because he'd had two martinis at
lunch and was paying some attention to the gaps between the ties.
They'd eaten at the Breckinridge Club, where Judge Dupree played cards
with Sunbeam and Hateful and the Stork, where black waiters in white
jackets stepped softly across the creaking floors with trays loaded with
high-cholesterol food. Lazaro had once been a waiter at a beach hotel in
Mexico. Now he was an illegal immigrant—he was hoping to get a student visa—carrying a jar of ashes onto a defunct railroad bridge that
crossed the Ohio River. His eyes were behind sunglasses. He was wearing
a pale blue summer suit, which he must have found in the closet of his
late patron and employer—it didn't quite fit—and a white shirt and a
pair of tasseled, hand-stitched, calfskin loafers. Morgan had been with
Lazaro in New York when Lazaro bought the shoes. He'd worn them out
the door and then he and Morgan had strolled uptown, Laz with his

jacket hung on his shoulders European-style and his eyes trying to keep up with the scenery and his feet a good inch off the pavement. They had stopped at a hotel on Madison Avenue where they drank two bourbons apiece and where, as they were leaving, passing through the lobby, they saw Mickey Rooney on the arm of a blonde a half foot taller. At least Morgan thought it was Mickey Rooney. What he was more certain about, both then and now, was Laz saying in the bar, "If Louis die, I come to New York to live," and then dolefully tapping cigarette ash into the glass ashtray and some minutes later grabbing Morgan by the wrist and saying, "You like to buy watch, mister? No? How about nice hombre with beautiful shoes?" Morgan had laughed and then realized that the latter offer was not a joke.

When Morgan first saw the ovoid-shaped urn, he thought of an egg in an egg holder, having just that morning watched his father eat his very soft-boiled brown egg from a ceramic one. (His father eating breakfast was, all in all, not a very appetizing sight; it was what happened to the thick, yeastless whole wheat toast—it was broken up into Communion-size bits and dipped into the undercooked egg—that got to Morgan.) The urn was about a foot high, a cherrywood egg rising out of a square cherrywood pedestal. It had brass handles and an acorn on the lid and it seemed too grand for Uncle Louis. Of course, it was true that Uncle Louis's funeral instructions, written in pencil on a sheet of sketchbook paper on which there were doodles (clouds? a sleeping dog?), had not specified a type of urn for his ashes. What he had written was: "My dear Laz, I don't want a church service or anything like that. Just bake me and then sprinkle me in the Ohio. The Big Four Bridge would be a nice bridge to be sprinkled from. My cousin Billy will help you with the details, if there are any."

ONE AFTERNOON TWO months earlier, in February 1985, Lazaro had called Morgan at his office in New York. Morgan was putting the finishing touches on a profile of the owner of a chain of budget motels. The man was a buttoned-down, tight-fisted jerk who waved his Wharton MBA in your face, but Morgan had softened his edges. It was an accommodation you made when you worked for an editorial arm of the lodging industry.

Lazaro had traded pleasantries with Morgan and then put Uncle Louis on. Uncle Louis had by that point submitted to chemotherapy. The herbal potions prescribed by the Belize witch doctor had not stemmed the tide.

"When the oncologist told me the cancer was 'indolent,' what I thought he meant was that it was like some lazy, mild thing, you know? Like an indolent tropical breeze." Uncle Louis had said this to Morgan on another occasion. Perhaps he'd forgotten. Not that Morgan minded. "But what he really meant was that it wasn't going to go away; it was going to sit on my couch, like some shiftless, no-account guest, and eat me out of house and home." Uncle Louis made a throaty noise that was possibly a chuckle and then he started coughing.

Morgan sat with his feet propped on the windowsill, his six cleanly typed pages of mostly factual piffle in his lap, and listened to his father's cousin cough. It was four in the afternoon in New York and it had been snowing hard for two hours. The city was supposed to be buried by midnight, and Morgan was excited by the prospect. He looked forward to sleeping with Gina as the snow fell past his windows, as wolves came out of their burrows in Central Park and howled their mournful howls.

When Uncle Louis stopped coughing, Morgan said, "That's what all those chemicals are for, right? To rub out that no-account guest?"

"So they say. Sometimes I think their primary purpose is to make me bald and sick to my stomach. You should see me—I look like Casper the Friendly Ghost after a month of upchucking."

Morgan had seen Uncle Louis in December. The Duprees (minus Crawford, who spent the holidays in Washington) had gone over to

Louis's on Christmas afternoon. He was wan and his hair had been reduced to a patternless scattering of grayish stubble, but there was still a
belly beneath his cardigan. He sat glumly in a high-backed chair. Jacques
was at his feet, in a quilted, plaid dog bed (a Christmas gift). Judge
Dupree had tried to entertain his cousin with a tale of a railfan trip he'd
taken that fall, an adventure that involved chasing a steam engine across
Iowa by car, but Louis had interrupted twice to ask where Laz had run off
to. When Morgan had gone into the kitchen to get himself a soft drink,
he'd found Laz slicing a ham. Laz was wearing a bow tie (a Christmas gift
from Uncle Louis, rather silly looking) and tears were running down his
face. He said he missed Mexico and the sea and his mother. He babbled
in Spanish and a tear dropped among the black cloves that pimpled the
top of the pink ham. In New York, late on the evening when they had
seen either Mickey Rooney or his double on the arm of the tall blonde,
after they had had dinner at a tandoori place on Columbus Avenue with
Morgan's wife-to-be, after Gina had gone home to her little efficiency
and Morgan and Laz had one more drink at Morgan's apartment (where
Laz was staying until Uncle Louis returned from Belize), they had a
round of sex, which Morgan had regretted and also found too tumul-
tuous to dismiss. Two months later, Morgan, with one hand in his pocket
and the other holding a glass inscribed with the names of the Kentucky
Derby winners from Aristides to Sunny's Halo, had resisted the impulse
to put his arms around his father's cousin's tearful boyfriend.

Snow hurtled by Morgan's window, as if it were fleeing something.
Morgan asked Uncle Louis if Laz was taking good care of him.

"Sometimes the poor boy goes out and gets *muy borracho.* Don't you,
Laz?" If Laz made an answer, Morgan didn't hear it. "It's not much fun
looking after a sick person. I wouldn't mind getting *muy borracho* myself.
Except I have been sober as your proverbial dad for most of a decade
now and also I have to leave room in my veins for cytosine arabinoside
and other things I couldn't pronounce if you paid me. Did I tell you that

Laz found my pistol, that teeny-weeny one I bought to defend myself against criminals with long ago?"

Morgan said, "No."

"It was in a benne wafer tin in the pantry. I told him to throw it away."

"Good idea," Morgan said. He noticed a typo in his profile. He had made the motel tycoon's hair "salt-and-peeper."

"But enough about me," Uncle Louis said. "I was calling to ask what you and Gina might like for a wedding gift."

The wedding was scheduled for May, which, given the weather, seemed very far off.

Morgan said, "You shouldn't bother about that." Morgan was thinking he would walk home through the snow. That would make arriving there more pleasurable.

"A waffle iron? An asparagus platter? Cutlery?" These things were all presumably jokes. Or perhaps not. "Tell me your heart's desire and Laz and I will get it for you."

"If you and Laz came," Morgan said, "that would be great. I like waffles, too."

Later, as he was walking home through the snow that got into his ears and down his neck and under his pants cuffs, a slog during which he imagined himself as a typo, a mistake that was slowly being whited out by some diligent editorial hand, it occurred to him that he might have asked Uncle Louis for one of his paintings or drawings as a wedding gift. There was a charcoal of Laz, a nude, which Morgan had seen last summer. Gina might have liked to have it.

THE BIG FOUR BRIDGE, which was built late in the nineteenth century, had not carried rail traffic since 1968. It had been abandoned when its owner, the New York Central, merged with the Pennsylvania Railroad, and nobody had yet figured out what to do with it. At lunch, Judge Dupree said he'd heard it might be turned into a pedestrian mall, except that some people from Indiana had objected on the grounds that they didn't want Kentuckians to be able to walk into their state. The Ohio River was there for a reason.

Crawford said to Laz, "They don't want our rednecks to mix with their rednecks. And they want our dark-skinned people to stay over here. Don't want to mess up the gene pool."

Laz, who was eating a cheeseburger for lunch, smiled genially. Some of the terms Crawford used were probably new to Laz.

Anyway, it was illegal for a person of any state (not to mention a Mexican alien) to walk on the bridge, a fact that Judge Dupree ordinarily would not have turned a blind eye to. If he'd been willing to pull strings, he might have gotten permission to disperse his cousin's remains from the bridge. He wasn't totally above pulling strings, but he preferred not to, and he hadn't done so in this case.

It seemed to Morgan as they were driving over to Indiana—the bridge was not easily accessible from the Kentucky side—that the day couldn't go by too fast for his father, even if he'd had trouble keeping up with Crawford, who had led the two-car caravan. (Crawford, who some years before had climbed the middle span of the bridge, stoned, said he knew the way.) When Judge Dupree got out of his Toyota, after wedging it into a spot in front of a porch full of hookey-playing boys listening to Lynyrd Skynyrd at a high volume, he had said to Morgan, "I guess we shouldn't dawdle." When Morgan had reminded his father of the time, twenty-some years before, when he had led his sons and Uncle Louis into the L&N yards, an adventure that involved criminal trespass, Judge Dupree said, "That was bad judgment on my part. Let's hope this turns out better. At least it's not raining."

It was a fine April day, the sky blue with high clouds, the warm air as soft as a bird's breast. Walking out onto the bridge, Morgan smelled the river below and none of the pollutants that normally plagued the local air. It was that kind of afternoon—certain things had been suspended or set aside. Though it was a workday, the river was full of pleasure boats buzzing about. The calliope on the restored nineteenth-century paddle wheeler docked at the Third Street wharf was playing something gay.

Morgan walked behind Lazaro and ahead of Crawford and his father. As Morgan saw it, it was youth and beauty first, age and (possibly) wisdom at the rear, and confusion in the middle.

Crawford said, "You still afraid of heights, Morg?"

Morgan said, "Yeah, sort of." He was studying Lazaro's back, thinking of the train that had plunged off a burning trestle in *The General.* His father had taken him and Crawford to see *The General* when they were children. The city's lone art theater, now long gone, had shown it. The movie had helped to shape Morgan's views on bridges.

Judge Dupree said, in a small voice, "Maybe we should stop here."

They were perhaps a hundred yards off the Indiana shore, under the second span. They stepped out of the tracks and onto a steel-plated platform. Two of the span-supporting beams came together here in a **V**. The spot apparently served as a picnic site: a pile of chicken bones and a brown-bagged quart bottle of beer sat in the **V**.

For a moment, the four men stood in a huddle, looking at the urn, looking at each other's shoes. Lazaro, who was sweating along his upper lip, held the urn out from his chest, as if he were inviting someone to take it from him. Morgan thought of himself when he was an acolyte in his parents' church, standing before the altar in his baggy-sleeved surplice, waiting for the preacher to relieve him of the offertory plates or a Communion vessel. Morgan remembered that Crawford had told him about being chewed out by the preacher, Sandy Broyles's father, for "one-handing" the pitcher of water used to dilute the wine. "This isn't a boardinghouse, son," the Reverend Broyles had said.

But there was no preacher here to take the urn from Lazaro's hands or to read from the Order for the Burial of the Dead. For a moment, Morgan, a nonbeliever, wished there were.

WHEN LAZARO HAD called to say that Louis had died, Morgan was sitting at the window in his darkened apartment, watching the Saturday night pedestrian traffic on his Upper West Side street. Gina had gone to the Thalia to see a horror double bill. Morgan didn't like horror movies. Also, Gina had said to him that night, as they were eating his *omelette avec champignons* (which he had for some reason tried to spice up with horse-radish), that she wished he wouldn't be so jealous of her friendships with her *New Yorker* colleagues. He'd made a remark about all the *New Yorker* people on the wedding reception guest list—"Do you really know Andy Logan well enough to invite her? And that Hamburger guy, too?"—after spending some time on the phone with his mother, who'd said he really should consider inviting this couple from Louisville and this old family friend from Baltimore ("It's not that far away, they could easily come up for the day") and that distant cousin from Raleigh and his cousin Gee who lived right over in New Jersey. And so, after Gina had done the dishes and called Cletus, an ostensibly gay fact checker who lived in the neighbor-hood, to see if he would accompany her to the Thalia (he would), she'd gone out. That had been four hours ago. During that time, Morgan had watched a basketball game, listened to a scratchy Janis Joplin record, re-moved several fuzzy-gray items from the vegetable crisper, and read part of a *New Yorker* piece about the space shuttle. During the last hour, he'd showered and brushed his teeth and poured himself a bourbon.

"He die now, Morgan," Laz said.

"Just this minute?" Morgan asked. The window was cracked open. It was early April. Spring had advanced to within a block or so of Morgan's apartment. He could feel its breath on his bare legs.

"*Sí.* Today. I hold his hand. *Esta muy fría.*"

This answer raised questions, though all that really mattered, he sup-posed, was that Uncle Louis was dead. Morgan took a sip of his bourbon and felt it tumble down his throat to his chest, where it dispersed like fireworks fizzles.

On the stoop across the street, a couple was kissing. One brownstone to the east and three floors up, the man who paraded about his apartment in a kimono or less stood at the window and drank a glass of what was white enough to be milk.

"Is the nurse there?" An in-home nursing service had been hired some weeks ago, after the cancer had been found to be spreading, after Uncle Louis had refused to enter the hospital. Morgan's father had helped with the arrangements and the bills.

"She watch tele-bision." Laz had trouble with the letter *v*. "She eat KingFish sandwich on couch in libbing room. She do not prepare new bags for Louis—glucose, you know? Maybe she sleep now. Maybe she went to Sebben-Elebben. Who knows? And so he is died."

Morgan was confused. How long had Uncle Louis been dead for? Laz's preference for the present tense befogged matters.

"Call my dad," Morgan said. He was remembering the warm smell of the inside of Uncle Louis's fedora, which had briefly been on his head that Thanksgiving night in 1961. He gazed at the man in the kimono, which was untied; he appeared to be wearing tiny black underwear. Maybe the milk, if that's what it was, was warm, a sleep aid.

"Yesterday he say, 'I love you, Laz.'" He wrestled the *v* into that word. "Maybe I go home now. Be *camarero*."

What had happened at the end of the night they either did or didn't see Mickey Rooney popped again into Morgan's head. He saw himself slumped in the stuffed armchair in his apartment that he'd found on the street, his eyelids listing under the weight of too much liquor, and then he saw Lazaro coming across the floor on his knees, barking like a dog, wearing the wraparound mirror sunglasses he'd bought in Times Square, and then, almost incredibly, licking Morgan's crotch through his L.L. Bean corduroys. Sober, Morgan might have resisted, but the long and short of it was that he didn't—he even put his hands in Lazaro's silky black hair during the act. A moment later, he was considering, as far as he was able to, the possible consequences of what had just happened (as well as noting that the window blinds hadn't been pulled all the way). What if Laz reported this to Uncle Louis? What if Gina somehow intuited —she was good at intuiting—that her husband-to-be had betrayed her with his father's cousin's boyfriend? The most immediate consequence, as Morgan could not help noticing, was that Laz hoped Morgan would return the favor. Laz had stood before him on his two tasseled feet, smiling a big drunken smile, and unloosened himself from his souvenir "I ♥ NY" briefs. *"Por favor, hombre,"* he said. And Morgan had done it, eyes shut, and then had gone to bed, leaving Lazaro to watch Johnny Carson on his own. Morgan had hardly talked to Laz the next day. His head ached terribly.

"Call my dad, Laz," Morgan said. "He can help you with the funeral parlor and things. And get the nurse off her ass."

"OK," Laz said, and then he started to cry. His cries were tremulous yips mixed with Spanish Morgan didn't understand. When he stopped, he said, as if he'd just bumped into Morgan on the street, "How is Gina?"

"She's OK." The man in the kimono had retired from the window. The couple that had been embracing on the stoop had parted. A man in a trench coat was being led down the block by a troika of borzois. The budding jazz singer who lived above Morgan was loudly making love with her boyfriend. Morgan was waiting for the night when she would break into scat. "You OK, Laz?"

*"Sí,"* Laz said. "I bring gift to the wedding, OK? He sends me to Ox-moor Mall to buy it. You know? There is store with beautiful fish in tanks. Sometimes I want to be one fish swimming. But then the big fish come and eat you for *desayuno.*"

Morgan said he liked tropical fish, too. It was calming to watch them.

"Maybe I have store with fish someday."

"You know my father's number, don't you?" Morgan said, trying to steer Laz back to the topic at hand.

"I call now? Not too late?"

Morgan said never mind, he would call.

He replenished his drink first. When he dialed the number, he got his mother, a night owl, who said, before Morgan could get a word in, "I'm glad you called. I was wondering if you should invite the Bagshaws. They've watched you grow up from the time you were a baby."

After Morgan got his father on the phone and repeated the news that his mother had relayed in the course of waking her husband, after his father had hung up (just before, Morgan judged, he lost it), Morgan had sat in the armchair from the street—the fabric was like horsehair, a scratchy texture, a chair in which you could almost do penance—and waited for Gina to come home. He loved her, he really did, even if he was not to be trusted.

ON THE BRIDGE, before they scattered the ashes, Judge Dupree told a story about being in the Kentucky militia with Louis during World War II.

"They sent us out to near Shepherdsville one weekend to march around and shoot at some targets. The captain, a short man named Sherman— Louis called him Tecumseh—was all over Louis. Louis's boot heels weren't together when he was standing at attention, his helmet wasn't on right, he lunged incorrectly when we had bayonet practice. Sherman said, 'You aren't going to kill any Japs that way, Mudge. You think this is Arthur Murray?'"

Morgan had a memory of Uncle Louis telling this story, except the person whom Captain Sherman was all over in that version was Morgan's father. No doubt Sherman had found both men deficient in similar ways.

Judge Dupree, standing a hundred feet above the Ohio River in a lightweight olive suit and a tie decorated with steam engines before the Civil War, the spring sunshine bathing his unsmooth cheeks and his long straight nose that was like a sculptor's idea of probity and his mild brow that gray hair fell onto, said, "It rained most of the weekend. We were wet as rats by the time we went to bed. We slept in a gym, thank goodness. Louis saw Tecumseh slip out in the middle of the night. 'Maybe he's gone to get another haircut,' Louis said. Tecumseh was bald, you see."

Crawford, who had relieved Laz of the urn, grinned at this. Morgan put a hand on his head and said to Laz, "*Sin* hair. The captain had no hair."

Laz nodded. Morgan wished he would take off the sunglasses. They made him look slightly criminal.

"Louis and I were lying on the floor, talking, and I said, 'Louis, if Hitler walked into this gym right now, what would you do?'

"And he said, 'Well, Billy, the first thing I'd do is tell him that if he laid a hand on my cousin, I'd blow his brains out. And the next thing I'd do is blow his brains out.'"

The riverboat calliope was playing something cheerful and old-timey. A gull landed on the span above them, then flew off, calling raucously.

Morgan said, "Thanks, Dad."

Judge Dupree had removed his glasses and was dabbing at his eyes. "You're welcome," he said.

LATER IN THE DAY, near sundown, after each had taken his turn with the ashes, after they'd been escorted off the bridge by a Jeffersonville, Indiana, policeman, after they'd been taken to the station (the officer was young and zealous, and Judge Dupree had refused to pull rank), after Judge Dupree had made a call to a federal marshal in his jurisdiction and had also vouched for Lazaro and after they'd been freed to cross back over the Ohio, Morgan noticed a gray smudge on Lazaro's shirt. Laz and Crawford and Morgan were by then in the Pine Room, one of Uncle Louis's watering spots before he'd quit drinking. Judge Dupree had gone home.

The smudge was between the second and third button on Laz's shirt. Morgan looked at his own hands finning on the table, like fish waiting for something to float down to them. Probably he had traces of Uncle Louis under his fingernails. There was a residue in the urn, which was out in the car. Morgan tried to remember if they'd locked the car.

When Crawford went to use the restroom, Laz said, "Morgan, I make you dinner tonight?" He was still wearing his sunglasses.

Morgan said, "I think I better eat with my parents." Tomorrow he would fly back to New York and sleep in Gina's arms. He took a sip of his bourbon, the first drink of the day he'd allowed himself. "Crawford and I will work on Dad to get your visa situation expedited."

Lazaro seemed unimpressed by this. Or perhaps he didn't understand the word "expedite." He said, "OK."

"I hope you'll come to the wedding," Morgan said.

"Maybe," Laz said.

They talked about money. Uncle Louis had left some to Laz, but he wouldn't receive it until certain debts had been paid. The house would probably have to be sold.

"I'll find somebody for you to stay with in New York," Morgan said. "When you come for the wedding."

"Boy or girl?" Lazaro was having his third martini of the day. He stirred it with a finger. Morgan felt a loafer on his foot.

Crawford returned to the table and said, "Guess who I saw in the john?"

Morgan didn't guess. He let Laz's foot rest on his. What was the harm?

Crawford said, "The Reverend Alfred Lloyd Broyles Sr. You know how it's a law of thermodynamics that two men standing before urinals with their dicks in their hands can't pee? So, after about an hour of this, I said, 'Reverend Broyles, it's me, Crawford Dupree.' And he said, 'Well, goodness gracious, Crawford, what a pleasant surprise!' And he asked all about you and me, said he'd heard Sandy was going to officiate at your wedding, and told me what he was doing with his golden years, shot a ninety-two today, said that he didn't know Uncle Louis had died, missed the notice in the paper somehow. I said we'd just scattered him in the river and he said, 'God bless you, Crawford, and God bless Louis.'"

"And God bless Morgan and Gina," Lazaro said, raising his martini glass.

"And Lazaro," Morgan said. "And Jacques."

"And that waitress over there," Crawford said, "who smiled at me as I passed by."

# 14

# World Ever After

WHEN THEY PULLED into Crawford's driveway, Mrs. Dupree asked Lavell to leave the car running for a moment. There was a story on the radio that she wanted to hear the end of. It was about a young man from India, a Christian, who had been in the north tower of the World Trade Center when it collapsed. He had made it from the eighty-first floor to near an exit on the mezzanine when concrete and steel came pouring down. He had told the terrified people he was huddled with, many of whom he took to be nonbelievers, to shout out the name of Jesus. He said that acceptance of the Lord would bring them everlasting peace. He said they must plead for the blood of Jesus to save them. He said that he knew he was soon going to be in heaven and that he had asked only that something soft kill him. (What soft thing could he have been thinking of? Lavell wondered.) Of all those who had proclaimed Jesus' name on the mezzanine of the north tower, only the man from Calcutta was spared. Now he was taking his story to churches around the country. He was on a mission to bring people face-to-face with Jesus. He said the only name that could save you was Jesus'.

The voice of the Indian man gave way to a choir singing "Ein feste Burg." Mrs. Dupree had sung this hymn just last Thursday at the funeral for her friend Kitten Crutcher, the daughter of Aurelia, whose prize magnolia Crawford had struck with a car in 1966. And she'd sung it at another funeral earlier that fall—she couldn't remember whose. And it had been the recessional hymn in the service for her own husband ten months ago. She'd had to choose the music for Bill's service, because, even though she'd told him to write down his instructions, he'd never got around to it. Once he'd said, "The standard Order for the Burial of the Dead will be fine," and she'd said, "I need to know more than that." He'd been forgetful in his old age. Or was it more that he'd been willful and stubborn? She'd suggested he make an appointment with a neurologist and have his memory checked, but he'd ignored her. Well, that was water under the bridge, wasn't it?

"Imagine," she said, looking at Crawford's house. It was still a weather-beaten gray and it was still small and no doubt it was still drafty and also still contained the cat whose fur made her eyes water. On the stoop were three jack-o'-lanterns, a few days past their prime. One seemed to sneer at her. It had slit eyes and two triangular fangs.

Lavell, who had driven Mrs. Dupree's Camry all five hundred miles from Kentucky, never once exceeding the speed limit, said, "Yes, ma'am." He tapped the steering wheel, giving no hint of what he was imagining.

Kendra said, "Can we get out now, Dad?" Kendra was with them because Claudette, her mother, was in Hawaii with her new husband. They'd been married in September, but had postponed their honeymoon until now, the second week in November. They'd gotten a deal on airfares.

"Sure," Lavell said, turning off the engine but leaving the radio on.

"Faith is all we have, Lavell," Mrs. Dupree said. "You remember how Jesus slept through that terrible storm when he was on the little boat with his disciples? And how he calmed it with a word?" Sometimes, as she lay alone at night, after she'd said her prayers, she conjured up Jesus on the rocking fishing boat, water sweeping over the sides. She tried to concentrate on his sleeping face, mild but masculine, bearded but not ungroomed, none of the pain and dismay that would be there when he was hanging naked on the cross. Each time she hoped Jesus would take her hand and lead her into the land of Nod, and on some nights he did.

"It's a story that makes you think, yes ma'am," Lavell said. She'd cited this bit of scripture to him before. He opened his door and the warning bell ding-dinged. He took the key out of the ignition, glancing at her, hoping she'd finished listening to the radio. She was gazing at Crawford's house. She was wearing a black beret and a maroon turtleneck sweater; in between, almost like a surprise, like someone peeping out of a hole, was her small face, smooth in places, wrinkled like an old piece of fruit in others. From her nose hung a silver drop of moisture. She had the beginnings of a cold. She'd been drinking her distilled water all day, sometimes mixing powdered vitamin C into it.

"I'll get the bags," Lavell said.

"We can't be afraid," she said. "We can't live like that."

She saw her son standing at the door, on crutches. He'd fallen off a ladder while cleaning the gutters and had broken his ankle. She didn't know why he was so accident-prone. Of course, he'd always been temperamental, moody, and thus more likely to tumble from high places or walk heedlessly into the path of a bicyclist—not that she thought he had it coming to him. She worried about the damage that might have been done to his brain by the bicyclist. He was on an antidepressant now and had taken a leave from his teaching job. She didn't know what he did with himself during the day. She hoped he wasn't drinking. He'd restrained himself when he'd visited her in the summer, but who knew what he did out of her sight, in his house that was hardly big enough to accommodate one guest, not to mention three. Maybe she shouldn't have come. She didn't think he really wanted her to, hobbled as he was, grumpy as he'd sounded on the phone. But she'd wanted to see her grandchildren. And she wanted to see what Crawford would make of Lavell, whom she'd recently offered one of her empty bedrooms. Lavell was being evicted from the cottage he rented from the real estate agent. She'd surprised him with her offer. She'd surprised herself—it had just come out of her mouth, unbidden almost, like a wish that had become too big for its hiding place. Later, she'd qualified her offer, saying he was more than welcome to stay until he found something better. She would give him everything free—room, board, telephone, laundry—in exchange for yard work and a few odd jobs. He'd said, "It's mighty tempting, Mrs. Dupree," but he hadn't said yes.

Crawford came out on the stoop, crutches and all, as if to welcome her and Lavell and Kendra, who had gone next door to befriend the Effs' papillon, which was barking and dancing at the end of its chain.

THANKSGIVING WASN'T FAR off, but the grass was still green and vinca was blooming in the border garden and the backyard magnolia was budding. Crawford had planted the tree three falls ago, in a fit of nostalgia, thinking that if he stood alongside it in May or June (when spring came to his part of Wisconsin) he'd be able to smell April in Kentucky. But the tree's flowers—it was a hardy variety, bred for the north —had been disappointing, with little scent. The big, creamy blossoms that appeared on his mother's two magnolias were as fragrant as a girl's neck, a girl dressed for a party. Not that he'd had a particular desire three falls ago to put his nose in the neck of a girl dressed for a party. He and Michelle, who didn't believe in perfume and didn't own party shoes or even a little black dress, had been getting along fine then.

Mrs. Dupree, leaning on the cheap metal cane she'd gotten to replace the one she'd run over with her car one day last week when everything had gone wrong, inspected one of the magnolia's fuzzy green buds and said to Michelle, "The world is so strange, dear, sometimes I'm not sure where I am."

"You're in Wisconsin, Mom, among friends and cows," her son said. "Can't you smell the cows?" There *was* a hint of cow pasture in the air.

Michelle frowned at Crawford, who was standing by the garden with Lavell. A week ago, she'd told Rolf, the symphony tubaist, that they had to stop their affair. She'd said she was sick with guilt; she had rashes on her throat and bottom, which she took to be manifestations of her infidelity. But she already missed him, the prickly short hairs on his nape, his grabable paunch, his gentleness. Crawford had been so remote since he'd been run over by the bicyclist and then he'd disappeared into grief for his father. And now he was hopping around on one leg when he wasn't sitting in front of the TV watching Donald Rumsfeld and Rear Admiral Stufflebeem or doing whatever he did on his computer.

"What'd he say?" Mrs. Dupree asked Michelle. "He talks so low."

"Oh, nothing," Michelle said. "I have a friend whose roses are still blooming, if you can believe that."

Michelle and Mrs. Dupree walked to the other side of the yard, under the sugar maple. In September, following a brief cold snap, the leaves had turned golden—they were like tuba notes, sumptuous. When it warmed up again, Michelle had spent hours on the deck, wishing the light falling through the tree would fall on her in perpetuity, trying to read and not think about Rolf, whom she hadn't yet given up. She'd been on the deck when Crawford fell from the ladder. She'd only half-registered it, a body falling out of the blue autumn sky filled with golden maple leaves, and didn't immediately get out of her chair. When she did get up, realizing that it was her husband lying next to the cotoneaster pyracantha, with its orange berries that the birds loved, his face all twisted in pain, she thought, Maybe it's because I'm cheating on him that he fell. Does he know? Later, after she'd taken him to the hospital and brought him home and was making dinner, her daughter, Caroline, had said, "You broke your leg in March, Philip got a black eye in August, and now Dad breaks his ankle, plus he'd already broken his head. So when do you think something will happen to me?" Michelle had said, "I think you'll be spared," but she'd wondered.

Mrs. Dupree was saying something about hot spots in the ocean and then she was saying something about the Muslims and the war in Afghanistan and then she was talking about Ida, her maid of forty-some years, who had given notice last month—as if all these things were somehow related. The weather was strange, the Muslims wanted to kill all the Christians and the Jews, and Ida was going to leave Mrs. Dupree before Christmas, though she'd promised to cook the Christmas turkey and help put up the decorations before she went. Mrs. Dupree hadn't told Crawford about Ida's quitting, because she knew Crawford would blame her, his mother, for Ida's departure, even though Ida had become difficult in her old age. She hadn't told Morgan either, because Morgan was up in New York, visiting his son. Divorce was so hard on children— by the way, did Michelle know that Morgan had been seeing Lucy?

Michelle said she did know. Morgan and Lucy had come for dinner at Mrs. Dupree's last summer, when Michelle's family was there for a visit. Lucy had been rather quiet.

"I just don't know what to think about that," Mrs. Dupree said.

"Will you get someone to replace Ida?" Michelle asked, looking west. The sun was going down, leaving in its wake streamers of pink and orange. It seemed almost too gaudy to be midwestern, but then, as Mrs. Dupree had suggested, you couldn't be sure where exactly you were nowadays. Wisconsin, where the snows of Michelle's childhood had sometimes fallen even before she'd decided what she was going to be for Halloween, may have been sliding southwest for years without her knowledge.

"I don't know where I'd find anybody like Ida at this stage of the game," Mrs. Dupree said. "But Lavell may come live with me."

"You mean he'd be your"—she wasn't sure what the right word was—"tenant?"

Mrs. Dupree said, "His landlady is putting him out on the street and I invited him in. Do you think Crawford would mind if I gave Lavell his room? It's a little bigger than Morgan's and the mattress is firmer. Of course, I could put him in Bill's office. There's a TV down there, in case he wants to watch sports. But it seems a shame to put him in the basement when there's so much space upstairs, don't you think?"

Michelle looked across the yard at Lavell. He seemed like a pleasant man, polite, a little shy, more at ease outdoors than in. Indoors, he'd kept his hands mostly in his jean pockets. He had accepted a glass of tap water from her, but only after he'd declined everything else she had in her refrigerator.

"It might be good to have someone around," Michelle said. "In case something should happen." She looked up through the not-quite-bare branches of the maple. A tree surgeon had recently advised her that the maple was ill, being eaten from within by a fungus, and might have to come down, but she was not ready to part with it. And look how it had rewarded her this fall!

"He's a brick," Mrs. Dupree said, taking a ball of Kleenex from her pocket and touching it to the tip of her nose. "He looked after his mother when she was on her deathbed."

A mob of starlings flew over, peppering the air with squeaks. Michelle watched them go and then she saw, up on the roof, near where the chimney that was in need of pointing poked out, her daughter. Kendra was with Caroline. They sat with their knees drawn up, hands flat against the gray asphalt shingles, balanced just so. They looked like paper dolls against the eastern sky darkening behind them. Between them and the edge of the roof was Button, his tabby belly flat to the shingles. He seemed to be frozen there. The pitch of the roof was steep. Michelle heard her daughter say, imploringly, "Oh, Button, come, please. Be a good sweet old cat and come to me right now."

Michelle said, "Caroline, you can't be up there. What are you thinking?"

Crawford said, "Caroline, get down."

Lavell said, "Kendra, come down, no fooling."

Mrs. Dupree said, "Oh, Lord, help them down!"

Caroline said, "Button got out through Daddy's window and we're trying to rescue him."

Michelle guessed the first part of this statement to be untrue. Button, being thirteen, was no longer adventurous; he could barely rouse himself to swat at one of those orange beetles that had been fluttering about the house this fall. The chances of him slipping out one of the windows in Crawford's office—which were screened, weren't they?—in order to walk on the roof in the last of the day's light, pleasant as it was, were not good. No, like the bear that went over the mountain, Caroline had probably climbed out on the roof to see what she could see, and taken Button and Kendra along for company.

Mrs. Dupree said, "Crawford got so high up in a tree once when he was little that we had to call the fire department to get him down."

"I don't think we need to call the fire department yet," Michelle said.

"I could've gotten down myself," said Crawford, whose ears were as sensitive as a rabbit's. "I just didn't feel like it." He addressed the rooftop. "Girls, go back the way you came. Button will follow you."

"No, he won't, Daddy. He's scared. I think he had a brain seizure."

"His eyes are bugged out," Kendra said. Kendra was a gangly girl, all bones and angles. She had a sharp voice and strong opinions.

From the ground, in the fading light, Button was a bump on the roof, his eyes imperceptible.

A train on the freight line that ran over to the Mississippi River sounded its horn.

There was a discussion about how to rescue Button, and it was decided that Lavell would do it, even though Lavell, as Kendra pointed out to everybody below, didn't even like cats.

"Be careful, Lavell," Mrs. Dupree said, as Michelle led him into the house. "We can't afford to lose you, too."

"Am I lost?" Crawford said.

"What, dear?" Mrs. Dupree asked.

Michelle and Lavell stopped in the kitchen and got an opened can of chicken-flavored Friskies out of the refrigerator. "Ambrosia," she said. "No cat on a roof can resist it."

They climbed the two flights of stairs to her husband's attic office. It was a low-ceilinged room, with a couple of east-facing dormered-out windows. There was a desk, bookshelves, file cabinets, and a cot, which Lavell would be sleeping on tonight. Suitcases and lamps and framed posters and boxes of old toys and LPs and the bongos Crawford got for Christmas in 1964 were piled together in a corner. The jumble of things depressed Michelle, but Crawford didn't seem to mind. It was where he read and napped and (when he'd been able to hold down a job) prepared for school. His broken ankle hadn't deterred him from coming up, even though the stairs were steep and narrow. He wouldn't let Michelle bring his laptop downstairs. "If I fall," he'd said, "you can trade me in for a more agile model of spouse. Or sue me for self-abuse. Or both." Sometimes she imagined her husband wrapped head to toe in a white body cast—peepholes for his eyes, a slot for a drinking straw, some improvised opening for his pecker, which she hadn't seen in months. Immobilized, he'd be safe from harm, wouldn't he?

Lavell and Michelle stood by the window from which the screen had been removed, listening to Caroline make further appeals to Button. A beetle flew in and landed on the space bar of Crawford's laptop. It seemed to Michelle that the sky had gotten darker in the last few minutes.

It was her plan to have Lavell entice Button with the cat food, but how would he carry the can and also negotiate the roof? Maybe it would have been simpler for Lavell to go up on a ladder and approach Button from below. Or maybe they should just let Button figure things out for himself, assuming he was not actually having a brain seizure. Though that would still leave the problem of getting the girls off the roof. Caroline would not easily abandon her post.

"I'll tell you what," Michelle said to Lavell. "Why don't you go up there and see if you can get the girls to come down and I'll bang on the can. Button salivates at the sound."

"We'll give her a try," Lavell said, and he slid out the window. He was a slender, compact man, just the shape of person who might slide out a window without bumping his head. His hair was slightly longer than a buck private's. He had a small, cute nose. Only his ears stuck out in a vulnerable way.

She went over to Crawford's desk to get something to bang the can with. The orange beetle that somebody had told her was an Asian species had moved from the space bar on Crawford's PowerBook to the V key. The beetle had lovely black spots, like a leopard. Michelle took a pen from a drawer, stood at the window, and rapped the pen against the rim of the Friskies can. She leaned out the window and in her most cheerful part-time homemaker's voice yelled, "Dinner, Button!" And then she went back to Crawford's desk and looked again at his computer screen. She touched the Shift key and the screen brightened. Crawford had started an e-mail to somebody named Sidney. "Dear Sidney," it said. "While hopping around on one foot today, while waiting for my mother and her gardener and her gardener's daughter to arrive from Kentucky in their one-horse shay, I thought of thirteen ways. . . ." The letter went no further. Who was Sidney? She could not for the life of her think of a single Sidney of her acquaintance. It was a name that, like Herb or Myron or Chet, seemed not of this era. It might have been the name of one of her father's golfing buddies. She thought of Sydney Greenstreet, the portly actor who wore the fez in *Casablanca*. And then—duh, to quote her daughter—she remembered the young woman from whom Philip had taken ventriloquism lessons for a few months, whom Crawford had driven down to Kentucky for that convention in July. Wasn't her first name Sidney? Was this the Sidney Crawford was writing to? Her e-address was Ventingsid@mailpouch.com. Michelle gazed at the screen and tap-tapped the can—nothing an old cat on a roof would be able hear. She looked at the photograph above Crawford's desk, of his grandfather with his swollen, cantankerous head wrapped in a bandage. The human head was such a strange and delicate thing. Perhaps, she thought, Crawford's relationship with Sidney was one that lacked an illicit element, if she could put it that way. She wanted to put it that way. She decided not to go trolling through her husband's e-mail. She studied the spots on the beetle's wings. There were eight on one and nine on the other, an asymmetry that she chose to find not puzzling.

When they came in the window—cat first, Lavell last—Michelle, angrier than she meant to be, said to her daughter, "I'd appreciate it if you stayed off the roof from now on. I mean, crimini, Caroline."

"We were trying to rescue Button, Mom," Caroline said. She held out the palms of her hands to show how the shingles had marred them. "Did you want him to die?"

"Safe and sound," said Lavell, who had a scratch across his cheek.

On the second night of her visit, Mrs. Dupree had a dream in which her late husband passed before her eyes in his old tan raincoat and a railroad engineer's cap, a little striped thing that didn't fit his head right. He was walking in what she took to be her backyard, though she didn't know where the glads or dahlias came from (she didn't raise such flowers), and the cunning little pagoda had been appropriated from a movie she'd seen when she was sixteen or seventeen. "What was the name of that movie?" she asked herself, as she glanced at her wandering husband, who looked younger than he'd been in years, younger even than he was in the picture of the robed sixty-year-old man the newspaper had run in its obituary. He waved to her, smiled at her, his smile traveling all the way across the yard as quick and easy as light coming through a just-opened slat. She didn't wave back or say anything. She was busy sharpening pencils, which perhaps he couldn't see—he'd always been oblivious to life's boring details. The sharpener was one of those five-cent, thimble-size things that she used to buy at the Rexall store for the boys to take to school. The lead kept breaking off as curls of pencil shavings collected at her feet.

When she awakened, she smelled the flowers that Michelle had put on Philip's bureau. The flowers were lilies and the scent was thick—a bit too sweet for her taste, frankly. She raised herself from Philip's too-soft mattress and sat on the edge of the bed, waiting for the room to clarify itself. Her ophthalmologist had advised her to have a cataract removed—it was a simple operation, he'd said—but she'd balked at it. The words he'd used—"emulsify," "irrigate," "aspirate"—had made her feel like a lab specimen. The furniture emerged from the dark like animals coming out of the woods. Over in a corner, leaning against a bookshelf, was Philip's dummy. It had a beanie on its plastic skull and a noose around its neck. She had asked Philip about his ventriloquism last night and he'd said that he wasn't taking lessons anymore; he did it on his own a little, in private. Last summer in Louisville, he'd turned down a request to perform for her and Uncle Morgan and the rest. Crawford had said, "St. Philbert the Abbot of Nuts is a bit of a recluse," and Philip had said, "Yeah? Well? So?" and then he'd headed for where he wouldn't be visible, at least to his father. There was something going on between them that she didn't know the depth of. She hadn't inquired about it; she hadn't inquired about the noose either.

She put on her bathrobe and slippers and went slowly down the creaking, uncarpeted stairs, caneless, gripping the banister, thinking that the movie with the pagoda must have starred Fred Astaire, who had been built like a sharp no. 2 pencil, hadn't he? His feet, wherever he set them, spelled his name in flawless script. Bill had always been ready to dance with her, back in the days when dancing was as normal as breathing. Bill danced—what was the word?—gamely, shuffling his feet, letting her lead almost. Anything faster than a fox-trot was beyond him. She wondered if Lavell had ever done any ballroom dancing. He was nimble, nicely proportioned. He'd look handsome in a suit, she bet. She wished he would make up his mind about whether he was going to live in her house. It made her anxious, not knowing. Crawford had had little reaction when she'd told him that she'd offered Lavell his room. "Fine" was all he said.

At the bottom of the stairs she found herself in moonlight, silver lapping at her veiny ankles and threadbare shins. It was moonlight shed by a waning moon, but it held her for a moment, distracted her from whatever purpose she'd had for leaving her bedroom. She felt in her bathrobe pocket for a Kleenex—her nose was dripping again—and gazed at the clutter of things in the living room, where earlier that evening they had all (with the exception of Philip) watched *Rear Window.* The Raymond Burr character, who had chopped up his wife like stew meat, had reminded her a little of her new plumber, Mr. Betz, a dour, heavyset man who had been recommended to her after her plumber of four decades had died. This kind of thing was another reason she hoped Lavell would accept her offer. People were always taking advantage of widows. Some of the stories she'd heard were appalling, such as the one about how Georgieanne Shawcross had let her hairdresser's husband take over her finances and then lost tens of thousands in the stock market before you could say "Jack Robinson." She, Mary Louise Dupree, couldn't be expected to take on the entire world herself. She was eighty years old, for Pete's sake. God would watch out for her, of course. He had put up a hedge around her, as He had around Job, though the hedge, as Job had learned, could not keep out all who would do a person ill.

On the far side of the room, where the moonlight didn't reach, she saw a lump on the couch. During her stay, Philip had been camping out in the basement—the cat slept down there, too, thank goodness—and she guessed the lump wasn't him. Maybe it was Michelle. She and Crawford had seemed to be giving each other wide berth; not a word of endearment had passed either's lips in two days, as far as Mary Louise had heard. She moved closer, her head cocked in a worried way. On the floor next to the couch, standing as if waiting to be filled with a Frankenstein-size foot, was Crawford's boot-cast.

She peered down at her son. The blanket was drawn up to his chin. His mouth hung open, as if something fantastic had just fetched up before him. What did he dream about, she wondered. Did he ever dream about his dead father? Did he ever dream about her? He had rarely ever, even as a child, told her any of his secrets, though, the Lord knew, there had been plenty of times when his feelings (especially about her) had come pouring out. She wondered if he didn't hate her, for all the times she had let her temper get the better of her and for all the times she had browbeat his father and for all her failures to follow Jesus' teachings and love others as she loved herself. She leaned over her son in the hope that she could see through his skin to the workings of his mind. She had this notion that she would hear something like the sound of Bill's old Bell and Howell film projector whirring and that the images she'd see would be something like Bill's home movies, except that the images would not be cheerful. In Crawford's head, she suspected, there would be no movies of, say, the Easter egg hunt on his grandparents' lawn in 1956 or of the Christmas when he gave her a little ceramic pot with a jade plant in it, which still lived, miraculously, forty years later.

She went into the kitchen and got a glass of the bottled water she'd brought with her from Kentucky and came back into the living room.

She sat in the one armchair that Button didn't like to nest in and watched her older son sleep. He'd be fifty-two next month, five days before Christmas. His birthday had gotten lost more than once in the holiday rush. She remembered him saying—he must have been thirteen or fourteen—"I know I don't rate like the Christ child." She had reacted badly to this comment, it was true, telling him that Christmas was a time of giving, not getting, and that she had not forgotten his, Crawford's, birthday despite her many tasks; he would receive his presents, and if a couple of them came five days late, she hoped he would forgive her. Sitting in Crawford's stuffed chair, she heard how shrill her voice of almost forty years ago was—preposterously, she had asked him to imagine the magi crossing the cold desert on their camels with their carefully selected gifts for the little Lord Jesus: she was like them, she'd claimed—and she saw again the anger pinking Crawford's cheeks that pimples had begun to speckle, his mouthful of new braces and rubber bands that were always popping out and that inhibited his speech so that he didn't always finish sentences. One summer a few years later, when his hair was falling down into his face, he had tried to give up talking entirely. He'd taken a vow of silence; it seemed to be part of his experiment with Buddhism, a college flirtation. Though she'd wondered if it wasn't simply hostility, a way of silencing her. Nonetheless, she and her husband and Morgan had tried to respect Crawford's wishes. The second night of his journey into monkhood, she heard him talking on the phone to his girlfriend.

"What are you doing up?" His voice startled her.

"I'm up and down all night. It's the way it is when you're my age." She thought it better not to ask why he was on the living room couch. "Does your ankle hurt at night?"

"About the same as day." By December, he'd said, he should be able to jettison his crutches and prowl around with a cane. She'd imagined them dueling with canes, like children with wood swords. It was such a silly thought she couldn't believe it had come into her head.

It pleased her when he asked about her hip. She went on for several minutes about her health, about some problem she was having with her lower GI tract and how her alternative doctor (whom she consulted in addition to Dr. Fawcett, her apathetic internist) had prescribed an organic hormone for something and a daily dose of kelp for her thyroid, just a tiny bit because too much of it interfered with sleep. "Some days I hurt like the dickens," she said.

Crawford said he was sorry to hear that.

She sipped her water. "Does the drug you take for your head—is it helping?"

"I get up in the mornings with a smile on my face and a song in my heart."

She doubted there was any truth in this wisecrack.

"Actually, I have fewer headaches. I'm making it."

She wanted to lean over and touch his head, where it had struck the pavement in New York. But she was deep in the chair and it was a long lean for a short old woman.

"Do you remember Dad's home movies, how we'd watch them in the basement? He would set up the projector on a card table and put the screen back by the Ping-Pong table and then he'd call us to come downstairs."

"Usually he'd send Morgan or me upstairs to get you. And then we'd sit in the dark until you arrived."

"I had kitchen detail, my dear," she said, her voice rising. It had been a habit of hers to run late, but sometimes she had a reason. Her children were impatient. "Anyway, we'd always have to move the screen a little or Dad would have the projector in the wrong position and the picture would be half on the ceiling. And Morgan would be saying, 'Focus, Dad.'"

She looked across the room and there at the bottom of the stairs, where the moonlight lay, silvery as the surface of Bill's portable movie screen, stood a person. Judging by his poor posture and the whiteness of his hair and the smile that was the smile of a man free of most earthly burdens, the person was her late husband. There was no way to confirm this except to check it with Crawford.

Crawford was looking at the ceiling. He said, "The thing about those movies is that Dad isn't in any of them. The person you would most like to see isn't there."

She didn't think she needed to point out that his father was always behind the camera.

"Sometimes I feel he's in the room with me," she said, stretching the truth a little, for tonight was the first time she'd seen him in anything other than a dream. He was still over there, at the bottom of the stairs. She noticed that he was wearing the red cable-stitched sweater he'd had on the night he fell down in the kitchen, the last time he was ever in the house. She'd given him the sweater for Christmas or a birthday—she couldn't remember which. It had come home with one of the boys a few days after he'd gone into the hospital. She'd known it wasn't going to come home on him.

Crawford didn't say anything.

She wasn't certain what it meant that Bill was here, as solid as flesh almost. She didn't believe in ghosts and she didn't have visions, though now and then, during prayer, she'd felt the presence of the Holy Spirit, a tingling in her spine, which couldn't be explained only by the fact she was on her knees or humbly bent forward (being on her knees was too painful nowadays). Was Bill signaling to her that in the world beyond, the world ever after, that in God's infinite arms, he was fully himself? Was that smile, which went on and on like some boundless thing (it wasn't painted on, was it?), a signal that he had forgiven her for making him get down on the kitchen floor to clean up that spill of acidophilus, forgiven her for all her other sins?

She looked at her son, his hands folded on his chest. She was afraid to ask him if he saw what she saw. She couldn't have known how alike they really were.

She heard a train whistle, far-off, lonesome. Three toots—two longs and a short. When she looked across the room again toward the stairs, she saw nothing but light.

# 15

# One of Their Heads Was Green

Morgan was working on a fire. Crawford was in the pantry, clumping around on his bad foot, hunting for a dish to cook the meat loaf in. William and the dog were down by the lake, checking out the ice. Sidney was on her back on the living room sofa, listening to a band called Modest Mouse. Modest Mouse came out of its mouse hole and sang about a blood transfusion. Freeze your blood and stab it into me, Modest Mouse pleaded.

Lucy was in the kitchen, running water over a green pepper, a pepper so pretty and shiny, its curves so inviting, it might have been a mock-up of a pepper. She saw herself in the window above the sink, washing this vegetable she'd bought that morning from a Korean man in Manhattan, and looked away. Was she going to have a moment this weekend when she concluded that Morgan's professed love for her was too good to be true, just a kindness extended to his father's spinsterish law clerk, a piece of condescension? What was the meaning of all his throat-clearing in her presence?

Lucy was still tired from Thanksgiving and from the day before that, when she'd flown to New York, and from the days before that, when the phones at the West End Legal Clinic had rung off the hook. (She'd taken a job at the clinic after the one with the public defender fell through.) When she'd arrived at Morgan's apartment—Crawford and Sidney were already there—Morgan was in the throes of cooking. There was sweat on his brow and a mixture of flavors (but mostly bourbon) on his breath. He'd kissed her quickly, given her wine and pizza, and let her help him peel boiled chestnuts. Later that night, he'd sucked on her raw, chestnut-stained fingers individually. In the morning, he'd risen early to tend to the turkey. He made stuffing with the chestnuts and dried cranberries and sausage and some rooty thing she'd never heard of. He fixed yams with a lemon sauce and the spoon bread that Ida, the Duprees' now retired maid, was celebrated for. He went at the job a bit nervously, as if he were responsible for the happiness of a whole houseful of people— an extended family, say, with ex-spouses and stepchildren by the bushel —though there was only the four of them. (William ate dinner with Gina.) Morgan had given his older brother and his girlfriend the task of preparing dessert. Sidney had proposed they buy a pie at the grocery, but Crawford said he would make something. During dinner, Mrs. Dupree had called—she couldn't believe what Crawford had done, leaving his family, and she kept saying so until Crawford hung up on her—and Crawford's banana cream pie had come out of the oven scorched, the crust like earthenware.

The remains of the pie had not come north with them to this house at the foot of the Shawangunks. The house belonged to a friend of Morgan's, a woman named Melanie. It was a second home, a lakeside cottage that had been added on to and spruced up until it might have passed as the first home of a lawyer who represented people in the film industry. This was what Melanie's husband did. Or was he now her former husband? Lucy couldn't remember all of what Morgan had told her, though she did remember that Morgan had said he himself had had a crush on Melanie at one point. The husband, or ex-husband, was of Chinese descent. There were no pictures of him in the house. There was a snapshot of Melanie and her twin boys on the refrigerator, alongside a 2001 calendar from a New Paltz well digger. The boys, who were shorter than the canoe paddles they held at their sides, had dark, solemn, beautiful faces, though their cowlicks suggested they were hatching plans to lead secret lives. Melanie's face flickered beneath a cloud of black hair; in sneakers, she was slightly taller than her paddle. Morgan had said she was a sportswriter. Lucy imagined her in a locker room, nose-high to a defensive end's navel.

Lucy diced the pepper. She sliced an onion, and it made her eyes water, made her remember her father saying "An onion that doesn't make you cry is a nonion." Her father believed that onions made you stronger; he ate them for breakfast, along with his eggs.

Lucy ventured into the pantry. Crawford had got himself and the contraption that protected his wounded ankle up on a chair so that he could search a cabinet.

She said, "Maybe Sidney could do that." She didn't want to disapprove of Crawford's liaison with Sidney. Morgan had said, "I think my brother is having a brain spasm. It won't last. Though she is appealing in her own way." Lucy didn't want to disapprove of an allegedly appealing young woman who lay on a couch listening to music while her hobbled, almost elderly boyfriend searched the pantry for a meat loaf dish. But she did. Perhaps tugging on Sidney's nose ornament would get her off the couch. Did Morgan find nose ornaments "appealing"? Or green toenails, which matched the color of her top? Why would a ventriloquist even bother to paint her toenails?

Crawford said, "I found a Power Rangers lunch box and a bunch of candles."

From Lucy's angle, Crawford looked somewhat like his father. Was it because they were both accident prone, both a little hapless? Or was it because Crawford, like his father before him, had fallen in love with a much younger woman? His Adam's apple seemed large, like an inflamed gland.

"Here," Lucy said, extending a hand. "Let me help you down."

Modest Mouse came out of its mousehole and sang—rapped, chanted, somethinged—about the beauty of dirt.

Morgan said, "Burn, baby, burn."

Crawford handed Lucy two dusty yellow candles, their wicks black. "We can have meat loaf by candlelight."

AT DINNER, DURING the portion of the conversation that was devoted to world affairs, William said he knew a boy named Ben Laden who got picked on at school.

"He's kind of a dweeb, anyway," William said.

"Dweebs of the world, unite!" Sidney said.

Zeke, William's chocolate Lab, looked up from his spot by the fireplace. Sidney and Zeke had rapport. So did Sidney and William. It seemed to Lucy as if the three, a youth brigade, composed a kind of alliance against her. William hadn't given her the time of day, Zeke shied away from her, perhaps suspecting she was a cat person, and Sidney seemed to regard the adult company (with the possible exception of Crawford) as not what she'd bargained for.

Morgan's fire was guttering, but the candles cast cozy light. The wine in Lucy's juice glass—she'd decided they shouldn't use Melanie's stemware —appeared golden. Lucy looked across the table at Morgan. If she married him—not that he'd proposed—what would it be like to look across the table at him every night? What would he do with the next thirty years of his life? He didn't have a job and seemed disinclined to get one, even though he was a more or less employable sportswriter. She wondered if living off of inherited money, as Morgan did, would cause you to recede behind your eyes, as if behind a hedge, to escape detection.

Morgan asked William who had come to his mother's Thanksgiving dinner, and William said, "Nobody you would know, except for me and Mom and Nonna." Gina's mother lived alone in Providence now; Dieter, the anthropologist, had been killed in a plane crash in Guyana. This had happened not long after Gina and Morgan split up permanently. Morgan had gone to the memorial service in Providence but had not sat with Gina and William.

"Eric?" Morgan asked. "Was he there? Eric the Red-Handed Editor?"

"No."

"They're not seeing each other anymore?"

"I don't know."

"The fencing teacher? Mr. Mylasz? The Polish Flash? Did he come? Is your mom still taking fencing?"

"I guess."

"You guess she's still fencing or you guess he was at dinner, slashing the poor turkey with his épée?"

"What are you—the FBI?"

"Yeah, Morg, ease up," Crawford said.

"If you were on a desert island," Sidney said to William, trying to be helpful, while failing to note that William was already on a desert island, "what CDs would you want to have with you?"

"I don't know," he said, sticking his fork into a hill of mashed potatoes. It stood there, like a toy shovel in sand. Crawford had been in charge of the potatoes. He liked them thick, not thoroughly mashed, it seemed.

William left the table and sat in front of the TV, the one thing he might not be able to survive on a desert island without.

"Well," Morgan said. He tipped his empty glass toward his mouth. Then he went into the kitchen and got another bottle. Lucy caught his hand before he poured wine into her glass.

Crawford said to Morgan that he'd recently heard from their old high school French teacher, Mr. Bassett.

"Monsieur Le Chien? What prompted you to get in touch with him?"

Crawford told a story about running into a classmate in Louisville, a lawyer who had tried cases in their father's court, who had run into another classmate, also a lawyer, who lived in Atlanta, who had bumped into Mr. Bassett at a restaurant in Orlando, Florida. Crawford had run down Mr. Bassett's e-mail address and written him. He was retired now, doing a lot of bowling and attending philately conventions. He lived in a nudist camp in Florida during the winter and in a nudist camp in Illinois during the summer.

"Is that possible?" Sidney said. "A nudist camp in Illinois?"

"The guy was hung like a stallion," Morgan said, and then seemed to retreat behind his beard to consider why he had offered this observation. Perhaps he was just having an off night.

"Ooh-la-la," said Sidney.

Crawford said to Lucy, "Morgan might be a good source on that. Monsieur Le Chien used to take a bunch of his students to Europe every summer. He'd do like fifteen countries in fifty days, a lot of them on bicycle. Morgan got to go twice. He was one of Bassett's faves." Crawford grinned at his younger brother, who had gone through life without being run over by a bicycle messenger and without having to resort to antidepressants and without running off with a very young ventriloquist.

"I walked through Mad King Ludwig's castle two summers in a row," Morgan said. "In Tangier, there was a boy who followed us everywhere, who kept saying, 'Muhammad Ali *est le roi.* You want to see Casbah? You want kef? *Allons, allons.* Muhammad Ali *est le roi.*' He was there the next summer, too, I swear, as soon as we got off the boat."

Lucy had once stood on a beach in Spain and looked through the shimmer toward North Africa. And now here was Morgan, this man whose true feelings she couldn't quite make out.

"When you got laid in Amsterdam the second time, Morg, was it the same girl, same price?"

"I didn't get laid in Amsterdam, Craw."

It worried Lucy that she couldn't tell whether he was lying. Why would he lie about five minutes in 1968 with an Amsterdam sex worker? If he didn't love her, Lucy, would he be too embarrassed to say so?

"I thought you did," Crawford said. "All of Bassett's other boys did, except maybe Goldstein."

"The token Jew?" Sidney asked. "The token Jew couldn't get laid? Unfair!"

Crawford said, "That was the scuttlebutt."

They had bought a pumpkin pie for dessert—Sidney's treat!—and Lucy went out to the kitchen to get it.

AFTER SHE'D SLEPT with Morgan for the first time, Lucy didn't see Judge Dupree in his ghostly apparel. For a couple of months, she'd kept an eye open for him, particularly when she was near railroad tracks, but she didn't really believe she'd see him. She hadn't mentioned the sightings to Morgan; she was afraid he might think her featherbrained. She had discussed with him her little romance with his father, though she had been careful not to tell him everything. He'd said he wouldn't put it in his book, if he ever wrote his book. (She wasn't sure she trusted him on that count.) She had asked him once if he believed in ghosts or spirits, and he'd said, a little pompously, like a sixteen-year-old who has just discovered the void, "I believe that you live and then you cease to live. The afterlife, angels, all that stuff, is pure invention." Anyway, Lucy was mostly relieved that the Judge no longer manifested himself to her. It was a perplexity she could do without.

Though there was the odd moment, such as about ten seconds ago, with Morgan inside her, when the Judge would rise up in Lucy's mind and she could hear him say, almost as if he were in the room, "If you would cast your eyes upon this, Lucy, I would be forever grateful." And she might for an instant almost feel inclined to reach out for the petition or brief that he held in his mottled, veiny, unmanicured hands, which she could see with her eyes closed. Though now, as a practical matter, with Morgan gripping her hands—her arms were outflung; she and Morgan were like Popsicle-stick crosses Elmer's-glued together—she couldn't very well reach for anything.

She opened her eyes and saw a portion of Morgan's hairy head and a smaller portion of his naked back as he silently and diligently went in and out. She saw the unmoving blades of the ceiling fan and the outline of the framed movie poster on the wall to her left. There was no white-haired gentleman holding papers out to her. This was a venue, she thought, where a ghost like Judge Dupree would be careful not to tread, even if he had something urgent that needed seeing to. If for some reason he'd found his way here, to this house in the New York countryside, he'd be polite enough to wait outside the door, or more likely down the hall, out of earshot of them.

She pushed aside the thought of her former employer and freed her hands from Morgan's and turned him on his side and then onto his back. She hoped the change of position might help him along. For the past few minutes, it had been as if he'd been trying to do a job that he was not entirely suited for—darning a sock, fixing a faucet, assembling something for which the instructions were in Japanese—and as if she had been watching him grow quietly exasperated from across the room. She was sympathetic to his difficulties, though it was his own fault for having opened that third bottle of wine. She was tired, ready to go to sleep, having had a pleasant shudder of an orgasm some time ago.

She went at it with pluck, but it didn't do any good and eventually, after he'd stopped moving, she leaned down and kissed him near the center of his forehead, where she'd once seen something like a nerve throbbing, as if with ambition or desire.

He said, "Maybe I'll give up drinking for Lent."

"Lent's three months off. How about for Advent?"

"Could I have a glass of wine on Christmas?"

She lay alongside him, holding his hand, listening to the furnace hum. The air that came through the vents whistled.

Morgan cleared his throat and said, "You remember when my dad had that operation for his bladder in 1997 or '98?"

"It was '99," she said. She didn't add: about a year after your dad and I kissed on my red couch.

"Right. I came down from New York with William. I promised him that if he went with me to see his grandfather, I'd take him to the races at Churchill Downs. So we went to the hospital on Saturday morning, the day after the operation, and one of Dad's bridge buddies was there, the one known as Sunbeam. And my dad was in this strangely ebullient mood—given the circumstances, I mean, such as the fact that the urologist had just snipped off a piece of prostate tissue and the fact that when Dad peed he did so through a catheter and the fact that the urine in the bag hanging off the side of the bed was the color of blood. Maybe it was the pain medicine he was taking that made him giddy or the simple fact that he'd survived the operation. Of course, he was also a person who refused to be unhappy if at all possible. Anyway, Dad and Sunbeam were chatting and at one point Dad said, 'Bemis, I thought they were going to make a Jew of me when they put this darned catheter on.' And they laughed and talked about something Hateful had said over at the club about Bill Clinton and then Sunbeam went out the door with his Ben Hogan hat—he had a golf game to get to—and it dawned on me that by my father's definition I and my brother and our sons were Jews. And that my uncircumcised father had probably not even noticed that his offspring were different."

"Probably he averted his eyes when the opportunity came up, assuming he even had his glasses on and could see anything at all," Lucy said, wondering why Morgan had told her that story, looking past his ribs at the sore little tuckered-out puppyish thing curled up at the base of his belly. She hoped it would sleep the whole night through.

"Do you think that remark was anti-Semitic?"

"I'd guess it was innocent," Lucy said. It had occurred to her that she'd known Morgan's father better than Morgan had. "Your dad was an innocent in a lot of ways. He once told me a story about a Jewish lawyer he'd known in college and how he had to overcome his provincial prejudices. He didn't have a mean bone in his body that I ever saw."

"He didn't care for drunks," Morgan said. "Though I guess he did make an exception for Uncle Louis."

"He had a few flaws. He didn't seem to mind letting me take Duff to the vet's on the government's time, to get his nails clipped, though this may have been your mother's idea."

"That alone should keep him from beatification," Morgan said.

"Your dad was full of love," she said.

"'What Do You Love More Than Love?'" Morgan said. "Do you know that song?"

"Is it by Modest Mouse?" Lucy said. "Down with Modest Mouse."

Morgan hummed something. She thought she said, "Did you and William win at the track?" but she didn't hear his answer. The little movie theater behind her eyes had emptied out except for one person in a raincoat who was watching the credits roll. The projectionist was thinking of the bowl of corn flakes he would eat at home before going to bed. Lucy's father had often snacked on cereal late at night, giving the leftover sugary milk to the dog, Red. When she came into the kitchen in the morning, the plastic yellow bowl would be on the floor, under the table or back in the corner, by the broom and dustpan. Red would have pushed it all around, trying to get the very last lick out of it.

Sleep—but that was all—covered her from head to toes. When she awakened, she found herself shivering and alone. She got under the blankets. Several minutes later she was still awake enough to hear Morgan say, "I didn't get laid in Amsterdam, on either trip. I was too afraid. I bought some pornography in Malmö, however, and carried it across numerous borders."

He went below the covers to suck on a nipple and she sighed, in a not quite agreeable way.

"Do you think," she said, unable to ask any of the questions she wanted answered before he climbed on her again.

"This is what I think, Lucy," he said, his bearded face suddenly rising up to within inches of her eyes. Had he gargled with something? His breath was cinnamony, appley. "I think I will love you now, next week, and until you are an old lady with dazzling white hair and orthopedic shoes. I think William will figure out at some point that you're cool and can tell him everything he needs to know about the Alien and Sedition laws. I think Zeke will lick you on the face—probably tomorrow. I think Sidney and my brother will have an argument, and then Sidney will take a bus into New York and fall in love with a cab driver from Yemen, possibly a terrorist, and Crawford will drive back by himself to Michelle and his children."

Lucy didn't say anything.

"Do you know how I know all this?"

"No," she said, a "no" so soft it seemed made entirely of air.

"It came to me in the kitchen when I went to get something to drink. Apple juice—good for the moral fiber."

She heard a train in the distance, but it didn't comfort her. Morgan's face was so close that she couldn't really see it; it was like having a spotlight in her eyes.

Maybe he noticed her anxiety. He lowered his head and kissed her throat.

She said, "When you were drinking your apple juice, did anything come to you about Melanie?"

"Huh?"

"Now that she's free again or getting divorced and you're fancy-free and everything is like some crazy midsummer's night dream with your brother and that way-too-young ventriloquist." Lucy told herself not to get worked up. He had told her that he loved her, hadn't he? Was it true?

"Late autumn night's dream," Morgan said. He brought his scented mouth to up near her sour-feeling one and offered some information about his long-ago crush on Melanie and then he said, "You'll see that it's nothing when she comes out tomorrow."

"She's coming out here tomorrow? You didn't tell me that. I thought she lived in California."

"I told you I picked up the keys from her on Tuesday. She came to New York to see her father for Thanksgiving. It's OK, Lucy. I love you. The earth is round and spins on its axis and I love you."

The lawyer in her wanted to object—on the grounds that he was protesting too much—but she kept her doubts to herself.

AT SEVEN IN the morning, on her way to the bathroom, Lucy heard Sidney say to Crawford, "I need to see my mom."

It came as a surprise to Lucy that Sidney had a mother. She gave the impression of being not even lightly tethered to anything so mundane. Maybe it was this quality that allowed her to be a ventriloquist.

"I'll drive you," Crawford said.

"No," Sidney said. "I'll take the train. Can you lend me a little cash?"

At 7:05 or thereabouts, on her way back to bed, Lucy saw a deer, a doe, in the backyard. The deer stood absolutely still, all eyes. Perhaps the deer smelled Zeke or had heard Morgan snoring.

At around 9:30, Sidney put her backpack and the valise that contained her dummy Jayne in the trunk of Morgan's car, his father's old Toyota. Sidney gave a peck on the cheek to Crawford, who stood in the driveway without aid of crutches, his bare injured foot in a rubber sandal. It had been decided that Morgan would drive Sidney to the railroad station in Poughkeepsie. Crawford had said to Sidney, "I might try to kidnap you and take you to Niagara Falls or something. You better go with my brother. He's more responsible."

By ten, Lucy was sitting on the deck, wrapped in Morgan's ski sweater, drinking coffee, skimming the copy of *Ethan Frome* that she'd found in Morgan's apartment. It was a 1930 hardcover edition, the boards water stained, the pages giving off a sweet, decrepit scent. It had once belonged to Morgan's mother: the bookplate, which had a drawing of a young woman looking thoughtful in a bower full of birds, said so. Morgan had taken the book from his parents' shelves some years ago, but had never read it.

Lucy had read it in ninth grade in Nebraska. She remembered that there was something important about a pickle dish. She found the passage where Ethan's wife, a shrew, discovers that the dish is broken, and then Lucy read the scene where Ethan and his cousin ride the sled down the hill to their doom. Illicit love was true love and true love had nowhere to go except straight into a tree. Was that right? Well, here, in the shadow of the Shawangunk Mountains, a hundred years after Edith Wharton steered Ethan and Mattie smack into a New England elm, illicit love, which was perhaps true love only on Crawford's part, had ended with a whimper rather than a bang. Crawford was now sitting on the living room sofa with William and Zeke, watching Sports Center, men flying through the air, dunking basketballs. Crawford sat with his wounded foot resting on a stack of magazines on the coffee table. Had Sidney ever kissed Crawford on the foot? He'd fallen off that ladder, he'd told Morgan, at least partly because he'd been thinking about Sidney. Too bad that hadn't brought him to his senses.

It didn't surprise Lucy that Morgan's prediction regarding Crawford and Sidney had come so quickly true. (Anybody could have predicted it and maybe even gotten fewer details wrong.) What did give her a small jolt was when William and Zeke came out on the deck, and William spoke to her. "It's boring here," he said, almost amiably.

"You mean by the lake with the birds singing and the sun shining?"

"Yeah." Zeke, who was built like a bear cub, descended the deck stairs.

"What would make it less boring?"

"If we were leaving for the city in about five minutes."

"Too bad there isn't ice for skating," she said. The necklace of ice along the lake's edges would be gone by noon.

William shrugged. He was barefoot, in a T-shirt and low-riding cargo pants. However, his head was covered with a stocking cap, the sort a muttonchopped Victorian papa might take a long winter's nap in.

"Of course, we'd need skates." Lucy hadn't skated since she was a girl in Nebraska. There was a pond shaped like an hourglass in the town park. To get from one end to the other, you had to skate beneath a stone footbridge that was a memorial to a resident who had gone to Hollywood and swum in some Esther Williams movies. More than one speeding adolescent boy had misjudged the height of the bridge.

"Yeah, we would," William said, and he went back inside, the black pom-pom at the end of his cap swishing across his vertebrae. Zeke sniffed along the lakeshore. Despite the sun and the birds—a cardinal was singing avidly, as if spring had arrived—and despite the fact that she'd had her longest conversation to date with William, she suspected that things were going to take a bad turn. She felt like a novice skater— a stage she'd never advanced beyond in Nebraska—who was trying to figure out how to stop before she banged into a stone bridge.

She shut her eyes and when she opened them again, she saw that Zeke had laid something at her feet. It was a mud-encrusted rubber duck. It wheezed when she squeezed it. She said, "Thank you" to Zeke and flung his gift to her off the deck. She threw like a girl—sports had not been her family's strong suit—but she got off a pretty good one. The duck shed sparkles of dog slobber as it traveled out over the yard.

THE TEMPERATURE HIT FIFTY by two in the afternoon. Morgan and William and Lucy went into town and played Putt-Putt golf. William made a hole in one on the third, the windmill hole, and pumped his fist. It took Lucy seven tries to get her green ball past the warped blades of the asthmatic windmill and three more to put it in the hole. Nevertheless, William wrote a five on the scorecard next to her name. On the eighth hole, Morgan and William mock-fenced with their putters while Lucy tried to get her ball around an Alp that rose out of the carpet. On the thirteenth, an unimaginative dogleg to the left, William said, "Lucky thirteen, Lucy. Bear down." She did, aiming where William told her to aim, but she took a four, a double bogey.

When they came home, with dinner provisions for seven (Melanie was bringing her boys), they couldn't find Crawford. His car was in the drive and his crutches were in the living room, but he was gone.

Lucy walked down to the lake with Zeke. The lake glowed like an ember in the dying sun. A hundred yards out, a man was floating in an aluminum canoe, not paddling. He was hunched forward, like he was studying the contour of the thwart. He fit the profile of Crawford. He didn't look up when two ducks flew over. She wanted to shout at him, How can you not have looked at those ducks? One had a green head, for God's sake!

She went back up to the house. William was on the couch, listening to the Modest Mouse CD that Sidney had left behind. He waved to her and she waved back.

She went out to the deck with an apple and a book Melanie had written about some drug-addled basketball misfit. It was entitled *Rejected*. There was a breeze. The canoe that contained Crawford had been blown west. He needed a fishing pole, she thought, or a radio to listen to, with Duke Ellington on it, playing "Mood Indigo"—some prop.

Morgan appeared with two beers and a jacket, which he draped over her shoulders. She said, "Thank you," for the jacket, a better idea than the beer, and pointed out Crawford.

"How did he even get the canoe down to the lake?" It had been stored under the deck. "Christ!" He shook his head. "Do you know what Sidney told me? She said he'd written her a check for a thousand dollars to help her out with her career—seed money. She wanted to know if she should return it?"

"What'd you tell her?"

"I said she could return it when she hit the big time, and she said, 'Don't hold your breath.' At least she's honest."

Lucy bit into her apple. It was tart.

Morgan exhaled, took a gulp of beer, and said that Melanie had called to say she was going to stay in the city with her father, who was ill. "She said we should keep our eyes open for a pileated woodpecker."

He sounded disappointed that she wasn't coming. He gazed in the direction of a stand of old ash trees.

"Have you ever seen one? They're as big as crows, with a red crest like a Mohawk. I saw one at my parents' house once. In Faulkner somebody calls it the 'God Almighty bird.' Or is that the ivory-billed woodpecker?" He took another sip of beer, perhaps in the hope that it would jog his memory. "One of them."

"Maybe Crawford would know. The English teacher," Lucy said.

"I wonder if he took a life jacket." He was wearing a hat and a bulky sweater—Lucy could see that much. "Probably not. Not his style."

Crawford had apparently taken his cell phone, a recent acquisition. His voice traveled across the water and up the grassy slope straight to their ears. He might have been right there on the deck instead of fifty yards away. "I'm in a canoe on a lake," he said. "Somewhere near Poughkeepsie, New York. An old flame of my brother's let him have her vacation house for the weekend."

"Who's he talking to?" Lucy asked, keeping her voice low. If she could hear him, couldn't he hear her? Or did her voice get lost in the grass and trees before it hit the water?

"Don't know," Morgan said. "Did you know that moments before the bicyclist whomped him, he'd been making out with a woman in a bar? For a long time he couldn't remember anything about what happened right before the accident, and then one day he was walking through Marshall Field's, after buying some socks, and he saw this saleswoman at the men's fragrances counter and he remembered it all. It was the first time he'd been unfaithful to Michelle, he said."

"So God punished him?"

"Only if you believe in that sort of tit for tat." Zeke came zigzagging up toward the deck, hot on the trail of something. Then, barking joyfully, he veered off, toward the stand of old ashes where the pileated woodpecker must have gone knocking for bugs on occasion. "I kissed Melanie once and didn't get hit by a bicyclist ten minutes later. It's true, however, that I kind of made my marriage wobble."

Lucy had long ago realized that she was involved with a family of men who did not take kissing lightly. A certain amount of preparation and thought went into a kiss, as if it were a college admission essay. Perhaps they all had some ancestral memory of a disastrous union erected on a seemingly minor, impetuous kiss.

Crawford said, "Have you ever heard of someone running away with his son's ventriloquism teacher, Darla? Maybe violin, but not ventriloquism. And I'm still in love with her. Do you think I'm irredeemable crud?"

"Speaking of old flames," Morgan said. "Darla was Craw's girlfriend twenty-five years ago. She's some sort of Washington think tank philanthropic foundation type. He met her at college. She was his first and only half-black, half-Jewish girlfriend. His very first serious girlfriend was one hundred percent Jewish. Sixth grade. He gave her his ID bracelet and she gave it back to him a few weeks later. My brother and I seem to have this thing about Jewish women, though we marry only Gentiles. Do you think we're compensating for something or is it all simple happenstance?"

"If you have a nickel, Lucy the psychoanalyst will tell you."

He pretended to search his pockets for spare change.

"I doubt you fall in love with somebody because she's Jewish or not Jewish."

Morgan said, "My late ex-father-in-law told me on my wedding day that married love is basically a fraud. He quoted Schopenhauer to me."

"I suppose it would depend on who's marrying whom," Lucy said. "May I have my five cents?"

"I'm such a screwup, Darla," Crawford was saying. "I even broke my ankle a few weeks ago. For Christmas I'm hoping to get a cane or else a gun to shoot myself with."

"Or," a big male voice from somewhere around the lake shouted, "you could just fall out of your fucking canoe and die right now. Christmas is a month off." Laughter, the guffaws of menfolk standing around a barbecue grill, spilled out across the lake. Lucy smelled smoke. She tilted her head back and saw that the first star had come out, a mote in a darkening blue eye.

Morgan walked down to the lake. The fact that he walked somewhat like his father—slowly, meditatively, slightly bent forward by obligation and duty—moved Lucy. Sometimes she liked him more when he was walking away from her than toward her. She stood up. She felt chilled. She stuffed her hands in the pockets of Morgan's jacket and bounced on her toes, which were in old brown oxfords. Morgan's pockets were full of things—scraps of paper, keys, a paper clip, a chalky, sticky, ovoid thing that was possibly an Altoid. He sucked on Altoids sometimes. It was a quibble she had with him, the fact that his breath was often flavored.

She heard him talking to Crawford, but she could make out only snatches of what he said. The breeze was blowing in now, dampening

any voice that went out. One thing she thought she heard Morgan say
was "We love you, Craw."

She didn't hear Crawford answer. She could hardly pick him out of the
dark engulfing the lake. But she heard a paddle bump against the side of
the canoe, a paddle dipping into water.

# 16

# Eye of a Needle

BETWEEN THE WINTER SOLSTICE and New Year's, Judge Dupree rode
trains, mostly in the South and Southwest, where the weather was balmy,
where it was possible to sit in an open boxcar with no more than a raincoat on your shoulders and a pith helmet on your head and not feel
chilled. Of course, he didn't really *get* cold now. He stayed at a constant
temperature, which was an improvement, in some ways, over how he'd
been during his last years, when he was subject to fevers and bone-
rattling chills. Once, back in the late nineties, when he and his wife had
gone to Wisconsin to visit their elder son's family, he had found himself
in a natural foods store called Magic Sunlight, shivering uncontrollably.
His wife had sent him there to buy lecithin and an item that had gone
out of his head as soon as she mentioned it. His granddaughter, Caroline, had walked with him to the store. He remembered that she wore
pink earmuffs—it was March and the wind made the limbs of the un-
green trees creak—and that she'd skipped ahead of him a couple times
and also that she had told him that her father had seen a coyote by the

playground one morning, hunting for rabbits. Somewhere between Magic Sunlight's front door and the bulk food bins Judge Dupree lost Caroline. As he stood in front of bins that contained whole wheat flour and groats and oat flakes and something called quinoa and rice and organic pitted prunes, so cold that he couldn't get his hands deep enough into the pockets of his coat, shaking so violently that his glasses teetered on the tip of his nose, trying to remember what the second item on his wife's list was (seaweed? sea salt? fish oil?), he wished he could become nothing. When Caroline, a brave and resourceful eight-year-old, had appeared with a young woman who had a ring in her lip and asked if he needed help, he'd said no, because he knew yes would mean a trip to the hospital and enduring dreadful devices such as catheters and in general making trouble for everybody when all he wanted to do was get under ten blankets and sleep. But Caroline had persisted ("Grandaddy, you have to listen to me!") and somebody (was it Crawford?) had driven him to the hospital—he turned out to have a bacterial infection that was caught before it developed into septic shock—from which he was released some days later to experience more fevers and more chills as well as states in between.

It was pleasant to be beyond those vicissitudes, beyond the sense that you were a chemical experiment that could go wrong at any moment. It was nice, too, not to have to run errands for your wife, to have your docket cleared, and to be able to ride trains at the drop of a hat. If he happened to be in, say, Memphis, which is where he was on the afternoon of Christmas Eve, wandering the downtown streets with his cardboard suitcase (empty except for some out-of-date timetables; he needed little), he could take a notion to hop a freight to New Orleans, where once as a boy he'd spent a weekend with his father eating puffy, sugary beignets and riding the streetcars, where later in life he'd gone for lawyer conventions, which could be fun if you avoided the 8:00 A.M. breakfast seminars and dinner tables dominated by hard-drinking securities-law specialists or a cigar-smoking fellow judge. (One time when he came home from one of these taxpayer-funded junkets and attempted to kiss his wife on the cheek, she pulled her head away and said, "You smell like a pool hall. What *have* you been doing?") The line from Memphis to New Orleans was the one that had carried the Panama Limited back in the days when America had passenger trains instead of buses that ran on rails. It was also on this line that Casey Jones, a Kentuckian, had had his famous accident. Casey had started in Memphis, three hours late, but by the time he took the reverse curve north of Vaughn, Mississippi, he was only thirty minutes behind schedule. Judge Dupree, standing on wobbly legs as his poky freight approached the curve, imagined the collision of engine with engine. What a way to go! He didn't have much of a singing voice, but all through Mississippi he sang "Casey Jones," the verses he could remember, that is.

At other times he sang snatches of Christmas carols, and once, when he saw a house trimmed in red, white, and blue, he let go with a few bars of "America the Beautiful." During the last few months, he had noticed an upsurge in patriotism. He knew something about the events that had given rise to these displays of Old Glory, though what he had learned (mostly from oral sources along the railroads) seemed so fantastic that he was hardly able to credit it. He had always been a little naive. It was his nature—forty years of sitting on the bench notwithstanding—to believe in the essential goodness of humankind. Of course there were rotten eggs, and they had to be isolated before they inflicted even more harm. He prayed for their transformation. He believed in the possibility of transformation. He had few responsibilities now, but one, as he understood it, was to be prayerful.

As he rode through Mississippi, singing in his wizened voice that sometimes hit a note by accident, he thought about his family. He wondered if Crawford or Morgan would accompany his wife to one of the Christmas Eve services at St. John's-on-the-Hill. (She liked the late one, to which some people came in their tuxes and evening gowns and with Scotch on their breaths, but he had always preferred the afternoon service, with the pageant and all the restless, twittery children.) He tried not to dwell on his family. They were on their own now. He had plans to check up on them before the year ran out. That would be enough—just a quick visit, then he would let them go entirely.

He didn't lay over in New Orleans for long. It was a bit damp there, and Christmas morning on the Toulouse Street wharf, where he heard two tattered men discussing the quality of the leftovers in a Dumpster on Chartres Street, was not uplifting. As it happened, there was a freight leaving for Los Angeles in the afternoon. The trip was two thousand miles and forty-eight hours, but the distance and time were hardly deterrents. He looked forward to riding past the bayous and climbing through the Del Norte mountains and then charging across the desert. He liked open spaces, long vistas. They clarified the mind. Not that his mind needed much clarification at this point.

Now and then, Judge Dupree shared a boxcar with another rider. It was a hazard of being what he was, imperceptible to virtually everybody, not simply to the self-absorbed and preocccupied. Generally, he didn't object when he found himself not alone; he had always been companionable and hadn't changed much in that regard when he crossed over. And of the dozen or so people he'd traveled with, only one had been by all appearances a rotten egg, someone whose picture was likely to have been found in post offices around the country. This low percentage of criminality he attributed to the nature of rail travel; it attracted, even at the bottom end, gentler people, people not in a terrible hurry, people whose baggage, if any, didn't include cell phones. He remembered the airlines with a shudder.

The train he caught, which followed the route of the old Sunset Limited, was near New Iberia, Louisiana, when he heard voices. A woman said, "Babe, you awake?" and a man said, "Huh?" They were in a tangle deep in a corner of the boxcar, which was owned by Southern Pacific, which had most recently carried a load of hot tubs. His head was shaved; it emitted a soft light. She had a face that was so sweetly pretty, heart-shaped practically, it might as well have been outlined in neon.

"Is it still Christmas?" he asked.

She kissed him on his skull. "Yep."

They were former convenience store clerks. He was originally from Indiana and she was from a Louisiana town the Judge had never heard of and they were going to Las Vegas, where she had hopes of getting a job as a dancer or cocktail waitress and he had a second cousin who was a limousine driver. They appeared to be unmarried. He seemed to be slightly older than she was, but neither could have been much over twenty. They were by far the youngest people the Judge had ever ridden with.

Carla and Kirk—those were their given names—made love three times between New Iberia and the old railroad division point of Sanderson, Texas, which averaged out to about once every two hundred and fifty miles. During these sessions, the Judge, who had always been a firm believer in the right to privacy, concentrated on the scenery and removed his hearing aid. Sometimes, however, Carla raised her voice to such an extent that the Judge could not help glancing over and noting one or two things before returning his gaze to the outdoors of Texas. And he could not help remembering his own unabundant experiences with sex, to use a word that in his previous existence he'd used hardly at all. (He used it once when Crawford gave him a book by Judge Richard Posner called *Sex and Reason.* It was a birthday present. He said, "I wouldn't have thought that sex was among Judge Posner's interests.") All of those experiences had been with his wife of fifty years, and two had resulted in children. One that had not resulted in children had taken place on the South Wind to Florida in 1954, in the lower bunk of their compartment, and was memorable for the bump he got on his head when he suddenly reared up. (A northbound train had rushed past at a certain moment.) There was a part of him that regretted that that aspect of his life had not been richer, more exciting, whatever the word was. He had had longings from time to time, particularly toward the end of his life, but one kiss with his clerk was as close as he'd come to fulfilling them. On the other hand—and wasn't much of life "on the other hand"?—he hadn't found the sexual act itself all that rewarding. What he had really hoped for more of was kissing, nuzzling, hand-holding, things that women (as opposed to men) were supposed to require. He'd had a craving for that, though he'd tried not to let it show. Anyway, it was all past him now. He was not a player—he could watch, think, pray, meditate, even sing a little (though the sounds he made were not noticeable in the world), have feelings, but he could not *do*. And the longings he still sometimes experienced were, strictly speaking, not corporeal.

Carla and Kirk disembarked in Phoenix. Kirk's stepmother lived there. She worked at the dog track. Carla was excited about taking a shower. "You could use one, too, babe," she said to Kirk, and she kissed him just below his earringed ear and they walked across the rail yards through the desert twilight toward a highway aswarm with traffic. Kirk carried their baby-blue Samsonite suitcase.

It surprised the Judge that he missed Carla and Kirk. Even now, it seemed he wasn't entirely sufficient unto himself. He got off the train in the Coachella Valley in California, when it stopped to take on cars packed with grapefruit and dates. He would have liked to have seen the Pacific—he had swum in it off Long Beach in the summer of 1960, when he and Mary Louise took the boys on a tour of the West; Crawford had been stung by a jellyfish—but he could always see it later. He wasn't bound by the clock or the calendar.

He caught a freight that carried him back to New Orleans on the same track he'd come out on. He saw antelope in New Mexico and dust devils in Texas and a boy in Louisiana riding a bike with his hands on his head. He himself had never ridden a bike with fewer than two hands. He prayed that harm would never come to the boy, that he would get good grades and not have to fight in wars, that he would be kind to animals and never cease loving his children, if he should be so lucky as to have any.

THE JUDGE CAME UP from Nashville on the old L&N line, through Bowling Green and Glasgow and Elizabethtown and Lebanon Junction. In the Louisville yards, he caught a freight loaded with new Toyotas and vats of mysterious chemicals. It was headed for Toledo by way of Cincinnati on track now owned by the CSX Corporation. (He had an instinct for where trains were going.) As he guessed it would, the train slowed to a creep about five miles east of the city limits, which was as close as any rail line came to his former home. He had often sat, contentedly, in his automobile behind the dinging crossing gates here, noting the logos of the railroads emblazoned on the sides of the cars, those combinations of letters and symbols that seemed magical to him even at an advanced age, sometimes counting cars, along with his boys, who never seemed to come up with the same number, and waving to the cabooseman before the time came when the cabooseman and his toylike hut were deemed extravagances.

The Judge had never jumped from a train, even from one doing five miles per hour, but he was without fear, and the landing he made in a ditch strewn with Dizzy Whiz hamburger wrappers and flyers promoting a church bake sale and other trash was painlessly easy, almost as if he were as light as one of those things that had floated into the ditch. He might have caught a county bus near here, though it was a fact of his situation that he could board one only where paying riders got on or off, and this evening, the last of 2001, buses and riders looked to be few and far between. Anyway, he decided to walk. He had no difficulty walking long distances now, even though he walked as he had as an old man—slowly, somewhat aslant, looking as if a gust from a passing truck would topple him. He had stamina, vast reserves of it, but had you seen him—or imagined you'd seen him—you wouldn't have said, "That is one peppy old guy."

His walk took him past the Episcopal Cathedral Home, a one-story, many-winged, red-brick structure whose entrance was across the street from a Swifty filling station. The Judge knew people who lived there—at least he assumed they were still there—including Hateful, his old bridge colleague, and Bishop Grady Leonhart, with whom he had once attended a Cincinnati Reds game on a hot day, the Judge in a seersucker suit and the Bishop in his collar, which he loosened in the bottom of the first to make it easier for the Hudepohl beer to slide down his throat and so he could shout "Cesar Geronimo!" when the Reds' centerfielder came to bat. The Judge's wife had several times suggested that they put themselves on the Cathedral Home waiting list—"How can I possibly take care of this house," she'd said, "with you barely able to walk?"—but he'd done nothing about it. He wondered if she'd put herself on the list after he'd gone. No, he thought, that was unlikely, her complaints notwithstanding. She would have to be in a bad way, all but dithering, before she gave up her gardens, her closets of dresses, the piano that nobody ever played, the china that never came out of the cabinet, the towering secretary in whose cubbyholes she would put photographs and Christmas cards and trinkets. What sane person would walk away from that? He hadn't. He'd had to be carried away on a paramedic's stretcher.

When he jumped from the train, the sky had been purple-blue, a color that made daylight seem almost like a shabby memory. Now, as he climbed the hill toward his wife's home, the sky was past all color and stuck about with stars and planets. The moon was up, too, as round and luminous as it ever got. It shone on the slate-roofed Tudor revival mansion that had been the first house to be built on the hill, twenty rooms, which presently contained a couple from Atlanta and their daughter.

(The Judge had been to Hannah's bat mitzvah the year before he died, and at this grand event had had his very first bite of lox. Later, when his wife would send him to the store, he would sometimes buy a package of lox and eat all of it with Carr's table crackers in his Toyota.) The moon shone superfluously on the Griffins' smaller house—Christmas lights outlined every eave—and on the Maypothers' modern confabulation, which they shared with a couple of Russian wolfhounds as big as horses. Gerald Boardman's cottage sat dark behind two large magnolias. Not even the porch light was on. Gerald, a longtime widower who had sold the Judge a high-premium, tax-dodging piece of life insurance a few years back as well as assorted other policies, often went to Florida during the holidays. The Judge hoped that was where he'd gone now. He'd been fond of Gerald.

The Judge hadn't been home since, well, the night he'd been hauled off to the hospital. He was rather shy about appearing where his loved ones, his so-called survivors, might see or imagine they'd seen him. (He himself had once been skeptical of the idea of ghosts, phantasms, the soul fleshed out. To be honest, the Resurrection of Jesus Christ had always troubled him, though he had eventually assented to the idea of it, the notion that you could be transformed in life as in death. Anyway, it was certainly hard to argue against such things now.) It was true that he had once or twice passed near where his clerk, Lucy, was living. He had even seen her on Frankfort Avenue in her church clothes, and he'd had the impression that he'd given her a bit of a shock. He had also seen his older son this summer, going into a convenience store in Covington, Kentucky, at three in the morning. He felt as if he'd somehow caught Crawford in flagrante delicto. And then there was the night last month when he entered Crawford's house at an hour when he thought they'd all be in bed, when he'd been overcome by a desire to gaze at their sleeping faces. (In hindsight, he'd concede he crossed a line; it was the first time he'd gone inside anybody's home.) He hadn't wanted to be an imposition on the living; they had enough to think about, as it was. Which was why he intended this visit to be brief.

But what if none of his family were here? He didn't have advance notice of where they'd be, he wasn't endowed with paranormal skills. He operated on common sense (and the occasional hunch), and it had seemed likely to him that his widow would be at home on New Year's Eve, and that she might have the company of one or both of his sons and one or perhaps all three of his grandchildren. When he was still around, he and Mary Louise had tended to celebrate New Year's Eve by staying home, though once or twice in his later years she'd taken him to a prayer vigil at St. John's. The thought of seeing his grandchildren—and Duff! old arthritic Duff!—prickled his scalp (or that aspect of him that might be construed to be scalp).

In the driveway, parked where he'd often left his car when he didn't pull it into the garage, was an old model pickup truck. Even in the forgiving light of the moon the truck looked raggedy. The driver's door had taken a battering. Rosettes of rust were everywhere. Touching it, the Judge tried to recall who among his acquaintances drove such a vehicle, but he came up with nobody. He walked around the side of the house, past the holly that in previous years had been strung with lights, remembering to go slowly down the little slope that was bordered with creek stone. (He had fallen there in 1996 and given his wife a fright when he came stumbling in through the back door with mud on his hands and a scrape on his chin.) Electric candles burned in the windows of the living room, which was otherwise dark. In the room where the TV had its niche, where he'd often sat and read while also keeping tabs on the Reds or Cardinals or Wildcats, a Christmas tree twinkled with white lights. It was a small spruce, not much taller than a shrub. There was a festive skirt under the tree and on the skirt was a handful of unopened presents. His wife believed in the idea of the twelve days of Christmas. There had been years when she hadn't got around to opening a gift from him until long

after the magi had departed Bethlehem for eastern realms. He had sometimes wondered if she'd delayed this because she knew she wasn't going
to get what she wanted. It was a fact that he'd given her the same gardening book two years in a row and that a wood angel he'd purchased
was possibly gimcrack, as he once heard her describe it to Morgan.

Lights were on in the kitchen. The counters were mostly clear, but
there were wineglasses on the table where he'd eaten thousands of break-
fasts while reading *Blondie* and James Reston. Had his olfactory organs
been sharp—it was the one sense of his to have gone totally kerflooey—
he might have detected, through the ajar window above the sink, the
scent of roast beef. (Oh, what he would have given during the last quarter of his lifetime for some red meat!) But he guessed that the platter
covered in foil—the oven door had been left open—contained that low-
fat holiday staple, turkey.

He was turning away to consider his next move when he heard a dog
bark. It was a puppy's yip, fretful, excited, far from the croak that was all
that Duff could manage late in life. It came from inside the house. When
he turned back, he saw, over in the corner, where the bucket of birdseed
and a trug laden with gardening tools were kept, the cage to which the
incontinent Duff had been relegated at night. There was a little black dog
in it—a fluffy, poodleish dog. Duff had passed on, it seemed. (It was a
fact of afterlife—or, of the Judge's so far, anyway—that one was not necessarily reunited with dead friends or dead relatives or beloved dead
pets.) But it struck him as surprising that his wife had replaced Duff.
She'd often stated she didn't want to take on another dog after Duff
went. "Aren't you tired of getting down on your knees to clean up after
him?" she'd said.

The puppy put its forelegs on the bars of the cage. It yipped as if it
could see him, as if its release were imminent.

The Judge walked back around to the front of the house, humming a
Doris Day song, remembering what it felt like to have his hands on his

wife's waist when she was twenty-seven and he was a thirty-year-old lawyer hoping for work other than the drafting of wills. He had looked forward to coming home to her then—home was a small brick house in the Highlands until the district attorney hired him—and giving her the kiss that he'd been saving up all day, a kiss that entailed gripping the scant flesh above her hips. (He had to hold her in place or she might slip away.) She permitted him to do this until she became pregnant with Crawford. Thereafter his lips found only her cheek, which to his mind was akin to eating lemon chiffon pie without the chiffon. When she was seven months pregnant, he brought home a puppy he'd seen in a shop window, and she withdrew her cheek, leaving him to breathe in the hot, anxious air around her. But she didn't make him take the dog back. And for five years, until the milkman hit him with his truck, the dog, whose name was Whitey, had jumped all over the Judge when he came home in the evenings.

LUCY WAS HAVING A PARTY. From where he stood, off to the side of the front porch, behind some bushes that were possibly rhododendrons and that would not have given him cover had he been the kind of Peeping Tom that you could call the police on, he had a clear line of sight into her living room. On the couch, which had been red when he had kissed Lucy on the lips in 1998, which was now veiled with an Indian print covering (as if to hide its blushing surfaces), sat a bearded man and the Judge's granddaughter, Caroline, and a dark-skinned man in a green sweater-vest and bow tie whom the Judge believed to be Lazaro. The Judge, who had presided at Lazaro's naturalization ceremony in 1989, had not seen his late cousin's companion often during his last years. Lazaro, who had started a tropical fish business with some money Louis had left him, had run in circles that didn't often intersect with those the Judge had moved in. When they did bump into each other, the Judge had been less than effusive, if always polite. Though he had not been a jealous man, he had never quite gotten over the loss of his cousin to Lazaro. Louis had been his best friend, and then Louis had found this Mexican boy with beautiful shining white teeth and beautiful black hair. The Judge had not thoroughly considered the notion that his cousin might be a homosexual until Lazaro came along, at which point the Judge discovered that he felt unkindly toward homosexuals in general, if not toward Louis in particular. Homosexuality had deprived him of a year or two of cribbage games and conversation with his cousin. Later, he had modified his views, partly because of what Crawford had said during a dinner-table discussion. "Would you love Morgan or me less if we were gay or something?" Crawford had put this question to his mother, who had implied that a landscaper who had given her bad advice was homosexual. Mary Louise had said, "Well, of course not—a mother loves her child through thick and thin." The Judge, who had kept quiet during this exchange, had thought, There is love and there is also love that surpasses all understanding.

It took the Judge several moments to see that the bearded man on the couch was his younger son. His beard was thick and serious, a beard that a pickup-driving roughneck might sport. (Could the truck at his widow's house have been Morgan's?) The beard made him seem older— older even than his clean-shaven older brother who was standing next to the Christmas tree with a beer in one hand and a cane (a cane!) in the other—and as if he might have lost his bearings. During his lifetime, the Judge hadn't worried much about Morgan—he'd saved his worrying for Crawford, who had almost routinely made unfortunate decisions. And then Morgan had split up with Gina, whom the Judge believed to be a prize. (She was, among other things, a crack bridge player.) The Judge hadn't asked Morgan to explain the breakup or even allowed himself to speculate much about it. (His wife had done both, and come to the conclusion that the fast life in New York, which allowed no time for spiritual endeavors, was the cause. The Judge thought there might have been an ounce or two of truth in this.) Later, lying on his hospital bed in his polka-dotted, backless gown, having finished the last book he would finish (a history of the Union Pacific Railroad, given to him by Gina), listening to the noises of the hospital (monitors ticking and beeping, the murmurous voices of medical personnel, oxygen hissing through the tube to his nose, his emphysemic roommate snoring), knowing that he wasn't going to go home again, it seemed to him that love that lasted from its first little flare-up until death—that survived decades of marriage, that is—was a most amazing thing. It was easy to love your child, even a mistake-prone, hotheaded child staggering through adulthood, but loving your spouse, "cleaving" to your spouse, until your heart stopped beating, "through thick and thin," as his wife had put it—well, who but a saint could help himself from wanting to kiss his clerk on the lips just once, who but a crusty old dogmatic saint could keep his heart from bursting in the presence of someone he loved who was not his wife? Not that he, lying in his hospital gown, had been proud of his romance with Lucy or had approved of Morgan's divorce from Gina.

The Judge didn't see William, his namesake, among the partygoers. Nor did he notice his other grandson, Philip, or Philip's mother, Michelle. He missed each of them. His eyes were hungry for the sight of them. He hoped they'd appear from the back of Lucy's apartment, like rabbits out of a hat, like parts of a family that had gotten lost in the fray.

He did see his wife, though, sitting in a high-backed rattan chair. His wife looked as if she had shrunk, or perhaps it was the chair that diminished her. This was so despite her hat, a tam-o'-shanter that had a fuzzy red ball, like a cherry, in the center. Of course, they'd both shrunk over the years, he more than she. Once, in a light moment, she'd said, "Honey, if we keep going this way, there won't be anything left to bury."

The Judge guessed that there was still about ninety pounds left to bury—or burn, since, like him, she'd chosen cremation. (But she'd said "bury" instead of "burn," the thought of bones and flesh and eyeballs roasting being perhaps too vivid for her to offer up to him, even in a light moment.) And the ninety pounds that was left was still in its own way formidable. He remembered a moment in the hospital when she was washing his hair, using some sort of powder she'd found at the natural products store whose owner had been able to invest in race horses partly as a result of her loyalty to his business. She was massaging his sore, worn-out head, a kindness in her fingertips that he'd not felt for years, and on the other side of the curtain his roommate was eating lunch, his cutlery clattering against plate and bowl because he had the shakes as well as an emphysemic cough. Crawford was sitting in the corner, not reading the newspaper on his lap though his head was bowed in that direction. And a doctor came in, a specialist in pulmonary disorders, who monitored the Judge's pneumonia-riddled lungs. (There was some speculation—or so the Judge had gathered from the murmurings of nurses —that he had caught a hospital-borne staph infection.) The doctor was a robust middle-aged man from some Spanish-speaking country (he'd said which country, but the Judge had forgotten), with a genial, rumpled, fleshy face. He filled his visits with chatter, for which the Judge was grateful, preferring it to the ominous silent probing of many who treated him, though this geniality somehow also gave the impression of carelessness. When Dr. Chela entered the room, his stethoscope lying on top of a florid tie, his light brown forehead shining as if with hope, he said, without first acknowledging the Judge's wife, "And how is our patient this morning?" The Judge, who rarely thought of or tried to tell jokes, had thought of one following the doctor's previous visit, and he was going to try to tell it today. He was going to say, "Shouldn't you be wearing a staphoscope, Dr. Chela?" But before he was able to muster the strength to tell the joke, before he even remembered that he had a joke to tell, his wife said, "I'm afraid our patient isn't doing very well." She had removed her small hands from her husband's yellow-white hair that was now full of the powdery shampoo. She went on to say that "our patient" was a "distinguished federal judge, you know" and that she was outraged by the care he was receiving in this tiny little room he had to share with that poor man over there and that she could never get any of the doctors or nurses or so-called hospital administrators to return her calls and that she knew a lot about health ("You all just fill people up with drugs") and that she was tired of being condescended to by so-called medical authorities. At some point, Crawford had said, "Mom, let the man do his work," and the doctor had said, "I understand your concern," and the Judge had said, "It's all right, honey, everything's fine," which set her off again, because everything was not fine, it wasn't even close to fine. And the upshot of this outburst—by which time a staph infection had been confirmed—was that the Judge got his own room, which you couldn't enter without donning a gown and mask and latex gloves, which had a view of the expressway and the clusters of suburban housing on the other side.

The Judge looked at his wife in the high-backed rattan chair, her cane hanging on the armrest, the little cross around her neck shining sweetly among the folds of her royal blue sweater, and he thought she could have commanded armies, or at least given the order to have a traitorous subject dispatched. Once, the Judge recalled, she had slapped Crawford for talking back to her, and Crawford, who was fourteen then, had said, "I can't believe you hit me," and she had said, "Oh, that didn't hurt. You don't know what hurt feels like."

There were two men alongside her. The one who was crouching looked like Sandy Broyles, the Reverend Alfred Lloyd Broyles's son, who was also a preacher, who had run around with Crawford when they were boys. (One Saturday night in the midsixties, the Judge had run into Al Broyles downtown at the police station, where each had gone to pick up his intoxicated son. "Bring him to church tomorrow, Judge," Al had said, "and I'll make his ears turn red.") The other man—who was standing, looking around the room as if for a place to sit—the Judge couldn't place, though the jacket the man was wearing looked familiar. It was the Harris tweed one he'd worn to the courthouse hundreds of times, that he'd put holes in the elbows of and that his wife had eventually taken away from him and had patched. The Judge looked more closely at the man. He was balding, trim, though broad in the shoulders (the jacket was a bit tight on him), with something about his posture and the set of his mouth that suggested taciturnity. And then the Judge, whose memory for everything except obscure foodstuffs and popular culture figures younger than Doris Day or Ingrid Bergman had always been excellent, remembered handing a check through the window of a blue, beaten-up truck to a man named Lavell, who had a tattoo on his shoulder, a jester or something. Lavell had been one of his wife's yardmen—she'd gone through a number. It seemed as if she'd always been on the lookout for the perfect one, the one who could make a bare, sunless patch of yard bloom and also solve her mole-deer-groundhog-rabbit-squirrel problem and who would listen to her talk and keep all his promises to her about showing up on a regular basis and not go flying off on a bender or leave her for another client. It was almost as if, the Judge had thought, she had been hunting for a beau. He recalled her saying once, "Lavell and I don't see eye-to-eye on every little tulip, but he doesn't bully me, thank goodness, like some of these know-it-alls do. I just wish he could give me a few more hours a week."

The Judge was not sure what to make of Lavell standing alongside Mrs. Dupree, like a retainer, a sentinel. Nor did he know what to make of the fact that his older son was using a cane and was without his wife and his son. He wasn't sure why Lazaro was here (though when he looked again, he didn't see him). He didn't recognize the man with the hair down to his waist, who was talking to a young woman whose belly button had a gem gleaming in it, or the black woman in the leopard-skin hat or the little bespectacled black girl whose pigtails stuck out like antennae. And wasn't that man with the sheep finger puppet, which was roaming the air in front of Caroline's nose, wasn't that old what's-his-name, Randall Laidlaw, the assistant federal defender? And where was Lucy, the hostess? And why did Morgan, now sharing the couch with Randall Laidlaw and Caroline (who turned her cheek to the sheep when it tried to peck her on the nose), seem so lonesome and befuddled?

Well, how much could you know about people, really?

The Judge went for a walk. He heard sirens, horns, fireworks. A man came out on his porch and said, "Yahoo, baby!" A woman followed him out and, offering him her mouth, said, "Be the first on the block." It was a new year—2002.

The Judge waited for the light at Mercer and Frankfort Avenue to turn, felt nothing when a tank-size vehicle that had run the light grazed him, and took a seat on a bus bench on the other side. The railroad tracks were at his back. As he saw it, one of the problems of his present existence (to use the term loosely) was that, while he was free of pain and annoyances and fears and the burdens of everyday life, he also felt perpetually restless, as if he were still somehow in the grip of desire and hope. Of course, he liked to travel, to move about, but was it possible that he was everlastingly condemned to it? Where was the peace that surpasses all understanding? He recalled that Crawford, his irritable, anxious older son, had once attempted to practice Buddhism or some version of it during one summer when he was in college. Though the Judge had not said so then, though he had been somewhat offended by the ten-page rebuke of Christianity that Crawford wrote while observing silence, he had also been moved by his son's effort to make his restless soul less restless. He himself had had Jesus thrust on him as a boy, and then, in late middle age, after years of lukewarm belief (or was it disbelief?), he had chosen Jesus as the Light and the Way, though even then he'd not been without reservations. He had often thought it was harder for any person, no matter his wealth or lack of it, no matter the depth of his faith, to enter the kingdom of heaven than it was for a camel to pass through the eye of a needle. And based on his present experience, he wasn't wrong.

Across the avenue was a restaurant that for many years had been a movie theater. It was where the Judge had seen, with his cousin Louis, *Abbott and Costello Meet Captain Kidd,* and, with his two young sons, *The General.* Those occasions had preceded by many years his embrace of Jesus, but he had been happy then, in the dark with his cousin and two children, almost ecstatically at peace, if that was possible. Who needed more?

He got up from the bench and walked back toward Lucy's house. He couldn't leave town until he'd seen her. It had nagged at him that he'd left Lucy nothing in his will. He had given the job of drawing up the will to Clifford Barnhill, one of his first law clerks, a kind-hearted boy and a decent bridge player, and after he had bequeathed everything he possessed to his wife and children and Ida and assorted charities and libraries, after all "absolute" and "discretionary" powers had been handed out, Clifford had said, "Well, Judge, do you think we've got it all covered?" They were sitting in Clifford's office, a half-dozen floors above the Ohio River. He hadn't felt well that day, a gorgeous June afternoon, the river glinting in the sunlight like an unspoiled natural wonder. His legs had ached, his bowels were in an uproar. Lucy had driven him over from the courthouse and was waiting for him outside Clifford's door. He had more than enough money lying around to make the rest of her life comfortable, whatever work she should find after he passed away, which he knew he was doing, as surely as he knew the Ohio flowed southwest into the Mississippi. He had said to Clifford, "Let me sleep on it and I'll give you a call in the morning." He'd slept on it in a fitful way, and at 4:00 A.M., when he wobbled feverishly through the dark toward the toilet, he had every intention of leaving Lucy a hundred thousand or so. But he didn't call Clifford in the morning—he didn't go into work—and when he finally signed the will, several months later, Lucy wasn't in it. There were too many complications. He feared the possibility of his name and hers being smeared together. He didn't want to bring their love affair to light.

Up ahead, a couple was embracing. The Judge politely stepped off the sidewalk, out into the street, into the path of a car that suddenly swerved, as if the driver—the Judge almost chuckled at this—had seen a ghost. The driver was Crawford. In the car were Mrs. Dupree and Lavell and Caroline, who twisted in her seat in order to better see something—the couple kissing on the sidewalk, perhaps, or a shatter of red fireworks in the sky or whatever it was her father had swerved to avoid. He remembered that Caroline had once said that when she grew up she was going to be either an astronaut or a veterinarian. The Judge had tried to imagine his granddaughter floating weightless in space, her beautiful green eyes magnified behind the visor of her helmet. He himself had never been much for air travel. Gliding along the surface of the earth suited him just fine, though he understood the impulse to escape gravity and all that went with it.

When he looked again, after he'd returned to the sidewalk, he saw that the two people who were embracing, who were kissing each other thirstily, like two people at the same tap, one bearded face against a smooth one, were Morgan and Lazaro. The Judge studied this scene for a moment, long enough to notice how the moon (or was it the street-lamp?) silvered the hair of both men, before he turned away, as if from an accident. He continued up the street, wondering if what made Morgan kiss Lazaro was love or something else that he, Judge Dupree, couldn't get his mind around. He hoped it was love.

Lucy was standing on the porch stairs, gazing out at the street. She was wearing a dark dress that stopped a couple inches above her knees. He could see the shape of her knees through the fabric of her stockings. Over the dress, which was cut lower than anything he'd ever seen his law clerk in, though not so low that anything other than the lovely skin be-

tween her throat and the tops of her breasts was exposed, she was wearing a coat. He wished she wasn't wearing the coat, not only because it
looked like the shabby thing he'd kept at the courthouse for rainy days.
He would have liked to have seen her bare shoulders and her arms and
her wrists. He remembered contemplating a cluster of moles just above
her elbow (there were five, in a Little Dipper sort of pattern) while they
pored over an opinion by Justice Cardozo that applied to aspects of a
breach of fiduciary duties case. He remembered hearing her voice, the
authority with which she cited cases, the sound of the words "defraud"
and "despoil" in his ears as the spots above her elbow seem to whirl.
She'd taken off her suit jacket and was working in a plain white blouse.
The library was hot, or felt that way to him. Perhaps it was all those
brown volumes of the *Federal Reporter* that made the room seem op-
pressive. He didn't understand why so fine a person as Lucy should be
going home at nights to only a cat.

He wished she wasn't wearing a coat, but it was a winter's night and
only the reckless or delirious would leave their shoulders uncovered.
Lucy was a sober woman. She was not the sort who would tipple in secret or exceed her limit in public, even on a festive night. Here, a few
minutes into the New Year, with the air bursting with cherry bombs and
bottle rockets, she looked decidedly ungiddy. Perhaps it was the drab, too
large raincoat that gave this impression. Had she claimed the coat as a
souvenir? Did she actually wear it about town or did she keep it in the
closet, like a Halloween costume from years past? What else of his did
she have? The thought that she might have taken one of his courtroom
robes and worn it on occasion—to bed, say—came to him. No, that was
a gross fantasy. It was unworthy of him. He sent it packing.

Music came from her apartment, saxophones parting the air and then
a trumpet growling like a dog not wishing to relinquish its bone. Was
this Duke Ellington? Lucy always played Duke Ellington at her New

Year's parties, in honor of her father, she had told him. Maybe she had come outside to see if the music had brought her father here from wherever he was.

Or maybe she'd come outside to look for Jumbo, her cat, though she hadn't called his name. Or maybe she'd stepped out simply to see what the New Year had wrought. She peered up at the sky when something exploded there. She didn't seem impressed.

Judge Dupree stood not ten feet from Lucy, on a patch of frosty-stiff grass, close enough that he could see her hands moving in the pockets of his raincoat. From one pocket she took a little black thing that he immediately saw was a canister of film. He'd often carried a roll of film around for weeks or even months before getting it developed. The pleasure for him was taking the picture rather than seeing the result—that was one reason he was dilatory, anyway. He tried to think of what might be on this roll of film, which Lucy had already put back in her pocket. It might have been those fall foliage pictures his wife had asked him to take of her yard. It might have been the last set of train pictures he'd taken, when Amtrak innaugurated service from Chicago to Jeffersonville, Indiana. It might have been the Christmas pictures from 1999, when all three of his grandchildren had come to town, when William and Philip had decided to set fire to one of Caroline's dolls and had also scorched the trunk of a sycamore. (The Judge hadn't caught that moment on film.) It might have been the roll that included the only photograph of Lucy he could remember taking, at a law school luncheon at which he'd been honored. (He was the only honoree to have brought his camera.) No, he'd had that roll developed, he remembered, had even had an extra copy of the shot of Lucy (underexposed, alas) made.

Anyway, whatever was on that roll of film was not his now. It was a peculiarity of his situation that nothing, not even his pith helmet or cardboard suitcase or the bleary, ancient eyes with which he observed what he couldn't have, belonged to him. He could know whom he might have loved more or better before his time had elapsed, but he couldn't atone for it now.

Lucy was looking right at him. She wasn't wearing her glasses, he belatedly realized, which seemed to leave her unprotected, vulnerable to whatever might come her way. She didn't give any sign that she saw him, as she had on that Sunday back in March, when he was strolling the railroad tracks. Of course, it was true that he was, at most, ephemeral, all but gone.

She turned back toward her door, toward trumpets and trombones. She had a life to live. And there was a man waiting for her inside, nodding his head to the music. It might have been her neighbor, the salesman of artificial knees and hips. It might have been somebody who would love her until she died.

*In memory of my father,*
*Charles Mengel Allen (1916–2000)*

# Acknowledgments

I will be forever grateful to my editor, Shannon Ravenel, for her care, encouragement, and wisdom. Many thanks to my agent, Betsy Amster, and to my friends Judy Goldman, Dana Sachs, and Elizabeth Macklin for casting their good eyes on the manuscript. I am grateful, too, to John Holyoke, Mark Singer, Mary Norris, Michelle Huneven, Richard Sacks, Charles Castner, Jeff Apperson, Dar Williams, Jo Ann Dale, Janet Shaw, Dale Kushner, Lisa Ruffolo, Ann Shaffer, Rosemary Zurlo-Cuva, Steve Finney, Michael Taeckens, Dana Stamey, and Courtney Denney. For love and support and otherwise putting up with me, thanks to my mother, Betty Anne Allen; my sister, Angela Allen; my son, George; and my wife, Nancy Holyoke, the best writer in the house and a reader this writer is lucky to have.